ALMOST PERFECT

ALMOST PERFECT

A DYSTOPIAN LOVE STORY

TAMARA MARTIN

THE HENRY MAYBERRY GROUP
Adelaide

First published in Australia 2018 by The Henry Mayberry Group

www.thehenrymayberrygroup.com

Edited by Cathleen Ross

National Library of Australia Cataloguing-In-Publication data:

Martin,Tamara, 1973-

Alexandra Deen / Tamara Martin

1st ed.

ISBN: 978-0-6480250-9-2 (pbk.)

Cover Design: Kristyn McGuiggan, Drop Dead Designs

For Amanda

Who loves this book as much as I do

*Who has cheered me on and kept me from quitting
every single day of this beautiful journey*

*They say you can't choose your family but I'd choose
you every day* ♥

CHAPTER 1

_____

It was 2026 when the world as everyone knew it fell to pieces. The worst war we'd seen in a lifetime or two. Not my lifetime, I hadn't been born yet. I came a few years after we closed our borders, put ships out in the ocean guarding us like a ring of fire. But we were reminded often enough of where we'd come from, why things had to be the way they were, why the part we would play would be so important to the future of our nation.

By the time we'd closed our borders though, we'd lost so many people. We'd lost our brand new, first president while he'd played on the Kirribilli lawns with his cocker spaniel, Bob. They were blown to bits, just like that. Our new president, Sheila Smith, took charge like an army general and saved us from annihilation by closing the borders and reallocating anyone who didn't play by her rules. Those people were sent to the farms, the ships, factories in faraway places and never seen again. So we're told.

The rest, those that were left, were skill tested and allocated jobs accordingly. If you were on the perfect side of creation, beau-

_____

tiful, brilliant and kind, those women and men were sent to the breeding program. Everyone else, to a career, to fulfil their part in rebuilding our broken nation, put the pieces back together and begin again. But only the women.

So many men and boys had died, there just weren't enough to spare for anything but the breeding program. They were treated like gold dust and kept separated from society until there were enough to add in the entertainment program. Someday numbers would be enough, maybe, but there were too many benefits to society now to go back, I deduced, it was too easy, too uncomplicated to go backwards, but I'd never say. I'd seen what happened to those who questioned the way our society was built. A girl in my dorm asked too many questions and suddenly, in the middle of the night she was desperately needed somewhere else even though she hadn't graduated yet.

'Shhhh...' called headmistress as the lights dimmed.

The auditorium fell into a hush, filled with all of us who'd come of age in the last month. We'd turned eighteen, been tested as a birthday gift and allocated a role in society, and now we were ready to be shipped off to do our part in keeping the country running, keeping it self-sufficient because our borders were still closed. The President trusted no one and there was still so much work to do, so much to protect us from.

I took a deep, fortifying breath as the departure video began with footage of explosions as the videos usually did. I looked down to my brogue clad feet like I did every time as body parts flew past the camera. I wondered if anyone ever became desensitized to it? What would it mean for our humanity if they did?

I looked up as President Smith's face filled the screen. She was young, for a president, although no one ever mentioned her actual age. She'd never aged in any of the videos though, like there was a magic wand somewhere that kept her face fresh and wrinkle free. She had fine blonde hair pulled casually into a feminine side knot and her pretty face was perfectly made up with just the right amount of makeup, as always.

I often imagined she woke up looking exactly the same every morning, that maybe someone painted her face while she slept. She spoke with a kind, soft voice that even though it suited the rest of her face, rarely felt as authentic as it should. But I was smart, smart enough to know to keep that thought to myself. We adored our president. She saved us from annihilation. We were reminded too often to forget.

'Ladies,' she began, smiling brightly. 'It is now your time to take your place in our society,' she said, the camera panning to show a beautiful city behind her full of pretty, tall buildings surrounded by grass and fruit trees, and lakes bathed in glorious sunshine. 'We are ready for you but we need you to be ready for us.

'Our cities have rebuilt in the twenty-one years since the war but there's still rebuilding to do, still so much work to do. We lost a lot of people in '26, too many. We're replenishing well enough through the breeding program. Just look around at your fellow classmates, all beautiful and brilliant, all with their own part to play. Some of you may have been allocated to our precious breeding program because you are the best of humanity. Perhaps your gifts lie in replenishing and fueling your nation's bodies. Perhaps you are destined to beautify the nation through art or keep order amongst our people. Maybe your mathematical brain will help build our homes or advance our technology. Whatever your allocation, trust you are exactly where your gifts and your country need you to be. No person, no task is a waste in the world we have built for you.

'We have rebuilt so much of what we lost, we've rebuilt it better than it was, it is now time to advance on those builds, to take our technology to the next level. You bright young women, purposefully born within our breeding program have been designed to do more than anyone that's come before you. Your gifts and your talents will be nurtured to bring out your very best. We are a completely self-sufficient nation relying on no one else for anything. We have everything we could possibly need right here and right there in that very room in which you sit. We don't need anything but you.

'What we've built for you is nothing short of extraordinary. Your ancestors, those that died for our freedom, your freedom, would be proud of what we've done, the nation we've become. When you arrive in each of your destinations, you will be greeted by your relocation specialists, gifted and kind organisers who will have sorted out your homes and your wardrobe and will provide you with everything you will need for your new life.

They will guide you through the societal etiquette of your region, your allocated transport requirements which evolve as you evolve. They'll go through the extra-curricular activities on offer, which are not too different to what you already do, art, fitness, cooking. You'll learn how to take care of yourself in this beautiful world we've built, just for you, for you to excel and fulfil your destiny. Doing work you are perfectly designed to do, will fulfil you in ways your predecessors could only dream of.

We have eliminated the stresses of love and family. You won't worry about money or a lover cheating on you, being disrespected or stabbed in the back, wanting for anything or children playing up while you're trying to fulfill your destiny.

Those are trials of the past.

We've moved beyond that. We've evolved because we are evolution itself. Adult needs are taken care of by the men not quite up to the breeding program standards. They'll help you relieve those built up endorphins you'll accrue from fulfilling your daily destiny. Some of you may have more access to them than others, but we encourage every one of you to partake as often as possible to keep your head clear and your minds focused on the tasks at hand.

'The men are well trained. You just need to show up, like a manicure or a haircut, all the work will be done for you.'

I stifled a yawn as I doodled in my notebook, drawing a stick figure image of a man like we'd seen in the textbooks on how this mind clearing theory worked. It didn't nearly look as effective as running. I decided running would be all I needed. I couldn't see how anything resembling a mani or a haircut could achieve anything, anyway. I hated sitting still for a haircut, it was so unproductive. But the woman insisted the same thing every time we had to listen to one of these videos and every time I tuned out her pretty, melodic voice.

'You've been prepared for this,' she continued. 'and all the other tasks that await you. We are so excited to have you join us out here,' she said waving her arms into the sunshine and twirling like a girl. 'We are ready for you. Come and fulfil your destiny.'

The screen went blank and the sounds of fidgeting filled the dark room moments before the lights came back on. My destiny awaited but I was anxious, uncertain and although I'd never admit it to another living soul, afraid.

'Come, come, ladies,' Headmistress commanded from the front of the room.

The girls who'd sat towards the front had already begun forming a queue to exit. Supervising the only way out of the building stood Nurse with her needling machine followed by Dawn from the front office with her rows and rows of envelopes containing our fate.

One by one arms were put in front of Nurse. Nurse scanned the chips in our arms to update our medical and activity data and then the machine struck into the pale flesh of our inner wrists, inserting a new chip, the departure chip that would hold our money and create access to our new worlds. We'd had no need for it in the college, but out there in our perfect society, everything cost something and there was no wandering around in places you didn't belong.

I walked away with my wrist stinging from the new strike and smiled at Dawn, a sweet, middle aged woman from the prewar time as she handed me my envelope. There was no time to stop and read it with a queue of excited young women behind me eager to fulfill their destinies so I kept walking, kept the line moving and followed everyone else to the departure point where we waited behind the signs labelled, A, B, C, D, each corresponding with the letter in the left corner of our envelope.

The white vans taking us away from the only home any of us really remembered stopped in front of the benches on which we sat, sending a cloud of dust from the driveway rising into the air. Patrice and I coughed, waving it away from our faces as Helen flopped down beside me. Two other girls, tall, broad shouldered, came to stand beside the bench without even glancing at us. They were from the defence and protective services program like Helen but were clearly not her friends.

'Shippers,' she whispered with a smirk, referring to the ships that protected our borders. Even though we didn't discuss our allocations, if we'd been brave enough to open the envelopes, until we got in the van to avoid anyone we left behind knowing where we were going, some destinations were easy to guess. Some people were just born for the ships.

'Come along, ladies,' chirped Ms Cally, our assigned chaperone, before losing her smile as she looked at the shippers as though the word didn't quite apply to them.

We reluctantly boarded the van like the sulky teenagers we were forcibly leaving behind. I chose a seat by the window and Helen chose the seat next to me. We weren't friends but we were friendly. I looked up at the beautiful old mansion and saw my carer, Ms Milly, the closest thing I'd had to family in the last thirteen years, in the upstairs window. I put my hand against the window in a wave and blinked away, the tears filling my eyes. When I looked back, she was gone. It was the way it was meant to be. No families, no ties, it was less stressful, it gave you the power to fulfil your destiny without the detriment of emotion.

It began because of the war. Families were threatened and people forced to do unthinkable things to protect them, sometimes traitorous, treasonous things, so no family to protect meant no leverage for the bad guys if there were any left. It kept us all safer in a time when people were so desperate they'd trust anything. No one had questioned it since. Everyone knew not to question the President's rules.

There were consequences.

No one spoke of them, we weren't taught them but we all knew they existed. By now everyone knew someone who had disappeared, who'd been quietly reallocated during the night to somewhere better suiting their skills. The President did what she did for our benefit, we had to now do our part and we had to trust her to do hers. That's what we were taught.

We followed the busload full of engineers that were going to take our technology to the next level through the big wrought iron gates and onto the smooth solar panelled road that helped power the college. I held my envelope in my sweaty fingers, afraid to open it, watching everyone else open theirs instead. Patrice from the culinary program stared at her letter, tears running down her face.

'Oh dear,' cooed Ms Cally. 'What did you get, love?' she asked kindly. Clearly this wasn't her first time chaperoning.

'Grain Farm Seventy-Two,' Patrice mumbled.

The van fell silent. Everyone knew a life on the farms was worse than death. The farm hands were society's cast offs. If you weren't pretty enough for a restaurant in the city, or beautiful enough for a vacation resort, if you weren't lovely enough to be seen in a café or takeaway, you were sent to a farm. The farms ran seven days, fifteen hours a day and the cooks and cleaners kept the cogs of the farming machine running. It was hard, thankless work. Patrice would have no need for visiting vacation resorts, there'd be no men to relieve her endorphins, she worked a hard enough, physical job to relieve them herself, so the theory went. Where would she find the time anyway? We'd all seen the videos as children while being taught where our food comes from, we'd seen the sun hardened women with calluses on their hands, their faces wrinkled from the long hours, the sun, their hair as dull as the look in their eyes.

There was nothing I could do for Patrice but wish her well, I thought as I turned the envelope over in my hands, a lump forming in the pit of my stomach.

The two girls destined for the ships confirmed their appointments with pleasure. Helen confirmed her appointment with the Federal Police, not surprising really, they never sent women as beautiful as Helen to the ships.

'What'd you get Coté?' Helen asked.

I tentatively opened my envelope and read. *Congratulations on your appointment to La Ferme. Your career will begin in the important role of booker as we train and guide you to play an important role within our breeding and entertainment programs. A bright future awaits you and we look forward to welcoming you to this valuable path.* 'La Ferme,' I whispered.

Helen gasped. 'You did not,' she said, snatching the letter from my hands as I turned to look out the window at the passing fruit trees. 'I can't believe it,' she gushed. 'Congratulations.'

'Yes, Courtney, congratulations,' said Ms Cally, breathlessly.

'Thanks,' I mumbled. I didn't really care where I was going. I suddenly didn't want to go anywhere at all. Leaving left me filled with too many emotions I was unable to process, people I loved even though I wasn't supposed to love. Love was an unnecessary, inconvenient emotion that had caused too much trouble in its history, caused people to do absurd, irrational things but I felt it anyway.

A brusque woman named Mary collected Patrice when we arrived at the train station. Mary had grey hair, pulled into a bun so tightly, it pinched her face. She had no patience for emotion and quickly hurried Patrice along. *Dinner wasn't going to cook itself,* she instructed. Patrice dropped her head in defeat as she quickly scurried after Mary, her fate sealed, her freedom over.

There was nothing I could do but wave and smile. Her fate hadn't been fair. Her food was fine, she baked a fabulous apple pie but she was too stocky, too manly by acceptable standards, a flaw in her DNA, which in no way measured her kindness or her generosity. But it was our way. It worked. The country flourished, there was no disputing the facts, so despite the uneasiness in my tummy, I waved and smiled like a cartoon character.

The shippers left with few farewells, following the signs to their designated transfer point.

Helen and I followed Ms Cally as she pushed through the swarms of people who were shouting and talking and laughing as they went about their business, the noise mingling into one big cacophony of indecipherable sound. We swiped our wrists against a scanner attached to a long metal barrier and followed Ms Cally onto a waiting train. She pushed past more people milling and chatting in the walkway until she found an empty cabin that smelt of polished leather and stale coffee, with two bench seats facing each other.

'This will be a long journey, ladies, so you might want to get some sleep,' she suggested, handing each of us instructions, our exit points, the names of our relocators and then she was gone.

Helen left me some hours later as the train pulled in to the hub-bub of the Sydney station. She was too happy to be joining the throng outside the window and was gone with barely a farewell. I was thrilled to remain inside the safety of the carriage.

A woman born of the prewar time took Helen's place in the cabin but didn't speak before pulling out her bag of knitting. We sat quietly together as I marvelled at the solar farms that glittered like seas of diamonds in the red dirt outside the windows, the cattle farms that stretched wide and deep, the lushest, greenest orchards, trees with branches heavy and sagging with coloured fat fruit.

The woman opposite promptly packed away her knitting moments before the perfunctory voice announced our destination over the loudspeaker. As the woman stood, making her way out into the hallway, I followed close behind as though she were my friend or companion, even though we hadn't shared a single word.

Standing in the doorway of the train, ready to step onto the platform though, I couldn't move my feet. The sea of people had quickly swallowed my silent travelling companion, now it was my turn. But there was nowhere to place my feet. The platform was full of people hurrying here and there and I couldn't see a way forward. I had to move but my legs wouldn't cooperate. I couldn't see a placard with my name, I couldn't see anything past all the people.

'Come on, love,' someone begged from behind and I had to move so I grit my teeth, taking my first tentative step into my new life.

Instantly, I was swallowed by the crowd, unable to escape, moving with them, a part of them. Before a fresh surge of panic took hold, I summoned my strength and pushed through the crowd until I reached the solid wall of a pillar. I sucked in lungfuls of air, glad to finally be able to breathe again as I looked around for the placard but I could see nothing.

The stifling heat of the Brisbane station sent rivers of sweat into unmentionable places. The noise of people, chatter, coming and going, trains and food sellers calling to passers-by assaulted my ears too used to the controlled quiet of the ladies' college. Like a frightened child, I near clung to the pillar as I looked for the placard with my name on it. My relocation specialist was supposed to be waiting for me but I couldn't see her anywhere.

The train blew its whistle in the distance as it rode out of the station and I was officially stranded here in this new and strange place with nowhere to go, nothing to do but wait.

For the first time in my short life, I wished for a friend or that someone I knew could have come with me. But I'd left everyone I knew back at the ladies' college. I should be used to leaving people, being alone. I hadn't seen my mother since I was five. It created resilience, strength, made us reliant on no one but ourselves, it made us stronger. And I was. Strong. Most of the time. It was how I was built. A leader among my career path. But today, as I craned my neck for that placard in this unfamiliar place with the hordes of people rushing from one place to the next, with the food smells hanging thick in the sticky air, I wished for a different life, a different world, a different time.

This perfect world that had been created for me, full of perfect people was suddenly an overwhelming deluge of emotion and my breath became lodged like a rock in my chest. Not that I was perfect. I'd be in the breeding program if I was. I'd never say so because it was supposed to be what we all aimed for, one of the greatest honours to be bestowed upon our generation but I was glad for it. For the freedom to live and do mostly as I chose in the city with people and everything that was on offer.

As unfamiliar tears threatened to fill my eyes, a little voice asked, 'Courtney?'

I looked down at the pint-sized woman radiating sunshine and I nodded.

'I'm Stacey, your relocation specialist. Do you have everything?' she asked kindly.

I nodded, holding up the small suitcase I carried that contained what was left of my snacks and the few belongings I'd been allowed to bring, a book Ms Milly gave me as a graduation gift that talked about stars in the sky that held the power of dreams, the nightdress I'd squirreled into a ball and stuffed inside my beloved runners, almost run bare but loved anyway and the shawl, now too small for my breadth, my mother had knitted for my departure to the college. I'd long since outgrown it but it had decorated my bed ever since. I'd have to find a new purpose for it, I supposed. I doubted such sentimentality was allowed in the new world.

'Come on, you look like you could use some air,' Stacey suggested with a kind smile as we walked out of the train station and into the warm sunshine.

Stacey was expert at pushing through the crowds of people and by the end of the street, it was just us and finally, I could breathe again. 'That's better,' I said.

Stacey smiled. 'It's a lot, I know. Come on, let's walk.'

Stacey made the long walk across the river look easy. Everything about Stacey was tiny and perfect and easy. She had shoulder length, shiny blonde hair, crystal blue eyes, a tiny frame and a warmth that exuded from her that made you want her to be your best friend.

'Did anyone travel with you?' she asked conversationally as we walked, pretending our skin wasn't melting.

'Patrice left us in Perth. Helen rode the speed train with me but left Sydney.'

'What'd they get?' she asked referring to their papers.

'Patrice, a grain farm.'

'Oooh,' she cringed. 'And Helen?'

'Federal police.'

'Wow, she must be impressive.'

I nodded, 'She is,' I confirmed without elaboration. I'd remember her for always being quick with a joke and just as quick to pull you to the ground if you stepped out of line. I'd seen her take care of a potential shipper or two in my time and those women were more like men than women, but they had nothing on Helen in a fight.

'What did they say when you told them what you got?' she asked.

'Helen didn't believe me, ripped the papers out of my hand to read it for herself. Ms Cally gripped her chest like I'd won a lottery,' I said with less enthusiasm than I knew I was supposed to have.

'Rightly so, too,' Stacey smiled. 'La Ferme is a very prestigious appointment.'

'Oh, I know, really, I'm honoured they chose me. It's just, it's been a really big day,' I told her, subconsciously rubbing my wrist where my implant still ached.

She smiled kindly, patted my hand. 'I remember how hard it was. But I promise, a few days and you'll be right at home.'

Stacey chatted as we walked over the bridge, pointing out landmarks, telling stories, pointing to the apartments swimming under the sun on the river bank on the other side of the bridge that would be my new home. I was grateful for her chatter. It passed the time and I didn't feel so lonely with her beside me talking as though we were old friends.

I was accustomed to much more walking than here to there. Exercise had always been one of my extra-curricular activities. But it was hot, so hot, the moisture-laden air sucked my lungs dry, sucked everything dry while at the same time making every pore on my body swim with sweat.

I took off my cardigan, draping it over my bag, fanned my face with my hand.

'You'll get used to the humidity,' insisted Stacey as she motored along, breezy and sweat free, not a drop of moisture showing on her pretty face.

'How long have you been here?' I asked, trying to keep up, glad for the white shirt that wouldn't show all the sweat marks on my body.

'Just a year,' she said. 'It feels like forever though, everything moves fast here,' she smiled.

'So you which year of the program born graduates were you?' I asked.

'Second,' she corrected. 'But you'll find there's not much difference between those of us program born and those from the pre-war time who were reallocated after the war. Everyone takes their part in rebuilding our country as seriously as everyone else.'

'Of course,' I agreed.

Halfway over the bridge we stopped to drink from the water fountain. Looking along the river we could see all the way to the next bridge. 'That building there she pointed to one side, the Director of La Ferme lives there and throws the most wonderful parties. Over there,' she pointed to the other side of the river, 'is full of the best eateries. You're really going to love it there,' Stacey told me as the pounding of feet on cement interrupted her.

I turned in the direction they were coming, from where we, ourselves, had just come and there was a group, a swarm of men in loose fitting tank tops and shorts running towards us. I flattened myself against the railing as they passed, their feet pounding on the pavement, my heart beating so hard in my chest I thought it might make a run for it too as I inhaled their scent and something I couldn't name twitched about inside my body as I drew it deep into my lungs.

I hadn't seen a real live male since I was five and had left for the Ladies College, and even then, it was only my brother Alec and the other pre-schoolers from our village. My heart pounded through my body, my mouth turning bone dry as I realised those sweet chubby faces of the children I'd once known had turned into stubble jawed, chiselled faces of men who took up too much space, too much air.

As the men passed, two turned, running backwards for a few steps tipping an imaginary hat as they chimed, 'Ladies'. A man with hair so dark it almost shone purple under the sun's rays winked at me then they both smiled, as bright as the sun, before turning around and again running in time with their companions, sweat beading over their perfectly sculpted muscles.

'Well,' I gasped, my breath caught in my chest.

'You'll get used to seeing them around,' Stacey smiled.

'What, they just run about and...and...behave like that?' I asked, appalled.

'Well of course,' she smirked.

'Isn't that a little inappropriate?' I asked. 'Aren't there rules or something?'

'Seems we have a lot to talk about,' she said as we resumed our walk along the bridge. 'You know about entertainers, right?' she asked.

I nodded.

'Well, that's what they were, a group of entertainers, just out for a run, getting some fresh air. We don't lock them up like rats, you know. They perform much better when they're fit and full of nature's nutrients,' she grinned as though seeing something I couldn't see. Anyway, you'll get used to them, you won't even notice them after a while,' she added and I don't think she believed her own words for a second. I certainly couldn't imagine ever becoming so unaware of something so beautiful.

The subject closed, Stacey began pointing out the highlights of where we were headed as we exited the bridge and began walking along the esplanade with the river sparkling under the sun beside us. The green bank of the river was filled with restaurants and bars, herb and vegetable gardens, tranquil walking trails, people and so much activity, watched over by a long row of tall apartment buildings, identical in a variety of pastel colours looking like giant cupcakes. We stood before a pretty mint green building that rose high into the sky.

'Well, this is you,' Stacey said.

I looked up, taking in the magnitude of it, the size, the shininess. Each balcony ledge was home to vegetables and herbs, which looked greener, richer, against the mint green walls. In a self-sufficient country with so many people to feed, we didn't waste space. We grew food on the sides of buildings, on rooves, in the median strips and the edges of the solar panelled footpaths. Fruit trees, apples, pears, oranges and lemons shaded walkers wherever they went and everywhere was lush and green and beautiful. It wasn't for helping yourself, it was for harvesting and storing and for us to buy from the market with whatever food funds we were allowed.

I swiped my wrist on the scanner by the door to the building as Stacey instructed and the doors slid open. Stacey waved to the security guard just inside the door. The guard nodded and went back to reading her newspaper. I swiped my wrist again to call the lift and then again inside the lift to go to my floor.

'You only have access to your own floor. If you want to visit someone on another floor or in another building, they'll have to give you access as you will for them if they come to visit,' Stacey instructed as the mirrored cube rose.

We walked down a soft, carpeted hallway, all the way to the end and stood outside my door where I swiped my wrist against another scanner, waited for the lock to click then pushed the door open.

We stepped into a light filled room. A living room with a white leather couch and bright yellow and blue cushions directly in front. A vision screen imbedded in the wall in front of the couch, a white galley kitchen with grey stone tops behind the couch. To my right was a glass top dining table with tall white leather chairs.

I walked through to the living room, dropping my bag by a closed door on the left, walking to the other side of the living room and throwing open the long caramel drapes. Sunlight poured in through the floor to ceiling glass doors that led to a wide balcony. Opening the door, the room filled with fresh warm air and I breathed in deep.

'Are you okay?' Stacey asked.

'I'm sure I will be. Is this really all for me?' I asked.

'It is,' she smiled.

'It's a lot for just one person, isn't it?'

'You're on an important path now, you need accommodation that reflects that. It may change as you rise through the ranks but this will see you through the next few years. Are you sure you're alright?'

Mentally shaking my head clear, I reminded myself of the rules, who I was, the expectations. 'Of course. I'm just tired from travelling,' I smiled, despite feeling the heavy weariness return to my bones.

'Of course you are, it's a long journey,' Stacey said. 'Well, how about I leave you to settle in, then. Bedroom and bathroom are through there,' she said, indicating the closed door. 'There's food in the fridge if you need it or there's plenty to choose from on the riverbank. Your wardrobe and bathroom are stocked with everything you'll need so you're all set up and ready to go. My number has been sent to your tablet if you need anything or have any questions at all, otherwise, have a look around, make yourself at home and I'll be here to collect you at seven thirty in the morning, okay?'

'That sounds perfect,' I said.

'Alright then, settle in and get some sleep. I'll see you in the morning,' Stacey smiled, touching my arm in comfort before letting herself out.

After the door closed I stood on the balcony, listening to the sounds of people talking drifting on the breeze, cutlery clanking in the restaurants below, empty bottles smashing as they were thrown into recycle bins, the sounds all mixing together in a beautiful melody of life. I closed my eyes and let it all in, absorbing it, the sounds of my new life.

I wandered the small galley kitchen, opening cupboards filled with jars of food and bottles of sauces, spreads and spices, the fridge with milk and cheese and deli meats. Other than some basic recreational cooking classes, I'd never taken care of myself.

I'd never had to rely on myself for anything. I'd just focused on excelling at my studies. Other disciplines took care of the cooking and the cleaning as part of their training. There were dining room schedules and meal plans prepared by the culinary students. Other than a couple of classes on how to make a stir fry, I'd never set foot in the kitchens. It would be enough, I supposed, everything else was down on the river bank. It was the way our life was designed, focus on what you are best at and let someone else take care of the rest.

I was too wound up to eat though, too overwhelmed with all that lay ahead of me, my new responsibilities, to bother with even a cheese sandwich, so I switched on the kettle and found some peppermint tea leaves and a mug with an infuser. What I really wanted was to run, like the men we'd seen on the bridge, burn off some energy, make my muscles quiver just a little, clear my head, feel free, in control, for just a little bit but I didn't dare leave the apartment.

Sitting on the balcony with my tea, relishing the slight breeze that found its way up as the sun sank, I watched the people below, heading to dinner, drinking at the bars, the occasional car driving along the otherwise quiet road.

Once the roads had been made of asphalt. Cars had filled the streets, consuming precious resources, many of which were imported. Solar energy powered our cars now. Only important people had the travel funds that allowed for them, though. I would find out in the morning what my allocation was. I was sure mine would not allow for a car, despite the prestige of my employer. There was nowhere to go that wasn't accessible by foot or high-speed train, anyway.

When the tea was gone, I closed the balcony doors and took my bag through to the bedroom suite. The bedroom was to the right, bathroom to the left and in between, joining the two, was a long wardrobe filled with the necessary items of my new life. I resisted touching all the clothes that hung in there, looking in the drawers and boxes on the shelf. It was too much. For thirteen years, all I'd had were my college issued school uniforms and college issue nightgowns. The wardrobe in front of me held more clothes than I could wear in a year, dresses, jackets, pants, shirts with colour.

I rummaged through my bag for my nightgown. I'd left all my uniforms behind for someone else to use. The travelling uniform I was wearing was the uniform we wore for dinner, a navy skirt, a white shirt, a cardigan but now I had no use for it or the pair of clunky shoes on my feet. They'd be sent back to the college for someone else to use, but the nightgown, I'd needed to keep something, something familiar, something that smelt like home.

The bedroom had the same floor to ceiling windows as the living room, hidden behind the closed drapes. A giant bed sat in the middle of the room filled with too many pillows and covered in a white quilt and a textured purple throw artfully draped over a corner. There was a purple velvet wing chair in the corner and a shiny black chest of drawers against the wall. I was sure the drawers contained more appropriate sleep wear, but today I needed the familiarity of the college, of home, so I slipped into the long, pale pink, cotton nightgown, climbed into my new bed and laid my head on the poufy pillows.

It was quiet. Too quiet. I was used to other people, their movements, their snores, their breath. Now it was just me and the quiet seemed too loud and too empty. There was a need, deep inside my belly to reach out and touch someone but there was no one. There would be no one. Just me. I was all alone and it was terrifying.

CHAPTER 2

Sitting on the balcony of my apartment, overlooking the muddy river, watching the shirtless men row by, I revelled in the sun warming my shoulders, breathing in great lungfuls of the thick heavy air as I sipped my coffee. Would I ever get used to seeing them? We'd been segregated my whole life, told in no uncertain terms fraternisation was against the rules. Now here they were running all over the place.

People milled around below, chattering like monkeys in a zoo, all busy with somewhere to go, someone to see because that is our way. Wasted time was wasteful and unacceptable. Friends were networking opportunities, opportunities to build community, for the good of the nation, for the good of our survival as long as you didn't cross too many boundaries, get too attached. It was a fine line. But we'd all spent thirteen years living the rules, we knew no different until the rare moments where our hearts ached in the quiet, ached for something to hold onto. That's when I craved the comfort of my mother, what I remembered of her, her smell, the feel of her arms. But it had been so long. Memories faded and you just had live with the ache. No one ever spoke of that. It was just better to pretend it didn't exist, brush it aside and move on. The ache always dissipated soon enough, anyway. I put the thoughts of loneliness out of my mind, it was an unnecessary emotion in a perfect world, a waste of my energies, detrimental to my purpose. Instead I soaked in the noise and the sounds and the activity. The apartment, my apartment, my home was too empty, too quiet, this was better. Soon I'd be among them, one of them down below involved in monkey chatter and this unproductive feeling of loneliness would be a distant memory and I'll have regretted wasting a beautiful sun filled morning on outdated emotions. I moved my chair closer to the railing so the sun covered my whole body. I leant my chin on the top of the rail and watched the people, what they wore, how they greeted each other, how the water sparkled like jewels under the sun's morning rays and instead gave gratitude for all that had been bestowed to me.

'Well, I'm impressed,' Stacey said, looking me up and down when I let her in. 'Not everyone can put together a decent outfit on the first go. I blame those darned woollen dress things they make you wear at the college. Argh,' she shivered. 'Hideous things. Now, you'll need a handbag and your tablet and you're ready.'

'All good to go,' I said, holding up the handbag I'd left on the couch packed and ready. It wasn't that hard, a skirt and a matching shirt or a dress didn't require a genius IQ. Thankfully we'd had lessons on how to walk in heels and accessorise appropriately for our vocation. They trained us well, set out very clear guidelines for us to follow. I was very good at following rules, whether I agreed with them or not. Most of the time, I just tried not to think, but it was hard.

'Well done,' she praised. 'You're going to be great at this job. I can already tell. Come on then, let's go,' Stacey said with a kind smile, opening the door to let me pass.

Once we waved to the security guard and opened the door onto the street, the nerves hit me. I broke out into a sweat and jitters filled my stomach. This was it. My new life. No turning back. No reclaiming my childhood. No time to even adjust.

'Alright, now you have to pay attention okay? This is the route you'll take to work each day so keep up,' Stacey said as she started scurrying between and around people going in all directions as we headed towards the river.

I put the fear rippling through my body out of my mind and hurried to keep up as Stacey weaved between people like she owned the world until we arrived at a busy landing dock.

'Now we wait,' she said, leaning against a rail. 'You doing alright?'

'Ahuh,' I smiled, or tried to, my brain was desperately trying to take everything in and my insides were screaming holy moly. All the activity on the riverbank, the people, the noise, it was all so far from the college where a part of my brain and heart still lived as it tried to catch up to the rest of me. It was hard to comprehend the two existing in the same world.

Stacey laughed. 'You'll be fine, I promise. Come on,' she said as people instinctively prepared for the water taxi moments before it appeared from up river.

'Try not to stand outside, the wind will mess your hair, you'll get water spray on your clothes and this is not a job you want to arrive at wrinkled, okay?' Stacey instructed as we made our way aboard the boat, finding seats under the canopy.

I nodded like a mute because that's what I did now. I was so overwhelmed with the strangeness of my new life, I could no longer form sentences and speak like a person.

'Once you move up the ranks your transport funds will increase but for now, you're better off saving your money to get the train into town at night and just get the free water taxi to work.'

As the boat slowed and gently rocked its way level with the dock on the other side, I went to stand but Stacey grabbed my arm, pulling me back into my plastic aisle seat.

'You're not an ordinary person anymore. You need to remember that, okay? You don't hustle and bustle with everyone else. You work for La Ferme. Best you wait until they all leave to avoid getting squashed in amongst them. You must remember your place and your status or it will look poorly upon the company and trust me, you do not want that.'

'Right,' I said as we sat and waited for everyone else to squeeze their way out like cattle racing for feeding bays.

After we stepped off the boat, we followed the riverbank, walked through a tunnel, up a hill and finally stopped in front of an enormous mirrored building, which reflected the world beyond its panels as though it had a super power. The building was much wider than it was tall. Each floor was wrapped in the greenery of the food being grown on the ledges, each floor doing its part to feed our self-sufficient nation and glistening in the sunshine.

We pushed through the glass door into an unexpectedly warm, inviting room. Plush, off-white carpet softened our footfalls. Fancy art depicting landscapes from places most of us would never get to see, hung on the perfectly off-white walls. A few sofas sat against the walls and directly in front of us was a glass desk that almost looked afloat before a cream leather chair.

A security guard walked out of the room behind the reception desk and smiled when she saw us.

'Hey, Stace, how are ya, love?' she greeted Stacey warmly.

'Hey Jen, good thanks. It's been a while. You good?'

'Yeah, you know me,' she smiled.

'Glad to hear it. I have Courtney here to see Trish when she's ready,' Stacey said.

'Of course, the new recruit. How are ya, love?' Jen asked. Without waiting for a reply, she pressed a button on her earpiece and something on the tablet she was holding, then announced, presumably to Trish or perhaps Trish's assistant, my arrival.

'She'll be right with you, ladies, have a seat,' Jen insisted, waving towards the sofas on the opposite wall.

Stacey led me to the chairs. 'You'll be fine, Courtney. You'll get used to it all,' she assured me, somehow sensing and understanding my inner turmoil.

It seemed there was a lot I was supposed to get used to any second now but I doubted I was going to get used to any of it any time soon. It was too much. They should have prepared us better at the College before setting us free. It was unfair to expect a person to go from the drab, mundane, quiet, overly organised life at the Ladies College to this and to be fine. My brain couldn't keep up.

'Staceeeey. Courtneeeey,' cooed a tall, willowy brunette with shiny, neat, shoulder length brown hair blow dried to perfection. She wore a black dress that hung comfortably on her willowy frame, big heels and smart, black-rimmed glasses. I could only assume this was Trish.

'Trish, how are you?' Stacey greeted Trish familiarly, kissing her on each cheek.

'Good to see you, Stacey, it's been a while,' Trish smiled. 'Come, come,' she insisted, ushering us past the empty desk and through the door she'd appeared from, down a long, warmly lit corridor lined with more art and into a bright room with soft blue velvet chairs. 'Sit, sit,' Trish insisted before pressing a button on her ear piece and asking, 'Coffee for three if you can, please.'

'Right, then,' she said. 'How are you, Courtney? We're so happy you're here and ready to begin your journey with us. You may feel a little overwhelmed for the first few days, but don't worry, I've seen your test scores, you'll find your feet in no time. There's also a few perks that should make it easier to acclimatise,' she said, winking at Stacey who smirked like the proverbial cat.

I thanked Trish for her confidence just as a woman, a little older than Stacey, knocked on the open door then wheeled in a tray of coffee and related paraphernalia.

'Hi, I'm Zoë,' she smiled, introducing herself. She was taller than Stacey but shorter than me. She was slim, had long brown hair that waved perfectly, big brown eyes and a kind smile.

'Courtney,' I said taking her outstretched hand and shaking it, totally taken aback by the abundance of friendliness. I really hadn't expected anyone to be so nice in such a fancy place.

'Welcome. We'll catch up when you have a chance,' she offered.

'That'd be great, thanks,' I said.

Zoë nodded and went to leave as Stacey poured the coffee.

'So how are you feeling?' Trish asked. 'A little nervous, I suspect,' she smiled kindly. 'But you needn't be, we'll take good care of you,' she insisted as we fell into a few minutes of friendly, polite conversation.

Stacey placed her cup and saucer on the table and giggled as Trish told a story of someone they both knew. The story finished, Trish placed her cup and saucer on the table as well.

'Okay, shall we get started then?' Trish asked.

'That's my cue to leave,' said Stacey, swilling the last of her coffee.

'You're leaving?' I asked, suddenly terrified.

She smiled kindly, 'You'll be fine. I'll be back at five and we'll head back to your place together and get some dinner and you can fire all your questions at me then, alright?'

I nodded like a sulking child as she left.

'It's a little overwhelming, isn't it?' said Trish. 'Don't worry though, we've all been through it. We remember it well. Why don't I get Zoë to show you around and then we can meet for morning tea? You can meet the rest of the team then. We can run through some particulars and after that Zoë can get you started on the bookings desk out front. Sound alright?'

I nodded then Trish led me back down the hallway, through a door on the right and into a large square room. On each wall was a door and in front of each was a desk, each manned by a woman tapping eagerly at keyboards or talking into their earpiece as Zoë was doing at one of the desks. There was a kitchenette in the corner and in the middle of the room was a sunken cube of beige couches surrounded by lush green plants.

Trish clapped her hands and all the girls behind the desks looked up and smiled. The three I hadn't yet met tapped something on their tablets but said nothing. The doors behind them then opened and three immaculately dressed women came out to stand beside the desks.

'Alright then,' Trish said to me. 'You already know Zoë and that is my office behind her. I'm available any time as your mentor, just check in with Zoë, she'll always know where I am. Then we have Di who heads up our R&D department and her right hand, Rosie. Erica heads up medical with Tess. Last but certainly not least, in fact probably the most important, next to me that is,' Trish whispered the last part, 'is Catherine who heads up the breeding program for the region with the support of Jules.'

They each in turn raised a hand in hello, smiled warmly then went back to their business.

'Alright, Zoë, can you show Courtney around?'

'Sure, no problem,' said Zoë gathering up her coffee and her tablet.

'Thanks. I'll see you both for morning tea. Don't be late,' Trish said, before disappearing into her office and closing the door.

'Right, then, where shall we start?' asked Zoë. 'Do you have any questions so far?'

'Trish didn't say what your department does,' I said quietly, feeling stupid, as though I was already supposed to know.

'Ah, we take care of the Entertainment Department and your role as booker supports us. Without us, our perfect world goes mad,' she winked. 'Just remember, you'll get used to the way of things and it'll all make sense before the week's out.'

'I'm not sure anything's going to make sense any time soon,' I laughed.

Zoë laughed. 'I remember the feeling. It's a lot to take in. But we're lucky, this really is the life jackpot. Most people don't have it as good as us. You'll see. It's worth being a little overwhelmed in the beginning. Come on, then,' Zoë nudged good humouredly. 'Let's see if I can help sort some of it out. We'll go see what's what, hey?'

We went back down the hallway, past the room where we'd just had coffee and through the door at the end and into an enormous open room. The room was filled to capacity with people squished into little, brightly lit cubicles, seemingly unaware of each other or the constant noise of typing, ringing phones and talking.

'This is the nest,' Zoë said. 'We call it that because it's filled with all the analysists and data processors for every department. They're like the worker bees that keep the hive going. They make sure everyone's where they're supposed to be and everything is working as it should. You'll never remember who's who or where they are or what they do. Here,' she said, handing me her coffee cup and taking my tablet from under my arm. 'I'll install the map for you. See here,' she said pointing to the search bar now showing on the screen of my tablet, 'you put in the name of who you're after and their seat will light up on the map and a green light will come on above their desk. If they're kind, they'll stand up so who-ever's looking for them can see them but sometimes they're so focused they might not notice or some of them,' she whispered, 'just don't have any manners.'

Zoë typed a name into the search bar and I watched as a green light came on across the other side of the room. Almost instantly a curvy blonde with long, thick curly hair stood and looked around the room. When she spotted Zoë, she waved.

I followed Zoë as she crossed the floor, ignoring the curious glances from those not so focused on what they were doing, to the girl who was now taking the opportunity to sip her coffee.

'This is Rachel. Rach, this is the new booker, Courtney,' Zoë introduced.

'So new but yet with so much power,' she giggled. 'Hi, nice to meet you. Fresh off the train, then?' Rachel asked.

'Yesterday,' Zoë answered for me. 'She's a little overwhelmed.'

'Which is why she didn't laugh at my joke,' Rachel giggled. 'I'm not surprised though, it took me weeks to stop shaking once I'd been shown my seat in here. You'll be right though. Anything you need, you just come find me, okay?' she offered.

'Thanks, appreciate it,' I said, grateful for her kindness.

'Rach and I started the same week,' Zoë explained. 'We have lunch now and again and often go out for dinner and drinks, see a game and whatever.'

'You'll have to join us sometime,' Rachel offered.

'Thanks, that'd be great,' I said, thinking I just wanted to spend the rest of forever curled up in my apartment where something made sense, where I wasn't constantly assaulted with unfamiliar people and buzzing nests full of people that overloaded my senses. But I knew I had to make the best of it. This was my life now, the new rules I had to follow. Like everyone kept saying, I'd get used to it all in a few days.

'Who's your relocation specialist?' asked Rachel.

'Stacey,' I said.

'Blonde, tiny little, firecracker, Stacey?' she asked.

'Yeah, that sounds like her,' I smiled.

'She'll have you sorted in no time. You'll be right with her. What's your genetic code?' she asked.

'CA-5,2,' I told her.'

'Oh really? There's a very talented CA-5,2 in the basketball team at the boy's college who's about to receive his allocation.

Looks very promising for the breeding program although, his testing could go either way, yet.'

'Right, Alec,' I guessed, remembering he'd been sporty even before I'd left for the college and wondering what exactly Rachel did at La Ferme to know such a thing but too afraid to ask any more questions. Or more so, I was afraid of the answers. I wasn't sure I wanted to know where he ended up, not sure how comfortable I was with either answer.

'Alright, we'd best get moving before you overload her with company secrets. Besides, we have to be back for morning tea,' Zoë said.

'Argh, you execs and your bloody morning teas,' Rachel laughed, rolling her eyes. 'It's not fair, you know, you shouldn't be allowed to come in here and tell me such things if I can't come too,' Rachel sulked.

'I know, I know,' smirked Zoë. 'You all wish you were me,' she laughed as she walked away, waving her arm in the air in farewell.

'Everyone wants to be us, get used to it,' Zoë told me. 'As the booker you fall under the exec banner so "us" includes you, too. Sadly, we only get morning tea when there's something to celebrate, like a new employee,' she said nudging me. 'Or a birthday, if we reach monthly or quarterly targets, that sort of thing. We try really hard to find reasons as often as we can, you'll see why,' she giggled.

'So, what did Rachel mean by me having so much power?'

'I'll explain it all when we get to it, but you book the entertainers, you are the key to their sanity, probably one of the most powerful women in town right now.'

I'd never thought about this job that way. I didn't know what to do with power.

'It's fine, I'll go through it all. You just follow the rules and you'll be fine.'

'Well, that I can do,' I smiled.

Zoë showed me through the cafeteria, a huge cavernous room with long tables like the dining hall at the college, full of similar smells and ladies bustling behind the serving bays as they prepared and cooked the food for the day.

'Is the food any good?' I asked, trying to make conversation, wondering what kind of hierarchy and protocol ruled the seating.

'Probably. Who knows? We don't eat in here,' Zoë scoffed as though the idea was repulsive. 'We get our food made to order and delivered to the pod and eat in there.'

'Right,' I answered. 'Why?' I asked, thinking the cafeteria looked perfectly fine to me.

'Oh, honey, you've so much to learn,' she smiled. 'We are not the same as the people who eat in the cafeteria like school children. It is the perk of being an overachiever, achieving something none of them could dream of. An analyst will never find themselves on the same path as us. They'll never have the same advantages. It's just the way it is. Trust me, it's much easier if you just go with it and don't think about it too much.'

'But you're friends with Rachel, isn't she an analyst?'

'She is. But she's my friend so I don't care. Another perk, there's some rules we can bend if we choose and Rach doesn't really care that I have access to things she doesn't, as long as I share every now and then. Key is to not think too hard about it, but I'll help you figure it out, don't worry,' she added as I could feel my face scrunching as I tried making sense of it. There were no hierarchies at the college, no one was better or worse than anyone else. It was the point of being tested and allocated career paths, so that everyone was equal, you spent time with people in your same block, you stayed focussed on your path. Wasn't that the whole point of this structured society? For everyone to be equal and purposeful. 'You'll give yourself a headache, Courtney and trust me, you can't change any of it, you just have to live with it. It's not that hard once you get the hang of it, I promise,' Zoë added kindly.

Finally, we went through our pod. She gave me a run down on the coffee dispenser and showed me the toilets allocated to just us and showers, 'Should you be the sort that insists on going to the gym in the middle of the day,' she scoffed.

Note to self, no gym in the middle of the day. Even though I'd never been to the gym in my life. I was a runner, there was no need to lock myself in a small room and run on a machine. It defeated the purpose in my mind. The fresh air that filled your lungs and cleansed your soul was part of the running benefits.

'Alright, we'd best get ready for morning tea. Trish hates it when someone's late.'

'What about the rest of the building?' I asked, remembering how enormous the building was from the outside, we hadn't even seen a third of it.

'There's not much else for us to see. Upstairs are the directors' offices. We don't really get invited up there but sometimes one of their people will come down or call and you'll have to drop everything to support them. Below are the training rooms, gyms, living quarters and what not for the entertainers and breeders. Zoë's voice dropped to a heavy whisper, 'We absolutely don't go down there unless specifically requested by a manager or Grace,' she said, pointedly, waiting a moment to make sure I understood. Then added, 'Sometimes Grace will need help on a Saturday when she's doing health checks, mainly just to carry stuff, not for anything interesting. But you'll need a manager to set your access to go either up or down and you go down, you do as you're asked and you leave.'

'Got it,' I assured her. Then we went back into the pod and sat on one of the sofas in the middle of the room.

'We have quite a welcome surprise for you,' sang Tess as she wiggled her bottom into the cushion on the sofa opposite. Tess had a bob the colour of caramel and wore her purple fitted dress and soaring heels effortlessly. She was almost too beautiful not to be in the breeding program. I wondered what had excluded her as everyone took a place on the sofas. Each of the four sofas had four seats but only two people were sitting on each. I sat on one end of the same sofa Zoë chose as Trish opened the door to the pod.

'Ah, right on time,' Trish cooed as a group of men walked in carrying trays of morning tea supplies.

Men? More men? I had expected a cake. That's what people do. That's what Ms Milly did at the college. If there was something to celebrate, she organised a cake. Not contraband men to carry it. I'd knew the men entertained women, kept them focussed, their heads clear. But I'd just arrived, my head didn't need clearing, my endorphins were perfectly proportioned.

A very handsome, very shirtless man with chocolate brown eyes, floppy hair and beautifully tanned skin, placed a tray of freshly brewed coffees on the table in the middle, looked up at me and winked. The blood in my veins froze as I had an intense need to look away and stare at the same time. Then another put down two trays of tiny muffins before joining the others standing in a line behind the sofas.

'I think I'll take my morning tea in my office,' Trish sang from where she stood. 'You,' she said to one of the men standing behind the sofas waiting for instructions, 'if you could bring me a muffin and a coffee, it'd be greatly appreciated.'

'Of course,' he smiled.

The chosen man quickly scurried to the table, collecting a coffee and putting a few muffins onto a little plate before disappearing into Trish's office, firmly closing the door. The remaining men each found a vacant seat and began handing the rest of us coffee and offering muffins, chocolate chip, bran and banana, something for everyone it seemed.

I'd seen the man beside me on the bridge when I'd been walking with Stacey but he didn't seem to recognise me. He had hair that looked like the night sky and the darkest blue eyes that glistened when he smiled. I had to keep looking away because they were truly magnificent.

He passed me a coffee and offered a tray of muffins. I took the coffee and a chocolate chip muffin and tried not to look at him because I knew I'd blush beetroot. No one else was blushing. They seemed to be happily cosying up beside the array of tanned, muscular men who surrounded them. A couple were blonde, a couple brunette, all perfectly chiselled and lovely. What on earth was going on, I wondered as my heart beat so fast I thought it might explode? What on earth was I supposed to be doing here beside this lovely man? A slice of chocolate cake would have been easier to manage. I knew what to do with that.

'Are you alright?' asked the lovely man beside me with the wavy midnight hair.

'Ahuh,' I mumbled.

'You might need to go easy over there cowboy, Courtney's fresh off the train,' Catherine joked from the next couch before returning her attention to the perfectly designed brunette beside her.

'Brand spanking new, hey?' the man beside me asked, trailing a finger down the side of my face, leaving goose bumps in its wake and my breath lodged in my throat. 'Didn't I see you on the bridge yesterday?'

I nodded, answering both questions, unable to actually form a sentence. What does one even say to a beautiful man, any man, especially one sitting so close you could feel his breath? There was a warmth spreading up from my toes. I desperately wanted to abate it before it reached my face and sent it pink, telling all manner of things that didn't need to be told.

I looked to Zoë, desperately hoping for guidance, some idea on what was going on. What the hell I was supposed to be doing? To the others, hoping someone was paying attention but they were busy wrapped in the arms of their men, gazing into their eyes, stroking their stubbled jaws. Rosie was completely ensconced in a forbidden kiss and I couldn't tear my horrified eyes away. When did fraternisation become acceptable?

'It's okay,' smiled the man beside her. 'This is one of the perks of working in the exec team here.'

'What exactly is the perk?' I whispered, not wanting to look a fool but having the feeling I'd missed a pivotal conversation somewhere along the way. Probably at one of those relocation seminars where I drew pictures of the surf instead of listening.

'Us. Entertainment to do with as you please,' he said, taking my hand in his and then bringing it to his mouth to kiss as he looked into my eyes and sent my knees to jelly. 'You get to sample the offerings. Have a little play, take it as far as you like, if you fancy,' he winked.

We'd covered entertainers in our departure education. Just like getting a mani, you just sit there and it's done, that's what the

President said. That's what we were always told. This wasn't just sitting there and being tended to. Rosie's mouth was fixed to her entertainer's as she was wedged beneath him, his hands roaming inappropriately over her body. It looked neither comfortable nor pleasant.

How did one even breathe while doing such a thing? I was beginning to suspect the education we'd received had been lacking, the anatomy books not as clear as we thought, the process skimmed over.

'We don't have to do anything you're not comfortable with. At the very least you have the pleasure of my company for the next fifteen minutes. Anything else is entirely up to you,' he smiled, leaning back comfortably against the sofa. 'Would you like some more coffee?'

'Sure,' I answered, thinking at least that'd give me something to do. Although I doubted I needed anymore caffeine fraying my nerves. I felt ready to explode as it was.

He passed me the mug, his fingers brushing mine, sending shocks of electricity up my arm and straight to my heart. I looked up into his eyes and he was smiling. 'It's okay,' he whispered. 'Anything you're feeling, it's okay, just trust in that.'

I trusted in nothing right now. I didn't trust myself to speak. I didn't trust myself to look at him. I didn't trust myself to look at anyone else. I wanted chocolate cake and to laugh over the latest Miriam and Kate movie, not to have this beautiful man who liquefied my body with a single touch to be looking into my eyes like I held all the secrets to the world, like I was a beautiful piece of art to be admired, to be treasured while he trailed his strong, perfect index finger down my arm and my entire body begged for that finger, that hand, to trail in other places on my body, forbidden places.

Trish came out of her office and her entertainer took her hand, bent over almost in a bow, kissed her hand and gave a signal to the other men that it was time to leave.

'I promise it will be painless,' winked the man beside me as he took my hand, bringing it up to his lips. My stupid heart fluttered irrationally as his warm breath stroked my hand, as his soft lips sent sparks through my entire body. 'Until we meet again, milady,' he smiled and he rose and they all left.

Everyone went back to work. Trish cleared her throat from her doorway, untangled what had become of her hair and asked, 'Zoë, why don't you show Courtney how to work the switch, I need a few minutes here.'

'Sure,' Zoë smiled. 'I bet you do,' she mumbled as we walked out the door.

'I don't understand,' I whispered as we walked down the hall-way towards the reception room.

She giggled. 'It's quite a curveball, isn't it? They don't cover that in those stupid relocation seminars, do they?'

'I was sure I'd have noticed if they did,' I told her.

'Don't worry, it's all part of the game,' she grinned, putting her finger to her lips to shush any further talk of it as she pushed open the door.

'Hi ladies, all good to get started, are you?' asked Jen who was hovering in her doorway.

'We sure are,' grinned Zoë, not saying anything else and I understood clearly, she didn't want to talk about morning tea in front of Jen.

'Your job is mostly to answer all the incoming booking calls. They tried automating it when the program first came into effect but people found ways to hack the system to get free dates. It was a free for all and people were messing with the whole foundation of life, so now we have a dedicated booker.'

'Nothing for free, right?' I smiled.

'Right,' she agreed.

'Okay, if it's a new customer, it means they're either fresh off the trains like you or they've been transferred and need to register and have their files moved over to our office. Occasionally, they've just resisted as long as they can before registering. They're always a laugh.'

'Why do they resist when the President encourages it?'

'Everyone's different, I guess. Sometimes they grew up in the pre-war times and they just weren't raised this way. But I think for some, they find being that close to a person, naked and vulnerable, too much to take, it's easier to keep the emotional lines clear if they keep control of their bodies but it gets too much for all of them at some point,' she laughed.

'I'd forgot about the naked part,' I mumbled, remembering the pictures in the books and realising that was going to be me, and I understood the women who wanted to keep things simple and uncomplicated. 'What happens to people who resist?'

'I think they go a little mad,' Zoë joked conspiratorially.

'Actually mad?'

She chuckled. 'Maybe not literally. Although... I'm kidding,' she added as my face must have paled a little. 'It's a lot to take in, I know. But you'll be fine. You'll be nervous the first time, we all are, but it's just like a getting a mani, you're just in the nude, but just lie there and he'll take care of the rest,' she smiled.

I nodded. 'Just like a mani, sure,' I whispered, no longer believing a word anyone said on the subject. I'd seen what was going on at morning tea, none of it was anything like getting a mani.

Zoë smirked and I knew she knew it was all rubbish but she was spinning the line she was supposed to spin.

'Alright,' Zoë said, turning the conversation back to work. 'All the new customers and transfers you put through to me. Any complaints or oddballs you put through to me. We man the phones from eight in the morning until nine at night. Reception closes at five so there's a roster for the evenings and weekends. You can do the night shifts remotely but you'll have to come in on the weekend because Dr Grace will have appointments, which she'll have a lot of during the days as well, which is why your desk is out here, to keep them company while they wait and make sure they don't go wandering off,' she smiled.

'Where would they wander off too?' I asked.

'You heard me when I said the men are all downstairs, right? Under our feet are the living quarters for the entertainers. It takes all my energy some days to not go wandering myself,' she laughed. 'The breeders are a few floors below the entertainers, but trust me, that is not something you need to see,' she said, her eyes doing a funny twitch.

'Why?' I had to ask. We'd been taught that becoming a breeder was the highest honour in our society. Wouldn't the breeders be treated like kings and queens?

'They tell us a lot of things, Courtney, not all of it is true. Just trust me on that,' she whispered, casually checking over her shoulder. 'Breeders are treated no differently to the cows and sheep on the farms. They have one purpose and one purpose only.'

'But I don't ever remember my mother being sad.'

Zoë looked at me like I'd grown a second head. Then it dawned and it felt as though my entire existence was crumbling before me.

'One purpose and one purpose only. She wasn't my mother. Or not the woman whose womb I grew in?'

Zoë shook her head.

'My brother and sisters?' I asked, my heart breaking.

She shook her head. 'Although in your case, your brother was your brother, you were twins, a package deal.'

I had a twin. My sisters weren't my sisters. I felt something inside me cry like a baby.

'I have a lot to learn, don't I? I feel so inadequately prepared,' I said, trying not to let what was happening inside me show.

She smiled. 'Didn't we all, don't worry about it. That's why you have me. And Stacey. It sounds worse than it is, I promise,' she said, a little too forcefully.

I smiled, let her off the hook and let the subject drop. I wasn't sure how much more I could take before I broke down in a world where I was supposed to be so well cared for there would never be a need to be sad.

Zoë added an app to my tablet. 'Here's the booking system. When someone calls, they'll give you their customer number, you type it in here and then as long as it has a green dot next to it, you can go ahead and type in the request number they give you,' she said, using herself as an example and adding in a random number.

'What does the green dot mean?' I asked as I scrolled around the page looking at the different symbols.

'The first one shows the booker is healthy and they have available funds so they're permitted to make a booking. Once the system matches the details of the booker and entertainer, it makes sure they don't come from the same heritage line because even though we don't have families and emotional connections anymore, the idea of having sex with your brother, is just too much, even in this wacky, fabulous world we've built. Somethings will never change,' she smiled. 'So, if you get the green light, you can add in the date and time and it'll drop the booking into the calendar.

'If any come up with an x through the dot, it means they're not a match, apologise but don't say why, just say they're unavailable and ask for another number if they have one. If you get red dot, it means something is wrong with the booker, so you transfer it to me. If they don't have a request number and they want a random selection, you go here and you can press randomly select and let the system choose, or you can go here and do what we call a lucky dip, there's no going back on one of those though. If they have an idea of what they want, you can open up the advanced selection and put in some parameters like blonde, stubble, tall and the system will lucky dip based on those parameters.'

I watched as she demonstrated each of the actions. 'Do they really care about the specifics, isn't one just as good as another?'

Zoë shrugged. 'Of course, they're all well trained. But people like a bit of variety, I guess. It's like food, if you've had too much apple pie, perhaps you just want a brownie one day or ice cream. It's the same, really.'

I nodded as though it made sense. But I felt like I'd landed in an alternate existence. The college had made it seem so simple, so banal, I thought. I'd pop into a store front, sit and have whatever these needs were taken care of and be on my way. It was far more complex than they'd let on, that was for sure.

'Everyone's payment details have already been put into the system so they'll automatically be charged the booking fee as soon as you confirm the booking and then after their treatment, or whatever you're comfortable calling it,' she smiled. 'They'll be charged the full rate. Is it making sense?'

'Yes,' I answered as the phone rang. 'Shoot,' I mumbled.

'It's alright, just answer it like I showed you,' she said as she exited out of her file without confirming the booking, setting the tablet back on the booking home screen.

I pressed the answer button flashing on my tablet. 'Welcome to La Ferme, this is Courtney,' I said cheerily into the air, hoping it made it to the tiny microphone attached to the earpiece hooked over my ear.

'Hi, this is one, one, eight, three, I'd like to book, zero, two, three, nine for Friday at six.'

'Certainly, one moment,' I said, following the process Zoë had shown me while she watched on.

The caller's customer number came up with a green dot, so I typed in her request number, which also came up green. 'Lovely, it's all booked in,' I told the caller, adding it all into the calendar.

'Thanks,' she replied and hung up.

'You did great,' Zoë commended. 'Not so tough, right?'

'Nope, not so bad at all.'

Zoë ran through some other scenarios and office ins and outs in between calls until midday came and we switched the phones over to Jules whose turn it was to cover the lunch break.

Zoë phoned the cafeteria for grilled salmon salads and we went to wait for them in the pod where we ate with Rosie and Tess who were intent on sharing office gossip that although highly amusing, meant nothing to me, without knowing who they were actually talking about.

Zoë sat with me for the afternoon, watching on as I took calls, put through some more bookings and explained some of the intricacies of the queries that came with the calls.

'How's it all going out here?' asked Trish while we were enjoying coffees we'd made in Jen's security office instead of walking all the way out to the pod. The coffee wasn't quite as fancy but it did the job.

'I think I'm getting the hang of it,' I said as I took another call.

'She's doing great,' Zoë added once I'd hung up. 'She's a natural.'

'I'm not surprised,' Trish smiled. 'We don't give these jobs to just anyone, do we Zoë?'

'Absolutely not,' she said proudly. 'I was five years in it myself,' she said.

'Really? How did you get from here to there?'

'A chain affect really, one person retires at the top of the chain and everyone in the line below jumps up a spot, if they're skilled and dedicated enough.'

'So this is your job I'm taking?' I asked.

Zoë and Trish shared a look before Trish answered. 'No, Zoë's been with me for six months now. The last receptionist didn't work out. She wasn't right for the position, wasn't able to keep her emotions out of her work, out of her life, so we sent her back to the college to work in their administrative team when Ms Ilsa retired. It was the best solution for everyone.'

My stomach twisted uncomfortably as I wondered what my predecessor could possibly have done to have her sent to the dungeons, which is how we referred to the inner workings of the college. Sure, there was a lovely reception area on the ground floor manned by the rosy cheeked Ms Laura who snuck cream cakes into her drawer and the principal, vice principal and the teachers all had office space on the ground and first floors but the rest, the workers, they were all in the windowless basement where wine was once stored. It was only a slight upgrade from being sent to the farms.

We called it the dungeon and we pitied any poor soul who was stuck down there all day every day, typing up menus, class schedules and teaching notes. They ordered the food and supplies down there, scheduled building maintenance and maintained student records. You'd see them standing stunned on the beach in the late afternoon, looking up to the sky, letting the sun warm their faces like rats set free. Those of us in the business services program lived in fear of such a fate, just as those in the cooking program feared Patrice's fate.

She must have broken unspeakable rules to have been banished to the college. I couldn't even begin to comprehend what she'd done, what she could have done that had been so bad she'd been sent there.

Zoë gave me the slightest shake of her head. *Stop thinking and don't ask questions.* So, I followed the rules and smiled.

'It's nothing to concern yourself with,' Trish added. 'Once in a blue moon the recruiters are wrong, there's a DNA flaw no one spotted and the pace and the necessities of this job get the better of them, a place like this isn't for everyone. It's only the best of the best who can manage it and clearly you're already a natural, so you've got nothing at all to worry about,' she assured me. 'Alright, I'm going to steal Zoë for a while, will you be okay out here on your own?' she asked.

'Sure,' I said, there wasn't really that much to it.

'Excellent. Jen's in her office if you need her or you have Zoë's number if you get into trouble.'

'Thanks,' I said, as they left me to it.

As they left I felt the heavy weight of knowledge settling on my shoulders. Everything I knew was nothing but a mirage, smoke and mirrors. But I couldn't give voice to it. Zoë was right, it would do no good. Is that what had happened to my predecessor? Had it all been too much? I could see how. But I pushed all of the thoughts aside, hid them in the dark spaces of my mind. Instead I spent the rest of the day familiarising myself with the things Zoë had loaded onto my tablet, trying to feel comfortable sitting behind my desk, taking calls and before I knew it, the front door opened and Stacey walked in full of smiles and contagious energy. Suddenly everything was better, the weight that had hung over my heart despite my efforts, lifted.

'So how was your first day?' Stacey asked as we left the building and crossed the river.

'Fine, fine,' I answered.

'Fine?' Stacey asked with her eyebrows raised.

I shrugged. What did she want me to say? I suspected she knew what had gone on at morning tea. Did she know everything else as well? She seemed to know everything that went on everywhere so I wasn't sure why she pretended to be surprised.

'You have questions?'

'I do,' I told her. I had to ask someone about all I'd learned, what had happened at morning tea, somehow make sense of it all before I became like my predecessor and was sent to the dungeons at the college like a serviceable rodent. Zoë had told me to save it all for Stacey, that she would explain it better than anyone. It was her job, after all.

'I thought you might. I've booked dinner at Ora's. You can fire away once we're there. You might need a cocktail. I know I do,' she smiled.

The sun had disappeared by the time we took our seats in Ora's. People watched us as we were led to our table. 'I had to book but you'll find you have certain advantages in your position and one of them will be getting a table despite the waiting queues. 'Don't worry about it, you'll find your place,' Stacey told me before I could get too lost in my thoughts.

I focussed on the loud chatter, listened to the laughter rumble around us as cutlery clanged. There were distant shouts from the busy kitchen and waitresses running here and there, carrying trays of food and jugs of drink. Stacey ordered a jug of sangria and an array of tapas and paella and the waitress scurried off to fill our order.

'The Spanish might not be able to visit us anymore or us them, but thankfully we got their recipes for Sangria and Paella before we closed our borders,' Stacey smiled. 'There are a few of the restaurants still around from before the war like this one. Some things were just too good to give up, even if they are controlled by the government now.'

We talked of polite, everyday things, how everyone was, who did I meet, how Trish was treating me, nothing too important even though the big questions hung unasked in the air until the waitress returned with a jug of Sangria and glasses.

After Stacey had taken a few quick sips, she said, 'Alright, hit me with it, fire away, first question.'

'I don't even know where to start. I feel so underprepared. For all of it. Not just the sex and boy, it doesn't sound like popping out for a mani at all,' I told her.

Stacey had to cover her mouth to avoid spurting sangria over the table. 'Are they still throwing out that line?'

I shrugged. 'I saw Rosie kissing an entertainer, her body pushed up against his. Lay back and let them do all the work, we're told, just like a mani or a haircut, they said. If none of that is true, exactly how does it work?'

'You've seen the pictures, right?'

I nodded.

'Good. Well what he does will bring you pleasure, the most exquisite please,' she smiled, then cleared her throat and continued. 'It's the culmination of that pleasure that results in all the head clearing. It burns off the built-up endorphins from fulfilling your daily purpose and that's how you're left clear headed and refocussed. You know, there was no control over who reproduced, regardless of their DNA or capabilities. Men and women were doing whatever they pleased, whenever, no matter the detriment to their lives, their work, their purpose. It was mayhem. This way works better for everyone. You'll see. All the benefits, none of the complications.'

The waiter brought our paella, taking away the plates of tapas we'd already eaten and replenished the jug of sangria.

'And what's this about my mother not being my mother? My sisters not even related? Why all the secrecy?'

Stacey looked a little sad as I served myself some paella and shook her head. 'That's the hardest one of all to learn,' she agreed as a group of five or six truly beautiful men walked in to the restaurant. The restaurant fell silent as every woman stopped what they were doing to watch them.

'Are they allowed to just walk around like that any time they please, go anywhere they want whenever they want?' I asked, getting frustrated with the interruption and all the things I didn't know.

'They're not animals, we don't cage them,' Stacey laughed. 'But in a group like that I'd say they're advertising.'

'Advertising what?'

'Themselves.'

'Really? How exactly?'

'They lounge about handsomely, laugh and eat and drink and show everyone how well trained they are.'

'They sound like monkeys,' I interrupted.

'Trust me, monkeys can't do what they do,' she said smirking. 'Anyway, if you see something you like you ask for their number.'

'We're allowed to phone them?' I asked.

'Oh, hell no! There's absolutely no unauthorised fraternisation under any circumstances. That's the fastest way to land a ticket to the dungeons or out to the ships. You ask for their entertainer number so you can book them.'

'Right,' I said, watching the men sit with perfect manners, laughing gregariously but not too loudly, each looking like they'd be fantastic company. They all wore fitted t-shirts and jeans that hung snugly on their hips and thighs, showing off each of their most beautiful assets. They were handsome and those darned butterflies took flight in my stomach as the man from my morning tea entertainment looked up and caught my eye. He winked, sending waves of electricity through my body.

Blushing, I looked away, down into my paella, trying to fake some nonchalance.

Stacey laughed. 'Someone caught your eye, then?' she asked.

Utterly humiliated at my lack of control, I shrugged.

'It's alright, you know,' she said. 'There's always one or two that you'll find more attractive than the others but they're all well trained to do their job, so you'd be satisfied with any but if there's one in particular, you should book him when Trish offers you your first week bonus.'

'My what?'

'Your bonus. One of the perks of working at La Ferme. You get a bonus at the end of your first week in the shape of a tall, dark and handsome entertainer, or whatever look tickles your lady bits. You also get a nice discount on your bookings and quarterly bonuses. Not to mention your morning tea treats, you lucky bitch,' she said, envy dripping off her tongue.

'Lucky? That is still to be determined,' I smiled.

'Your first time would be better if it was with someone you had some sort of connection with, though, so you should ask him for his number. Go on,' she encouraged.

'No, no, I couldn't,' I insisted, still trying to comprehend everything I'd learned. It was too much. My head was swimming. But even so, there was no way I was getting up and walking over to him to ask for his number. I doubted any words would even come out of my uncooperative mouth.

I was busy hanging my head in shame, blushing at the mere thought, focusing on the food on my plate, when I saw a pair of jean clad legs headed towards me. I looked up to see my morning tea treat stop in front of me. He leant down, took my hand and pressed a card into my palm. I looked at it. It was white with only the numbers, one, eight, five, nine printed in black.

He whispered in my ear, 'I'll make sure your first time is mind blowing. I promise,' he said, with that deep velvety voice of his, his warm breath doing all sorts of naughty things to my ear and insides, and causing my breath to catch in my chest.

He stood up and winked before returning to his friends. Captivated, I couldn't help but watch how his body moved in his jeans.

Stacey laughed. 'Don't get too attached there but you should definitely take him up on his offer. Every girl should have her mind blown the first time out,' she grinned.

'So how often does one hire an... entertainer?' I asked, curious.

'Whenever you want. Everyone's needs are different as are our budgets, of course. Your salary is more generous than some, so you might be able to afford one or two entertainers a week if you felt the need. Ordinary people either wait 'til they're really randy or if they have an event to attend then they can kill two birds, so to speak. But my dear, you are not ordinary.'

'Why is that and what does that even mean? Zoë says things like that and I don't know what she means. Why am I so special and why can't I be like ordinary people?' desperately hoping I could be in the ordinary category and just order an entertainer when I had an event that required a date? I certainly couldn't imagine booking one or goodness, two, every single week. 'Surely that many entertainers each week is a little excessive? To have sex with that many men doesn't sound right. It certainly doesn't sit well in my stomach,' I told her. I felt quite ill at the thought of so many men touching me. 'Not to mention the cost. Zoë mentioned a beach resort she and Rachel are planning to go to later in the year, to sit on the beach and drink cocktails and have fun for a week. She'd said I would be welcome to join them, so I'd rather spend my money on the holiday than an array of entertainment every week. That makes far more sense. Doesn't it?' I asked, almost desperately.

'Some nice theories, but no, you are not ordinary and will never be ordinary. You tested highest in your class, in fact higher than any one has in a while, not just academically but across the board.

That's why you're here at La Ferme, one of the most prestigious companies in the country, on track for a career people would beg for with perks 'ordinary' people can only dream of. That's what makes you more than everyone else Courtney. It's a good thing.'

'But who would even know where I work, my trajectory, any of it?' I asked.

'An important lesson here, everyone knows everything. The public know who you are, or they will if they don't already. Your face was in the weekend paper as the newest, brightest recruit in a decade, people were predicting you'd rise to the top, before your career was done. It was just a few degrees here and there in the make-up of your body and temperament that kept you out of the breeding program. Some even suspected too smart to breed, your brilliant brain would be dulled, they're having similar concerns about your brother, I hear. All that and you hadn't even started yet. You'll be seen at the best events in the best seats, at the best parties wearing only the top shelf clothing. That outfit you have on, cost more than a month's wage of any server here. They know who you are, trust me. And people expect people like you to behave a certain way, set an example. And when you have the perks you have and access to the best entertainers before they get snapped up, you are expected to not only make the most of it but to be seen, to be flaunting it, so that everyone else will follow suit. Some things never change. They pretend all the emotions are dead and buried but some will never die. They're imprinted in our DNA from centuries of evolution and envy is one of them, and we exploit that when we can, for the good of the nation. People mightn't go to the extreme measures they once did but they see you, they follow your lead and their focus and productivity increases.

'Yeah, I still don't get how any of it achieves that,' I admitted.

She smiled. 'You wait. You will. You like to run, right?' she asked.

I nodded.

'Well, how you feel after you run, your head is clear, your body is alive, it's kind of like that. But times ten,' she grinned stupidly.

Well that was an analogy I understood. Running never failed to clear my head shake things up, shake things free and I always felt better for it. I wondered what ten times that would be like.

Stacey paid the bill and walked me back to my apartment building. 'Will you be alright? Any more questions?' she asked.

'Nope, I think I'm good. For now,' I lied, still trying to find a way, a place for it all to sit in my brain. I'd manage, everyone else managed, didn't they?

'Good girl. Do you remember the way to the office?'

'Yeah, I think so.'

'Good, you'll be on your own tomorrow but I'm just a phone call away, alright?'

'No problem,' I said, almost believing it.

There was so much to take in. It wasn't just a whole new world, it was an alternate universe where nothing made sense. Nothing was as I'd imagined or expected. I needed it to make sense though and fast. The last thing I wanted was to be deemed incompetent like my predecessor, get caught up in unnecessary emotions and sent to work in the dungeons. All it had taken was one mistake, she gave in to an outdated emotion, no one had been clear about it, but like Stacey said, I was smart, smart enough to read between the lines and I'd read enough to know it'd had something to do with a man and just like that, she'd lost everything. Zoë had made it clear, fitting in and playing the game exactly as I was expected to play it, was necessary to my survival.

I threw on the running gear Stacey had bought for me. I kitted up and headed back out into the balmy night to burn off some endorphins before they took over my body and I really did go mad.

The air was still warm but the humidity had eased so it was clean and fresh or maybe I was acclimatising already?

I ran, feeling tremors in my legs as my feet hit the pavement, slowly picking up pace, flushing out the negativity and confusion. As my muscles burned I felt them strengthen, felt my mind strengthen and knew I'd be alright. I just had to go with the flow. There was a reason we lived the way we did and I just had to trust in it and know it was for the best and that I'd be fine. I would always be fine. I only had to look around to know that everyone acclimatised. Sure, I worked for one of the most impressive and most sought-after companies in the country but I'd been recruited because I was the best in my class at what I do. It was just the first step in my career. I just had to remember that, remember that I was exactly where I was meant to be.

I ran along the river front, past the bars filled with people, the empty dock for the water taxi the fake beach, the sand now empty, the water glistening under the moonlight. I ran until there were no people, just me and the sound of my feet hitting the ground. All the way to the big bridge. At the bridge I bent, putting my hands on my knees and sucked in air. It felt good to feel everything burn from exertion. I felt in control. For the first time in days, I felt like me. Once I'd caught my breath I turned and ran back the other way.

I ran for home, looking at the row of restaurants in the distance where one eight five nine had been lounging with his friends as though I had no say in what my eyes did. Then I saw him and his friends walking along the path towards the river. Catching a river taxi back to La Ferme, I supposed. He looked up and saw me watching him, our eyes connecting. He smiled and I swear my heart skipped a beat and my breath caught, lodged somewhere in my chest.

Quickly turning, embarrassed, ashamed, I ran straight into an oncoming pushbike. Stupid distracted reflexes. I didn't even realise what was happening until it was too late. I'd tried to dodge the cyclist but I was just too slow and I was on the ground before I knew it, everything hurting, aching.

Slowly, comprehension set in and I opened my eyes to a sea of handsome male faces who all began checking my limbs were still connected and in working order. I scanned the faces until I found the lovely, dark ocean-blue eyes of one eight five nine looking into mine as he lifted my head from the pavement.

'Are you alright?' he asked, kindly.

I don't remember ever being more embarrassed. Immediately I sat up, looking for the cyclist. She was fine, the front wheel of her bike a little buckled.

'I'm so, so sorry,' I said, apologising profusely for not watching where I was going.

She waved me off, 'As long as you're alright then all is well,' she insisted.

One of the entertainers helped her straighten her wheel. She asked for his card and rode off with a smile on her face.

'Let me walk you home,' offered my dark-haired, white knight.

'No, no, I'm fine,' I insisted, trying to stand but wobbling when the pain shot up my leg. I caught my balance but my ankle was too sore to put all my weight on.

'I insist,' he said.

'But your friends, you have to get back,' I said, trying to buy some time and think of another solution.

'It's alright, they'll wait for me. There'll be another taxi,' he smiled.

I nodded reluctantly but only because I couldn't think of another solution. There was no one else to offer assistance other than the entertainers and I was unsure how I'd make it home without some help, my ankle just wouldn't take my weight.

He draped my arm across his shoulders and wrapped one of his strong arms around me so he could take my weight. We walked along the river towards my apartment building, the moon above bright, the stars twinkling, unaware of the twinkling happening inside me from the feel of his arm around me, of his touch that burned through my clothes, searing my skin in the most incredible way making everything inside me shimmer and dance.

'How was your dinner?' he asked.

'Very nice,' I said shyly, too aware of every single contact point.

'Quite a change from the college, isn't it, all this choice and opulence?'

'It is,' I smiled, glad someone finally seemed to understand.

'It takes some getting used to but you'll get there,' he assured me as we walked and talked about how surreal it was to go from one place to the other.

'How long since you left the boys' college?' I asked.

'Only a year,' he said. 'And yes, I'm still getting used to it,' he said with a small, kind smile.

'How do you manage?' I asked him.

He shrugged. 'When you don't have a lot of choices, it's easy to just let go. You can't control any of it, anyway. Then you find someone you can trust; one or two people you can call a friend and it just gets better. Tolerable anyway,' he added quietly with just a hint melancholy. 'But you,' he said with more cheer. 'Look at where you're beginning. Nothing but bright shiny lights ahead for you,' he gushed.

'Yes, nothing but bright shiny lights,' I agreed with much less enthusiasm.

'It's not what you expected?' he asked.

'I'm grateful, really I am. One of my fellow graduates went to a grain farm, so I'm very grateful to be here, to have a lovely apartment and beautiful clothes and a wonderful career planned out for me.'

'But?'

I shrugged. 'But I just found out my mother's not my mother, my sisters not even genetically related among other things. Things I thought I knew, are not what I thought they were.'

'The key is to not think about it,' he winked as we approached my building. 'You can't change it, so it's best not to, it'll be easier that way, I promise,' he assured me kindly.

I nodded

As we walked up the path towards the doors of my building, he said, 'I meant what I said earlier. I'll take good care of you. I'll make sure your first time is something to remember,' he insisted.

I nodded, realising that this chivalry of his was just part of the game, just part of the advertising and schmoozing for customers. I supposed everyone had targets to reach and this was how his part of the world made theirs.

The disappointment must have shown on my face as I felt the

blood drain downwards. 'Hey, are you sure you're alright? Do I need to call you a medic?'

'No, no, I'll be fine,' I insisted, no longer wanting to be a part of his silly game.

'Hmmm...' he mumbled. 'Well, make sure you ice your ankle. There'll be bruise cream in your bathroom, use it as much as you need, your housekeeper will replenish it. Anyway, I better go. Don't want to get either of us in trouble for unauthorised fraternisation now.' He smiled and suddenly the whole world lit up, my insides lit up and I was stunned, wordless.

Don't be a fool, I told myself when I finally caught my breath. He's an entertainer. He's supposed to make me feel like I was the only woman on earth that mattered. 'Thank you, you were very kind, I shall consider your proposition,' I told him.

He looked around at the quiet street, put his finger under my chin, tilting my face so I had to look at him. He looked into my eyes for a heart stopping second too long before whispering, 'I'm not playing. Yes, you could have me detained for what I'm about to say, but I don't think you will,' he suggested, looking at me curiously. When I mutely shook my head, insisting I wouldn't, he lowered his voice until it was so low it could have gotten lost on the breeze if I hadn't been paying attention. 'If it wasn't against the rules, I'd like nothing more than to kiss you right now.' But it was against the rules, so he didn't. He watched me a moment more, a strange, sad, longing filling his lovely eyes before he turned away and walked towards the dock. Damn rules.

'Courtney?' called Margie, the security guard, interrupting my incredible view of one, eight, five, nine's retreating rear, whose words sinking into the place in my chest that ached at night.

'Oh, hello, yes,' I replied, regaining my senses and hobbling through the door she held open.

'Are you alright?' she asked, looking from my retreating white knight and back to me.

'Oh, yes, thank you, just an unfortunate spill with a cyclist, I'm afraid. I'm not used to so much activity at night,' I smiled. Which was true, no one was out on the trails after dark at the college. 'Luckily there was a group of entertainers heading to the docks and one was kind enough to help me hobble back up the path,' I added, to ensure the security guard didn't have an inkling of what was going on inside my head. Not that I was even sure what was going on inside my head but I was sure it was against the rules.

It certainly didn't make any sense to me. I stepped into the lift and all I could think was he'd wanted to kiss me. He'd said he wasn't playing. What did that mean? I should have been horrified that he'd say such unlawful things, that I was feeling so many banned, outdated, unproductive emotions but all I could only wonder if it was real? That he felt it too? Or was the flirting and the suggestion all a part of the game he supposedly wasn't playing?

If so, he'd played me like a master.

CHAPTER 3

―――――

My ankle was fine in the morning thanks to a good icing and a lathering of the bruise cream I'd found in the bathroom cabinet just like one eight five nine said I would. My ankle was a little stiff but loosened easy enough after a hot shower. I don't know how I'd have managed to walk in heels if it hadn't been okay and there weren't many other shoe choices in my wardrobe.

When I opened the door to reception, Zoë was sitting at my desk, absently twirling her long, chocolate brown waves around her finger, staring into space.

'Good morning,' I called to her.

'Well, good morning. It's always a good sign when they come back,' she smiled as though I'd had a choice.

Rosie pushed open the door on the other side of the room and wheeled her chair through with Tess and Jules right behind her, creating a tangle of chairs so Tess nearly tripped over as they tried to fit them all behind my desk.

'Come, come, quick,' hurried Zoë, patting my empty chair waiting beside her.

'What's going on?' I asked, kicking my handbag under the chair and sitting down.

'Just wait, you'll see. Any second now,' cooed Jules dreamily.

Tess passed me a coffee and I noticed they all had coffees in front of them. How nice of them to make sure there was one for me too. I was about to comment on how kind and welcoming they all were when I spotted movement from the corner of my eye and the girls all gasped with relief.

I turned to the big windows where they were staring, and hanging from a pulley was a shirtless, beautifully tanned, sculpted man picking strawberries from the row of plants hanging along the top of the window. There seemed to be hundreds of plants and he just hung there with the sun glistening over his body, happily moving side to side as he collected strawberries.

Zoë leaned over to whisper in my ear. 'They use the entertainers to pick the fruit, and do the little planting jobs so we don't have to look at the farmers. This is much nicer, trust me,' smiled.

The girls watched him dreamily. 'He's my favourite, I think,' cooed Tess.

'You say that every time,' laughed Rosie who very much suited her name. She was more robust than the others with pretty green eyes, rosy cheeks and wavy black hair.

'I liked last Thursday,' said Jules. She was usually a smart, no nonsense woman and had apparently lost all her smarts at the sight of a beautiful man. 'But this'll do too,' she added dreamily.

'We should get his number,' said Tess.'

I watched closely, interested to see how they would go about it. I could feel one, eight, five, nine's card burning my leg through the pocket of my skirt where I'd absently put it. I had left it on my nightstand the night before and the thought of leaving it there, out in the open did something unexpected to my insides, so I'd hidden it in my pocket where it would be safe, from what I hadn't figured out yet.

'Quick, Courtney, where's your tablet?' Jules demanded.

I put one eight five nine's card out of my head, swiped open my tablet and passed it over. Jules opened a blank page and wrote on it then went to the window, knocked on the glass and held my tablet up as the fruit picker looked her way.

He smiled, held up his fingers, two, one, three, two.

Jules wrote the number down and instamessaged it to herself and Tess, then deleted it from my screen as she sat back down.

'I could just book it in for you now,' I offered.

'Thanks, but that's one of the luxuries of working here, we all have access to the booking system so we can book in our own entertainment and stay anonymous. Not sure why it even matters, it's not like when you see someone at a party with a man you don't know where he's come from,' Jules said.

'It's so those who book in a lot of dates and don't want the world to know, can be anonymous and if the guys add notes to the files about what the women like or how difficult they are, they don't want us to know who they are,' Zoë clarified.

'I know, I know. The perverts don't want anyone to know they like being handcuffed or what toys they have hidden in the cupboard,' laughed Jules.

'What do you mean toys?' I asked, horrified.

The girls giggled. 'You know, like dildos and stuff,' Rosie said.

'Balls and bullets, beads and whips,' added Tess. 'Some people are into some crazy shit. Who knows what they have stashed away for a bit of mid-week fun,' she giggled.

'What?' I sputtered. As if the sex itself wasn't quite the revelation to contend with.

'I don't know what's wrong with the regular stuff myself,' said Jules. 'It's not like the olden days before the war when you got stuck married or living with any old bloke because they were nice or whatever. These ones know what they're doing. The boys' college makes sure of it. They're not done until you're done,' she giggled.

'The President reckons if you're satisfied in the bedroom your productivity will be better, you'll be sick less, you'll be happier, more focussed and less inclined to find yourself involved in mischief,' informed Zoë.

'Burning off the endorphins, like getting a haircut or a mani,' I repeated.

'Certainly burns off the endorphins but a mani doesn't come close, trust me. But yes, the President is quite adamant about every woman partaking to do her bit for society, if our heads are clear, we'll work better, faster, harder, be more committed to doing our bit for the rebuilding of our nation.'

'I heard,' Tess said conspiratorially, 'she was ditched by her childhood sweetheart. He went to war like everyone else and ran off with an English princess and she was royally pissed,' she giggled at her own joke. 'He was declined one of the flights home, was left standing dumbfounded on the tarmac. Now she just likes to use and abuse at her leisure,' she said.

'Who said that?' asked Zoë.

'My mum, my carer, whatever you want to call her, said it. I heard her and her friends talking about it once before I was sent away,' Jules said, smiling at her memory.

'It's all poppycock,' scoffed Tess. 'Silly old bitch just likes to get laid,' she whispered so softly if you weren't paying attention you'd have missed it.

'Are you complaining about your lot in life?' Rosie asked raising her eyebrows and smirking.

'Absolutely not and you know it,' laughed Tess. 'I'm not quite sure how they managed in the olden days with the same man for every party. A man's like a handbag, you have to keep it new and fresh instead of having to use the same one every day for your whole entire life. How dull it must have been in the pre-war times,' she mused.

I'd never really thought about it one way or the other. But I did wonder how long it would take to get bored having sex with the same person every time? Or would it be comforting to have the familiarity and the intimacy of knowing one person more than any other? I suspected I'd soon have the data to analyse. I wasn't yet sure if that was a good thing or not, mostly, I was just terrified at the idea of partaking in any of it but I would, I would do my bit as I was expected, terrified or not because the consequences were too great and I believed in what the President had done, the world she'd created and how great we were as a nation. That didn't happen by accident and if this was one of the ways we contributed to being a great nation, then I was committed to doing my part.

The strawberry picker moved up to pick broccoli from the floor above and with a moan the girls took their coffee cups and chairs and went back to their own desks, leaving me to man the front area on my own, which was just fine. I had so much information swirling about in my head that I didn't quite know what to do with and needed some quiet and space to at least digest it all and try to make some sense of it.

When we're twelve we take aptitude tests and personality tests to see what careers we'd be most suited to. Our lives then revolve around those results. Our friends, our studies, our hobbies. When we turn eighteen the recruiters come, we take more tests, we interview, we smile and are then allocated positions, housing, lives, in line with who chooses us and the positions we're given, then our lives begin.

Nowhere in that perfectly organised syllabus are we taught how to exist without a carer, how to exist in a world where men are for hire, status symbols, popular accessories like a fashionable hand-bag and ordered weekly as though milk for your morning coffee. And certainly, nowhere in that perfectly constructed education of ours do they prepare us for the sheer, incredible beauty of the entertainers who provide these services. Perfectly trained to pro-vide a certain type of stress relief for the women committed to their nation and who can afford them.

It was all only temporary of course, so our education had told us, until there were again enough men to go around, until the country regenerated, until the war was over, until the world was safe. That's what the President had said when she saved us from annihilation but twenty-one years was a long time to be tempo-rary but perhaps without the label, the promise of impermanence, no one would have accepted such a thing but now, people were forgetting or maybe they were just afraid. No one wanted to be the one reallocated in the middle of the night. We didn't even know for sure if the war was still being fought. We had no access to the outside world, just total, complete faith in our President and the fear of repercussions if that faith wavered. The newspapers though, they said we still had a way to go, that female births still outnumbered the male ten to one, despite the dusty forgotten history books in the back of the college library saying they were once almost equal but if people knew that, the foundations upon which we were rebuilding would or could become irreparably fractured, the people less compliant. But worse still, how far would the President take her programs if given the chance? Temporary or not, it didn't make any of it any easier to compartmentalise in my head. Zoë said I'd get used to it, to the men, the requirements, the activities, their place in our society, the role I had to play but I doubted I'd get used to any of it because it made no sense in my overly programmed brain. But it had to, I had to believe in our President if for no other reason that I didn't know what else to believe in. Anything else went against everything I knew and I'd already lost so much of what I thought I knew since I'd arrived. I had to keep something or what was the point? What would I have left?

The rest of the day was quiet and dull in comparison to the morning. By the time I headed home, I was exhausted. I hoped not every day would include some ridiculous revelation to contend with.

I made a stir fry for dinner, one of the few things we learnt during cooking classes at the college and I ate it on the balcony, listening to the sounds of life below.

When I was finished, I was too restless to sit still, to watch the vision screen or sleep. So, despite the previous night's unfortunate altercation with the cyclist, I tested my ankle, which felt fine, and put on a fresh set of running clothes and headed out into the night.

The riverbank was quiet. There were people around, but not too many, so I was able to run without any clashes but I kept my wits about me none-the-less. I took it easy to begin with, until I was confident my ankle would hold up and then I relaxed into it, breathed in the fresh air and let my body take over.

I felt a sense of relief as I reached the bridge. It was peaceful. Just the water recently disturbed by a passing water taxi, lapping against the riverbank. It felt like a haven. Perhaps it would be my safe place, my happy place, the place my mind could be quiet for just a moment. I'd had the beach at the college, no one ever went there late at night and I could watch the moon hovering in the sky above the water without the noise of other people.

I took some deep breaths, breathing in the quiet before turning for home but then there was movement, under the bridge, in the shadows and then he was there, standing in front of me.

Unauthorised fraternisation is strictly prohibited. No doubts. No confusion. No question. Prohibited. Against the law. You will be sent to a detention island if you're caught, prohibited. I knew it. The man standing before me knew it. We all knew it. But I stepped into the shadows anyway.

The muscles in my legs still burned from the lactic acid flowing through them. It was late and we both should have been sleeping, safe and sound in our respective beds on opposite sides of the river. But we weren't. We stood in the shadows of a bridge under a restoring moon with illicit transgressions filling our heads.

'Hello,' he said.

'What are you doing here?' I asked.

'Hoping to see you,' he smiled casually.

'Really? Why?' I asked dubiously.

'I'm not really sure,' he said, throwing me one of his brilliant smiles that outshone anything the moon could give on its best day. 'I just know I couldn't stop thinking about you today and something inside me kept begging to see you again.'

I know I wasn't smart enough for the breeding program, but I wasn't stupid either. Did one, eight, five, nine, really expect me to believe that our brief encounters had somehow embedded me into his handsome brain so much so he would break rules to see me again?

'Really?' I asked. 'How did you know I'd be here? I didn't know I'd be here,' I said.

'I didn't,' he said. 'But I hoped.'

He hoped. He hoped I'd go for a run and we'd cross paths? 'What made you think I'd run?'

'I run. If you run, you run, you can't help yourself, you need it. I hoped you were the same. I was counting on it.'

'Is that allowed? Orchestrating accidental encounters?' I asked, knowing it wasn't, but unsure what else to say.

'Absolutely not, but it seems you have me desperate to break all the rules,' he said. 'Will you report me?' he asked, concern etching the corners of his eyes.

'How do I know you haven't been sent here on some errand to test my allegiance?'

'To test your allegiance? An errand for whom?' he asked, his mouth turning slightly at the corners, clearly amused.

'Are you mocking me? I'm not stupid, you know. I've heard about what they do to people who break the rules. How they punish them. Send them away. So what if you're the most handsome man I've ever seen, it doesn't mean you're not a spy.'

'The most handsome man you've ever seen?' he asked, raising an eyebrow.

'Shut up. I've only been here three days, I haven't seen that many,' I added, defending myself.

'Well, I'm not a spy, I can assure you,' he scoffed. 'I just wanted to see you again.'

'Why?' I demanded, still not sure I could trust him. I was starting to wondering if I could trust anything. 'There are far more beautiful women for you to stalk than me. Why would you risk getting into trouble for me?'

He smiled, that brilliant smile that did crazy things to my traitorous heart. Bad things. Unlawful things. Things that felt too good. Things you read about in the banned stories buried in the back of the library, stories used as cautionary tales depicting the mischief and mayhem that arises from emotions, feelings, unauthorised fraternisation.

'I happen to think you're incredibly beautiful. But there's something about you. A kindred connection, I don't know. I find you intriguing, I like that things matter to you even though you know they're not supposed to, you think about them anyway and you think with your heart. I could see it in your eyes at morning tea and again when we were walking last night. It makes no sense but I can't stop thinking about you, wondering about you, hoping you're okay, that you're finding some people to trust, that you're not alone with that sadness that flashed at the back of those beautiful eyes when you spoke of your family. You looked as lost as I feel some days and I couldn't help myself, I had to see you,' he said. 'Not to mention, I haven't stopped thinking about the electricity that sparks between us when I touch you, and I haven't been able to think of anything else but running my hands up those perfect long legs of yours or kissing that perfectly delicious mouth,' he added, with a childlike naughty grin.

'I beg your pardon?' I asked, lost for any more words.

'It's not a crime to be beautiful, Courtney. And it's not a crime for me to imagine touching you. Well, it is but I'm choosing to pretend it's not. It should be a crime though for you not to accept the compliment.'

'Well...' I mumbled, trying to find the right thing to say so I didn't embarrass myself, so I could stop the fluttering in my chest and run home where it was safe but when I checked in with my heart, it wanted no such thing.

'I won't bite, you know. I just wanted to see you. This life can get dull and lonely sometimes. I felt a connection with you, something I've never felt with another single human being and I can't ignore it. I don't want to ignore it. I want to see what it is. I want to feel. Something. With you I feel and I want to feel some more. Will you just sit with me for a little bit?' he asked, almost begged.

I didn't know what else to say and if I was being honest, I knew exactly what he was saying was true because I'd felt it too. I'd felt those sparks shoot through my body when he touched me. I'd felt my blood heat and pump too fast through my veins. It's why I was running tonight in the first place, if I was being honest. I was trying to run him out of my brain. Trying to burn off the endorphins built up from thinking of him, of those dark ocean-blue eyes and that thick mop of midnight-black hair. If I was being honest, all I wanted to do for the rest of my life was to sit with him. To feel. That alone said I was in trouble. Big trouble. But I no longer had the strength to run in the other direction, not when he was asking me to stay. I couldn't think of a single objection. So I gave in like a fool.

'Of course,' I said, following him to a ledge deep in the shadows where it was cool and quiet. Where no one could hear us talk about anything and everything. Where we were free, just two people talking, sitting with a few inches between us, and our hands in our laps, like semantics made a difference to the law breaking.

I knew it was wrong. Everything inside me knew it was wrong, but when I looked into his eyes, as dark blue as the deepest parts of the ocean, there wasn't a thing I could do to stop any of it, so we talked.

'It's really pretty here,' I commented as the water shimmered under the moonlight.

'It is. They like to think they made it that way but most of this was here before the war. Some parts were damaged in the war, here and there and then rebuilt but most of it has just been upgraded or left as it was. They take credit for it, anyway. Not that it really matters, I suppose. Credit is ego, right? An unnecessary emotion in the structure of a perfect life,' he smiled.

I chuckled. 'If ego no longer matters then why am I wearing an overpriced state of the art running top and the girl I passed down by the gardens is wearing a daggy old t-shirt?'

He smiled. 'See? Interesting. Do you know how many people don't even think about that, don't even notice? They notice you're wearing an overpriced running top, that you're from a level of society they can never reach but they don't know why. They don't think about where that comes from, how ego based that is at its core. They're so well trained not to question any of it.'

'Are you saying you don't agree with the way the President has structured our society?' I asked curiously.

'I'd never ever say such a thing,' he grinned. 'Not out loud, anyway.'

I laughed because he said it with humour even though I knew he meant it. Even though I'd thought things myself. Questioned things I wasn't meant to question. I'd always thought I was a freak, that I'd been born wrong, they'd forgotten to adjust one of the chromosomes in my DNA but maybe what he'd seen in me was right, maybe we did have some sort of kindred connection.

I certainly felt something. It came off him in waves. It charged back and forth between us like an electrical current I couldn't seem to move away from even though we weren't even touching. It was like maybe our souls were reaching for each other. Was that even possible? I'd never heard of anything like it, not even in the banned romance books at the back of the library at the college. Whatever it was, soothed and calmed me, it filled me with something I couldn't name, something that felt so good, so pure and real, the first truly real thing I'd felt since I'd arrived, since maybe ever.

'You know once, this, whatever this is,' I said, indicating the two us. 'Friendship between genders, whatever, was allowed.'

'What do you know of those things?' he asked curiously.

'I did extra-curricular work in the library sometimes. There were books buried right at the back in the caged section. But there's was a key on the ring with the storeroom key so sometimes I went in and there were books that told the most beautiful love stories. People dreamed of it, they'd see each other across a crowded room, their eyes would meet and they'd fall in love and everyone would celebrate with a wedding and champagne,' I told him wistfully. 'Sorry, I don't know why I told you that,' I added, suddenly realising how inappropriate it was to talk of such things.

'You don't ever have to censor yourself around me. You know how I said you needed to find some people to trust. We mightn't be allowed to be friends but whatever happens, you can trust me. Kindred remember,' he smiled.

I smiled back. Comforted that there was one person in this place who got me, me, the bits of me I'd never shown anyone and it felt good. Even if I never saw him again, because realities were I probably never would, I knew that in this world, in this place where nothing made sense and I felt so out of my depth, he existed.

It was midnight when he kissed the top of my hand and I ran for home with a smile on my face and glow in my heart.

Three days. That's all it had taken for me to break the only rules anyone really cared about. Three days. Sunday, I was on a train crossing the country. Sunday, I marvelled at the solar farms that glittered like seas of diamonds in the red dirt, the cattle farms that stretched wide and deep, the lushest, greenest orchards, trees with branches heavy and sagging with coloured fat fruit. I'd marvelled at all of it, my eyes wide with wonder, my tummy filled with fear and excitement for what lay ahead.

Now three days later, here I was, a fool and I didn't care. I couldn't undo what I'd done. I didn't want to. I wouldn't, even if I could. It felt too good, too perfect to change it. He felt like home.

Like I said, I was a fool.

CHAPTER 4

The office, like everything else in our country, was perfectly organised with rules and structure, processes and procedures governing everything from how you answered the telephone, where you ate lunch and of course ascension through the ranks. Everyone passed through our office, one way or another at one time or another. They came to set up accounts or to see Dr Grace if they'd been sick. We had implants that not only kept us infertile but alerted all manner of systems if there was any change to our health, anything from a cold to leukaemia. The smallest of changes blocked your entertainment account for the protection of the entertainers until Dr Grace could check everything was back in order and cleared you. Dr Grace cleared all the new entertainers before they could be integrated into their new homes in the apartments below. There was always someone coming or going.

Jen, Head of Security, had her office right behind my desk. She sat in there all day watching the gazillion monitors that saw everything that went on at La Ferme. Jen was a hoot as long as you didn't divulge any secrets you didn't want everyone to know. She had smoky blue eyes and dark-blonde hair that she wore in a loose ponytail. She wore a lot of eye makeup that made her eyes look mean and dangerous, but she laughed like a hyena and gossiped like an old lady. She knew everyone's business. She either saw it on one of her screens or someone told her hoping to gain access to places they weren't allowed access. It never worked, she was a true professional, but she liked the gossip so she let them tell her things, anyway. I hated to think what she could use that information for so I was always careful about what I said.

I leant against the doorframe of Jen's office, sipping a freshly brewed coffee, having a laugh about Maria, an uptight accountant who'd just been in to see Dr Grace. 'Now there's one that definitely needs to get herself some stress relief,' laughed Jen as Zoë knocked on the door.

'Yooohooo,' Zoë cooed even though I was standing right there.

'Oh, hey,' I said. 'Want one?' I offered, indicating my cup of coffee.

'Sure, sure, why not?' Zoë accepted.

Once the machine had dispensed Zoë's coffee, we farewelled Jen, letting her get back to watching her monitors and returned to my desk. I sat in my chair and Zoë planted herself on the glass top of my desk as though she weighed nothing more than a feather.

'What's up? What brings you out here?' I asked her.

'Nothing', just thought I'd see how you were doing?'

'Really? You just saw me at lunch,' I said, suspecting something mischievous was brewing in Zoë's brain.

'It's nothing, really. I had plans with Rach tonight but she just bailed on me, so I have a spare ticket to the game and I was wondering if you wanted to come?'

'What game?' I asked, unfamiliar with the sporting schedules. We were aware men in the entertainment program played sport but they'd never showed us the games at the college or taught us the rules. It was becoming more and more apparent there was a lot they left out.

Some insight would have been nice, especially as exercise for women was purely recreational. We had a country to rebuild, there was no time for us to be playing competitive sport. So the available sports involved running, tennis, yoga, aerobics, that sort of thing, the sort of activities that keep you fit and looking your best, social activities that provided opportunities to build relations and community, but didn't require you to become too close or require too much time or emotional investment.

'Basketball. It's on over at The Cube. Big game. Great seats. What do you say?'

I shrugged. It would be great to get out, get out of my quiet apartment and out of my busy brain. It didn't really matter to where. 'Sure, why not? Hey, hang on, this isn't one of those events one needs a date for, is it?' I asked. I now lived in perpetual fear of this date hiring business, the rules and requirements and more importantly, the how to's of it all. My plan was just to avoid it all indefinitely.

Zoë laughed. 'No, not at all. In fact, it's best if you don't bring one. But there will be men, lots of beautiful men and people to impress, so wear something nice. Something fun and flirty,' she smiled.

'Fun and flirty,' I repeated. 'What is that exactly?' I asked. A week ago, I wore nothing but a grey woollen dress, tights and clunky brogues.

'Have a go, see what you come up with. I'll meet you in the

lobby at seven,' she said, sculling the rest of her coffee and jumping off the desk.

'How do you know where I live?' I asked, even though I suspected Zoë knew a bit of everyone's business.

'I approved it. And it's a few floors down from me,' she smiled.

'Really? How come I haven't seen you around, in the hallways, or on the water taxi in the mornings?'

'I get the train, my travel allowance was upgraded when I got the promotion to work with Trish, as yours will be someday,' she said. It would be nice not to have to worry about water spray wrinkling my outfit and frizzing my hair, that's for sure. I lived in fear every morning. But I wouldn't hold my breath, no one looked ready to die or retire, so I'd be booking entertainers and keeping an eye on Dr Grace's visitors for a while yet.

I tried asking Jen before she left for the day, what on earth fun and flirty was, but all she'd said was, 'Oh don't listen to Zoë. Wear whatever you want. The blokes don't care, the players are all in the breeding program anyway and the rest, well, they'll show up no matter what you wear. Zoë just likes to show off to the little people. It's just part of the game, so wear whatever you're comfortable in.'

Yeah, easier said than done. I wasn't comfortable wearing anything in my wardrobe. The entire contents, work wear, casual wear, sportswear, fancy frocks, shoes, jammies and jewellery, had all been selected by Stacey. Every day, I looked inside my wardrobe and wondered what she'd been thinking, that surely she'd had too many cocktails the day she shopped for me?

I was comfortable wearing that ugly, grey woollen dress the college issued and those clunky shoes. Zoë would have a heart attack if I showed up in anything resembling one of those outfits, so instead of being comfortable, I spent too long scouring the wardrobe Stacey had stocked for something to wear.

I decided on a pair of dark blue, stretchy skinny jeans that looked comfortable enough and paired them with an equally comfortable, floaty purple tank top. I finished the outfit off with a pair of black heels as there were no other shoes in my wardrobe other than my runners. I put my hair up in a loose ponytail, added some lip gloss and some fun, colourful bangles and figured I'd had an alright go at fun and flirty.

I waited anxiously in the foyer. This was my first real night out. Ever. Dinner with Stacey didn't count, neither did an illicit midnight rendezvous with a forbidden man. I didn't want to make a fool of myself. I didn't want to embarrass Zoë or she'd probably never invite me out again. I breathed a sigh of relief when Zoë exited the lift also wearing skinny jeans and heels. She wore a black tank top with something scrawled across it with a basketball logo, which I assumed, represented her team allegiance. Her chocolate curls fell effortlessly over her shoulders and she carried a big, black tote bag and a black denim jacket.

'Nice work, you look fantastic,' she complimented, making me twirl.

'Thanks,' I answered sheepishly. They didn't give compliments on how you looked at the college, not unless you were in one of the drama, arts or entertainment programs and seeing as we all dressed the same anyway, I'd never much considered if I looked nice or not but I think I liked the compliment.

'Come on, we have a train to catch,' Zoë stated, pushing through the doors and strutting down the street.

The train had just arrived at the station when we got there and a long line of people queued in the thick evening air waiting to get on it. Apparently, Zoë didn't wait. 'Watch out,' she commanded, pushing through the crowd that instinctively parted for her, dragging me along by the hand. No excuse me, no pardon me, just 'watch out' as she shoved her way through.

'We don't queue,' she told me.

'Right,' I said as though it made sense.

Zoë laughed. 'You'll get used to it. We're from the elite part of society and everyone else, well, isn't.'

Zoë effortlessly pushed her way through the crowds again when we reached The Cube. People queued for miles waiting their turn to get in through the turnstiles but Zoë just grabbed my arm, dragging me to the front of her chosen entry, waved to the security guard, swiped her arm over the sensor and walked straight through, ignoring the moaning and groaning of those still waiting patiently in the long queue.

We walked along the cement concourse paved with food vendors and bars with patrons already drinking and eating amid laughter and loud conversations. They hovered in pairs and groups, some with dates. They wore jeans and sneakers, heels, t-shirts proclaiming their team allegiance, caps that did the same. They were in good spirits as they greeted waiting friends, gathered around tall tables sharing cardboard containers of nachos, drinking beer and cider from big paper cups. We passed them all even though my stomach grumbled.

I followed Zoë up a flight of stairs, which led to a landing overlooking the court. Seats rose up behind us and down in front of us towards the court filled with sparkly dancing girls. Zoë stomped her way down a row of steps towards the court, waved her wrist over a sensor gating the five rows of seats closest to the court. We walked down a few more steps, Zoë waved to a couple of people in neighbouring gated sections until she arrived at the row of seats, directly behind the players' seats. I sat where Zoë told me to sit right before she exhaled from the effort of it all.

We'd barely taken a few breaths and settled into our seats before a perfectly handsome, clean cut, suited man approached, levelling a tray of champagne before us. Zoë passed me a glass before taking one herself. I sipped as Zoë sipped and let the fizzy sweet bubbles delight my senses.

'Good, huh?' Zoë smiled.

'Mmmm... very good,' I agreed.

While the girls danced on the court to a pop song about winning, the seats behind us filled with beautiful men. I could see them lounging handsomely over Zoë's shoulder, sensed them on the other side of me. I tried desperately not to look but I could smell them and feel them and hear them talking in their deep gravelly voices, laughing politely.

People watched us, or at least they watched the men around us, we were no doubt secondary, but were watched anyway. People approached, called or waved to the men from behind the gates, tentatively, shyly, some boldly, asking for cards. Zoë rolled her eyes and waved the suited man over for more champagne and ordered cheese toasties. Apparently when it comes to stadium food like hotdogs and nachos, *we don't eat that crap*, she told me. Shame, the mixture of cheese and bacon and onion smelt pretty good.

'Who are they?' I finally asked, unable to resist the ever-growing array of men sitting behind us.

'Who?' she asked turning around. 'Oh them,' she said as though she'd only just noticed we were surrounded by thirteen incredibly beautiful men. 'Entertainers. We always fill the box with them. It's good advertising. They get loads of requests and bookings out of it. Technically we're their chaperones,' she smiled. 'But there, that's the real talent,' she smirked as the bas-ketballers began to take the court.

The players, ours I'm told were in maroon shirts, took the court amongst a great deal of pomp and ceremony, their names called with dramatic air over the loud speaker, spectators clapping, cheering, stomping their feet.

Once all the players were on the court, our team came to take their seats in front of us. A man with skin the colour of coffee, black dreadlocks and hazel eyes looked up at Zoë admiringly, reached for her hand and then kissed her knuckles, 'Milady,' he cooed with a grin.

The lovely man then turned to me, reaching for my hand before realising I wasn't who he was expecting. 'Where's Rach?' he asked.

'Who knows,' laughed Zoë forcefully. 'You have my new friend Courtney here today instead,' she told him.

'Well, hello there, new friend, Courtney,' he winked, kissing the back of my hand before taking his seat in the team huddle to talk game strategy.

'Isn't that against the rules?' I asked Zoë, sure it came under the unauthorised fraternisation rule.

'Technically yes, but here, no. We're like a good luck charm and it is very important to people that our team wins, so they'll allow this minor infringement as long it stays here, courtside and it gets no friendlier than that.'

'Why is it so important that they win?' I asked. Surely it was a just a game of basketball for the entertainment of the people.

'Interstate rivalry,' she said. 'But also, the better our team does, the better each of them does,' she said indicating the team as a whole, 'the better their stocks. They're only allowed a certain amount of dates a week with certain, acceptable levels of women and only on certain days and you never know which days, it depends entirely on their playing, travelling and training schedule. Nothing can interfere with that but oh boy, can those men do magic things,' she grinned stupidly. 'So, you see, very valuable men indeed.'

'Right,' I said as though any of it made any sense.

Zoë tried to help me understand the game as it went on but the more she talked about team fouls and personal fouls, offensive, defensive, blocking and charging, penalty shots, and which ones were taken from the free throw line, and which ones from the side of the court, and then there was the random substitutions and time outs in the middle of play, the less sense any of it made. Who could possibly make sense of any of that? My brain was full, so I just cheered when Zoë cheered and that was fine enough for me.

Then just as we levelled our score with the other team, the buzzer echoed throughout the stadium.

'What's going on, is it over already?' I asked as the players all left the court.

'Half time,' Zoë told me.

The dancing girls replaced the players, dancing to sounds of another familiar song. Some people watched the dancers, a collection of beautiful women in flamboyant glittering costumes. A lot of people got up to use the bathrooms or buy more food. I took the cheese toasty and another glass of champagne from Zoë and happily consumed both, looking around the stadium, marvelling at the people, that so many people had gathered in one place just to watch a game of basketball, even though I suspected they gathered to watch some of the most beautiful, desirable, and near unattainable men do their thing. They weren't the only men reserved for certain standards of women, either she told me. Was anything in this world actually as equal as we'd been led to believe? Wasn't the whole premise of the way we lived, the way we were educated, allocated careers and homes and pathways supposed to alleviate class and societal divide?

Some people flirted with the dates they'd brought to keep them company, many drank beer and cider and whatever else from the paper cups, and ate nachos and hot dogs in their seats. They all seemed to be having a great time, enjoying their time out from the real world. As my eyes passed over the crowd, I saw my wavy, midnight-haired friend, one, eight, five, nine, drinking beer with his arm around a pretty girl in a pink summer dress that looked more suited to a picnic on the beach rather than a basketball game.

One, eight, five, nine looked up, his eyes locking with mine and a beat passed between us. My heart fluttered as though it had wings, my breath stilted as though caught and every cell in my body pounded. Just to see him across the stadium sent my head, my world into a tailspin, to see him with his arm around a girl, to see her grinning like a cartoon cat, did strange things that twisted my insides, something I didn't expect, nor did I like. Then, just as quickly as it started it stopped, the moment broken as the players returned and our coffee-skinned team captain came for his good luck kiss. I had to say, if this was the price of being an IT girl, I wasn't sure I minded too much.

Once the players had all taken their seats in their huddle, I looked back to one, eight, five, nine. He was frowning, apparently unimpressed over my obligatory IT girl antics with the captain. But then his date commanded his attention and he leant in to listen to whatever she was muttering in his ear and my heart sank to my toes.

I knew I wasn't supposed to be disappointed. This was the way of our world. This was his job. But it didn't change the way I felt. It didn't lessen the sinking feeling of devastation that hung heavily in my body. It reminded me I'd gone too far. I should never have stepped into the shadows to speak with him. I should never have let him in. Now I didn't know how to get him out. Maybe it was just a build-up of all the lady needs everyone kept crapping on about. I'd never felt them before but then I hadn't been in such close proximity to so many men since I'd shared a house with my brother. I would have to bite the bullet. I had to book an entertainer, any entertainer. Quench these needs, shake myself free of one, eight, five, nine and whatever was happening to my insides.

I felt sick as the rest of the game went on. I watched on as though inside a clear Perspex bubble that muffled sounds and distorted images. I partook in the rituals and the cheering as best I could, with as much enthusiasm as I could muster, but really, my heart was no longer in it. My heart was sitting somewhere around my toes bathed in disappointment.

Finally, Zoë declared the game over, a victory by a small margin and the elated spectators finished their cheering as the players left the court and everyone began filing out of the stadium.

'There's too many to push past now, look at them all,' Zoë scoffed, watching people pushing and shoving their way to the exits. 'We need our own exit,' she mused. 'But how would we rub their faces in anything if we snuck out some back door?' she scoffed. 'Anyway, we'll just finish our bubbles and wait for the livestock to depart. They'll flood the bloody trains, too so if we wait, we'll get the next one and enjoy some peace,' she said. 'What did you think of number three,' she asked, referring to a tall, well-built blonde who'd scored many points throughout the game.

'Nice,' I said, not really sure what else one was supposed to say. Weren't they all beautiful, after all?

She sighed wistfully. 'Damned shame they're near impossible to book,' she pouted as we finally handed back our champagne glasses and left our seats. I suspected she'd try anyway.

We descended the stairs onto the concourse, heading towards the exit when a group of girls blocked our path, their hands on their hips, their faces scrunched into unattractive scowls.

'You think you're something special up there on your fancy overpriced stilettos, Zoë? Well you're not, you know,' spat a particularly feisty girl in a black mini skirt and tank top with fly-away brown hair. 'You mightn't remember where you came from but I do and I know you are not nearly as important you think you are. You are no different to the rest of us, just with a shorter, more selective memory,' she accused with her hands on her hips and eyebrows raised in challenge. She was looking for a fight. I'd seen the shippers pull stunts like that when they just needed to channel some aggression. It never ended well.

'Shut up, Meg, you're making a fool of yourself,' Zoë said, calm as a cucumber as though she wasn't afraid at all.

'Just because you jag a job with La Ferme doesn't make you the queen of anything the way you think it does, sitting up there in your gated box drinking champagne. One of these days you're going to fall from your very high perch and I hope I'll be there to see you crash. Come on girls,' Meg snapped as her friends followed her out of the stadium.

The confrontation shook me but not Zoë. She stood stoically

watching them leave before bursting out laughing as though it had occurred purely for her entertainment.

'Are you alright?' I asked her, worried she'd lost her mind.

'Oh, yeah,' she said, waving it away as though it was nothing. 'We were some of the first under the new education and recruitment regime, born outside of the program. I was three and Meg was four. We didn't live in a wealthy part of town. Our dads died while fighting overseas, our mums reassigned. There was a care facility at the college then for girls like us, and that's where we stayed until we were old enough to attend as students.

'I didn't mind much because my mother was a bitch. I still have the scars to prove it. It's why I believe in the program. Not everyone is capable of being a mother or a carer. Anyway,' she said, composing herself. 'As unlikely as it is, Meg and I roomed together until she turned twelve and tested for the culinary career path. She moved dorms and we never spoke again. I guess the analysts missed our earlier connections, though because we ended up in the same city and she's never forgotten where we came from and takes every opportunity to remind me. She works in a restaurant on Parliament Street waiting tables because she couldn't be bothered putting in the work at college even though she must have had the skills to learn to cook. I guess she's bitter about how things turned out,' she smirked with victory.

'But weren't you afraid? I've seen shippers with that look in their eye.'

Zoë chuckled. 'She wasn't going to attack me. There are camera's everywhere. If she did it would be in the papers tomorrow and no matter what actually happened, she would not be portrayed well and she'd be reallocated before she could blink. I told you, hun, we are not like other people. When you work for La Ferme, it comes with many, many perks,' she smiled.

I took it all in, not sure what to make of even more clearly defined differences that made little sense. We'd all been equal at college. Different career paths, different disciplines but everyone had a role to play in rebuilding our nation, every role as important as the other, we were always told.

'So how is it you did so well and she didn't?' I asked, trying to figure out how these divides were decided, to somehow make sense of them.

'Sheer will and a desperate need to be something other than what I was I guess. I don't know. I'm also smart. Smart enough to know being the best, being the smartest always got you more. More attention, more rewards, just more. I wanted more, I needed more, I was never going back to the way it was before, so I worked hard and I made sure I was the smartest. No different to you. We might have had different reasons, come from different places but we worked hard, we were the best because we put in the work.'

'I did everything I was asked, followed the rules, did the very best I could. My carer always drummed it into my head that I had to be the best, only the best, that only the smartest would have the greatest opportunities. I never really knew what she meant, I suppose, until now. Somehow, she knew what waited out here I guess, some of these bizarre realities they don't teach us.'

'Some things just never change. No matter the changes to society, someone always needs there to be a hierarchy. If it was a true utopian society, it would be like it was at college but someone somewhere retained their ego. Perhaps when you program born graduates eventually begin to take over, things will change. You'll lead differently because you've been bred differently, purposefully.'

'Why, what do you mean?'

'You've had ego and emotion bred out of you. Those of us from the pre-war time, even though I was only three when I were reallocated, we still retain so much emotion, even though we pretend not to, you can't erase memories or thousands of years of evolution, it's just not possible, but with the petri dishes and their perfect humans, who knows what they're creating down there. Come on, let's go have a cocktail,' she insisted, closing the conversation.

How could we end it like that, though? It just opened a whole other train of thought I wasn't allowed to give voice to. But Jack would understand. Jack would help me make sense of it. Even though he was the one person I wasn't supposed to spend time with, the one person I wasn't sure I could look in the eye ever again knowing what he would be doing with the rest of the evening, he was the one person who understood.

It was close to midnight when Zoë and I parted ways in the lift. I needed to sleep, my poor overwhelmed brain needed to rest and I knew I'd regret it in the morning but I had to run. I had to clear the image of one, eight, five, nine with that girl from my mind. I was nothing to him but a girl he had things in common with. A girl who liked to run as he liked to run. A girl who thought like him and had some kindred connection we weren't supposed to have, that was supposed to have been bred out of us like emotion and thought and everything else that made us human. I was just a girl who thought the same. Nothing more. That's all it was, all I was, all he was, a raft in a sea of confusion. But somehow, I still needed to run the image of him with her and what they would now be doing out of my brain.

My feet took over once I was beside the river and they were pounding on the footpath, every step reverberating beautifully through my body. My mind cleared. I thought of nothing as I ran and ran, faster and faster, letting my muscles burn, my chest burn and pushing myself some more, welcoming the ache like a familiar old friend.

When I reached the bridge, I thought I'd stop, just for a minute. I'd sit for just one minute up on the ledge where it was cool and quiet and I was invisible and my mind could go anywhere I wanted and I could breathe, just for a second, without worrying I was doing it wrong, that there was something wrong with me.

'You came,' he said as I walked into the cool shadows of the bridge.

My breath caught in my chest. I hadn't expected him to be there. 'I did. As did you,' I said, trying to hide my surprise and pleasure at seeing him there. Had I really hoped somewhere in the back of my mind that he'd be here? Is this why I really came instead of crawling into bed and getting some much-needed sleep?

'I did,' he said, stepping off the ledge, still in the clothes he was wearing at the game, jeans and a fitted sky-blue t-shirt.

'What happened to your date?' I asked.

'You really want to discuss my date?' he asked, his eyebrows raised dubiously.

'No,' I laughed, realising I didn't want to know a thing, that in fact, I wanted to pretend she didn't even exist.

'I can't stay long,' I said. 'I'll never get up for work tomorrow, otherwise,' I said, wishing I had all the time in the world to sit with him.

'Then we'll just visit for a few minutes. How did you enjoy the game?'

'It was fun,' I told him, taking my place beside him on the ledge.

'You looked like you were having fun, caught yourself a few admirers on the team,' he said, frowning.

'Are you annoyed about that?' I asked him.

'Surprisingly, yes,' he smiled. 'I didn't expect to be, but yes. I didn't like it at all.'

'Well, I don't mind that you didn't like it. I didn't like seeing you with that girl, either,' I smiled.

'Well, it seems I don't mind hearing that,' he smiled, nudging me with his shoulder while keeping his hands firmly knotted together in his lap.

I smiled. Changing the subject, I said, 'It's so quiet here, isn't it? No where's quiet in this place.'

'I know,' he agreed. 'Even when I sleep there's the noise of other people sleeping.'

'On my first night, that was the first thing I noticed, the absence of other people while I tried to sleep. Now I'm grateful for it because there's too much noise everywhere else.'

'You get used to it. Sort of,' he said.

'There's a lot of things I'm told I'll get used to,' I said, looking at my feet.

'Some things are easier to get used to if you do them with the right people.'

I could feel him smiling but I couldn't look at him because I realised, I wanted to touch him too much. I wanted him to be the person I did those unfamiliar things with and it scared me just how much.

'Well, I best get back,' I smiled tightly.

He took my hand in his, raised it towards his mouth, 'Until tomorrow?' he asked.

I nodded, digging my hole a little deeper, 'Until tomorrow,' I agreed and he kissed my knuckles, then I left him watching me run for home.

CHAPTER 5

'Courtney, can I have a minute?' Trish asked as we were all finishing our lunch break.

'Of course,' I replied, my heart rate picking up a few beats as I quickly racked my brain trying to think of any indiscretions that would cause her to summon me to her office. Did she know about my late-night visits with one, eight, five, nine? No, she couldn't possibly. But I couldn't think of anything else. There hadn't been any complaints or cross words or errors, but I was weary after my late night and I'd been yawning a lot throughout the morning, so I hoped I hadn't missed something without realising.

Trish was in her thirties, which meant she was born well outside of the breeding program but had, like everyone else it seemed, embraced her new life and the new ways wholeheartedly. She was slim, pretty enough, wore glasses, had shiny brown hair, pretty blue-grey eyes and was kind. Clearly not kind enough, pretty enough or smart enough for the breeding program but I was glad to have her as my mentor.

Her office was very chic, lots of wisteria blue and silver brocade upholstery, glass and dark timber. It was sparse but welcoming. Beautiful art hung on the walls and a picture of a teenage Trish smiling beside the President, most likely taken on reallocation day when everyone was excited about the President's plan to regenerate the country, the day she would have arrived at the college. Everyone who'd arrived that day displayed the same photograph. Ms Milly had one in her bedroom. She'd had to leave her teaching job on the other side of the country, leave her son who was sent to the boys' college, but still, she was proud to display her picture with the President, proud of her contribution to the rebuilding of our nation.

Trish indicated for me to sit in one of the opulent, overstuffed visitor chairs, so I sat.

'Don't look so worried,' Trish said, waving my worries away. 'I just wanted to have a chat about how your first week's going,' she said.

'Right. And has it gone okay?' I asked.

'Well that's the question I'm supposed to ask you, dear,' Trish smiled.

'Well I think it's gone well. Everyone's been so nice and I think I've got the hang of things alright,' I said.

'Good, because I think so too. Everyone's been saying wonderful things about you. Jen says you're a star on the phones, a real natural. Zoë said you handled yourself well last night even though it didn't all make sense. So yes, I think it's been a great week for you indeed. I'm very happy as are the Directors, so well done you.'

'Thanks,' I said feeling quite chuffed with myself.

'As a reward, I've put some credit into your entertainment account, so you should use it to celebrate making it through your first week. Stacey said she's taking you to The Parlour tonight for a tizzy up so why don't you go and book something in for tomorrow night, enjoy the perks of your job while you're all freshly waxed and whatnot, you've earned it' she suggested.

'Oh, right, okay,' I agreed, not realising I'd have to go through with a booking so soon.

'Don't be so worried, dear. I've put a note on your file so whoever you get will know to go slow and explain what's happening. You'll be well taken care of, I promise,' she said kindly, not at all alleviating my worries.

I went back to the quiet of my desk. Jen was at lunch, everyone else busy with their own work. There were no clients waiting to see Dr Grace. Just me, all alone in the quiet reception area. It was perfect timing, who knew when I'd get another spell this quiet. I waited for a pedestrian to pass by outside as though she could see in through the window, see me and what I was doing, then I opened the booking system and typed in my own customer number.

My file appeared on the screen with a green dot. I took a deep breath and pulled the card from my pocket that he'd given me, even though I had his number memorised and typed it in, one, eight, five, nine and held my breath.

His file came up on the screen with a green dot. We were an allowed match, no genetic crossovers, no illnesses to be concerned about, and he was available for the date and time I wanted. I desperately wanted to book him. I wanted it so badly I ached. But I couldn't. With a sinking feeling in my stomach, I knew I couldn't. If I let him in any closer, into my personal space, into my bed, there'd be no turning back. No redemption. I could feel it. I was so close to the edge already, taking that next step with him would be the end of me.

After seeing him at the basketball with his date, knowing what went on at the end of a date, knowing that was our reality, meant I had to do something to protect myself. I had to do it for both our sakes. I had to flush him out of my head, out of my system. I had to free myself of him, of this incredible connection we shared. The only way to do it would be to do this whole unfortunate thing with someone else, no matter how ill it made me feel. No matter what it would do to him, how hurt he'd be. It was the best for both of us.

I arrowed back to the previous screen, clicking open the calendars. I sucked in a deep breath to alleviate the bile building in my stomach then I entered the date and time I wanted and pressed the auto select button, also known as lucky dipping, and waited to see what the system returned.

When you lucky dipped, you got whatever the system gave you. There was no arrowing back to change your mind, which is why you had to put the date and time in at the beginning of the search and it searched for whoever was free and from that pool of available men in your access category, then inserted a random selection into the calendar.

The little thinking circle went around and around on the screen while it sifted through the available men and my stomach flipped a thousand times. I swear it was taking longer than I'd ever seen it take. Then, finally, the selection appeared on the screen. No, it couldn't be. I blinked a few times to make sure my eyes were working. I leaned forward for a closer look to make sure the number I was reading was correct and not a figment of my wishful imagination. One, eight, five, nine glowed in its illuminated greenness as it sat in my calendar at 7pm Friday night. I hadn't selected him, but he was there in my calendar anyway. People had once spoken of fate, a silly, unnecessary, disruptive romantic notion we were told. Could there really be such a thing? My heart beat a little faster and I couldn't help smiling.

It was a second before I realised I'd been holding my breath and I exhaled just as Jen returned from her break.

'You alright, love?' She asked.

'Oh sure,' I smiled, ignoring the excitement building in my stomach.

'So, how was your day?' asked Stacey as we walked into a luxurious room of muted warm lighting, dark blue velvet chaises and tiny quiet women in pale pink coats rushing here and there without making a sound.

A pink-coated lady spotted us, greeted us kindly and sent us through to the change rooms to put on robes before I could answer Stacey.

I returned to the relaxing waiting room and Stacey was already reclining in her robe on one of the chaises with a glass of cucumber water. I sat down beside her and whispered, 'I did it.'

'Did what?' Stacey asked curiously.

'Trish gave me my bonus today and I booked it in.'

'You didn't,' she gushed, her eyes wide with excitement.

'I did,' I confirmed.

'And?' she asked.

'And now I'm terrified. I'm shaking in my darned stilettos,' I laughed.

'Well, right now it's fluffy slippers but it's okay, everyone's scared the first time. Did you book that guy from the other night, the one who promised to blow your mind?'

I nodded, sure I was blushing.

'Well done,' smiled Stacey. 'But don't worry, he'll take good care of you. They know what they're doing so just relax and enjoy it. What are you going to do?'

'What do you mean, do?'

'Are you going to go somewhere, have dinner or something or just get down to it?'

'I don't know. What am I supposed to do?' I asked. How the hell was I supposed to know, anyway?

'Whatever you want,' Stacey said.

'How do I know what I want? Can't someone just tell me?' I asked. Wasn't it enough I'd booked it?

Stacey laughed. 'Why don't you order a pizza and a movie and stay in. Have a glass of wine and something to eat, chat and flirt for a while, if you make it to the movie, great, if not, it doesn't matter. He'll most likely take over after you've eaten, anyway.'

'Okay,' I nodded, not sure I was really ready for any of it.

'You'll be fine,' Stacey insisted, patting my hand. 'Right now, though, you have other things to focus on, good luck,' she said as she waved me towards one of the pink-coated women beckoning to us.

The woman smiled kindly. 'Hello, I'm Annabel, come on through,' she said, leading me into a small room with very dim lighting. 'Pop your robe on the hook behind the door, lie face down on the bed and pop the blanket over you and I'll be back in just a jiffy,' she chirped.

Once she returned, I was massaged, scrubbed, waxed, mani'd, pedi'd, my hair was trimmed and highlighted, my eyebrows shaped and tinted. It was hours before I was set free, my stomach rumbling, my skin feeling raw and shiny.

'Was all that really necessary?' I asked Stacey when I found her in the waiting room.

Stacey smirked. 'As a matter of fact, yes it was,' she replied. 'Especially now you have some company coming your way tomorrow night. You're an IT girl now, you need to look the part and that includes perfect eyebrows, enviable skin tone, a hairless body and pretty nails.'

'Perhaps someone could have discussed the price of being an IT girl before it was thrust upon me,' I suggested as I looked at the results in the mirror. 'But I have to say, wow,' I gushed at my reflection.

Stacey laughed. 'I know, right? Nothing beats a good eyebrow wax and a facial, my dear. Now, on our way out, we'll book you in for fortnightly visits, okay, can't have any of this getting out of control,' she said, waving a hand over my face as though it were a work of art.

'Well at least next time I know to bring a snack. I'm starving. Is dinner a part of this catch up?' I asked hopefully.

'Absolutely,' replied Stacey. 'Right this way, ma'am. I've booked us a celebratory table at Francine's, a beautiful French inspired bistro that is to die for.'

'What exactly are we celebrating?' I asked. 'Because having hair ripped from my skin is not something I feel the need to celebrate.'

Stacey laughed. 'I'm going to miss you when our time is up and I have to leave you to fend for yourself. We might just have to stay friends, I think. But no, we are celebrating your first week and more importantly, your bonus. Just you wait... You'll understand why when you're done. Feel free to call me afterwards, no matter the time and tell me I'm a genius,' she laughed.

'Yeah, yeah, whatever,' I laughed, embarrassed I appeared to be the only person on the planet who had no idea what everyone was talking about. But I figured the only way I was ever going to know was to see what happened Friday night and then I could just forget all about the entertainment business. As it related directly to me, anyway.

I followed Stacey to a prime seat in the middle of the restaurant. I'd really wanted to ask more about Friday night but it wasn't a discussion I wanted to have with so many people around and I suspected it wasn't something I was supposed to ask in such a fancy restaurant. I'd find out soon enough, so I ordered a chocolate martini and enjoyed some amazing food, putting Jack and Friday into the far corners of my mind.

It was too late to run once we were done but again, I ran, anyway. I knew I shouldn't. I was trying to limit my exposure to him. I'd even tried booking someone else for Friday night. It wasn't healthy for either of us, but I couldn't help myself. It was as though I changed clothes and pounded the footpath through an out of body experience I had no control over.

It didn't matter anyway as it turned out. The ledge was empty except for his card. I'd missed him. My heart sank. You'll see him tomorrow night, I reminded myself. Then a whole other thing happened. Fear and excitement ran rampant through my insides and I had to put my muscles through their paces to rid my tummy of the butterflies that had woken at the mere thought of one, eight, five, nine, being in my apartment. I hadn't even been able to tell him I'd booked him. He'd soon know when he arrived at my door, I supposed.

As I climbed into bed, I was terrified of what lay ahead.

CHAPTER 6

'**Y**ou look like shit,' laughed Zoë when I walked into the pod on Friday morning to make a coffee. 'You're not getting yourself all worked up over tonight, are you?'

I looked at her no doubt with a little horror on my face, how could she know.

She laughed again. 'We've all been there and we all had that same look on our faces,' she said as the machine finished dispensing her coffee.

I breathed a sigh of relief. I'd never been so nervous in all my life. Not even the day I'd been put on the bus to go to the college.

She giggled at me and I'm sure I blushed, I felt the heat rise up and although I tried to stop it, I'm not sure I was successful.

'Well, you get a reprieve from sitting out there and dwelling on it while taking bookings today. Dr Grace is headed out to one of the local breeding villages and we thought you could use the outing. So, have your coffee and make sure you go to the bathroom, it's a long ride. You leave in thirty minutes,' Zoë declared, tapping

---

me on the shoulder as she took her coffee across the room to her desk.

'Have you ever been to a village?' Dr Grace asked conversationally as we walked to the train station.

'Only the one I lived in before going to the college,' I told her.

'Ah, yes, but that wasn't a breeder village, that was the preschool village.'

'Oh, of course,' I amended realising, again, that my carer wasn't my mother and the waves of sadness came all over again. 'I just thought they must exist together,' I corrected.

'No. They did in the first year but it caused too much unease amongst the breeders and carers. So we moved the breeders to a new area where they'd be happier. It's easier now the program born graduates are entering the breeding program. We're really excited by the results that we're seeing, but still, I think the program works better for everyone this way.'

'Right,' I said, trying to take that new piece of information in as we got on the train. 'Do you visit the villages often?'

'Now and then. They have nurses to do a lot of the work and we have the machines that keep track of their health, reproductive specialists on site. But general doctors like me are few and far between at the moment. We lost a lot in the war and the first round of program born medical students are only just getting ready to graduate. Most of the doctors that survived the war were retrained in reproductive technology if they weren't already specialists. A lot of them were though, certain disciplines just weren't needed during the war so they were some of the least affected in the medical profession. Handy for the President, though.'

'Handy indeed. Did you serve? In the war?'

'I provided aid up north. A lot of boats and planes tried coming in that way even though they'd tried unsuccessfully in other wars. They tried again. Did more damage this time around but still didn't succeed. But the damage gave me a lot to do. We lost a lot of people,' she said sadly.

'You lost people you cared about?' I asked.

She nodded. 'I lost my husband. I lost my best friend.' She composed herself. 'I would have lost them in the reallocation anyway and what good does any of that emotion do for me now, huh?' she smiled brightly but forcefully. 'No good at all. Everything is working perfectly. No regrets,' she insisted.

I nodded, even though she couldn't see me because she was looking out the side window of the train.

We rode in a single carriage along tracks that had grass growing right up to the edge, which told me not a lot of people came out this way. The further north we went, the greener everything became but it wasn't too long before we stopped with a start and a shudder in front of a quiet, small, lone brick building.

There was no one to greet us and I soon learned why I was accompanying Dr Grace. I hung a bag across my body full of Dr Grace's notebooks and stacked small boxes into a trolley that had been left by the building for us. The boxes were all equally sized so it made it easy enough logistically.

'Be careful with those, you don't want to be dropping them, some of those contain the nation's future,' she smiled as she nodded to the boxes.

I wasn't quite sure what she meant but I nodded, made sure they were all secure then followed Dr Grace as we headed to the village.

We stopped at the gate to the village, scanned our wrists and nodded to the attendant as the gates slid open, then kept walking.

The first buildings we came to looked older, were falling into disrepair in parts, chipped bricks, chipped and missing roof tiles or cracked, dirty windows. There was no sign of life but I knew enough to know nothing existed for no reason.

'I thought they'd be nicer,' I commented.

'Ah, these are just the retirement buildings, dear.'

'Retirement buildings?' I asked, unsure of the phrase.

'For breeders once their seasons are over. They have everything they need inside, no need to worry,' she insisted as she strutted ahead.

Then we came to a much nicer group of tall, wide beige apartment buildings surrounded by green space, with courtyards between the buildings and eateries but no sign of any people.

'Where is everyone?'

'It's a bit warm out today, I'd say they're inside taking care of themselves, keeping cool. Its hard to keep cool when you're carrying a child.'

'So they grow the children here and then they go to the preschool villages with a carer? Why don't they go straight to the college?'

'There's been a lot of research done over time and the first few years of a child's life can be some of the most formative. We need to create an environment of family and security so that when they become adults they integrate better into society.'

'And no one minds when they find out that wasn't really their family?'

'Not everyone finds out, Courtney. Only the really clever ones who ask the right questions,' she smiled.

I couldn't quite tell if I'd done something wrong, overstepped a line but I suspect by coming here I would have found out the truth, anyway, smart or not. It wouldn't be hard to put the pieces together when I saw there were no children.

'Come, come,' Dr Grace said as we entered the foyer of one of the buildings.

I could hear a vision screen in the distance but we went in the opposite direction, down a grey hallway until we reached a lift. I wheeled the trolley into the lift after Dr Grace and we descended.

'How many people live here?' I asked to make conversation.

'About two hundred or so per building so that's about eight hundred, which is standard per region.

'That doesn't seem like many. That's only about four thousand births a year.'

'Only about half that. Most of the girls only birth every second year, depending on how their bodies respond. We only want them seeding in tip top shape.'

'That's not many at all. I thought with the whole rebuilding thing, there'd be more.'

'We only breed what we need. In the pre-war time, when it wasn't controlled, there were too many births, too many people draining the resources. We have analysts now predicting what we're going to need and when, so we breed what we need.'

'You mean, if you think we're going to need more architects in eighteen years, you'll breed more of those and less of something else?'

'Exactly. Only what we need. It makes the most sense or we'd end up with an over supply of one discipline and not enough jobs, then we'd be back where we started, with overly competitive and unfulfilled people.'

'And what about the men, when will there be enough of them for them to re-integrate?'

'They're not things you need to worry about right now but it's coming along fine. The President and the Regional Directors are very happy with how the programs are going,' she insisted as the door dinged our arrival.

The doors opened, I followed Dr Grace out, past a queue of women in bright green, knee length kaftans. They chattered amongst themselves, a few throwing curious, sideways glances at Dr Grace and me when they thought we couldn't see.

At the front of the queue was a door. Dr Grace knocked and upon an ascent from the other side, she entered and I wheeled the trolley in after her.

'Ah good,' said a woman sitting on a chair in front of a computer.

I looked around the sparse room. There was the computer where the doctor in her white coat sat. A small sink and bright yellow chair with a high back and spider legs stretching out to the side. Beside the chair was glass cased shelving.

'Where would you like the seeds?' Dr Grace asked.

The new doctor stuck a list to the wall beside a rack of shelving. 'Here is the order, please stack them accordingly, carefully and quickly. The cupboard is temperature controlled and if you take too long they'll all die,' she said looking at me.

I felt my eyes going wide, what on earth had I been wheeling across town?

I didn't dare ask because Dr Grace followed the new doctor into the adjoining room and I quickly did as I was asked. Each box had a number on it, which corresponded to the numbers listed. I could feel the temperature-controlled packs inside each box but I supposed they, too had a life span. It was easy enough and I worked as fast and as carefully as I could. When Dr Grace and her colleague returned to the room I was done. They were neatly stacked in order, the pretty symbols of triangles lining up nicely. Every tenth box had a square and together they all formed a nice pattern. 'Oh good, you're done,' smiled Dr Grace. She and her colleague was seemingly pleased. I felt like maybe I was finally getting ahead at something in this crazy world.

'Alright Joanie, I'll leave you to it. I'll go check on those few girls up in the clinic and we'll be on our way. You have a nice day.'

'Nice, huh,' scoffed Joanie. 'You know exactly where my face is going to be for the rest of the day. There's nothing nice about that.'

Dr Grace laughed and we left.

I followed Dr Grace back down the hallway to the lifts. It was much easier to keep up without the trolley full of delicate boxes. We didn't use the lift this time, instead walking up one flight of stairs and down a corridor that looked the same as the one on the floor below where Joanie worked. We reached a room with some chairs that adjoined another room that looked like Joanie's but without the yellow chair.

'You can sit out there with the girls, just don't talk to anyone, okay,' Dr Grace said as she closed the door to the doctors' room.

The waiting room only had half a dozen girls, much better than the long queue that waited for Dr Joanie. I sat as far away from everyone as I could and stared at the wall.

'All the same, you lot,' commented a girl with long dark hair with a machine pumping white liquid from her breast into a small bottle.

I looked at her but didn't speak.

'Too good to speak to the breeders?'

'Dr Grace said I should just be quiet.'

'And of course you all always do exactly as you're told. Don't want to be reallocated now, do we?' she laughed.

'Don't you?' I asked.

'We don't get reallocated. This is it for us.'

'But it's beautiful here,' I told her.

'Ahuh,' she smirked.

I looked around the room, some were watching our exchange, one girl, her belly big and round like a watermelon, was picking at the quick of her nail, another girl sat with her feet on the chair her knees pulled tight to her chest.

Dr Grace stuck her head out and called the girl with the long black hair into the other room. Dr Grace gave me a poignant look as the girl removed the pump and pulled her shirt over her breast then Dr Grace closed the door, so I leaned my head back against the wall and closed my eyes. It would do no good to speak to anyone, to know anything else. Behind my eyes though was the haunted eyes of the girl with her knees pulled to her chest. She'd looked devastatingly sad. I wanted to know how anyone could be sad in this beautiful place but I didn't dare open my eyes. Dr Grace had obviously heard my brief exchange with the black-haired girl. I didn't dare say anything else until she was done, the girls gone and we were walking back to the train carriage.

'Why did they look sad?' I asked Dr Grace.

'Oh honey, they weren't sad. They were fine. The seeds had taken and when that happens their hormones go a little nutty for a bit. That's one of the many reasons not everyone can breed, not everyone can cope with the fluctuations and recover.'

I nodded. It sounded right enough. I remember overhearing one of the girls in the breeding program at the college saying things about hormones and fluctuations and things once at the dessert cart. It hadn't made any sense then but it sounded reasonable now.

We didn't speak much on the return journey, just a little about the impending weekend. Dr Grace had the weekend off and was looking forward to yoga in the park and a little shopping. She talked enough about her weekend that we were back before we had to talk about mine. I was glad because I just didn't want to. I was feeling off and anxious and I just wanted to go to sleep.

Back inside La Ferme, I went to my desk and checked on my messages but there weren't any. Who would be messaging me when everyone I knew, knew I was out for the day. I only had an hour to go and then I could go home and see if I could make some sense for the day. It was a relief to know the day was nearly over.

'Hey, you,' called Zoë, sticking her head into reception.

'Oh, hey, what's up?' I asked.

'Can you come help me set up for Friday night drinks?' she asked.

'Yeah, of course,' I said, following her into the pod.

'How was your day?'

'Interesting,' I told her.

'I thought you might think so,' she smiled.

'It wasn't what I expected,' I told her.

'Nope. I think they do it to all new people as a test.'

'What do you mean?' I asked, suddenly going over everything that had happened to see if I'd done anything wrong.

'Don't look so worried. You're here, aren't you? I bet you were fine. The next few days will show for sure.'

'What's supposed to happen in the next few days?'

'How you react.'

'How am I supposed to react?'

'As though you saw nothing out of the ordinary.'

'I can do that.'

'Good. But you definitely see some unexpected things,' she whispered.

I told her about the girl extracting a liquid from her breast.

'It's milk. Once they've birthed the seed, their breasts fill with milk. Its good for the babies, so they fill jars for as long as they can and the jars are sent to the preschool village for consumption.'

I nodded as though it made sense.

'Was it at least distracting?' she asked.

I giggled. 'Very.'

She smirked but said nothing else on the subject. 'Chips and bowls are in the first cupboard in the kitchenette and the wine's in the fridge, glasses in the cupboard by the fridge,' she instructed as she poured pretzels into a bowl.

I piled as many of the supplies in my arms and my hands as I could. Two bottles of white, two of red, two packets of potato chips, one chicken, one plain and three bowls. I'd have to come back for the nine wine glasses.

'You lot aren't going to spring anymore surprises on me, are you?' I asked as I poured chips into a bowl, the revelations of the week still too fresh. My frayed nerves couldn't take the stress of anymore surprises.

She laughed. 'Nope. Friday night drinks is just us. A chance to touch base with each other. You don't have to look so relieved,' Zoë laughed.

'Come on, it's been a big week and it's not over yet,' I defended.

'Stop worrying, it'll be fine, trust me,' she said, wiggling her eyebrows.

As I opened the wine, it was like a whistle went off at each of the work stations. Everyone switched off their monitors. Trish, Di, Erica and Catherine all came out of their offices, and everyone converged on the sofas in the centre of the room. I got some more wine out of the fridge and when I returned, Zoë handed me a glass.

'To Courtney,' Trish toasted once everyone had a glass. 'To your first week. You've fit in so well, it's like you've always been here,' she said. 'Oh, and to your first entertainer, enjoy,' she winked and they all toasted.

Frankly, I didn't think it was anything we should be toasting. I was still terrified and the fact that everyone knew what I'd be doing in a few hours made me feel queasy, but by the time I'd finished the thought, they'd already moved on to another subject as though it were no big deal at all. I supposed it wasn't. It was just something we did to clear out the cobwebs, freshen up the brain.

Rosie had some swanky party to go to and that then commanded the conversation as everyone talked of dresses and makeup. I happily sculled my wine and waited for the grapey goodness to numb my senses while they talked and then we were all waving goodbye as we went our separate ways.

After almost tripping into the river from nerves and distraction as I disembarked from the water taxi, I walked up the path towards my apartment building. I could barely breathe, my stomach so full of butterflies in flight I could hardly walk.

Sex was supposedly a good reliever of tension and stress, which is how it increased productivity and focus, which would have been helpful after the day I'd had but from all I'd seen so far, all it did was increase stress, blood pressure and was extraordinarily distracting.

I didn't want anyone interrupting my night or sticking their nose around my front door and peeking at the goings on. I'd heard how easily gossip started and spread like fires, and enough people knew what I was doing already. I didn't need them gossiping about my underwear as well, so I had the pizzas delivered early and kept them warm in the oven.

Stacey insisted I would feel better if I put on some of the ridiculously skimpy underwear she'd purchased for me under a nice simple black dress, nothing too constricting and something with a zip in the back. She'd even told me where to find just the dress in my wardrobe. I hated that someone else knew my personal belongings better than I did. It was creepy. I made a mental note to rearrange the whole lot over the weekend.

I rummaged through the pile of underwear in the allocated drawer, and found something that looked like it'd at least fit. It was purple and black with lace bits and satin bits. I put on the dress Stacey suggested and felt ridiculous. Why was I getting so dressed up, anyway? It's not like one, eight, five, nine was actually going to care what I wore. He'd do his job regardless of what I was wearing. He'd seen me sweaty and gross in my running gear and still told me I was beautiful. But apparently feeling sexy was necessary for the evening's proceedings so I dressed and poured myself some wine and waited for the sexy feeling to come.

I'd just taken my glass of red wine onto the balcony where I was taking comfort in the sounds of the street below and the restaurant strip and pubs beyond where people were going about their business as they always did, when there was a knock at the door. My heart nearly bounced right out of my chest. I sculled what was left of my wine, stood, straightened my dress, took a deep, supposedly calming breath and walked to the door.

My hands shook as I opened the door. On the other side, one, eight, five, nine leant against the doorframe. All two hundred and something centimetres of him lounged as though he owned every particle in the space he occupied. He wore a perfectly tailored black suit. His wavy midnight hair had been mostly contained and his dark, ocean-blue eyes scavenged my body like a starved man. He offered me the perfect, long stemmed red rose he carried and smiled so brightly he lit up the dim hallway and liquefied my insides.

When I hadn't moved after a moment, he raised his eyebrows, the corner of his mouth twitching in a smirk. I somehow found my legs, stepping aside to let him in and closed the door before any of my neighbours could peek. I didn't care if this behaviour was encouraged by the President, it felt like something I should be keeping to myself. He felt like something I should be keeping to myself.

I stood, stuck, by the door watching as one, eight, five, nine moved through my apartment in his perfectly tailored suit until he walked through to the balcony. He turned to look at me, a smile spreading across his face. 'I don't bite, you know. Well, not unless you ask me to,' he winked.

'That's not helpful,' I muttered.

He grinned lazily, apparently enjoying himself.

The least I should do is offer him some wine, I thought. I walked towards him. One, eight, five, nine walked towards me, meeting me in the living room. He hooked his finger under my chin, tilting my face to his. His eyes caught on mine, sending sharp bolts and sparks through my body with such intensity, such force, I could hardly breathe. He carefully took my hand in his, slowly bringing it to his mouth, never breaking eye contact, not even to blink. He kissed the back of my hand, searing the skin where his warm, soft mouth touched. 'You can breathe now,' he smiled.

I audibly exhaled, then laughed at myself, at the silliness of my behaviour. I knew this man. How could I be so nervous? 'I'm sorry,' I whispered. 'This is a lot to take in.'

'I know,' he said calmly, his deep voice soothing my frayed nerves as he brushed a stray hair off my face. 'It will be okay, though, I promise,' he insisted. 'Why don't we start with some wine?' he suggested.

'Thank you,' I said, grateful he was being so kind.

I led him out to the balcony, pretending I couldn't feel his eyes intently ogling me from behind. I just had to not think about it, be okay with, feel it, accept it, trust it and go with it. He'd admired me before, he'd said flattering things before and I'd still been able to function, just.

I poured him a glass of wine, refilling my own and taking a long sip.

He sat in the chair next to mine, turning it so we faced each other. Our knees touched as he comfortably leaned back in the chair, owning his space, unbuttoning his jacket, none of which went any way towards alleviating an ounce of the anxiety taking over my body, nor the increasing need to see what was hidden beneath those layers of packaging. It was the latter thoughts that caught me off guard. What was I thinking? Where had that come from? But I couldn't help it, he looked incredible and my fingers twitched, desperate to pull off his shirt, to see him, to touch him, to feel him.

'What is it you're thinking?' he asked, curiously.

Shoot. It was as though he could read my mind. That's the way he was looking at me, anyway, his eyes watching me intently as though they saw right inside me, deep into my soul, reading every thought I'd ever had. It was unnerving, electrifying. I tried to speak but my throat was dry. I took a sip of wine, thinking of what to say. I didn't dare tell him what I was really thinking, that I was wondering what it would be like to have those big hands touch me, his mouth on mine, what his chest would feel like beneath my hands. Instead, I asked, 'What is your name? What do I call you, surely, I can't keep calling you one, eight, five, nine?'

'Jack. My name is Jack,' he smiled.

'Jack,' I said quietly, trying it out on my tongue.

I liked it. It suited him. It was simple and strong like he was.

He leaned forward, taking both of my hands in his and suddenly there was too much contact, not enough space, not enough air and I couldn't breathe. All the air left my body and no more would enter. Jack watched me closely for a moment, as though thinking, considering.

'Why don't you serve up some of that pizza I can smell,' he suggested.

'Sure,' I said, grateful for something to do.

I managed to get the pizzas out of the oven and onto the bench with only a minor burn on my arm. How I burnt myself, I've no idea. I wasn't paying attention. I rinsed my arm under the water and looked over to where Jack sat, hoping he wasn't watching me but he was. He was watching me far too closely, his eyes fixed on me.

'Are you alright?' he asked.

'Sure, sure,' I mumbled.

Suddenly my entire body shook. I pretended otherwise of course, bent, retrieved the plates out of the cupboard and as I went to put the plates on the bench, I knocked the spare bottle of wine that was on the bench breathing, with my clumsy, shaking hands. I was so startled, I dropped the plates and crockery and fermented grape juice went everywhere, shattered glass and china spreading far and wide across the floor.

Tears immediately flooded my eyes. I stood still, willing them away but they sat there, threatening to overflow. I bent, took the little dustpan and broom from under the sink, squatting to sweep up the shattered crockery and suddenly it was all too much and the tears spilled over, a sob escaping.

I couldn't believe I'd made such a fool of myself. Not in front of just anyone, in front of Jack. I fell back on my heels, defeated, embarrassed, ashamed, wishing the floor would open up and swallow me. As I was about to give in to the pull of gravity, the pull of humiliation, Jack caught me from behind, held me against his chest, his strong hands holding my arms as though holding me together.

I froze.

'It's okay,' Jack whispered into my ear from behind me as he led me to my feet, his hands sliding up and down my arms leaving trails of goose pimples. 'It'll be okay, I promise. I'll make sure of it. I'll take good care of you, Coté,' he whispered in my ear, using my nickname from the college, assuring me, his deep, velvety voice stroking me, calming me, making things happen to my insides that I'd never felt before but that felt amazing.

Jack's warm mouth began a trail of kisses along the side of my neck, moving up to my ear, taking the lobe in his mouth. My insides ignited, fire burning through my body, every cell, every nerve ending alive. My breath stuck in my throat. All I could think of, all that existed in that moment was Jack's mouth on my skin and I needed it, wanted it, wanted to feel more, wanted him to take me, somewhere, anywhere. I wanted to offer myself to him but I didn't know how.

As I was about to explode from desperate need, he turned me, taking my mouth in his before I had time to think, and I melted into him, my mouth instinctively moving with his. One of his hands, cupped the side of my jaw, the other rested on my lower back, holding me to him, against him, and I only knew I wanted what was to come more than I wanted air or food or life.

I pushed his jacket off his shoulders and he took his hands off me to let the jacket fall amongst the debris, before returning both hands to my face, pulling my mouth to his as though he couldn't get enough, couldn't get close enough and needed more as desperately as I did.

My hands fumbled with the buttons of his shirt. I had to open my eyes, leave his mouth, concentrate to unbutton them. His mouth hungrily moved along my neck and it took enormous focus to concentrate, to make my shaking fingers wrestle with his shirt buttons. When I finished unbuttoning the last one, I pushed his shirt from his body, sucking in a sharp breath as I looked at the sheer beauty before me. Tanned, chiselled, perfection. I ran my hands across his skin marvelling at the flawlessness. He shivered and checking to see if I'd done something wrong, I looked up to find him smiling.

I couldn't help smiling back. He was magnificent. I gasped again as he pulled my mouth to his, greedily taking from me as one hand cupped the back of my head and the other reached behind and slowly, interminably slowly, he unzipped my dress.

He stood back then, watching as my dress fell to the ground. I stood in only the next to nothing underwear Stacey had insisted I wear as he took in his own view, shaking his head before trailing a finger across my collarbone, and down between my breasts. He looked at my mouth, all over my body as though not sure what he wanted first, as though there were too many choices.

Then he grabbed my legs, hoisting me up, my legs instinctively wrapping around his waist as I nudged my shoes to the floor. He found his way to my bedroom by sense not sight because his mouth was fixed to mine, my mouth melting into his.

He gently sat me on the end of the bed, expertly taking my underwear from my hips as he did, then falling to his knees and weaving them down over my legs like he was playing a kindergarten game of skill.

He moved his way up my body, his mouth leading the way from my instep up my inner calf, to my thigh. His spare hand following the trajectory on the other leg. My skin was flushed, the sensations almost over powering and then his hands and mouth met in the middle. His eyes met mine and he grinned before draping my legs over his shoulders as he buried his mouth in me.

I gasped, from surprise, from delight, I wasn't sure which, both and more. My breath caught then quickened but still he continued. Electricity raced across my skin, under my skin, through the blood in my veins. I wanted to push myself into his mouth and pull away at the same time. Then conscious thought left and the sensations took over, building and building until the most extraordinary, unexpected, concentration of muscle contraction, of sheer, uncontrollable pleasure exploded at the point of contact, echoing throughout my entire body. Still his mouth worked and the subsiding shocks of pleasure built again and exploded again and stars bounced around in the blinding light behind my eyes as I fell back onto the bed, a depleted puddle of delighted exhaustion.

He stood up, watched me a moment with nothing short of adoration and pride before removing his pants and setting himself free and standing before me in his beautiful, naked glory. We'd studied the human anatomy. Women and men. We'd taken a perfunctory, textbook based departure class on what happens during a stress release session. But nothing I'd seen in the books looked like Jack. Nothing I'd seen in the books was as beautiful as him. His body perfectly sculpted. His penis thick and hard and that look on his handsome face, there were no words in any dictionary, old or new, for that.

The moonlight snuck through the window, between the gaps in the drapes, glistening over his skin, golden from the sun. I couldn't look anywhere but into the ocean-blue eyes that were home and safety, even though I wanted to, whether it was right or wrong, I wanted to see him but I was afraid.

'It's okay,' he nodded, telling me to look, that he wanted me to.

So, I allowed my eyes to stray, to scan down, past his broad, strong shoulders, over his beautifully defined pecs, his chest. His stomach rippled, every muscle clearly defined as though Michelangelo himself had crafted each one. I knelt on the bed before him, counting each ripple with the tip of my finger. Six.

My fingertip followed the defined vee that led downwards. I hesitated as I looked at his erection, watching it for a moment, as though it might jump or make some sudden movement, but it didn't move, it just stayed there.

I looked up into Jack's handsome face, searched for those ocean-blue eyes, found them darkening to near black. I waited for him to nod, to permit me, before I touched him, felt the soft, silky hardness of him, watched how it moved as I trailed my fingertip down its length.

Jack drew in a sharp, short breath. A groan as guttural and feral as any wild animal escaped from deep inside him as my fingertip circled the tip of him.

I gently touched the softness that hung behind but he took my hand, kissed my knuckles and edged me back onto the bed, his mouth taking mine, slow, long, deep.

Jack trailed his hand along my collarbone, over my shoulder, down my arm, skimming my breast before taking the skimpy excuse for a bra with him. He trailed his finger over the soft flushed skin underneath, causing me to gasp, suck in air from the surprising, electrifying pleasure his touch gave. His hand kept trailing down my side, as he watched my face, over my belly, my hip, the length of my leg, as far as he could reach, then he came up again, skimming over the soft sensitive skin of my inner thigh, slowly, torturously slow, until he hovered just on the edge of my soft centre.

My heart pounded and heat spread through my body from my toes. Then slowly his fingers spread me, stroked me then they were inside me.

I closed my eyes as the sting of pleasure shot through me. He smiled then dipped his head to my breast, his mouth taking a nipple, his tongue doing beautiful things, as his finger, one then two moved in me, stretched me, little by little, then more and more until I could feel my eyes rolling in their sockets then his thumb rolled over my centre and I exploded around his fingers as that exquisite pleasure filled me to overflowing.

His mouth found mine and he kissed me, deep, long, slow as he moved, hovered over me and I felt him, his hardness pressing where his fingers had just been. Then slowly, so slowly, he entered me. Nothing happened for a moment as he seemed to give my body a moment to become accustomed to him being there, filling me and it did, my body, uncomfortable at first, eased at the invasion then he moved and those stings of pleasure shot around my body with every move he made.

'Coté, look at me,' he pleaded.

I opened my eyes and looked into his dark, ocean-blue eyes, trying not to get lost in them.

'It's okay,' he assured me. 'I've got you.'

I nodded as he moved some more. Slowly in, out, a swirl of his hips until he was sure my body had adjusted and I forgot what was happening, let him take control, let my body take control as I lost focus, as I lost conscious thought as the heat built again. When I thought I was already spent, it just kept going, kept building, light blinded behind my eyes when I could take it no more and my head fell back, my eyes closing to building, uncontrollable pleasure until it happened again, until everything contracted in that moment of indescribable pleasure. Moments before he let out a guttural groan, thrust in once more, twice, then stilled as he buried his head in my neck, silent, his breath heavy on my flushed and sensitive skin.

Eventually his senses returned and I felt him smile against my skin before he kissed it and removed himself.

'Are you okay?' he asked as he lay on his back, looking up at the ceiling.

'That was nothing like getting a mani,' was all I managed to say.

'A what?'

'They say in our departure preparations, to just lay back, the man will do the work, it's just like getting a mani or a haircut.'

He laughed, a loud belly laugh that shook his body. I couldn't help giggling too because saying it out loud after what just happened sounded as ridiculous and naïve as it was.

'That's what they tell you?'

I nodded but couldn't help smiling. 'Is it always like that?' I asked.

'It's supposed to be. It's what we're trained to do, theoretically. But that, that was so much more than I've ever known.'

'Why?' I asked.

'I don't think either of us want to explore the answer to that question,' he said and I understood his meaning. Whatever this was, whatever we were together, it had just exploded into something more the second our bodies had come together. The cautionary tales were told for a reason and we'd ignored all the signs and I wasn't even sure I cared. No, I know I didn't care because if I never felt another thing for the rest of my life, I had that. I had these beautifully exquisite moments with Jack, the memories that would keep my heart and soul full for eternity. But I couldn't stop. I knew I wouldn't be able to, that I'd always want more of whatever that was.

As we lay there, caught in the moment, I couldn't help trailing my hand, my fingers across his body, feeling it move and hearing his soft groans as I touched him and I suddenly wanted to feel what he felt. To feel what it was like to pleasure someone, to drive them to the brink of insanity. I gently took his hand away from my breast. He looked at me with confusion but I only smiled at him.

'Well that's a wicked look if ever I saw one,' he smiled. 'What are you thinking?' he asked.

'I'm thinking I want to see what it's like to make you squirm. Is that allowed?' I asked.

'Anything you want you can have. Just give me a minute to clean up and I'm at your service,' he winked.

Suddenly I remembered who he was, that he wasn't just Jack the beautiful, kind man who made me feel more alive than I knew possible, the man whose kisses made the world spin while at the same time grounding me and making me feel whole and complete. The man who made me laugh, who saw the world the way I did, saw the wistfulness and the beauty and the possibility. He was also one, eight, five, nine; entertainer; trained sex for hire.

'What's the matter?' he asked, concerned as I moved away from him, sitting, pulling the sheet up to cover me. He sat up, concern etched in his beautiful eyes. 'Coté, come on, you're scaring me,' he said as he reached for me.

I shrugged him off, leaning my forehead in my hand, feeling foolish and stupid as tears fell. This is just how life was, I thought. It was his job to make me feel this way. This was how I remained focussed and productive. For the good of the nation, my efforts to rebuild it, regenerate it, replenish it, and make it self-sufficient.

How was I supposed to remain focussed now? Ever again? How was I supposed to not think of Jack every minute of every day, of the way he made me feel, of how he touched me? The way my stomach filled with joy when he looked at me. The way my body came alive when he touched me. The way the world, our bloody nation, faded away to nothing, leaving just the two of us.

I knew it was wrong but it felt right.

I felt it so strongly, the wholeness he gave me was not just a flight of fancy, and I knew without him, I'd go mad. But I couldn't have him. He wasn't mine. I had to share him. This was the way of our world.

'Coté,' Jack whispered, turning my tear-stained face to his. 'What is it? Did I hurt you?'

I shook my head. 'It's nothing. It's silly,' I told him.

'Tell me. Please,' he begged quietly, tipping my chin so I had to look into his eyes. 'Please,' he pleaded.

'I just got carried away. I forgot where we were, what this was, who you were, that this was your job.'

'Coté, this wasn't a job for me,' he said, shaking his head. He tipped my chin back to face him when I tried to turn away. 'Coté, this wasn't normal. This isn't what a job feels like. I don't know what happened. It was my fault for losing focus and getting caught up in you. But man, look at you, you're incredible. I get hard just fucking looking at you,' he said breathlessly, running his hand through his hair. 'To hear your voice is like hearing angels fill my heart, soothing my soul. It's wrong, it's so wrong and we'll both be banished for it, I know,' he said, tracing my mouth with his thumb. 'But you do something to me, Coté, something I never thought could happen. They warn us about it in class, but I always thought, no, not me, never me. I'm too smart for that. I can control it. Then I saw you and my breath caught in my chest, and my heart pounded, and I haven't been able to think of anything but you since.

'This week, it's been the greatest week of my life. I can't tell you the relief I felt when I read your file in my booking calendar. Coté, I have no idea what we're going to do, but what you're feeling, what just happened, it's not what usually happens. It was better. It was fucking incredible,' he said, smiling, shaking his head.

I smiled, too, glad I wasn't alone in this foreign field of feelings. 'But it doesn't change who we are or the world we live in or how many other women touch you every day,' I said, gasping for air at the thought of another woman touching him, of him pleasing another woman as he did me.

He lent his forehead to mine. 'If I could change it, I would. I'd change it in a second,' he said. 'If I could run away with you, I would run until the end of time. But where would it get us? The country's surrounded by ocean, there's nowhere to run to.'

I melted into Jack's arms and he wrapped them around me, holding me tightly as we lay in my bed. There were no words to speak. There was nothing that could change our situation.

Falling in love, it was forbidden.

It's all there was to it. For the good of the nation. While there weren't enough men for everyone, we had to share. Love was an unnecessary, unproductive, antiquated emotion that resulted in nothing but bad things. So those were the rules. I wondered if the President would ever change her view even if there were enough men. Everything worked better this way, no marriage, no divorce, no children, no family, no distractions, only happiness and fulfilment and purpose, and a flourishing nation that was entirely self-sufficient.

'That was some pretty fancy talk there. Why aren't you in the breeding program?' I asked him.

'Ssshhh,' he whispered. 'Don't tell anyone I can string together a decent sentence or you'll condemn me to a fate worse than death,' he answered.

'You purposely hid that you're smart?' I asked.

He turned my face to his, tilted my mouth to his, kissed me soft and slow. 'Doing nothing but make babies by jerking off into a tube for fifteen years until they send me to the retirement houses with hundreds of other ageing breeders is no way for a person to live,' he said quietly. 'I chose the lesser of two evils. God, those poor blokes have their diet, exercise, body temps, clothing choices monitored twenty-four seven. They're not even treated like people. Who'd choose to live like that?'

Suddenly the whole process made me sick to my stomach. I brought his hands to my mouth and kissed them then pulled his arms tighter around me. He was a person. He deserved rights, choices. It didn't seem fair. Nothing seemed right anymore. Nothing was as I expected and I didn't know what to do with it.

'Are you okay?' he asked.

'I'm just thinking about everything, our world, the choices we don't have, you don't have.'

'Don't you worry about me, I'm okay,' he insisted.

'It's not just you. Well, it's mostly you,' I smiled at him and was rewarded with an appreciative smile in return. 'It's everything. Nothing is as it was supposed to be. Not this, this is no haircut or mani,' I laughed. 'And today, I went to a breeding village. I always thought I'd been raised in one, that it was where we come from, that the carer was my mother, my brother and sisters, my siblings. Turns out my brother was the only thing that was real. The rest nothing but an illusion.'

'What exactly happened at the village today?' he asked, his voice laced with concern.

'I was transporting seed. I didn't know it but I was. And there was a queue of women waiting for it to be planted in them. They lived in these beautiful buildings with gardens and swimming pools, cafés and everything they could need, just like a miniature version of where I live but when we got there, there was no one outside, no sign of life. Inside, they queued like cattle, waited to be planted. Others waited for Dr Grace and Jack, you should have seen these women, they were so desperately sad, they picked at their fingers, they struck out with their voices and held their knees to their chests like frightened children from the pre-war time.'

'What did Dr Grace say?'

'That it was hormones. And maybe it was. I heard the girls in the breeding program talking about them once. Dr Grace said not all women are strong enough to endure them and to not worry, it was part of the process but it didn't feel right, none of it felt right and I just feel, I don't know, lost, powerless.'

'You get used to it.'

'You didn't see their faces, Jack.'

'I don't need to. I'm an entertainer, Coté. I live in the same facility as the male breeders. I've seen their faces.'

My own must have drained of colour because he pulled me close to his chest and held me tight.

'It's okay. You learn to live with it.'

'I don't know if I can. I don't know if I want to.'

'You have to because I have to and I can't live in this world without you. I've finally found a light in amongst all this darkness and I need to know it's still shining.'

As the night noises outside subsided, I asked, 'so what other tricks do you know?'

'Distraction, now you're catching on,' he chuckled. 'The only way to tell you is to show you,' he smirked as he moved above me, pinning my hands above my head. 'Are you ready?' he asked, his eyes darkening with lust.

I giggled, nodded and that was the last coherent thought I had for the night.

CHAPTER 7

Birds chirped and the sun shone through the gaps in the drapes but my bed was empty. Something inside me had been set free and I felt liberated and alive, like suddenly I could see clearer and hear better and everything smelt sweeter. I felt whole and complete as I padded to the bathroom. I could still feel him, where he'd been in the most glorious of ways, pleasure sensations shooting through my core as I remembered the night before.

Two pieces of Pizza were missing from the box on the kitchen bench. The debris on the floor was gone, not a splinter of crockery or drop of wine left. On top of everything else he was thoughtful and sweet. Looking at the rest of the uneaten pizza on the bench, I suddenly realised I hadn't eaten any dinner the night before and was starving. While the kettle boiled, I ate a piece of cold pizza, ham, pineapple and cheese. Perfection.

I reached into the overhead cupboard for a mug and leaning up against the cute butterfly covered mug, one of a set of four Stacey had bought, there was a business card. On one side it just read one, eight, five, nine, on the other was just two xx's. I smiled, more smirked to myself, hid it inside a mug in the furthest corner of the cupboard and hummed softly to myself as I took my tea and pizza to the balcony to enjoy a lazy start to my Saturday.

The sun turned the river below my balcony into a sea of glittering diamonds. The sun itself was warm, the sky perfectly blue, cloudless. It was too beautiful a day to be up here watching it from afar. I needed to be down there, in it. I changed into my running gear and went for a slow run, enjoying the feel of the warm air on my face, the sun's rays caressing my arms, the vitamin D soaking into my skin.

On my way back, I stopped by a café with the most delightful pastries filling its windows; cream buns and iced delights, all manner of colourful delicacies that reminded me of the patisserie at the college. I ordered a flat white at the counter and a chocolate covered, cream filled delight from the cabinet in front of me, waved my wrist with the implant over the scanner to pay and then went to find a table.

When the waitress brought out my order, she asked, 'Are you new? I haven't seen you around before.'

'I am. I've only been here a week,' I told her. A week. So much had happened it felt like years.

'Fresh off the train, hey?' the waitress smiled. 'What were you recruited for?'

'La Ferme,' I told her.

'Oooh, fancy,' the waitress said. 'Best leave you to it, then, don't want to be ruining your reputation now,' she said, as she left the table.

The status thing was getting on my nerves. I didn't know how to change my own immediate future, so I wasn't sure how to even imagine changing an entire society, so I tried putting it out of my mind, stuffing it in the dark corners with all the other things I wasn't supposed to think about and couldn't fix. Instead, I tried enjoying the sunshine and watching people going about their business.

There were girls off for a day of shopping, giggling at the entertainers that jogged by. There were serious women returning from an early morning visit to the supermarket or the hairdressers, some off to do an extra shift wherever they worked. Just people and life, and it all spun on around me and none of them knew what I'd done, none of them knew of Jack or how he'd irrevocably changed me.

I knew it was wrong, against protocol, against everything I believed in because I believed in our nation and making it better and returning it to its previous glory, better than it ever was, but I couldn't ignore what had happened to me. I still felt him on me, felt the strain and tingling of where he'd been and what he'd done, and remembered as clear as day, as though it was a movie playing on repeat behind my eyes, the extraordinary, exquisite pleasure of it. I wanted more. I wanted to go back to my apartment and have him devour me all over again, all day long, every day.

I was in trouble. Big trouble.

Back in my apartment, I distracted myself from thoughts of Jack, from looking at the clock and counting down to when I could consider a night time run, by washing my sheets and rearranging the wardrobe Stacey knew better than I did.

I was a hot sweaty mess when I was finally done. I had a quick shower then sat on the balcony in the sunshine with one of the books Stacey had bought and left in a pile on top of the entertainment unit.

I was just wondering what I'd do for dinner when there was a knock at the door. I opened it to find Zoë and Rachel in jeans and cute tops.

'There she is, all flushed and rosy. Come on, we need all the goss from last night, so go tizzy yourself up, we're going out to dinner.'

'How did you get on my floor?'

Zoë grinned. 'I had to approve your apartment. I left the access open because I knew we were going to be friends.'

'Liar, you're a nosey neighbour,' I grinned, glad we were actually friends and there'd be no snooping.

'Well, now you know, you go can go get ready for DINNER,' she reminded me.

'Fine, fine,' I laughed.

It solved the problem of cooking but I'd really have liked to stay in, have a wine, go for a run and wait under the bridge to see if Jack showed. But I could tell from the look of Zoë, she wasn't taking no for an answer, so I went and quickly freshened up, dressed similarly to the girls, but I had to leave my hair up in a ponytail, removing it would have required a full blow-dry and I was not bothering with any of that to satisfy their gossiping needs.

I returned to find them on the balcony helping themselves to a glass of wine and watching the people below, gossiping about what people were wearing or who they were with.

'Ah, good, let's go,' insisted Zoë when she saw me. 'I'm starved, and I can't wait any longer to hear about last night.'

I ignored the last comment, the last thing I wanted to do was to talk about Jack. 'Where are we eating?' I asked instead.

'Ora's,' Zoë said.

Good, at least I didn't have to walk far.

'Mmmmmm, sangria and paella, my mouth is watering already. Let's go, come on,' hurried Rachel.

Despite the queue of hungry people waiting their turn, the suddenly chirpy waitress led us to a prime table in the middle of the restaurant that hadn't been there, a moment ago. Zoë didn't even blink, as though she knew it would happen, that it was an expectation but Rachel caught my eye and smiled. 'Gotta love the perks of hanging out with you guys,' she whispered.

'You work at the same place we do, Rach,' I reminded her.

'But I'm just an analyst, no one cares. They very much care who you two are. Keepers of the entertainment bookings remember. The most powerful women in town. But that's okay, I'm happy to be a hanger on,' she grinned.

Zoë ordered an array of food and a jug of sangria before the waiter walked away.

We talked of everyday things until the drinks arrived. By then, Zoë looked like she was about to burst. Amused, I stayed silent until she poured the drinks. I took a sip, deciding how much to tell.

Zoë couldn't take it anymore and demanded, 'Come on!'

'It was fine,' I lied. There was no way I was going to tell Zoë just how damned fine it was. How life-alteringly incredible it was. Especially after I'd spent the whole day trying to pretend it hadn't happened at all to stop myself going mad wanting it to happen again.

'Fine? That's it?'

'That's it.'

'No, no, I saw that man at morning tea and he was way more than fine,' she said, looking at me questioningly. 'Now spill.'

I sighed. It was clear that I was going to have to spill some dirt or Zoë would never shut up about it. 'Okay, it was more than fine, it was great. He had a great body, good moves, I don't know, what do you want from me? What more do you want?'

'We want the juicies,' Rachel insisted, leaning forward, her long, purposely messy blonde hair falling forward as she did, her big grey-green eyes eager.

'Exactly. Every detail,' Zoë insisted. I blushed. I felt it creeping up from deep within and spreading across my face. Damn it, I cursed myself. I hadn't wanted to give anything away, but my body had a habit of betraying me, and of course it was always at the most inopportune times, like now.

'Ooh was he that good?' Zoë asked.

'It was my first time, anything would have been good, wouldn't it?' I suggested.

'I suppose,' Zoë answered, disappointed.

I felt bad, everyone else seemed to share details, and I didn't want anyone thinking I wasn't a joiner or worse, catching on to the fact that I fancied the heck out of Jack, so I threw them a bone and said, 'He did this thing with his mouth, you know...' I trailed off. 'Do they all do that, like that?' I asked.

Zoë laughed. 'If you want them to. They'll do anything you ask, but yes, they all have their speciality. Was your mind blown?' she asked, finally satisfied I'd given something away.

'It was better than I thought, amazing, fantastic, mind blowing,' I said, in a bored monotone voice, in an effort to appease Zoë.

'Fine, don't tell us anymore, then,' Zoë sulked.

'My mind was suitably blown, okay? Is that what you wanted to hear?' I huffed.

'Yes, it is,' Zoë said smugly. Zoë finally appeared satisfied with the gossip and moved on to Rachel's date from Wednesday.

'What date?' Rachel answered, her eyes getting twitchy.

'Don't give me that,' Zoë admonished. 'There's no way you'd blow off a game, unless you were randy as a rabbit,' she said smirking.

I saw a look of something, sadness, disappointment, embarrassment, I'm not quite sure which, pass over Rachel's face before she answered, 'Oh well, busted, I guess. But do you know what? I enjoyed my mid-week treat so much I may do it again next week. What do you think about that?' she challenged Zoë.

'You're blowing off another game?' Zoë asked, absentmindedly twirling her long, chocolate waves around her hand and dragging them over one shoulder.

Rachel shrugged and smirked. 'Now, I think the true question is, why are you so interested in everyone else's dates? It sounds like you need one of your own if you ask me,' Rachel said to Zoë.

'I had one last night,' she groaned. 'Ah, it was fine,' she said, waving off an imaginary comment. 'But I'm just in a funk. I can't find one that's really giving me a good going over. They're all fine, don't get me wrong. They're doing their job but I just need a good scream fest I think. What about your guys, will I get one from one of them?'

'Not sure he gave me a scream fest,' I answered, a little too fast, chastising myself the second it escaped my mouth.

'Yeah, mine wasn't a scream fest either, think I'll lucky dip next week,' Rachel said.

'Argh,' groaned Zoë. 'I just need one who knows how to take charge, without me giving a list of instructions. One who'll just, argh. You know what I mean,' she said.

'Yeah, yeah, I know,' Rachel said. Then to me she said, 'You'll know what we mean in a year or two when the novelty of the ordinary wears off and you just need a good shag that rattles your bones and clears out the cobwebs.

'The guys are all trained to please you but sometimes they're trained too well. Sometimes they just need to think for themselves, go outside of the guidelines now and again.'

I nodded. I was pretty sure Jack went way outside of the lines but I wasn't telling them that, especially Zoë. The last thing I needed was to be comparing Jack notes with my friends.

Some girls Zoë knew joined us for a while before heading off for a night of dancing. Then Stacey and some of her friends stopped by. 'How are you getting on?' she asked me.

'She's doing great, freshly shagged and finding her feet,' Zoë answered for me.

Everyone laughed. Zoë was heading over the line of drunk. I was controlling my own intake of sangria by filling their glasses before mine had depleted too much. I didn't need to be loosening my tongue about things I didn't want to share, things that would see me in a great big world of trouble.

Stacey and her friends left when their other friends found them and they sashayed down the street to a party.

'What now?' asked Rachel.

'We need some dates,' Zoë said.

'Now?' Rachel asked, unconvinced. 'What kind of dates are we going to get now?' Rachel asked as though the whole idea was ridiculous.

'Hopefully some that know how to break the rules,' Zoë winked, pulling her tablet out of her bag.

Fear floated through my body, taking hold of everything. I couldn't go a round with another man. I didn't want another man in my bed. I wanted Jack. He still consumed my thoughts, the memory of him, what we'd done was still as fresh as though it had only happened moments ago. My lady bits still strained from him, still tingled from where he'd touched me. How could I replace all that with someone else? I couldn't. I didn't want to. What kind of stupid world did I live in where I had to?

'Come on, what's wrong with you two?' asked Zoë, clearly annoyed at our lack of enthusiasm.

I knew it looked bad and I knew I was in trouble. Big trouble. I fancied the heck out of Jack. More than fancied, I knew it but I couldn't even think it. If I thought it, I might say it, someone else might see it on my face. Perhaps it would be better, safer for us both if I just went ahead and cleared him out of my head, no matter how sick the thought made me. If we got caught, it was over, all of it. I couldn't be sent away. I couldn't lose all I'd worked so hard for. I couldn't risk him losing everything and being sent to who knew what kind of awful fate. So, I mustered up some enthusiasm, even if it was totally fake. 'Go on, then, spin the dice and get me a surprise,' I told Zoë.

'Ah, that's my girl,' Zoë smiled, suddenly cheered.

'Yeah, go on, then, dip for me too,' said Rachel.

'Excellent, we have 20 mins,' Zoë squealed once she was done. 'Just enough time to finish the Sangria,' she added filling our glasses.

I sculled my drink, hoping the sangria would work its way into my system and do whatever it was alcohol was supposed to do, and make it just remotely possible that I could get through what was left of the night.

We were loud and too happy as we walked back to our tall green, cupcake of a building, laughing at nothing, the sangria making the ordinary hilarious. Perfect. We took the lift to Zoë's floor, walked down a hallway identical to mine and then we were inside her apartment. It was strange to be in an apartment identical to my own but with different furnishings.

In contrast to my bright apartment with white leather and pops of colour, Zoë's apartment was homely and warm, decorated with dark timber, accentuated with pretty pastel throws and colourful pillows. Most of the buildings and the apartments in them were just copies of each other on the inside. It saved on design fees and just like everything in our country, it was done the most economically as possible. If everyone of each career path lived in a similar apartment, there'd be no envy and jealousy or misguided ambition and therefore less distraction. It didn't stop it from being strange and surreal though to walk through an apartment that was so familiar and yet unfamiliar at the same time.

Zoë was pouring some much-needed wine on the balcony when there was a knock at the door. My heart froze.

'I'll get it,' sang Rachel cheerier after her own serves of sangria and quite at home in Zoë's apartment.

I almost didn't dare look. I was terrified and repulsed to be with anyone other than Jack. But Zoë was so spirited about it all, I had to muster some enthusiasm, for my own self-preservation, if for nothing else. Against my better judgement, against the calls of betrayal beating from my heart, I forced a smile and I looked up.

My heart stopped and almost jumped into my mouth when I saw who was entering. Jack caught my eyes from the doorway and his mouth twitched in one corner, slowly turning into a lopsided, satisfied grin as though thrilled to find me there.

But then my world crashed, my breath was lost as though it'd been kicked out of me. What if Zoë or Rachel wanted Jack for themselves? Zoë had already asked about him earlier, looking for her good hard shag. I could only hope I'd put Zoë off enough with my lacklustre report.

With Jack was a man with shaggy brown hair and a good covering of whiskers on his jaw. His shirt hung casually, untucked from his jeans that gripped his body snugly. Everything about him was casual and effortless. He was who he was as though he had no control over it. In another era he may have been trouble, a bad boy. In any era he'd be considered ridiculously, dangerously sexy.

The third man had some native heritage, rich tanned skin, black, slightly unruly hair, dark, dark sexy eyes and a wide, mischievous grin. I suddenly saw how dangerous the situation could be. There were three women, three men. The question hung in the air unspoken, or at least in the leaden pit of my stomach. Which woman would get which man and in which order did we choose? Would I, the newbie get last dibs, scraps? Isn't that how things worked in packs? I noticed Jack looking at me quizzically, with concern as he stepped onto the balcony.

'Well, look who it is,' smirked Zoë when she saw them.

'Did you book him on purpose?' I asked her, suddenly angry.

She just shrugged her shoulders, her face full of mischief.

Zoë turned up the music and poured our guests wine. Polite conversation ensued while Zoë danced her way around the kitchen while preparing a plate of nibbles to go with our drinks. No one nibbled. Rachel refilled my fast depleting glass and Jack watched me carefully. I just wanted the whole thing over with. The suspense was eating me up. Someone had to do something. I couldn't stand it.

Rachel spoke for what seemed the first time in ages. 'Well, Zoë here needs someone who's going to rattle her bones and break the rules and shake free all the cobwebs.'

I nearly spluttered my wine.

'That'd be this one,' Jack said, offering up the bearded man.

'You sure?' asked Zoë. 'You don't just want to save yourself for another round with the newbie, do you?'

Jack laughed, tapping Zoë's chin playfully, 'I'd be very glad to rattle your bones ma'am, but out of the three of us, I promise you, he'll leave you gasping for air and forgetting your name,' he assured her.

'Well, then,' Zoë stammered, sculling her wine.

'Shall we?' asked the shaggy, bearded man, holding his hand out for Zoë.

'Sure, sure,' answered Zoë, looking far less sure of herself than I had ever seen her.

After she'd left, I whispered to Rachel, 'What do we do now?'

Rachel shrugged. 'To be honest, not sure I have it in me. Think I'm going to watch some telly. You,' she said to the dark and handsome one, 'come keep me company till I sober up a smidge and you can walk me home,' she said, reaching for his hand. Then to Jack she said, 'Why don't you walk this one home and give her some details she might actually remember this time?' she winked.

I wanted to smack her. How could she say that? I wanted the floor to swallow me and take me away. Jack's finger tilted my face to his, and he looked at me curiously and all I wanted to do was go, leave, with him. Could we? Just leave? Was it even polite to just leave after Zoë had organised the men? Wasn't this supposed to be a party?

'Come on,' he said, reaching for my hand. 'Or you'll soon have the pleasure of listening to your friend screaming the apartment down,' he winked.

'Well that I can do without,' I smiled, taking his hand. I certainly didn't want to be listening to Zoë's rattling bones and cobweb cleaning.

'So, what's going on?' he asked, when we reached the hallway and were waiting for the lift.

'What do you mean?'

'Did I not leave you satisfied enough last night?' he asked, raising his eyebrows doubtfully.

I blushed. 'You left me plenty satisfied,' I whispered. 'This was Zoë's idea. Rach and I just kind of went along to keep her happy.'

'So, getting me was just luck?' he asked.

'Very good luck indeed. Although I think Zoë may have had something to do with it. She did the booking,' I smiled. 'I couldn't believe it when I saw you walk in. I've never been so happy to see anyone in all my life,' I gushed. 'I really had no idea how the hell I was going to be able to go through all that with anyone but you.'

'Well, I'm very glad to hear that,' he smiled. 'I was wondering if you'd been as happy as you said though when your friend told me to make sure you remembered it this time.'

'Oh, I remembered every single moment I assure you, but,' I shrugged, 'I just didn't want to spoil it by telling them every detail. Somehow it just didn't seem right.'

He kissed the top of my head as the lift dinged its arrival.

'How were you all even available tonight?'

'Party cancellation I'm told.'

I nodded. 'Lucky us.'

'Lucky me,' he smiled as we arrived on my floor.

The door to my apartment closed, the lock clicking into place, locking the rest of the world out of our bubble. Jack took my face in his hands, kissing me, hard, deep. 'Aaahhh...' he groaned as though finally everything was better before taking my mouth again.

'Do you want to sit for a bit?' he asked when he'd finished reviving himself.

'Sure,' I agreed. 'Wine?' I offered.

'Absolutely,' he said, hooking his arm around my neck and pulling me in for a rough kiss that curled my toes before going over to the couch while I went to get wine and glasses.

How did he do it? I wondered as I hung a couple of wine glasses in-between my fingers and picked up a freshly opened bottle off the bench.

'Come here,' he said, once we were sitting with our wine, pulling me into the comfortable nook of his body where we fitted together like two halves.

'Is this allowed?' I asked him.

'Nope, snuggling is most definitely discouraged,' he said, kissing the top of my head.

I smiled. I liked that he wanted to break the rules for me. But it worried me, too. I was worried for him. 'Will we get into trouble,' I asked.

'Who will know? As long as neither of us report it, we'll be fine. But to be honest, after the last few weeks, I don't even care if they chain me in a dungeon. If it wasn't for you, this week, last night, tonight, I'd be almost ready to volunteer for the breeding program.'

'But you said it was a fate worse than death,' I said remembering his words from the night before.

'And it is,' he assured me. 'But sometimes I wonder if it's worse than this one. Until I met you that is. You my dear, you make it all worthwhile,' he said, tipping my chin so he could see my face. He watched me for a moment, his ocean-blue eyes seeing everything I was, sending tingles through my body and awaking the butterflies that lived in my belly before kissing me, slow and deep and long.

'They think they're in charge,' he said, drawing me in tight against him. 'In control of us, of everything, but they're not. For some of us, it's too much.

'They don't tell you about them, do they? One of my room-mates from college couldn't cope. They start the men breeding earlier than they'll admit to and it's too much, what they make them do. He ran one night, fed himself to the bloody crocodiles up north. That's what they do. There's not a lot of options if you want out. They get the freight train, drink a bottle of something they've stolen from someone and they jump in the river. It's a hor-rible way to die,' he said, shaking his head. 'I can't stand it some-times, what they make us do, how we always have to perform. How they control what we say and what we do and who we do it with. After a while, it just rips at your soul. Little bit by little bit, it starts tearing and tearing until there's nothing left,' he whispered, almost to himself.

'I'm sorry I booked you, made you perform, it must be awful for you,' I said, imagining how horrible it must make them feel, how worthless.

'No way, don't you dare,' he said. 'You, this, us, it's not like that. You're not like that. You take my breath away, Courtney. Being with you, you heal me. This, what I do, it makes you numb. Some guys love it, in the beginning, but after a while you feel nothing. Everything keeps working, it's how men are built, but we don't feel anymore, the pleasure in it is gone.

'It's been so long since I've felt anything, so long since I've had a single real human connection. Until I met you. With you, I feel. I feel so much it consumes me, it's overwhelming. But it makes the rest worse too because I don't want to be with anyone else. I don't want to be numb anymore.'

My heart broke for this beautiful man. This incredibly kind man who deserved better than the life he'd been given. I wanted to wrap him inside me, love him, keep him safe. I trailed my finger down the side of his face, getting lost in his sad eyes that saw all the way into my soul. I felt his pain through his eyes. I just wanted to love him, to love him forever. I didn't know how to do it other than to kiss him. I pulled his mouth to mine and got lost in him, lost in feeling, lost in love for him. I didn't want to be numb anymore, either.

We forgot about the vision screen as he positioned me beneath him and slowly, beautifully, languidly, did beautiful, magical things to my body until I couldn't see straight, until I didn't know what day it was, and until all I could pray for was an end to the world we lived in, so I could spend every day, every night, nestled in the nook of Jack's body, being devoured by him and pleasured by him and loved by him.

When he was done, he took me to bed and after showing me the moon and offering me the entire, vast, brilliant, star filled universe, I fell asleep wrapped in his arms, his breath on my neck, his heart beating against my skin.

When I woke, the morning sun was kissing the sky, the noise of a new day rumbling up from the street below. I reached out to the space where he'd been, where he'd slept, where I'd felt him in the early hours of the morning breathing, holding me to him. The empty space beside me was still warm. Was he still here? I wondered, hopefully.

I got out of bed, threw on my dressing gown, smoothing down my hair before padding out to the living room where Jack stood at the kitchen cooking blueberry pancakes in jeans, no shirt, no shoes, his hair still mussed and a dark shadow creeping across his jaw making him look too good to be set free on an unsuspecting world.

'Good morning,' he called.

'Good morning,' I answered, sheepishly, suddenly afraid of what I looked like, surprised I cared when I'd never cared. But then I'd never had a man in my home in the morning to see me.

Jack placed the last of the pancakes onto a plate, left it on the bench and came over to kiss me.

'Are you even allowed to still be here?' I asked, terrified we'd broken another rule.

'You get six hours, if we want to be pedantic about it, our booking didn't start until after midnight so you have me for another twenty minutes,' he smiled.

I snaked my arms around his shirtless body, resting against the warmth of him, taking in his smell and memorising how it felt to have his arms wrapped tight around me, how safe I felt in a world where little made sense and I always felt a heartbeat behind everyone else.

'Come, I've made you pancakes and coffee,' he said, kissing me before leading me out to the balcony where the sun warmed my bare arms and legs. 'And before you ask, no, it's not part of the package, so don't tell anyone or I'll be making bloody pancakes all over town and I only want to make pancakes for you,' he said, putting the plate before me. 'And now I do have to leave,' he said, kissing me one last time, one more mind numbing, toe curling, memorable time before putting on his shoes, throwing on his shirt and buttoning it as he walked out the door.

CHAPTER 8

———

'Oh shit! What's wrong with you?' Zoë demanded when she barged her way into my apartment Sunday night.

After Jack had left, I'd eaten the pancakes, changed into some loungewear and had spent the day lazing about, ignoring all the chores I was supposed to be doing. Instead, I watched mindless programs on the vision screen in an effort to not think of Jack and when I could see him again, counting down the minutes until my nightly run. Now Zoë had arrived, shattering the quiet and the perfection and the memories.

'What are you talking about? I'm fine,' I defended.

'Hmph,' said Zoë, not believing me. 'Here, can you cook this?' she asked, handing me a lump of beef.

'You want me to cook a roast at this time of day?' I asked.

Zoë shrugged. 'How long do they take?' she asked.

I laughed. 'I'm pretty sure more than the hour that remains until dinner. I can slice some up and do something with it, maybe and roast some veg at least, I guess,' I said, already scanning my table for recipes.

'Thanks,' Zoë said. 'I'm not great in the kitchen.'

'I'd never have guessed,' I laughed.

'Shut up,' laughed Zoë. 'How 'bout you tell me how you got on last night instead of laughing at me,' she said.

'Great,' I said. 'How about you? Did he rattle your bones?'

'Oh, my otherworldly goodness,' Zoë gushed. 'There are no words. Your man wasn't kidding.'

'He's not my man,' I snapped. 'You selected him and you and Rach chose your men first, and I got what was left,' I assured Zoë.

'Oh no!' said Zoë, her eyes wide. 'You like him. Courtney, no, you can't like him,' she said, grabbing my arms and pleading with me.

'Don't be so dramatic,' I told her. 'I don't like him. This is just how I look after a good shag,' I told her.

'No. Uh, uh, I've seen that look before and it only ever means trouble. Every time I mention him you get defensive and your eyes go all starry and stupid.'

'They do not,' I scoffed, going into the kitchen to start on dinner.

'Courtney?' Zoë questioned.

'I'm fine. It's all fine, it's nothing. I don't fancy him. It was just nice, alright? But I'm fine,' I insisted.

'That's a lot of fine,' she smirked. 'Well, you better be because if anyone gets wind of anything else, you're up shit creek. You know that, right? You know what happens if you get too attached?'

'Yes, Stacey told me, you get sent back to the dungeons at the college.'

'No, that was just once because Trish stepped in early enough.

Courtney, they send you to the detention islands to fend for yourself. If you're lucky, you're sent to a farm. You'll never see him again, if you even survive what they'll do to you.'

'It doesn't matter, anyway, its fine. I just had a nice time. Just feeling all nice and gooey from the sex, that's all,' I insisted. 'Can you just drop it?' I asked.

'Fine. I'm dropping it. But I have my eye on you, newbie,' she told me. 'Now cook me some food and let me tell you about that bearded stud and what he managed to do with his tongue,' she smirked.

'Shouldn't Rachel be here for this?' I asked, both desperately prolonging the story and wishing for a buffer. I suspected Zoë was about to unload a whole lot of detail my ears were not prepared to hear and my imagination did not want infiltrating it.

'I asked her but she said she wasn't up to it. Something's going on with her. It's not like her to pass up basketball games or free food. I just can't figure out what. We tell each other everything and I've been racking my brain for a clue.' Sensing she may have said too much, she laughed, 'But oh well, means it's your lucky day and you get all the goss for yourself.'

I suspected I didn't want to hear any such thing but knew it was better than being grilled about Jack or having Zoë suspicious about him and me. So, I poured us both some wine and while Zoë sat at the kitchen bench and I began peeling vegetables, the story of the bearded stud, as he would be forever known, was told.

After Zoë had left though, I slumped into a chair on the balcony. It was quiet without Jack. I liked my apartment better when he was there, taking up space, sharing the same air. I'd just have to book him as often as I could, I thought. But until then, there was the bridge, so I changed into my running gear.

I ran, with hope filling my heart but he wasn't there. I sat on the rocky ledge as the heavens opened and big fat drops fell down the sides of the bridge. I waited and I waited until goose pimples raced up my arms, until the rain stopped, until one day stretched towards another. Eventually I had to give up, he wasn't coming. Big fat grey clouds blocked the moon, only the soft orange street-lamps illuminating the slick pathway on which I ran. I ran home, my heart heavy, my legs refusing to move on a pathway I couldn't feel.

I sat on the balcony. I was alone. All alone. Just me. No Jack. No life filling the empty space around me. I watched the people below on the street totally oblivious to my aching heart. Could they even comprehend such a thing in their perfectly controlled worlds? I doubted it. I could never have imagined I could feel this way about another person, about a man, if it hadn't happened to me. These were the stupid feelings that happened to the silly women in the silly books used as a warning of what happened when love clouded your judgement, the mishaps and interference it caused.

But now it was me.

Not a silly woman in a silly cautionary story and it felt real. It felt amazing, not silly at all, but unlike those women, I could never have what I craved the most. There would be no miscommunication righted that would bring us together for a happy ever after.

I watched a couple walking by the river. In another time, they would have looked like lovers strolling in the moonlight instead of the employer and the entertainer they were. The man's hand guided the women by the small of her back. They stood beside the river, watching how it shimmered in the moonlight, seemingly oblivious to the fresh batch of fat grey clouds rolling overhead.

The man turned, looking up to my building. Looking directly at me. Could it be to me? For a moment I thought it was just an illusion but I knew those eyes. I'd know those eyes anywhere. They were shooting right into my soul. He didn't look away, as though he could see me, see right into my eyes, as though those dark ocean-blues knew, knew exactly what I was feeling, as though they were a little bit broken, too.

I couldn't breathe. I doubled over trying to suck in air. My heart sank, my body went heavy, bile clogging my airways. Gasping for air, I reached for the new wine bottle I'd left on the table and started drinking, big long gulps, as the reality of our world seeped past the blissful wall of the bubbles I'd been indulging in.

I drank and kept on drinking until the little people down on the promenade, on the river bank, in the bars and the restaurants all became a blur of colour. Until I no longer felt a thing and I stumbled to bed.

When I woke, my head was heavy, fog had settled in all the corners of my brain. Nothing seemed real. A thick layer of dust seemed to cover everything I looked at. Colours were no longer electrifyingly bright, sounds weren't clear and crisp, birds didn't put a song in my heart, and the sunshine didn't make me want to smile or dance. I wanted to pull the covers over my head and curl up into a ball and die. Not just from the repercussions stemming from the bottle of wine I'd drank before I'd stumbled to bed in the wee hours, but from the Jack ache that wouldn't go away, that I feared would never, ever, go away.

I buried myself in work. It was all I could do. Block out the rest of the world, zone out until I returned to normal. I'd have to return to normal eventually, right? So, I worked. I made bookings, I transferred calls, I watched Grace's visitors. But I could only think of Jack. The way he tasted, the sound of his voice, the way he smelt, the way he moved, how safe I felt curled into the nook of his body on the couch, falling asleep in his arms.

I shook my head, almost laughing at myself. It didn't seem real. The truth was, no matter what he said, it probably wasn't. It was all an act. It had to be. Anything else meant I was screwed. We were both screwed.

I sat behind my desk with the girls from the pod watching the entertainer harvest strawberries outside our window. The others sighed as the man moved on to another floor then went back to their desks but Zoë hung behind. 'You alright, Courtney? You seem off with the fairies this week?'

'Oh yeah, sure, just, I don't know, maybe I put my neck out on the weekend or something. I'm just, I'm struggling to concentrate, that's all,' I said.

'I'll give you the number for my alignment lady. You sure that's all? You sure, you know,' she said, clearly not wanting to be too frank in the open office.

'Let me ask you something,' I said, leading Zoë over towards the far window and well away from Jen's office. 'They all get friendly, right? They all make you seem like you're the only one, tell you that you make the world complete and such, right? They have KPIs just like the rest of us, they need the repeat business, yeah?' I whispered, looking out the window as though discussing nothing of importance.

'I guess, not the repeat business as such, they need the referrals though, but there are rules, things they say,' said Zoë, unsure.

'They tell you you're beautiful, that you made their day, blah, blah, then they do their business and get the heck outta there,' she said.

'Your guy Saturday night, we get six hours right? Did you get your full six?' I asked.

Zoë shrugged. 'No one ever uses it all. We did our thing till about four and that was that, a kiss on the forehead, thanks for the laughs and off he went.'

I nodded, taking it in, the difference, the coldness, the indifference.

'What exactly did your guy do?' Zoë asked curiously.

I shrugged, 'Yeah, much the same, poured me some wine before he left, he was nice.'

'They're all nice, you can't get attached to them, it's their job,' Zoë clarified.

'Yeah, yeah, I know.'

'You know what you need, you need a comparison,' Zoë suggested.

'Yeah, a comparison,' I agreed without any enthusiasm. 'Great idea.'

'You good, then?' Zoë asked.

'Yeah, I'm good. Thanks, I'll see you at lunch,' I told her.

'You bet,' Zoë said, waving as she walked out the door.

Jack hadn't been indifferent. Jack wasn't cold. Jack didn't just say stuff to be nice, I knew it. I didn't want to believe it, but I knew it, deep inside my heart.

I was hoping Zoë would say they all schmoozed their arses off, laid it on thick, the whole nine yards but Zoë wasn't even on a name basis with any of her entertainers. That alone changed things. But I didn't run again. I couldn't. I couldn't be disappointed again. But more importantly, after what we'd shared, after what I'd seen on the riverbank Sunday night, I wasn't sure I could look him in the eye and not crumble to dust. Or pummel him until he was black and blue. Either way, it was better if I just didn't run. The fact that this wasn't his fault either, didn't matter. I'd stupidly gone and felt things for this man that I wasn't even supposed to be capable of feel and I needed to get rid of them and fast before someone other than Zoë noticed and we both suffered the consequences. I couldn't stand the thought of what might happen to him, to either of us. We had it fine enough where we were, we were fed and clothed and housed, that would have to be enough.

During the afternoon lull, I scoured the catalogue of available activities Stacey had sent me when I first arrived. I'd ignored them all, forgotten about them this last week when I'd become so engrossed in this new world, with Jack. But activities, distractions, fresh faces, they were exactly what I needed.

I booked a cooking class for that night. I decided Tuesday after work I'd go and buy some painting supplies and create something beautiful. I'd always been good at art at the college. In fact, I'd been surprised I hadn't tested for painting instead of business services. Wednesday, I was going to the basketball with Zoë as Rachel was booking in another midweek date. Thursday, I booked into yoga, the stretching, core building and meditation were just what I needed. I designated Friday night as movie night. I could stream a few movies, invite Zoë over if she didn't have a date, make a pile of popcorn, order something nice for dinner, buy something naughty from the patisserie for dessert, have a nice glass of wine to end my week.

I felt lighter already. Distractions were just what I needed. Fill the hours and the emptiness and I'd be too tired to think of him, too tired to give in and go for a run.

The cooking class was in the community centre, a short walk to the other end of the mall. It was a plain, purpose-built building and the cooking room was fitted out specifically for the task at hand with rows of benches with metal tops, sinks, ovens and cooktops built in.

Most of the benches were already full when I arrived. I was a little late because I'd stopped to do my best to de La Ferme myself by making my hair a little less polished and putting on jeans and a t-shirt I bought from a big shop on the way instead of the boutiques Stacey had directed me to. I needed to fit in. I didn't want to be a La Ferme girl. For a few hours I just wanted to be me.

I chose the closest empty bench, dropping my bag onto the shelf under the bench and smiling at the girl beside me.

'Hi there,' greeted my cheery bench mate. 'I'm Pauline,' she said, introducing herself.

Pauline had a big laugh and big hair with big, dark, red curls. She worked for an advertising company. I told her I was a support person for a builder. Pauline filled her spare time with a load of extra-curricular activities. She volunteered at the hospital, the zoo and the community gardens. I wondered if she filled her time for the same reason I was filling mine? Or maybe that's just how everyone else lived, how they kept out of trouble?

We learnt how to make coq au vin and crème brulee from a sweet, rosy-cheeked instructor. Pauline and I drank more wine than we put in the coq au vin and creatively covered missing chunks of custard from our brûlée's when the instructor came to inspect.

'Will I see you next week?' Pauline asked hopefully as we exited the building.

'Sure will, see you then,' I smiled before heading in the opposite direction.

It had suitably filled my time and it was surprisingly good fun. Tiring too, which meant I arrived home, exhausted and went straight to sleep.

Tuesday night, I bought art supplies from a chatty girl called Bree, a blonde who'd just taken over the art supplies shop after her manager had up and died from a heart attack. She sold me all the necessary supplies, bagged them up, tucked the easel and a couple of canvasses under my arm and I lugged it all home via the water taxi, hoping no one important saw me struggling on and off the wobbly boat with my loot. People like me probably got such things delivered, but I hadn't thought about the practicalities until I'd left the shop.

I set up my new art station between the living room and the dining room. I could see both the vision screen and outside from where I sat on a stool I'd moved from the breakfast bar. I stared at the blank canvas for a while after I'd eaten leftover coq au vin from the night before's cooking class. Opening a bottle of wine, I took a glass to my stool and stared at the canvas a bit longer. Eventually, I felt in a yellow kind of mood, painted the entire canvas a bright budgie yellow, finished my wine and went to bed.

I hadn't thought of Jack for hours by the time I got to the basketball on Wednesday night in quite high spirits with Zoë. I sent our butler off to fetch me the biggest plate of nachos he could find despite Zoë's protesting and happily swilled champagne, enjoying the admiration of the players and suitably ignoring the entertainers filling the box behind and around us, praying he wouldn't be one of them.

Zoë gave me stats on every player on the court, how many points they scored last season, how they were doing this season, their defence stats and of course, her hotness rating. We were having a great laugh. The world had faded away and there was nothing left but the game. But then came half time and Zoë went off to the bathroom. The suited man brought me more champagne and my nachos and as I went about stuffing my face, I couldn't help but glance around the stadium to see if he was there, hoping he was there while simultaneously hoping he wasn't.

I desperately wanted to see his face, to see those dark ocean-blue eyes, even for just a second even though I knew it would set me back days, so I was relieved when Zoë returned to her seat that I hadn't seen him and could relax and enjoy the rest of the game, and ignore Zoë's mocking of my food choice.

No one spoke to each other Thursday night at yoga, which was fine by me. It had been a crazy day in the office. Every woman in the region was looking to book their weekend stress relief, and get their health concerns cleared by Dr Grace. The day had been non-stop. I was exhausted.

I happily stretched my core and eased my mind in the calm serenity of the studio surrounded by lush gardens a few streets away from the office. Stretching made me feel strong. The breathing, in, out, in, out, was calming and energising. We finished by lying on the floor, concentrating on our breathing, meditating, nothing but the sounds of strangers breathing. It left me feeling energised and ready to return to the world.

I went home and blended a green smoothie for dinner, drank it on the balcony in the balmy evening air and went to bed revived and cleansed, feeling good.

Friday, as I walked from the water taxi to the office with the warm sun beating on my back, I congratulated myself on making it through the week. I was feeling good. No matter how tempting it had been, I hadn't filled myself with wine and I'd only thought of Jack a few times. Well, maybe a few hundred times, but I'd grabbed a hold of each thought and cut it short.

It would do no one any good for me to think about him in any way, shape or form. That's what I'd told myself during the work-day lulls when he'd crept into my brain. The fact that it was his eyes I saw when I lay down at night and closed my eyes was of no importance whatsoever. A comforting face in a strange new place, I lied to myself. The image would fade as I built my life, as long as I steered clear of him. As I opened my office door, I was proud of myself, of how grown up and responsible I was being.

The morning was again busy with people making their last-minute plans and it flew by in the blink of an eye. I ordered a Thai beef salad from the cafeteria and it was waiting in the pod kitchenette for me at midday. I sat with the others and listened to them talk of their weekends. Dates, parties; Di was going to a yoga retreat which sounded heavenly. I asked her for the details, which she instamessaged me. It would fill an upcoming weekend, I thought. Zoë had a date after work, which was disappointing. I'd been hoping she'd help keep me distracted while we watched movies about the end of the world and alien invasions. But I didn't say anything.

'What about you, Courtney?' asked Rosie.

'I think I might just settle in with a movie tonight, go for a run tomorrow through the gardens. It's been a crazy couple of weeks, I could use some balance,' I said, using the popular buzz phrase.

'Oh, that does sound lovely,' agreed Jules. 'Well, something to look forward to, anyway. We best get back to it,' she declared, when it was time to return to work.

The afternoon was quiet. I guessed everyone had already made their plans, got in before the best men were all booked out if there was even such a thing, who knows, but it was quiet and quiet was bad. Quiet meant too much time to think and the closer it came to the end of the day and my empty apartment, the more anxious I became. Eventually I couldn't stand it a second longer. I gave in and I typed my number into the booking system and then typed in his.

His profile came on the screen and the little calendar below the words of 205cm, dark blue eyes, tan, fit, words that didn't nearly do him justice, showed the whole weekend was booked. All day, every day. How many women was that? A lot. A lot of women for him to please. A lot of women that weren't me.

My throat constricted and tears rushed to my eyes as I chastised myself for the millionth time. I had to get over it, get over him. This was the reality of our world. This is what made our world work. It's what made it sustainable. It was the key to its regeneration. I had to get over it, get over him. I took a deep, shaky breath. Somehow, I would get through it. I had no choice.

As the day drew to a close, all I could think about was the wine I had at home. I imagined myself drinking it while watching those movies about the end of the world. I'd drink until there was none left and my insides didn't feel so broken anymore. Perhaps I'd even stay that way for the whole weekend. What did it matter, anyway? This world the President had created, this world without love was empty and meaningless. There was nothing to strive for, there was no one to love, there was no hope, nothing but drinking and sex and basketball games. What kind of a world had the woman created? Wine would make it bearable. Wine would make everything okay. Wine would help me forget.

'We need to go dancing,' Zoë said, plonking herself on my desk and startling me from my daydreams of wine.

I shrugged. I wasn't in the mood for dancing. 'Aren't you getting your bones rattled tonight?' I asked, grateful for the reprieve.

'I am indeed,' Zoë said, smugly. 'But tomorrow night, we are going dancing. You, me and Rachel. No one gets to blow it off. Girl's night out. No dates, no worries, just dancing. You look like you could use some dancing and so does Rachel.'

I knew I had to muster some enthusiasm, and it was just the right way to shake myself free of Jack and move on, get myself into this new life I had to live. Dancing was perfect.

'Sure, let's go dancing,' I agreed, even managing a smile.

CHAPTER 9

'Y ou ready to do this?' Zoë asked with mischief in her eyes.

It had taken all day to feel human after drinking myself into numbness the night before. I'd walked in the early morning sunshine, gotten coffee from the local café, an extra to take home. I'd done chores and tried running but had only got as far as the dock before wanting to puke, so I'd gotten another coffee and walked home. Now Zoë stood in my living room bursting with energy and excitement. I was worried, very worried.

I'd somehow agreed to let Zoë loose, not only in my apartment but in my wardrobe and on my face and hair. We were going dancing. I had never been dancing. There was no such frivolity at the college and we certainly didn't dress for any events when all we had was a collection of the same woollen dresses. So, I was a definite fish out of water, and Zoë was clearly the master of dressing appropriately for everything.

'Where's the wine, we need wine. Nice painting by the way, it's very um, yellow,' Zoë said with a smirk as she helped herself to glasses, and then filled two large glasses with wine from the bottle on the bench.

'Alright, come, come,' Zoë demanded after a few big sips of wine. 'Come tell me what you got up to last night.'

'There's nothing to tell,' I told her.

'What do you mean nothing? Didn't you book a date?'

'Nope, I was exhausted. I took the night off, watched movies. I told you I was going to,' I defended.

'Right, I guess I just assumed there was going to be a date in there, too,' Zoë said, making me move to the bathroom so she could brush my hair.

'What's wrong with that? Am I not allowed a night off now? I wish someone would bloody well write these rules down for me. How am I supposed to keep track?' I asked.

'Alright, alright, no need to have kittens. Yeah, you're allowed a night off. It's just, I'm worried about you,' Zoë said. 'Just want to make sure you were really taking a night off for some R&R and not sitting in here soaking your sorry soul with wine, wishing for something you can never have.'

'Don't be ridiculous,' I scoffed, hoping Zoë couldn't see my face pale.

'Why don't you tell me all about your night?' I asked, hoping to deflect the subject from me.

Zoë smirked, her eyes full of mischief, 'Thought you'd never ask,' she said, before continuing to tell me things I really didn't need to hear, things that made me splutter my wine out of my mouth and want to hide in a dark corner, which only made Zoë laugh louder and tell more outrageous stories. Zoë was getting way too much enjoyment out of making me squirm with embarrassment, but anything was better than discussing me and how much trouble I was in.

By the time Zoë had finished with her stories of debauchery, my hair had been curled and teased and constructed into a fun, sexy do, that would last a night of dancing. Zoë then raided my wardrobe until she found some shiny black pants and a sparkly, silver, low-scooped neck tank top and killer heels that made my legs look twice as long as they were.

We both changed into our party clothes. Zoë was wearing a slinky red dress that made her look almost naked. I shook my head, I had no idea where Zoë got her courage from or how on earth she would dance in the miniscule dress, but I was just secretly glad she hadn't outfitted me in anything similar.

We finished our wine, made our way to the train where we stormed on past the waiting queues and took our seats while the train filled around us with women in their shimmering party finery.

Once we got off the train we walked the short distance to the club where Rachel was waiting out the front for us.

'Why didn't she just meet us at my place?' I asked Zoë as we approached Rachel. Rachel didn't live in our building but lived in a similar one a street or so back from the river.

Zoë shrugged, waving so Rachel would see us coming. 'Dunno. She had something to do over this way and said she would meet us here,' she said, her voice laced with concern, but it was too late to ask any further questions because we had arrived.

It was a non-descript building. No neon lighting like I imagined, just a square grey box like building with light and music escaping from an open doorway manned by a large and imposing woman in a cheap black suit. A long queue stretched along the grey cement wall, the women in all sorts of coloured and sparkly frocks ready to dance the night away.

Rachel was waiting to the side of the bouncer. She smiled widely when she saw us.

'Hey, hey,' called Zoë as she hooked her arm through Rachel's and we headed to the door.

Zoë air kissed the bouncer and we all walked in ignoring the eye rolls and dirty looks from those still waiting in the line. A waitress waiting just inside the door led us to a table right next to the dance floor without us even having to ask, and as soon as we sat, a bottle of champagne and three glasses appeared on the table.

'Ladies, please let me know if there's anything at all you need, anything at all,' the waitress smiled, pouring our drinks.

'Now that's what I'm talking about,' laughed Rachel 'Nothing but top shelf service for you too.'

Zoë smirked and I suspected even though she was always so nonchalant about the perks she more aware and grateful than she let on. 'Cheers,' Zoë said, holding her glass up for us to clink. 'Let's get this party started!'

I couldn't remember ever laughing so hard. The more we drank, the funnier we became, the funnier everything became. Zoë helped the laughs along with shots of something that tasted like creamy chocolate and burned all the way down, but felt so darned good, numbed the pain, made me happy, made the world a better place, made everyone better. We drank bottles of champagne that were cleared and replaced in the blink of an eye. We laughed over stories of colleagues and life, and stories of entertainers and mythical urban legends of what goes on behind the closed doors of some of the women that use them. We laughed until our tummies hurt.

And we danced. We danced until our feet were ready to fall off. The club was full of laughing, sweaty women all trying to find a place to sit, to stand, to dance. It was dark and the music loud. The walls, floor and chairs pulsated from the music and room echoed with the noise of people trying to talk above the rhythmic sounds. Many women had brought dates with them but some, like us, had just come to laugh and dance. Zoë was right. It was just what we needed.

'Come on,' Zoë said, dragging us back to the floor for a favourite song.

We were jigging on the dance floor to an upbeat tune, arms flailing as we moved with the rhythm, squishing against others doing the same when my eyes landed on a familiar face in the crowd. Sitting at a table on the other side of the floor was Jack. Another man sat with him but all I saw was Jack. He was leaning back in his chair watching me, his eyes scanning up and down my body like he was thinking about all the improper things he wanted to do to me. Our eyes caught and instantly I blushed, unable to stop it after all that champagne swilling in my veins.

'Well, well,' cooed Zoë. 'What's caught your attention, then?' she asked following my eyeline. 'Aaah,' she smirked.

I was about to tell her to shut up when two girls returned to the table and sat between the men. One putting her hand on Jack's thigh, whispering something in his ear. I stopped dancing, felt my face fall as my heart sank. He was on a date. Of course, he was on a date, I'd seen his calendar. Jack closed his eyes, when he opened them, they burned with pain and apologies and regret as they looked back into mine. Then he turned, kissed the brunette, reached for her hand and led her to the dance floor where the girl pushed herself up against him as she ground and swayed her body all over him.

I wanted to vomit. It took all my energy to remain upright. I just wanted to collapse onto the floor, curl into a ball and die. I wanted to close my eyes and never wake up. The pain burned in my chest like a hot poker from the very depths of hell and I could feel my heart breaking, literally splitting apart into tiny, irreparable pieces and I couldn't breathe, my ears rang, my eyes glazed over.

Zoë took my hand, grounding me, bringing me to the present, back from wherever I was floating to. 'You'll get used to it, honey,' she whispered sadly. I sensed we both knew the truth, that I was never getting used to it, that this was going to end badly, or at best I'd be a broken shell of who'd I'd once been.

'It's fine,' I spat. 'I don't even care, anymore,' I lied, almost roared, suddenly angry, angry at the world, the President, Jack, the stupid cow rubbing her body all over my man and even Zoë for knowing, for seeing, for being too good a friend. I was angry at everything.

Returning to our table, I began throwing back the shots lined up waiting for us, one, then two, then three and waited for the numbness to take hold.

'What's going on?' Rachel asked, following me and Zoë back to the table, confused.

Zoë indicated the area where Jack was with her head but didn't say anything as I threw another shot down my throat. Rachel turned around to see what we were looking at and before we knew what was happening she was pushing through the crowd, physically pushing people out of her way as she stormed to the ladies' room.

'What was that?' I asked, stunned back to reality.

'I don't know,' Zoë mumbled. 'Wait here,' she told me, disappearing towards the toilets.

I looked back to where Jack and his companion were dancing, the girl draping her hands all over him like he was a piece of meat, and I was sick to my stomach as white-hot anger bubbled through my body. I could feel the fury and bile and vomit churning, getting ready to erupt and had to look away, quell it all with a shot of numbing perfection.

When Zoë returned alone, I asked, 'Where's Rachel?'

'Being a fool,' Zoë mumbled.

I looked over to the table Jack and his companions had been occupying and saw there was a very angry girl sitting alone taking long gulps from her glass of cider. Jack followed my eye line, his face turning fast from concern to thunderous fury. His date, completely oblivious rubbed her body against his, her head resting longingly on his shoulder.

'Come on, let's go,' Zoë said.

'Fine by me,' I grumbled. 'Wait, what about Rachel? Shouldn't we wait for her?'

'Fuck Rachel. The stupid bitch has lost her mind,' Zoë spat.

I looked at Zoë, stunned. I would never have thought Zoë would be so cruel about a friend.

'Sorry,' Zoë said. 'You don't want to know. Let's just go, alright?' she pleaded.

I resisted one last look at Jack, one last stab to my heart, and followed Zoë as she made a path to the door.

I almost had to run to keep up with Zoë who was stomping along the footpath as though she was the one who'd just seen the love of her life on the dance floor with some desperate cow who was getting all handsy and gropey. I didn't dare ask what had gotten her so worked up. Obviously, it was something to do with Rachel but what was a mystery. It wasn't easy walking that fast, with that much ferocity in sky high heels, a belly full of shots and champagne and with feet that were already throbbing from dancing in said ridiculous shoes, but I didn't have much choice and kept up as best I could.

There was hardly anyone on the train. It was too early for people to be ending their night, so we didn't have to push through any crowds to find empty seats. We didn't speak and the fury radiating off Zoë almost made me sit in another seat. But I just let her be, let her stare out the window and settle down.

We rode the train over the bridge in silence. Walked the path to our building in silence. When we finally reached our apartment building, Zoë appeared to have lost some of her steam and fury. When the lift arrived at my floor, she embraced me in a hug. 'I hope you had a fantastic night. I'm sorry Rachel went and ruined it.'

I shrugged, if it wasn't for Zoë's anger, I'd have had no idea it was ruined. 'It's alright,' I told her, thinking the only thing that ruined my night was Jack and the gyrating woman but I knew better than to say that out loud, so I said, 'I had a fantastic time. Thank you for inviting me, it was a lot of fun.'

'Good, I'm glad you had fun. Now go up, get some sleep and pretend everything ended fine and we farewelled Rachel at the train station, alright?' she told me.

I wasn't quite sure what Zoë was getting at. What had gone on at the club with Rachel? But as Zoë appeared to be waiting for confirmation, I agreed. 'Sure, of course,' I said, giving my best polite smile.

'And don't get yourself upset about your lovely shag. You'll get used to seeing them out and about. Maybe we'll get ourselves a couple and go on a double date next weekend, hey?' I could tell she wasn't saying it with her usual good cheer, but I didn't know what to do about it or what was really going on. I just hadn't been around long enough to know such things, so I hugged my friend and thanked her again for inviting me and walked out of the lift.

Once I was alone, the full weight of disappointment from seeing Jack with another woman hit me as I walked down the hallway to my door. It wasn't the first time, not even the first time since we'd slept together. Maybe it was all the alcohol I'd consumed? Or maybe it was only ever going to get harder and harder seeing him rather than easier. All I knew was that at any minute, his mouth would be on that woman's body as he went about his job of pleasuring her, and it smacked me in the stomach, hit me like a wall of ice.

I opened the door to my apartment and finally I was alone to wallow to my heart's content in privacy and peace. I stripped off my clothes, leaving them in the path I took to the bathroom where I wiped off my makeup and stepped into a hot shower, washing away the smells of excess and the gunk out of my hair.

When I was done, I put on the familiar forbidden college issue nightdress I kept hidden in the back of a drawer. I left my damp hair hanging over my shoulders and went in search of something to eat to soak up all I'd drunk.

I stepped out from behind the counter, eating a block of cheese, already imagining the heavenly comfort of my bed. Something on the floor by the door caught my eye. My floors were clean and no matter how much I'd drunk, I knew there wasn't supposed to be something there.

I picked it up. It was square piece of foamy card, a drink coaster.

I recognised the artwork as that of the club we'd just been to, a cartoon cat in a tuxedo drinking from an oversized bottle of champagne. I'd thought it hilarious earlier in the night, now I wondered if I'd ever find anything hilarious again?

The realities of life were no longer agreeing with me. I was fast discovering, I wasn't a fan of sharing and not nearly as patriotic as I'd always thought. I was mad and sad all at the same time. How could a person even be both simultaneously? My life was supposed to be too perfect to even feel those emotions.

I turned the coaster over. The hand-written scrawl read, 'Bridge. Run.'

My breath lodged somewhere in no man's land. It had to be Jack. I had no idea how he'd gotten into my building, but who else could it be? It had to be Jack. Besides, no one else knew I ran to the bridge. It was our place. Mine and Jack's.

I left the half-eaten block of cheese on the bench and went to find my running gear. I had my sneakers laced up in record time and was heading out the door before my wine-soaked brain could even catch up. No one paid me any attention as I made my way outside. An advantage of modern society, no crime and no predators, meant you could run half drunk at two in the morning without any worries, without raising any eyebrows.

The night air was still warm and sweet but I didn't waste time admiring it, I ran. I sprinted along the river, around the hand holders pretending their romance was real. As fast as my feet, sore and squished from dancing in stilettos would allow me. My lungs burned. My legs throbbed and the wine in my stomach churned, but I kept running.

There were a few muted lights on top of the bridge, some nearby at the grassed picnic area nearby but none underneath.

No one milled about so I stepped under the bridge, into the dark shadows. It occurred to me then that maybe it wasn't Jack. Maybe it was a trick, after all. Perhaps the world wasn't as safe as I'd been led to believe. Nothing was as I'd believed it seemed, and suddenly my heart beat faster and my palms became slick with sweat as I looked around for someone. Anyone. Perhaps I'd waited too long. Perhaps he'd gone.

A shadow flickered in the furthest corners. I meant to walk towards it but my feet refused to move. They'd frozen to where I stood. From fear, hope, anticipation, I wasn't sure which. Then I saw him, just a small glint of light catching his face and I breathed a sigh of relief and ran to him. Jack held my face in both his hands, pulling my mouth to his, taking like a man lost in the desert for weeks finally finding water. Taking as though it was all that would keep him breathing.

Finally filled with what he needed, he rested his forehead on mine. 'Are you okay?' he whispered, his eyes closed, breathing as though drawing me in, as though afraid of the answer.

I reached up to hold his beautiful face in my hands, to hold his eyes to mine, every ounce of anger, sadness and frustration instantly evaporating. 'I'm okay. I think,' I told him. 'Zoë says I'll get used to it,' I said, as though the mere idea that I would get used to such a thing was ridiculous.

'Well, I won't,' he said.

'But you are used to it,' I said, looking longingly into his eyes.

'No, I'm not used to feeling this for you and having to do that. I'll never get used to that. I'll never get used to seeing you across a room and not being able to talk to you, to touch you, to kiss you,' he took my mouth, slow and deep. 'Never,' he whispered.

'What are we going to do, Jack?' I asked as he pulled me into his arms.

'I don't know, Coté, I don't know. But I'll think of something,' he promised.

'This isn't right. This world we live in, none of it is right. I don't want to have sex with a new man each week like Zoë. I want to dream about the future, have ambition and hobbies and choose where I live and where I holiday. Why shouldn't you get to choose those things, too?

'Why shouldn't you and the other guys get to choose who you have sex with? Breeder, entertainer or farmer, that's not enough options and not particularly fair. If the President wants to approve who breeds and doesn't, that's one thing, but you should have choices about the rest of your life. You and me, this isn't wrong. This feels too right to be wrong. We should be able to be together. It shouldn't be a crime. I can't not feel this for you. I tried stopping but it hurts. I feel too much and it feels too good. How do I stop that? I can't. I want to be with you, wake up next to you, every day and eat pancakes on the balcony. I don't want to go to bed every night wondering, imagining who you are with and what you're doing with her. It's killing me, Jack. It's tearing me to pieces.'

'I know,' he said, his eyes filling with tears. He closed his eyes on the tears and leaned his forehead to mine. 'Believe me, I know because it's tearing me up, too, every date tears me up a little more.'

'How did you even get here so fast? What happened to your date?' I asked concerned.

'You don't want to know and I don't want to tell you, but it's fine. I'm here now and that's all that matters.'

'Not if she gets you in trouble,' I said, worried.

'She was very happy when I left her. Now stop asking,' he said, frustrated.

'Fine,' I conceded, kissing him softly. 'How long can you stay?'

He smiled, 'Not long, but a little bit,' he answered, leading me to the rocky ledge deep in the shadows where we sat, where I curled up against him like I was born to do. We sat quietly, just needing to be near each other until the dancing queens began their pilgrimages home.

'I have to go,' he said, pulling my hands to his mouth, his eyes on mine, looking into my soul, filling me with hope and faith and something so good and beautiful, it kept me afloat like a life raft in this sea of hopelessness and uncertainty.

CHAPTER 10

I raced around the market in a blur of frenetic energy. I'd woken feeling hopeful and then reality set in. Now I was trying to outrun it, outrun the heaviness building inside me, the sadness that threatened to overwhelm me, and the hatred for a world in which I had no say or control over my own life.

It was all good and well for neither of us to like or agree with the situation we were in, but it still remained, this was the way our world was and no matter how much we hated it, I would continue to see Jack in public with dates. Images of him pleasing all manner of women would continue to fill my head. So now I had to fill my time with mundane chores like filling a shopping basket with milk, wine and comfort food to fill the gaping hole spreading in my soul.

At home, I filled a glass with wine and went about rearranging my wardrobe, my new favourites at one end, the stuff I hated hidden in the middle. I prepared my clothes for washing. The cleaning lady Stacey had organised would come while I was at work, so I made sure it was all ready for her. Except my contraband college issue nightdress. I rinsed that in the sink, hanging it over the shower rail until it was dry, and then I hid it at the back of my drawer. I couldn't have some nosey cleaning lady reporting back to Stacey that I'd held on to college issue clothing.

In the afternoon, I prepared a small piece of roast beef, potatoes, carrots and pumpkin just like the cooks had done at the college every Sunday and slid it into the oven to roast. I tried not to think of Miss Milly, my friends, everyone I'd left behind. I'd promised I'd never forget them. But I had.

I'd become so caught up in my new life, in Jack, in my misery that I'd pushed them to the back of my mind. That's what this life had done to me, the person it had made me.

Sarah and Mish were about to celebrate their birthdays and I hadn't even thought to send a card. They would be shipped off to their new lives, naïve and unsuspecting and no doubt full of excitement about what lay ahead.

I wondered who had recruited them. Where they would end up? They were both were smart. They'd have done well in recruitment. They'd land on their feet in prestigious positions. Neither would have any idea of the world that awaited them. I desperately wanted to tell them, get a message to them. But there was no way to contact them. Even a birthday card wasn't safe from inspection. They'd have to find out for themselves. I sent out a wish, hoping they'd never fall in love. It'd be easier that way.

There was a knock at the door that startled me so much I almost spilt my wine.

'Who is it?' I called, thinking if it was a nosey neighbour, I wasn't even getting up to answer it.

'Zoë,' she called.

Zoë, I had to answer, so I put my wine down and answered the door.

'You look like shit,' she said, as soon as I opened the door.

'Great. Thanks. Right back atchya. What's wrong with you?' I asked, as Zoë stepped into the light and I got a good look at her dark ringed, red, puffy eyes. She'd tried concealing them with makeup but there wasn't enough in a foundation pot to cover that much dark nor the blotches on her face.

'Zoë you're scaring me, what's wrong?' I asked, putting my hand on Zoë's in comfort once we'd settled on the couch with a glass of wine.

'She's gone,' she said, shrugging.

'Who?' I asked.

'Rachel.'

'What do you mean she's gone?'

'She's gone. I've just come from her place. She wasn't answering my calls so I went to check on her. Her security people know me so they let me in but she hasn't been home since she left to meet us Saturday night.'

'Well, where'd she go?'

Zoë shrugged. 'Don't know.'

'Have you reported it?' I asked, not even sure what the procedure was.

Zoë laughed, a menacing, mean laugh. 'No one will care. Either she ran or they busted her stupid ass. Either way, there's nothing to report. Besides, if she did run, the longer it takes for anyone else to find out, the better head start she'll have.'

'Head start for what? I don't understand,' I said, my heart sinking at the possibility of foul play against my friend, that there could be such a thing in our perfectly orchestrated world.

'Of course you don't,' grumbled Zoë, taking a long sip of her wine. 'But a lesson Courtney, this is what happens when you get too close to the entertainers. Be warned. Don't go booking yours again,' she warned.

I almost gasped at the shock of it. Surely not, surely you just get chastised and warned or something. Surely as long as everyone still played nice, no one really cared? We weren't planning any public displays, we weren't going to run away together, just the occasional booking to keep us connected and sane. Where was the harm in that?

'What do you really think happened to Penny, your predecessor?' she asked.

I shrugged, although I had a sneaking suspicion I wasn't at all going to like the answer.

'She fell in love,' spat Zoë. 'Stupid fools. Both of them. You don't fall in love. They know it. Everyone knows it. Penny was just lucky Trish stepped in and she got off easy but it doesn't always happen like that and she was just lucky she'd been discreet so far.'

I didn't know what to say. There was nothing to say. I served us up some food and then snuggled against Zoë on the couch, like I did with those I'd thought were my sisters when one of them was upset. It seemed to do the trick. Zoë had stopped sniffling by the time we'd finished eating.

'Do you think we can find her?' Zoë asked with the innocence of a five-year-old as though I had any idea.

'Maybe,' I answered, thinking Zoë needed hope. 'It's getting late, why don't you get some sleep and come over tomorrow night? We'll talk some more then. It'll give us a chance to have a think about how, and maybe you can think of anywhere Rachel might have gone if she was in trouble.'

'Okay,' she agreed.

'Do you need some help fixing your face?' I offered.

Zoë smiled. 'Thanks, but I'm just going upstairs. Thanks,' she said hugging me. 'I really needed a friend.'

'You're welcome,' I told her.

'Hey, are you alright?' Zoë asked as though finally looking at me. I shrugged. 'Too much wine.'

Zoë shook her head. 'We really do need to talk, don't we? Tomorrow night,' she said hugging me again. 'I'll bring chocolate. You need all the vices you can get, I'm suspecting. Alright, it is late so I will go. We could both use some sleep,' she smiled.

Once Zoë left, it was like the emptiness of my apartment was closing in on me. She'd told me I couldn't book him, ever again. I had planned to book him for Friday night. But it was off the table. Why? What was so wrong with it anyway? It's not like I was inhibiting progress by my stupid fancies, I was the only one suffering after all. Okay, and maybe Jack but he was still doing his job and no doubt doing it well. He was very talented and really, a girl could orgasm just from his smile.

It wasn't fair. None of it was fair. I'd forgotten where I'd left my wine glass so I drank from the bottle. I'd done well to get through most of the day filling my brain with mundane things but now there was nothing left to do. Now my apartment was empty and quiet, Jack flooded my brain. Images of him, his mouth on that girl's body, filled the space behind my eyes. I tried imagining him playing video games with the other guys, playing pool or sweating it out in the gym instead but everything came back to him in bed with someone else.

The idea of Jack being with someone else made me sick to my stomach. No matter what Zoë said about getting used to it, there was no getting used to it. I went to open another bottle of wine. The smell of the leftover roast beef sitting on the bench smacked me in the face. The smell made my head swim and my stomach churn. I needed the support of the kitchen bench to hold me up.

Suddenly, I was overwhelmed, my body wanted to collapse. It couldn't take any more wine, any more smells, any more sadness. My vision blurred as tears begged for freedom and my body reached its limits. I covered the meat and slid it into the fridge. I left the wine on the bench and stumbled to bed, crawling under the covers in my clothes, curling up, pulling the pillow Jack had slept on to my nose, and falling asleep before I became a pathetic weeping mess.

Monday came too soon. I was dead to the world when the alarm squealed. My heart jumped and then my eyes, dry as sandpaper, ripped open. My mouth was parched and tasted like something rancid from the rubbish bin. I sat up, my head pounding and I desperately wanted to crawl back under the covers and never come out but I knew better. I had to get up and find some enthusiasm.

I drank two big glasses of water before showering and letting the hot water run over my body, washing away my misery. I took painkillers with my eggs and did my best to rustle together a respectable outfit before walking slowly to the water taxi dock, arriving just in time.

I walked numbly onto the boat, taking any seat I saw, not caring who I sat beside or how close I was to the water spray. Between Rachel disappearing and the mess with Jack and all the wine, I just didn't care about stupid trivial things like water spray and wrinkled clothes. What did any of it matter?

When I walked into the office it was a miracle I was able to fake any cheer at all. I did my best, smiled when required, made polite conversation in the pod until I could escape. I should have been in the drama program, I thought, commending myself for my performance.

I skipped morning tea, sipping my fourth coffee of the day at my desk instead as I ate a handful of almonds. I couldn't avoid any one at lunch though, and went to join the others in the pod to eat the chicken salad sandwich I ordered at the last minute.

I released the pretence of happiness when I saw the only person on the couches was Zoë. She looked terrible, way worse than me, as though the fate of forever rested in her hands, as though she'd gone a few rounds with a storm and lost.

'Where is everyone?' I asked.

'Meetings and stuff,' she mumbled, taking a bite of her sandwich. She chewed the bread as though it were a mouthful of sand.

'You look like shit?' I told her. 'Any news?'

'Nothing. I didn't know if I should phone in sick for her or not. But I thought, if they've caught her then they'd think I was covering for her and I'd be in trouble. So, I had to pretend everything was normal and it makes me feel like shit because it's not and my best friend is in trouble. I can feel it and I just don't know what to do to help her. You don't look any better by the way.'

I shrugged. 'Too much wine, no biggie. So, no one's said anything? You haven't heard anything?'

'Nothing. Not even a person from the nest asking where she is or if she's alright. Which means they know something but no one's saying anything.'

'What do we do?' I asked.

'Nothing right now, just get back to work. I'll see you tonight,' she said cheerfully as Rosie headed over to have her lunch.

I put some extra vegetables on to roast as soon as I got home. Once I'd changed and freshened up, they were ready to add to the leftover roast beef from the night before. The smell of the warming roast was filling the apartment when Zoë knocked on my door.

I hadn't seen her since lunch so I wasn't sure what I would find when I opened the door but when I did, she looked far livelier than she had at lunch.

'Smells great, I'm starving,' she declared, making herself at home.

We ate on the balcony amongst the sounds of diners from the promenade below, their chatter and clanking of cutlery filling the air made us feel less alone, made the conversations we were about to have less prohibited and conspiratorial.

'Shall we start with you?' Zoë asked.

I waved her off. 'Nothing to say. Got a bit caught up in it all. Was a shock to see him with someone else, that's all. I'm fine now, I promise,' I said.

'Then what was with all the wine last night?'

'Nothing, it was silly,' I said, giggling for affect. 'I was reorganising my wardrobe and doing chores and things before you came over, and just lost track of how much I'd had,' I lied, leaving out that I'd guzzled straight from the bottle after she'd left.

Zoë watched me as though looking for the lie. 'Fine,' she conceded as I smiled back at her even though my insides felt like blackened piles of ash.

'Now, what about Rachel?' I asked, purposely changing the subject, unsure how much talk of Jack I could take before I cracked and fell to pieces in the corner.

'I don't know,' Zoë said. 'She was kissing some guy in the alley.

Told me to go back inside, so I did. She blew me off, two games in a row and she never blows off a game. So, I looked up her personnel number today and checked her calendar. She had a date both nights with the same guy. She never books a date on game night. Then she had another on Friday night with the same entertainer. She never books the same guy. She's the first to advocate variety. So, I checked her file further and she's been on eight dates with this guy in the last three months. She's had a few in between to try and throw the analysts off track, but I know her,' Zoë said.

'Analysts?' I asked.

'Yeah, there's a program that spots anyone who has too many bookings with the same entertainer and their files are flagged and the analysts go to work, scouring all their bookings, every move they make, sometimes for years. Some people do it for reliability, like if they have a business thing to attend they like to know the guy is going to behave just the way they want, they don't want to retrain a new entertainer each time, but usually they'll have enough other dates that it balances out. The analysts know which ones are which, though. They're trained to spot the signs. It's too easy to get attached, develop feelings or whatever if you have the same guy so they run reports on everyone to try and catch things before they get out of hand.'

I felt ill. I could feel the blood draining out of my body but I couldn't stop it. I couldn't stop the building of bile or the fear rippling through my body that I might never be able to see Jack again, to be with him, to have him in my bed, holding me, making me pancakes in the morning as the sun streamed through the windows. In an instant, it was all gone.

'I knew it,' Zoë said. 'Don't go there Courtney, don't. There's no way to hide it. No way around the system.'

'I'm fine, seriously,' I said, trying to shake it off.

'No, you're not,' Zoë said.

'Well, we're not discussing it,' I said, knowing that I had to stop the conversation. Zoë couldn't know anything, she couldn't know how far things had already gone with Jack because then it'd be too easy for her to slip up, accidentally say something, especially if the analysts started asking questions. I couldn't ask her to lie for me.

Zoë seemed to understand. She nodded thoughtfully. 'Fine. Last comment though and you'd better listen good. You have to book in another date with another entertainer. Do an auto search. I remember the number of the guy who picked strawberries last Tuesday if you want it. But you need to book in someone, anyone and soon. Because even if you book no one, they'll wonder why. You work at La Ferme. You get discounted prime entertainment. You have to have a booking at least once a week. They expect it. Lead by example and all that. Promise me you'll book something in the morning,' she said sternly.

'Fine, I promise,' I agreed, feeling sick at the thought of having to do what I did with Jack with someone else.

'Good, because I can't be looking for you too,' Zoë said.

'What do you think happened to Rachel?'

'I don't know, but I'm going to find out,' she insisted. I was suddenly very glad to have someone like Zoë in my corner.

'Where would she go if she was in trouble, is there a hideaway you like or something?' I asked.

'No, nowhere. We don't have secret hideaways. The President has made sure we don't. No cars, no access. We can only get to places the trains go and they're so overpopulated there's no way to hide from the cameras or go unnoticed.'

'He was the guy at the club, wasn't he? The other guy with...' I said, not daring to say Jack's name.

'I think so. Hey, do you think your guy knows Rachel's guy?' she asked.

'He's not my guy. But maybe.'

'Only one way to find out. What's his number?' Zoë asked.

'What?' I asked, resisting the urge to punch Zoë in the face at the mere thought of her and Jack having a date.

'Well you can't have another date with him so you can't grill him, but I can. What's his number?'

'No,' I whispered.

'I'm not going to fuck him Courtney, I promise. I'm just going to talk to him, I swear,' she pleaded.

'Fine,' I said, handing her the card he'd given me the first night we'd met.

'We'll find Rachel or I'll die trying,' Zoë assured me.

'Why is this so important? I know she's your friend and all, but why?' I asked, thinking she was risking a lot to do what she was suggesting.

'Because she's my friend. That's it. They mightn't like us to get close to each other so they can ship us wherever they choose whenever they want, but it doesn't change our natural human instincts, does it? We still want what we want and we need what we need. We need our packs, our herds, our family. Sheila can't change billions of years of evolution, no matter how hard she tries. This is who we are, it's ingrained in us, the need to connect. Rachel is like a sister to me. I need her. I'm not letting her go without a fight. She's my family.'

I hugged her. 'I'm so glad you're my friend,' I said, suspecting someday I'd need someone like Zoë in my corner.

'Me too,' said Zoë smiling. 'Now I have two sisters.'

CHAPTER 11

'Anything?' I asked Zoë when I saw her in the morning.

'Nope, nothing.'

'Nothing at all?'

'Nothing. I'm worried Courtney, I'm really worried. I've been thinking about it and there's no way she'd have run without telling me, without saying something, a note under the door to say goodbye at the very least, so I wouldn't worry.'

'It is strange. I don't think I'd leave without telling you and we've only just met. But we're family, it wouldn't feel right to leave without saying something, doing something, even if you didn't get it until after I was gone.'

'Exactly and Rach was the same. I'm going to go hang around the nest and see what I can find out. See you at lunch?'

'Yeah, sure. Good luck.'

I didn't see Zoë for the rest of the day though and my brain was running through scenarios. Could Rachel really have encountered foul play? What if her date was responsible? What if he'd hurt her like in the olden days? Men did those things all the time then. Before we had a concentrated breeding program that aimed to eliminate such genes. But who's to say there wasn't a rogue gene? It happened, it's how Patrice had found herself headed for a farm, she was supposed to be more beautiful, but sometimes the program failed, rogue genes found their way in, who knows. Rachel and her entertainer didn't have the benefits of the breeding program though, Rachel was born pre-war, maybe her entertainer was too? Pre-war born people didn't have the benefit of altered genetics and maybe a moment of jealousy unleashed pre-war emotions that hadn't been spotted in their DNA and one of them had done something stupid? I could certainly see how that could be possible. The scenarios were endless.

I tried working but every thought came back to Rachel. Why would she run without telling Zoë? Where would she go? And if she'd found somewhere, found a way out, why wouldn't she have taken Zoë with her? Was she protecting Zoë by not telling her? How would she even survive somewhere else? Wouldn't she be on the run for the rest of her life? How would she eat? Keep warm? Without the amenities the President provided, no access to transport, health care and groceries, how would you live? Was there really a better life than this? Was being with the person you love worth giving it all up?

Could I give it all up for Jack? Safety, warmth, food, health, friends? Yes. I wouldn't even have to think about it, I'd give it all up in a second. But I'd never ask him to give it up, the security and safety of this life.

I couldn't put him in a position where he had to look over his shoulder, wonder where his next meal was coming from, where he would sleep. No. No, I couldn't ask him to do that. I had to find a way to exist in this world. Knowing he existed here too had to be enough. Maybe once a quarter we could have a date. Perhaps when all this business with Rachel settled down we could go back to meeting under the bridge. A few minutes together would have to be enough. I loved him too much to ask for anything else. I really did. I loved him. Foolish girl, I laughed at myself.

'Lunching with the nest girls,' Zoë instamessaged me just before lunch.

I was disappointed. I'd been looking forward to hearing what she'd found out from Rachel's colleagues. I'd just have to wait longer to find out what she knew, if she knew anything at all.

'What'd you guys get up to this weekend,' Jules asked when I joined them on the sofas to eat my chicken salad. 'Zoë looks like shit, Rachel's a no show for work and you don't look so hot yourself. Must have been one big night of dancing. You should invite me next time,' she laughed.

'You know, Grace can rehydrate you, would help with the dark bags,' Tess suggested.

'Really?' I asked.

'Oh yeah, won't take ten minutes of saline. I'll book you in for two and take your calls if you like.'

'Oh, thanks, appreciate it.'

'So, where is Zoë anyway?' Rosie asked.

'Think she got held up in the nest,' I said, keeping it as low key as I could.

'Easily done, those analysts can suck the life out of you. Time evaporates in a bubble when those people are around,' Jules laughed.

I knocked on Dr Grace's door at two as scheduled. 'Oh, hey there,' she called. 'Tess said you're a little run down today?'

'Something like that,' I smiled.

'Come on then, let's sort you out,' Dr Grace said.

I sat in the chair and watched her ready a needle and a bag of saline, not so sure I wanted fixing anymore but I couldn't exactly get up and walk out, so I smiled and thought of other things while she found a vein.

'So, dancing huh?' she asked.

'Yep, dancing,' I confirmed.

'It'll get you every time,' she smiled.

Once Dr Grace had set it all up, she said, 'Alright, we just wait for the bag to empty, should only be about ten minutes. I'll be back then. Sit back and relax,' she said, picking her empty coffee cup up off her desk and leaving the room, dimming the lights and closing the door as she went.

As soon as the door closed I realised my mistake, there was nowhere to hide and nothing to distract me. Relax? How was I supposed to relax with everything that was going on? My world was spinning out of control and falling apart. Rachel was missing. Jack, the only person who made any of it bearable, was off limits. None of it made sense and I just wanted to curl into a ball and cry. How's a person supposed to relax with all of that going on?

My heart was pounding when Dr Grace returned, sipping her coffee, steam rising out of the cup. 'You alright, love?' she asked.

'Oh yeah,' I lied. 'Not a fan of needles, that's all.'

She smiled. 'No one is. Let's have a look at your implant while you're here, hey?' she said, getting her scanner out of the drawer.

My heart pounded. Why? Why would she want to check that? It's an annual thing unless it communicated a message to the system. I knew I had nothing to hide, I wasn't sick, it would have alerted her already if I was, so there was nothing that could show up but still, why was she even interested in checking?

I held my breath while I waited for all the green ticks to come onto her screen on the corner of her desk. One by one. Then there was a red cross followed by more green ticks. A red cross. I'd never had one before. 'What is it?' I asked, terrified.

'Oh, just blood pressure, nothing serious. It's a bit high but not high enough to have triggered an alarm so no need to worry. We'll check it again in a week, alright? Are you worried about anything in particular?' she asked.

Dr Grace had a curious look on her face. Is this the look all doctors had when you got a red cross? It was just blood pressure but she looked at me, waiting as though I was about to spill the secrets of the universe.

'There's a lot to take in,' I told her, which was true. 'I think it's probably up and down and I'm tired today after the weekend. You know, I'll get used to it all, I'm sure,' I said, thankful the bag of saline had just finished dripping into my arm. 'I really do feel better though,' I said, sitting up.

'Works a treat, doesn't it,' Dr Grace said kindly.

'It really does,' I said, surprised at how much better I felt. 'Thanks.'

'Anytime. Alright, well, have a great day. Why don't you book in some stress relief for the weekend and I'll see you in a week?' she suggested.

'Sure, same time?' I asked.

'Same time,' she confirmed as she added the appointment to her calendar.

I left and went back to my desk via the pod to thank Tess.

'No problems,' she said. 'Works a treat, right?'

'It really did. Where's Zoë, still not back?' I asked.

'She's gone home sick,' Tess said. 'I told her to go visit Dr Grace after you, but she insisted she just needed to sleep. Seriously, what did you lot get up to? I'm jealous.'

I laughed. 'We just danced. A lot! And drank, waaaaay too much. It was a lot of fun. I'll let you know next time,' I said.

'Make sure you do.'

Back at my desk I wondered about Zoë. She wasn't sick. What was she up to? What did she find out in the nest? And why wouldn't she tell me?

I was ready to walk out the door two minutes before five. Zoë had bugged me all afternoon and I needed to walk. I needed air, I needed to see her, see what on earth she was up to.

She wasn't answering her phone though so I was distracted and frustrated as I walked to the community cooking school. They'd rescheduled the cooking class I'd missed on Monday and let me attend the Tuesday one instead.

The walk and the air had been good and as soon as I walked in, I spotted Pauline's big mop of dark, red curls at a bench on her own so I joined her.

'Oh, hey,' she smiled, happy to see me.

'What are you doing here? You don't come every night, do you?' I asked.

She giggled. 'No, I had a meeting that ran late last night. What about you?' she asked.

'Yeah, much the same,' I said. 'I'm glad to see you here though, these people all look like they've known each other for years.'

'They do, don't they? They all looked at me like I was from another planet when I walked in too, so I am very glad to see you,' she said cheerfully as the lecturer handed out our recipes for beef bourguignon and apple pie.

We talked and laughed while we chopped beef and mushrooms and apples and went about following our recipes. Pauline had only been here six months longer than me, but had certainly made her way around town and gave me all the necessary information on the best extra-curricular activities, the art gallery, the museum, places to shop and eat, she was a trove of information. And funny too, she didn't mind sharing her amusing views on the world we'd landed in. I asked her if she partook in entertainers.

'Occasionally,' she smirked. 'It doesn't really fall into our budgets to do it too often,' she said, reminding me I'd lied about my occupation. 'But now and again I book someone. One must keep themselves well rounded and try all the activities on offer, right? And the President's right, it is a good stress reliever, and a lot of fun,' she said, blushing.

I left Pauline when we'd finished, saying I had to meet a friend across the river so I had a reason not to walk with her. Technically, we should have been residing in similar parts of town. I left her with a friendly wave, taking my container full of leftovers and headed for the water taxi.

I rang Zoë again after I got off the taxi but she still wasn't answering. I was getting worried even though she was probably sleeping if she really was sick. So I went up to my own apartment and sorted my leftover beef bourguignon and pie into portions. I was going to zap a portion in the microwave and eat it with some leftover roast veggies but when Zoë still wasn't answering her phone, I was worried. Too worried to eat. First Rachel, now Zoë. What if Rachel had contacted Zoë after all and she'd run too? I couldn't do this without Zoë.

I locked up and headed for the lift with a portion of Beef Bourguignon and a piece of pie in containers. The access she'd given me for her floor was still valid, so inside the lift I swiped my wrist and pressed the button for her floor. Everything was quiet as it should be and I walked down her hallway, and knocked. Nothing. No answer but I could hear voices on the other side of the door. Could it just be something on the vision screen? Of course it was. What else would it be? What else would she be doing? But then I heard it again and no, it was a man's voice and it was definitely inside her apartment, not echoing out of her screen. I knocked again and kept knocking until she opened the door.

'What are you doing here, I'm sick,' she said, faking a cough.

'No, you're not, you look fine. What's going on? Who are you talking to?'

'No one, it was just the screen.'

'Then why has it stopped?'

'I turned it off.'

There was something off about her face, her eyes were darting left and right. Her face didn't have the same light in it. Something wasn't right. Something was going on. She was hiding something from me. I caught her off guard and pushed the door open and forced my way in.

'What are you doing here,' I whispered when Jack looked up from couch.

I looked from Jack to Zoë, back to Jack, neither of them speaking.

'It's not what it looks like,' Zoë insisted.

I took in the scene before me, Jack's hair not as neat as usual, casually mussed, the top button of his shirt undone, wine and pizza on the table in front the small couch. I remembered a scene not too different that had occurred in my own apartment, how I'd pulled his shirt open, how he'd leaned back and let me unravel him. He looked half way to unravelled sitting there on Zoë's couch.

I tried to speak. To demand what was going on, how could she do this to me but I couldn't speak. My best friend and Jack. After everything he'd said about intimate scenes like this being discouraged. After all that talk Zoë had said about being family and now they were cosying up on the couch together. Suddenly I couldn't breathe. Suddenly my knees felt like jelly and stars danced in front of my eyes.

'Coté,' Jack whispered, catching me in his arms before I hit the floor. 'Coté, open your eyes,' he begged.

I opened them slowly staring into the dark ocean-blues that watched me cautiously.

'Coté, are you okay?' he asked.

I tried nodding.

'No, no you're not. Come on,' he said, helping me to the couch.

'Here,' said Zoë, handing me a glass of water.

I sipped slowly. Finally, the dark edges abated, the dizziness stopped. Jack's arm was on my waist and I could breathe again. 'What's going on?' I whispered.

'Nothing, I promise,' insisted Zoë. 'We were just talking about Rachel and Leo, I swear.'

'It's true,' insisted Jack.

'Come on, have something to eat,' said Zoë. 'That saline shit of Dr Grace's takes it out of you, and I bet you hardly had any water or food this arvo.'

I shook my head and took the pizza Jack passed me, taking small bites, waiting to see how each settled before taking another.

I felt better, almost normal again and looked into Jack's eyes. He was home. I wanted to touch him but I remembered where I was, where we were. I coughed self-consciously. 'Sorry, it must have been Dr Grace's treatment. I was just bringing you some food, I'll go,' I said, putting the containers on the table and getting up.

'Don't go,' begged Jack.

I looked at him, wanting so desperately to touch him, to be with him.

'I'll give you both a minute and then we have to talk, Courtney. Jack, both of you, before you get yourselves into trouble,' she said, leaving the room.

Jack lent his forehead to mine, breathing in deeply. I breathed him in too, that familiar smell, the warmth that came from him. I felt stronger with Jack. I felt whole. I wanted desperately to take him in my arms, to snuggle into the nook of his body and never leave.

He tilted my mouth to his and as our mouths joined. I thought there'd never be anything more perfect and right. He kissed me soft and slow but not long enough.

Zoë returned with a worried look on her face.

'I know, I know,' I mumbled.

'You'd better,' she said. 'Both of you.'

'We have it under control,' said Jack, defensively.

'Do you? Really? Or do you just think you do?' she snapped. 'Rachel and Leo thought they had it under control, too.'

'I know, I know,' said Jack. 'I promise, I won't let anything happen to Courtney,' he assured her. 'I won't do anything that risks her safety. I couldn't handle it if anything happened to her either,' he said.

'Good,' she grumbled, seemingly satisfied.

'Have you come up with anything?' I asked.

'Nothing,' Zoë said.

'My roommate might know something though so Zoë will see if she can book him for a date.'

'What about me?' I asked. 'What can I do?'

'Nothing,' they both snapped.

'Geez,' I moaned.

Zoe smiled. 'Come on, right now, there's nothing you can do but keep your head down and your ears open, alright?'

'Fine,' I conceded.

'You're too new,' said Jack. 'You have to just stay out of everyone's way. You have to stay safe. For everyone's sake. We can't be worrying about you too. I don't think Zoë could handle it. I know I certainly couldn't,' he smiled, kissing me softly.

'Ahem,' Zoë laughed. 'You two done there?'

'Sorry,' Jack smiled.

'I have to go, don't I?' I said.

He nodded. 'The cameras outside will be timing your visit.'

I nodded. Kissed him quickly and left before Zoë gave either of us any more grief.

CHAPTER 12

W e all sat in a row behind my desk watching the farmer harvest the last of the strawberries, and begin to replant one of the sections while the hot sun beat down on his body beading with sweat and glowing from the sun's goodness.

'Did you do it yet?' whispered Zoë.

I shook my head. 'I'll do it when you all leave.'

'You can't keep putting it off. Do it now,' Zoë insisted, pushing my tablet in front of me.

'Fine,' I groaned as I opened the screen and tapped in my number while the other girls watched the farmer obliviously.

Once my file came on the screen I pressed the auto search button, not even bothering with parameters or anything else. At this point it didn't matter who I selected so I lucky dipped, not even bothering to check his statistics once he was in my calendar. 'There, it's done,' I moaned to Zoë already feeling sick about having to have a date with someone other than Jack, but Zoë insisted I had to, to make sure I didn't pop up on the analysts' screens. Especially if they started looking at Rachel, I had to make sure there was nothing to see on my file.

'Good,' Zoë said, not taking her eyes off the farmer outside the window.

The phone rang while the farmer was planting the last of the seedlings from the pouch around his waist.

'Argh, that thing is annoying,' groaned Rosie.

I smiled, I didn't really care at this point. Any distraction from reality was a welcome one.

The farmer hauled himself up and out of sight before I'd even finished my greeting and the girls began gathering their mugs and chairs and filing out as the woman on the other end of the phone began shouting at me.

'Hold on, hold on, I can't understand you while you're shouting,' I told the woman.

Hearing my plea, Zoë stopped in the doorway, letting the other girls go ahead.

'He didn't bloody show, did he? I want to know what you're going to do about it,' the woman spat. 'I was standing there waiting and waiting and he never showed and then I had to go alone. Do you know how embarrassing it is to show up to such a function and be the only one without a date? Do you? Do you?'

'Okay, okay, what's the number?' I asked the caller.

'Two, four, one, one,' she said.

I typed the number in and waited for the file to come up. 'I'm so sorry,' I told the caller. 'I can't see anything wrong with the file. I'll have to transfer you to Zoë so she can look into it.'

The woman on the other end let loose an array of expletives that had my eyes opening wide.

Smiling at the look on my face, Zoë came over, took my earpiece and after a moment of listening to some more expletives, began appeasing the woman on the other end.

'I understand, I do,' Zoë said, trying to calm the woman. 'I assure you, we'll not only reimburse your account but I'll add in some credit for your next date.'

The woman calmed down after that. I couldn't hear her anymore. Zoë made the necessary notes in the customer's file, apologised again and ended the call with an exacerbated sigh.

'What was that?' I asked. 'Do they ever just not show up?'

'No. Never,' Zoë said. 'If someone's sick or can't make it, we phone the client, apologise and send a replacement.

'Was it? Do you think it was? You know?' I asked, not quite sure how to finish the sentences.

'Yeah, that was the number in her calendar,' Zoë said. 'If you get any more calls for that number though, put them straight through to me, alright?'

'Sure, of course,' I said.

'I gotta get back to work,' Zoë said. 'I'll see you tonight and we'll prep for Friday. And then maybe we can do a nice roast on Sunday again and catch up on what's what?' she said cheerily, waggling her eyebrows as though we were having an ordinary fun conversation as Jen walked out of her office.

'You bet. I'll cook, you bring the wine,' I said, forcing a laugh as Trish appeared in the doorway.

'Zoë, there you are,' said Trish as though surprised to find Zoë anywhere but where she was on a picking day. 'Do you have a minute?' Trish asked.

'Of course,' Zoë told her, giving me a worried look before following Trish out of the room.

Just before she closed the door, Trish turned back and said, 'Oh Courtney dear, would you mind giving me ten minutes at lunch?'

'Of course,' I agreed.

'Thanks,' Trish said, smiling a little too big, big enough to make my stomach turn.

I worked through the morning until lunch, distracted enough by work that I almost forgot about my meeting with Trish and how weird she'd been. When I entered the pod I saw Zoë sitting on a sofa alone, looking sombre, very un-Zoë-like. She turned around, catching my eye. She had a strange look on her face but before I could ask her about it, Trish stuck her head out of her office and called me in for my ten minutes.

'Shut the door would you, Courtney?' she asked.

'Sure,' I said, quickly trying to assess the situation as I did.

Everything appeared to be in place, but there was a woman sitting in one of the visitor's chairs. The woman was older than Trish. She had blonde hair she'd pulled back into a soft ponytail, and wore too much make up on her face that added years I suspected she didn't want to her face. She wore a black shift dress a size too small, enormous stilettos and an annoyed, bored scowl.

I smiled tightly at her as I went to sit and she smiled in return but I'd never seen anything as fake in my life. Not a single glimmer of the smile reached the woman's eyes, not a single movement occurred on her face, other than the mouth itself, signified an emotion other than intense boredom.

'Courtney, this is Christina, the Director of Operations. Director, this is our newest recruit, Courtney, she's only been here for a couple of weeks,' Trish smiled.

The Director only nodded. But I supposed there wasn't much else a person could do while radiating so much negative energy.

'I won't keep you too long, dear,' Trish said. 'But I believe you'd made friends with Rachel from the nest?'

'Um, I guess, yeah,' I said. 'I've only seen her a couple of times though.'

Trish nodded. 'You saw her Saturday night, yes?' she asked.

'I did,' I answered. 'We went dancing.'

'You, Zoë and Rachel?' she asked.

'That's right,' I said.

'And did anything unusual happen?' Trish asked.

I didn't quite know what to say. I didn't want to get Rachel in trouble but clearly, they already knew something so I couldn't lie either. I figured all I could do was tell the truth as I knew it. I hadn't seen anything. Rachel hadn't shared any secrets with me. I just had to say what I saw. 'Rachel left without us,' I told them.

'Do you know why?' Trish asked.

'No. One minute she was there, then I thought she'd gone to the bathroom but she'd gone.'

'How do you know she'd gone?' the harsh woman beside me asked.

'Zoë went to look for her, said she'd gone and it was time for us to leave.'

'Zoë was upset?' the woman asked.

I shrugged. 'I guess, her friend left without saying anything, I'd be upset too.'

'And you've no idea where she went, with whom or why?' the Director asked abruptly.

'Nope,' I said. After all, everything I thought I knew was only speculation anyway. I could only hope that Zoë had been just as convincingly evasive.

'Thank you,' Trish said.

'How are you finding the perks of the job?' asked the Director in her best attempt at friendly.

'Fine,' I answered.

'Fine?' the Director asked, her eyebrows raised with suspicion. 'Fine means we need to reassess our training program.'

I gave my best winning smile. 'Well, it's indeed more than fine, I just didn't think it well-mannered to say so,' I said.

'Courtney has only just had her first real experience of our perks,' Trish interjected.

'Really?' asked the Director. 'And do you think you might hire him again?' she asked, curiously.

Suddenly I saw exactly where they were leading me. 'He would certainly do just fine. He was very nice indeed but with so much variety, who could stop at just one? I made another booking this morning in fact, thought I'd try another random selection and see what I get with a lucky dip, seeing I had such good fortune last time,' I smiled.

'Well I'm glad your appetite has been suitably triggered,' the Director said. 'Don't forget to go into your calendar and offer feedback for each of them so their managers can keep track of how they're doing.'

'Certainly, happy to,' I answered as brightly as I could but curious considering this was the first I'd heard of anyone doing so.

'I hear you were quite an outstanding choice for this position,' the Director asked.

'So they say,' I replied. 'I just did my best when the recruiters came and I was very happy to be offered the position. Everyone's been so lovely. I'm very happy to be here,' I told the Director.

'I'm glad to hear it,' she said cheerfully, her face not moving. 'In fact, I have an opportunity you might be interested in,' she said.

'Oh?' echoed Trish and I together.

'I'm having a party, just a little soiree and I thought perhaps you could give my Anna a hand with the organising?' she suggested.

'Oh, of course, anything I can do to help, I'm happy to do,' I offered.

'Great, I'll have Anna contact you, then.'

No one said anything for a few awkward seconds. Was that it? Was I supposed to just leave? Trish put me out of my misery. 'You should go and have your lunch before the time's up,' she said, smiling, although, like the Director, the emotion didn't quite reach her eyes. It wasn't like Trish to not be kind and warm and thoroughly authentic. I didn't like it, didn't like the way it sat heavily in my stomach.

I couldn't get out of there fast enough. Trish's office was giving me the creeps. The fake smiles, the shared looks, the secrets and agendas that hung thick in the air. It all gave me the creeps. I was no longer the least bit hungry but Zoë was still sitting on the sofa alone so I dispensed a couple of coffees and took them over and sat beside her.

'What'd they say?' asked Zoë when I sat down and reached for my unappetising sandwich.

'Just asked if I knew why Rachel left. I said I didn't,' I told her, leaving the sandwich on the plate on my lap and instead picking up my coffee and passing Zoë hers.

'Thanks. Good,' Zoë said. 'Anything else? You were in there for ages.'

'They asked me about date night and if I liked my entertainer.'

'Please tell me you played it down.'

'Of course, and I told them I'm lucky dipping for a treat this Friday.'

'Good, good,' Zoë said, not taking her eyes off the magazine she was reading. 'Anything else?'

'The Director wants me to help someone called Anna organise a party.'

'The Director's assistant, Anna?'

'I guess.'

'Wow, she won't like that at all and the Director knows it. She's up to something. Be on your guard at all times. Give nothing away.'

'Sure, sure,' I mumbled, leaning back in the sofa, forcing myself to chew a bite of my sandwich as though we were talking about any old thing.

'That Anna's a witch, so watch your back,' Zoë added, when I was leaving.

I returned to my desk wondering what on earth I'd walked into and whether I was smart enough to survive it?

It was easy to pretend none of it had happened, was happening, as the afternoon progressed and I saw no one but an occasional glimpse of Jen as she came and went, but that was it, just me and my phone, not even any visitors to keep an eye on. It was easy to drift into an imagined world, one where Rachel was safe and Jack was waiting, somewhere, anywhere, at the end of the day to make it all worthwhile. None of it seemed real as I sat at my glass desk watching the street through the window beyond, as people called to make their bookings. One after the other they called. Some liked to chat, some were brusque and to the point but as always, there was a steady stream of them to distract me.

The phone rang as I watched an overly coiffed older lady pass by with a pink poodle. She looked into the window, scrunching her face up against the glass to try and see through the protective coating on the glass by the waiting area. When she was happy with whatever she could see, she righted herself and scurried off and I answered the phone.

'Two, four, one, one, for Saturday night,' the caller asked.

I recognised the number from earlier and the blood in my veins cooled as I typed it into the search engine, in case I'd remembered it wrong. There were a lot of numbers handed to me every day, they all swam around together in my head sometimes, so it was highly possible I was remembering the wrong combination.

The file loaded onto the screen and glowed red. I didn't quite know what to do with a fully red screen. The file earlier had looked fine and all I'd ever seen on a file was a little red dot in the corner where the green tick usually lived. I'd never seen this before so I asked the lady to wait and phoned Zoë.

'What do you mean the whole page is red?' she asked, doubtful.

'It's red, glowing red. The entire page, Zoë.'

She sighed. 'Fine, give me the number just in case.'

I read it out to her and I could hear the short, sharp intake of breath even though she'd tried to disguise it.

'Shit,' Zoë mumbled once the screen must have loaded over her side. 'Tell the customer he's unavailable, she'll have to have someone else.'

I went back to the customer and apologised, said he wasn't available and she booked someone else. As I hung up, Zoë appeared in my office, perching on the edge of the desk casually with a coffee in her hand.

'What was that?' I whispered, not wanting to capture Jen's attention.

'Something's wrong, really, really wrong,' Zoë said, almost to herself. 'I've never seen a file look like that. His file has not only been red flagged, it's red, the whole thing is red. That's bad, that's really bad.'

'How?' Courtney asked.

'My predecessor mentioned it once but I've never seen it. I never thought it could really happen. Thought it was just urban legend.'

'What is urban legend?'

'They've run. They've escaped. Somehow, they found a way out. They're wanted criminals.'

'No!' I gasped. 'If they find them they'll make an example of them.'

'I know, they'll send them to the islands to die. Just to prove a point,' Zoë agreed. 'I told her. I bloody well told her.'

'You knew she was running?'

'No, when I saw them Saturday night I told her not to be stupid. But she wouldn't listen. She told me to go back inside and pretend I'd never seen her, so I did. I just thought she was going to make out with him in the alley and then go home. I had no idea she was going to do this. I shouldn't have left her. I should have made her come inside. Now she's as good as dead. If they'd just apologise and accept their fate...'

'Would it really make any difference?' I asked, hopefully.

'Who knows. Maybe at the very least they'd be shipped to opposite sides of the country, maybe they'd be sent to farms where they'd at least get to stay alive, but most likely they'd be shipped to the islands anyway, never to see us or each other, no shelter, no food unless they grow it, catch it and cook it, nothing.'

'Maybe, but they'd be alive, wouldn't they? If they're running, they'll be running forever. They'll never have a moment's rest.

What happens if they find them? I can't even think about it. How did they think that would be better than separation?'

I suspected I was beginning to understand the repercussions of separation. I was barely getting through each day as it was and Jack was three floors under my desk. 'We have to find them first,' I said.

'No, not you, newbie. You're too green. You're still being monitored and evaluated and now you've caught the attention of the Director and she's put you in Anna's crosshairs, you can't put a foot out of place, okay.'

Zoë got up to leave.

'What are you going to do?' I asked.

'The less you know, the better,' Zoë said, placing a comforting hand on my shoulder.

'Just go on your date Friday and make sure you tell everyone how excited you are, then how great it was and how much fun you're having checking out the variety. Play nice with Anna no matter what she says or does and you'll be fine.'

I nodded, feeling the rumbling swirl of bile building. Zoë pushed a glass of water towards me and left.

I stared vacantly across the room at the fancy artwork but not really seeing, thinking how unfair everything was, wondering if Rachel was okay, hoping against hope she'd found her way out and was safe.

'You alright?' asked Jen, coming out of the security office.

'Oh sure,' I smiled. 'Booked myself another date for Friday night, was just wondering how he'll measure up to the other one. This is fun, isn't it?' I smiled.

'Oh, it sure is,' winked Jen, going out the reception door.

As soon as she was gone, I all but slumped onto my desk. How on earth was I going to get through it? Perhaps just dinner, company, I can be one of those women, I thought. Maybe I'd just kiss him once and fake a headache? I could do that, that'd work.

By the time Wednesday night came, I was so desperate to see Jack, I didn't even care if he was on a date. I just needed to see his face, to know he was okay, that the world was turning as it should. I looked for him in the basketball stadium, in the queues and the hallways. I discreetly looked around the stadium once we were sitting, hoping he was there, somewhere. But he was nowhere.

'Would you stop it?' Zoë nudged me as the commentator announced the players over the loudspeaker.

I smiled sheepishly and focussed on the game, pouring my energy into cheering our team on to their win.

Zoë hooked her arm through mine as we left. 'Eyes ahead Courtney,' she laughed as though she'd told a joke. 'People are watching everywhere. Everyone's nervous. Everyone's being watched. I've heard talk, important people are getting anxious. You need to be more careful,' she smiled as though we were just chatting and having fun.

'Sure, sure,' I smiled as cheerily as I could muster as we boarded the train, even though I desperately wanted to ask what talk? What was being said? Was it about me or just in general? But I couldn't ask, not with all these people and their flapping ears around.

Zoë laid her head on my shoulder. 'It gets easier. You'll find a way to live with it,' she told me as a loud trio squeezed into the two seats in front of us.

We walked to Ora's where we ordered an array of tapas and a jug of sangria.

'So,' Zoë started once we had our drinks. 'Friday night.'

I only just stopped myself from groaning and she laughed. 'You're getting better. Now, seriously,' she said. 'What are you going to do?'

'I don't know. Get it over with as soon as I can,' I said.

'Courtney, come on. You have to at least milk it for all it's worth. Especially if someone like Anna is looking for a way to bring you down and trust me, if you weren't on her radar before as the brightest new recruit in a decade, you will be now the Director has put you right in her path. You bring him here and flirt like mad for starters.'

'Flirt? I can't flirt.'

'Yes, you can. You have to. Everything depends on it. Any hint you're miserable or pining and Anna will use it to bring you down and you'll never see Jack again. Can you live with that?' she whispered.

'No,' I said, without even having to think about it. 'No, I can't live with that.'

'Then you put on that teeny tiny, fabulous hot red dress I saw in your wardrobe and you flirt your ass off and then you let him fuck you, and you tell everyone it was amazing and then next week, you do it again with another one.'

I felt violently ill and pushed away the potato cubes covered in spicy tomato sauce I was about to eat. How was I going to manage it? Not just Friday night but week after week? My stomach twisted and turned and the whole idea was vile and revolting. I couldn't do it. Not over and over. It wasn't right. I didn't care what the bloody president said. It wasn't right. I knew it in my heart.

Zoë put her hand on mine and smiled. 'It gets easier. I promise,' she told me kindly.

I went to bed not believing a single word of it. It would never get better. I was sure Rachel would understand. I bet she tried to move on, tried putting it out of her mind and crumbled under the weight of ignorance. But look where it got her. She was on the run. We hoped. She'll be running for the rest of her life, always looking over her shoulder. If they hadn't caught them already. If she wasn't already sitting in a correctional farm. It might have all been for nothing.

No, I couldn't let that happen to Jack. I couldn't risk it. A couple of dates a year and glances across stadiums were better than that, than losing him altogether, than having him live that life. So, I'd do my duty, at least until things blew over, until I was no longer the brightest new recruit in a decade, the enemy of Anna and friend of an escapee.

CHAPTER 13

I had a meeting request from Anna when I arrived in the morning, scheduled for ten thirty in Anna's office. Damn! I thought, wishing I'd known about the meeting before I'd gotten dressed for the day, before I'd been up half the night wishing and wallowing over things I could never have, ensuring I looked worn and haggard.

I went into the pod to see Zoë. She was busy typing but looked up as I approached her desk.

'What's up?' she asked.

'Do I look alright?'

'Of course, you're quite the master of office fashion,' she smiled. 'Look alright for what?' she asked, smirking when I didn't laugh at her joke.

'I have a meeting upstairs with Anna. Do I look alright?' I asked again.

'You look fine,' Zoë laughed. 'Just relax.'

'Sure,' I said doubtfully. 'I don't even know how to get upstairs.'

'Of course you don't,' Zoë smiled. 'That door in the hallway opposite the pod, it'll take you to the lift bay. You'll need to swipe your wrist. Anna will have already given you access to her floor so that's where the lift will take you. But don't go getting any ideas while you're up there, you're a long way down the food chain.' Zoë smiled.

'Fine, fine, I'll just be happy to get through the meeting in one piece,' I smiled. 'Alright, I'm switching the phones through to you. Wish me luck,' I said, waving as I walked away feeling the weght of uncertainty filled my stomach.

I opened the opposite non-descript door, which led to a vestibule and a lift. I pressed the call button and waited in the cold empty silence. Once the metal doors opened and I stepped inside, I swiped my implanted wrist as Zoë had told me to, the doors closed and the lift automatically took me to Anna's floor.

The doors opened to a plush carpeted walkway. A glass wall separated the hallway from the offices beyond. I walked through the doorway to the reception desk. The girl behind it looked smug. I told her my name and who I was there to see. The girl nodded, she didn't speak, tapped her tablet then told me to 'sit,' with one word, no emotion, no nothing.

Geez, I thought as I sat in a visitor chair, the animosity from the girl behind the reception desk filling the room. That was a little unnecessary. But I smiled politely when she scowled in my direction and waited.

Anna came into the waiting room a moment later. She was dressed in a skirt suit with a purple satin shirt underneath. She looked smart. She looked expensive and the perfume wafting off her smelt expensive. Her hair was pulled back softly as though with no effort but it sat perfectly, not daring to move. I suspected

Anna's perfectly applied makeup was similarly afraid to deviate from its perfection.

'Come, come,' Anna spat, waggling her finger, turning and walking, expecting me to follow but without bothering to introduce herself. Perhaps in this alternate universe, I was supposed to know who Anna was.

I followed Anna to a small meeting room with a square glass topped table and black chairs. In the centre was a jug of water and beside it two glasses. Anna didn't pour herself any water though, so neither did I, even though my mouth had gone dry.

'Just so you know, I don't need help with this party and if I did, Bridget is more than capable of helping,' she said. I assumed Bridget was the receptionist I'd just had the pleasure of encountering. It certainly explained the scowl.

'Of course,' I told Anna. 'I'm not sure why the Director asked me to help you, but I really am more than happy to help with anything you need.'

'Well, I'll see if I can find something for you to do,' Anna said.

'What sort of party is it?' I asked, trying to be interested.

'Well, that's not really any of your business, is it?' Anna snapped.

What was I even supposed to do with that? I was only being interested and courteous as was expected of my position. There was certainly no need for Anna to be so rude. What could she possibly have against me? I didn't ask for the task of helping her. Why didn't she spit her anger at the bloody director? It was her fault, not mine.

'We all know you're some sort of superstar on some fast track the rest of us didn't get access to, but if you think we're going to let you steal our jobs without a fight, well, think again,' Anna said, shuffling through pages on her tablet.

I was gobsmacked. 'Anna, really, I don't want to steal anyone's job. I'm very grateful for the one I have,' I assured her.

'Yeah, right, for now, until you're bored. Everyone wants to move up sooner or later. Mind you with the trouble you're in and the people you're associating with, I mightn't have to worry at all.'

'What does that mean?' I asked more defensively than I'd meant.

'That girl who's gone missing. Isn't she your friend?'

'Sort of, I guess.'

'Well, not really the sort of friend you want on the fast track now, is she?' Anna snarled.

'I just got here. I'm not on any track. I'm still just figuring it all out,' I said, trying to appease Anna somehow.

'Well, figure it out fast. I sure as hell don't need the likes of you tarnishing my good character.'

'What's wrong with my character?' I asked.

'Hmph, we'll see soon enough, I'm sure,' Anna mumbled. 'Here,' she said, taking my tablet and lining it up with her own. 'Here's the guest list and last year's invite. Put together something nice, something gold and glitzy, it needs to look exclusive and expensive, raining glitter or something, but make sure it's classy, not like some three year old's art project. Email me a proof and once I approve it, we'll look at sending them. That's all I have for you. You can go now,' she said, standing and leaving the room without any further courtesies.

I left the room, making my way back to reception. I tried saying goodbye to Bridget but she turned her head and looked in the other direction. I had never been so shunned, never been made to feel so worthless. I didn't quite know what to make of it.

I swiped my wrist at the call button but the lift was right where I'd left it so I didn't have to wait and stepped in as the doors slid open. I swiped my wrist and the lift descended, returning me to the reality of the ground floor.

Zoë was sitting behind my desk when I walked in. 'That bad, hey?' Zoë asked when she saw me.

'That bad,' I said, heading straight for Jen's office. 'Coffee?' I asked Zoë.

'Absolutely, I need to hear every word that bitch uttered.'

I laughed, never more grateful for a friend and dispensed some coffees.

When I returned, I told Zoë everything.

'Wow,' Zoë said. 'They really have their knickers in a twist over Rach, and looks like we're all going to be under extra scrutiny,' she said.

'What do we do next?' I asked.

'Like I said, there's no WE. There's only ME. And one, eight, five, nine and his buddy. Well, he's booked, not that I could book him again so soon anyway, but I couldn't get his buddy until Saturday night, and even that was only because someone cancelled him, so that means I'm free for tonight if you need to talk?'

'Nah, I'm good' I smiled, using every ounce of energy to do so. I hated knowing Jack was booked. It made me think about what he was doing and it made my stomach swirl. I'd rather not hear about it then I could pretend none of it was real.

'Hey, you can't think about it,' Zoë told me.

I gave her a small smile. 'I'm on call tonight, anyway, so its fine,'

I told her. Zoë was right though, I had to put it out of my mind and think of the greater picture.

I sat in front of the vision screen on call, allowing the continual flow of women on the other end of the phone to distract me while watching a variety show.

'Zero, Two, eight, seven,' the woman on the other end of the phone said. Ignoring how abrupt she was and smiling instead at the comic on the variety show I was watching, I typed her number into the system and took a sip of my wine. 'One, eight, five, nine,' she added with a snip. 'Please add in the notes that it is a corporate event and he should be suitably attired.'

'Of course,' I told her, my whole body shaking as I called up his file. I wanted to tell her, sorry, he's unavailable. I desperately wanted to say it and it nearly slipped out, but out of fear for our safety, the repercussions of Rachel falling in love still fresh in my mind, stopped me. Instead, I made the match for the following week and cheerily told the snippy woman on the other end, 'All done. Have a lovely evening.'

As I hung up, I couldn't even remember if my voice had shaken. I'm sure it had no matter how hard I tried not to allow it, but the whole call was like an out of body experience. I wasn't quite sure afterwards of anything that had occurred other than the fact I'd booked Jack a date.

I couldn't quite catch my breath. My head spun, my stomach churned. It was one thing to know he had other bookings but until now, somehow, I'd never been the one to have to make them. I poured some more wine, taking a long, mellowing drink. I wanted to wallow. I desperately wanted to wallow but the phones wouldn't stop ringing, and I still had an hour to go before I could switch them off for the night, so I continued mindlessly taking calls, one after the other, woman after woman needing to satisfy her lady needs for the good of the country. By cut off time I was sick to my stomach, my insides suitably soaked with wine.

I woke at midnight. On the couch. Still in my clothes. The drapes still wide open and my bladder full to bursting.

After peeing, I needed to replenish some fluids and went to the kitchen. I was on my way to the sink when I saw the piece of paper in the doorway, bright white on the warm caramel carpet. Instantly forgetting my water and need for fluids, I picked up the paper, which wasn't really paper but a serviette. There were no words written on it, just a picture of a bridge.

Shit! Did that mean he was there, now, waiting for me? Was he still there or had he put this here hours ago and I'd missed him? Had I missed him because I couldn't help but soak my insides numb with wine?

Stupid, stupid, stupid, I chastised myself as I quickly threw on my running gear, ignoring my spinning head.

'A late-night run, Courtney?' asked the security guard.

I offered her my very brightest smile. 'I was on call tonight and now I can't sleep. I need to burn off some energy and clear my head,' I told her

'What a great idea,' she said, making a note on something in front of her.

I ran as fast as I could without attracting attention until I reached the bridge, thankfully devoid of all life in the middle of the night. I stood underneath, in the shadows looking around. I couldn't see him. I'd missed him. I knew it. Tears were welling in my eyes when I felt his hands sliding down my arms, his mouth on my neck and my body instantly filled with the sweetest relief.

I turned, wrapping my arms around his neck and falling into him, my mouth joining with his. I pulled apart to look at him, to look into those pools of blue as dark as the deepest ocean and suddenly everything was okay. Finally, my twisted insides fell into their rightful places. My heart stopped its erratic beating. I could breathe again and I breathed deep, like I hadn't taken a single breath since I'd last seen him. I breathed him in, let him fill me as my hand reached up to touch his handsome face.

'Hello,' he smiled.

'Hello,' I smiled coyly.

'Are you okay?' he asked, brushing a stray hair from my face.

I nodded.

'Come,' he said, leading me to the rocky ledge hidden deep in the shadows. 'What's going on?'

'Rachel's gone. That guy's file's red and I have to go on a date with someone else,' I babbled as tears overflowed, as the reality of everything suddenly filled me and it was too much to keep in.

He gathered me into his arms. 'It's okay. Everything will be okay.'

'No, no it won't,' I sputtered. 'I can't ever book a date with you again, and all I can think about is being with you.'

'I know,' he said, sadly.

'I'm not sleeping with him though,' I said, suddenly determined. 'I'm not sleeping with anyone but you,' I said, taking his mouth.

'You have to,' he whispered.

'What?' I demanded. 'No! No, you can't be serious,' I said, shaking my head, unable to believe what I was hearing. Didn't he feel the same anymore?

'Rachel and Leo have made it tough for everyone. We're all

under microscopes. We're all being watched and monitored, our dates analysed, our enthusiasm and actions scrutinised.'

'What does that mean? And what does it have to do with me? Why do you want me to have sex with another man?'

'Oh baby, I don't want you to. Fuck, it kills me to even think about someone else putting his hands on you but you have to. If you don't have sex with him, they'll want to know why.'

'But why can't I just be one of those that likes the company of a man? Why can't I have a headache and call it a night?'

'Because only old ladies like our company, and no one has a headache when they're paying for our entertainment.'

He had a point. I hated it but he did.

'So you do feel it too?' I asked softly.

'Fuck Coté, of course I do. Just lie there and let him work his moves, make some noises and that'll be that. You'll be fine. Just don't ask his name. Don't make him a person. Follow protocol, thank him and send him home when he's done,' he said, joining his forehead with mine and trying unsuccessfully to hide the tears in his eyes.

I gathered him into my arms. 'Why do I get the feeling I'm not going to see you again?' I asked.

'Because you're not. Not for a while, anyway. God, Coté,' he said, taking my face in his hands, his eyes pleading, 'if anything happened to you, it would break me. I just need to know you'll be okay and staying away is the only way I can make sure that happens. Just until all this business with Rachel and Leo calms down.'

I nodded.

He tilted my face up to his and kissed me slowly, softly.

'Did anyone see you leave?' he asked.

I nodded. 'Security. I think she made a note.'

'Shit,' he said. 'You better go, she'll be timing you,' he said. 'I told you, everyone's nervous and everyone's being watched, particularly those of us that had anything to do with Rachel or Leo.'

'I don't want to go,' I sobbed, looking into his eyes, memorising them.

'You have to. I'll let you know when it's safe to book me, okay?'

'How?'

'You'll know,' he said, taking my mouth in his, hard and fast and greedily. 'Go,' he said.

I stood, walked a few steps, turned to take one last look at his beautiful face and ran like the wind.

CHAPTER 14

The next day I took a renewed outlook on doing anything to protect myself and Jack at the office. I flirted with the day's farmer alongside the girls, receiving a nod of approval from Zoë who was flirting and giggling beside me.

Once the girls returned to their desks, I put all my efforts into the invitation Anna was waiting for me to draft. I designed something spectacular, I thought. The brief had been gold, glitzy, expensive and exclusive. I designed something classy, chic, raining sparkling gold. I was so proud of what I emailed Anna that it was like a kick in the stomach when she replied saying she hated it and would do it herself. Of course she hated it. She'd have hated out of principle, loyalty to Bridget, whatever warped reasoning she had, but she'd have hated it and all I could do was smile and thank her for the feedback.

The new invitation Anna sent through late in the afternoon and looked no different to the one I'd done but I said nothing and emailed it to everyone on the list just as Anna asked.

'Man, she's a really messed up bitch,' I told Zoë at Friday night drinks.

Zoë only smiled. 'She's the self-appointed queen of messed up bitches,' she said.

'Lucky me,' I scoffed.

'How you doing?' she asked. 'You know, about tonight.'

'Trying not to think about it. Planning to get smashed on Sangria and the bottle of Shiraz waiting on the bench and then I won't even know what's happening or remember it.'

She laughed. 'Try to at least be able to participate or he'll put your inability to handle your drink in your notes.'

'Are you kidding me?' I asked.

'Nope. No secrets.'

'Shit,' I mumbled as Rosie came over and started to talk weekends and I put on my happy face.

The more I got to know about this world, the less impressed I was. Nothing was my own, even if it happened inside my own apartment. Who was I kidding? That apartment wasn't even my own. Zoë chose it. Stacey furnished it. She filled the wardrobe, she even selected my undies, my jammies, my soap and toilet paper.

I thought it made sense, to have a relocation specialist who knew the world and the requirements of your new life better than you, for her to do the choosing but it meant nothing was mine. Nothing felt like mine and now not even the things I did were mine. They were things for the analysts to consider, judge, report on. How could I not be angry? How could I not envy Rachel's escape? But for Jack, I had to find a way for it to be okay.

I put fat hot rollers in my hair, feeling ridiculous going to so much effort when I knew I could just wear my comfy loungewear and he wouldn't even care. But someone would care.

I pulled the red dress Zoë had told me to wear out of the wardrobe and stared at it. It was just a slip of silky material. What on earth had possessed Stacey to buy me such a thing? I left it on the hook on the wall and touched up my makeup, making sure it was perfect. Then I slipped on the dress, took each of the rollers out of my hair and let the tumble of black hair fall over my shoulders. I didn't even look like me. I felt out of place standing in my bathroom. But it was for the greater good, I kept telling myself. For Jack. I added a squirt of perfume and a single platinum, diamond set bangle.

I was fortifying my courage with a glass of wine, trying desperately not to think of where this dress was going to lead me when there was a gentle knock at the door.

As I crossed the floor, I remembered the butterflies I'd had the last time a man knocked at my door, the excitement of knowing Jack was on the other side. Knowing it was someone else filled me with dread and sadness, so I was nothing but disappointed when I opened the door.

The man on the other side was blonde, his hair a little shaggy, his jaw stubbled, the lazy smile on his face sexy and his chocolate brown eyes warm. He wasn't a disappointing date under normal circumstances but then would any of them be?

I let him in while I gathered my bag.

'So, what is your plan for me?' he asked smoothly.

'Let's start with dinner,' I smiled, grabbing my bag from the dining table ignoring the fact he was looking my legs up and down.

'Excellent,' he smiled, resting his hand on the small of my back as he led me to the lift.

It was weird being so close to a man other than Jack, but he smelt good, he seemed nice, maybe it wouldn't be so bad, after all?

I gave a friendly, knowing smile and a wave to the nosey security guard as I passed just in case she was keeping notes as I suspected. I wanted her to see happy, flirty Courtney on a date with a guy she hadn't seen before. It hurt, everything inside me hurt but I did it. I smiled brightly and walked to Ora's with my date.

Ora's was packed full of couples and groups of friends laughing, drinking, eating, having a fabulous time, with each other, flirting with dates as though flirting mattered. It was just a relic habit from the pre-war time where you had to behave like a peacock to get someone into bed, to feel beautiful and worthy. The old days where you could keep the man you loved. I shook the thought free, suddenly glad Jack was busy doing who knows what instead of eating in my local restaurant.

I ate my paella and had perfectly nice, polite conversation with the man opposite who told me how pretty I was, complimented the food, discussed knowledgably the latest movies and books and all the popular activities while I nodded and giggled, smiled and cooed as I saw the other women doing, feeling utterly ridiculous. But I must have done something right because the more I cooed and giggled, the more animated and flirty he became, stroking the back of my hand, playing footsies under the table, trailing his finger down the side of my face and looking into my eyes like I was a movie star. He was good. Very good. It made things easier. Because no matter how much I giggled, all I wanted to do was hide under the covers until a new era dawned in which I could be with Jack.

I ignored the call of more sangria when we'd finished eating. Instead I settled the bill with a smile and let him lead me back up the path with his hand resting protectively on the small of my back.

I waved again at the security guard as she looked up. When we made it into the lift, even though there was another, vaguely familiar girl in there, I remembered what Jack had said about cameras and traced the stubbled jaw of this man with my finger while looking lustfully into his eyes. I pulled him by the tie so his mouth met mine, ignoring the smirk from the girl in the lift, silently praising myself for a game well played.

I almost forgot him though once I was safely inside my apartment. I dropped my bag on the dining table and went in search of wine. I remembered after I'd poured myself a glass that he was there and got another glass out of the cupboard and poured him some wine.

'So, how would you like this to go?' he asked smoothly, trailing his hand down my bare arm.

'However you like,' I smiled. 'Why don't you show me what moves you've got?' I suggested, remembering what Jack had said about just letting him run through his moves and make the right noises.

He smiled lazily, and I could see how it would make most women melt, their knees turn to jelly but he had nothing on the way Jack lit up a room, the way Jack's dark ocean-blue eyes drew you in. But I stepped closer anyway and let him take me, let his mouth take mine, let it wander over my neck, let his hands slide my dress from my body. I stepped out of the dress, leaving it on the balcony and coyly looked up into his eyes as he drank me in.

He smiled, not so lazily this time, more like a man about to get something he wanted. He took my hand, kissed it and led me into the bedroom. I knew this was where I was supposed to remove his clothes but I didn't have it in me. I sat on the bed and nodded to him, hoping he'd understand and do it himself. He understood and slowly he unbuttoned his shirt, his pants, all of it until he stood before me as perfect as a chiselled sculpture.

I nodded for him to continue. He crawled onto the bed, following his procedure, seemingly unaware of my inner cringing every time he touched me. I made all the right noises until the end goal had been achieved then he rolled off me with that lazy grin of his, pleased with himself.

When he'd caught his breath, he kissed me softly, stroking my arm. 'Okay?' he asked me.

'Oh yes,' I cooed stupidly. 'That was fantastic,' I said, smiling up at him.

'Would you like me to lie here a while?' he asked.

I kissed him on the side of his mouth and said, 'No, no, I'm good. I'm going to have a wine though if you'd like one before you go?' I offered, not really sure what else to do. It didn't seem right to ask him to leave.

'Sure,' he said.

I put on my blue satin gown and led him into the kitchen where I topped up each of our wine glasses from the bottle I'd left on the counter. The image of Jack in my kitchen, in the place where this stranger now stood, hit me like a slap to the face and I froze. I pushed the tears away, the sinking feeling in my stomach, I pushed them both further down. I had to focus. I had to finish this date respectfully. I couldn't think of him anymore. I had to stop comparing the two experiences or I'd collapse where I stood.

'Are you alright?' he asked kindly.

'Oh, yeah, sure. Just a bit dopey now I guess,' I smiled, quickly regaining my composure and passed him his wine.

He kindly lightened the mood, sitting on the balcony with me, talking and laughing while guessing what was happening between the people on the streets below. Under any other circumstances I could have been friends with him. Another time or place. Perhaps he'd be a good match for Zoë and we'd be able to have double date dinners and go to the basketball and the beach for holidays. I smiled at the thought. Another time, another era, a pre-war one I'd never get to see in my lifetime.

'Are you sure you're alright?' he asked again.

I smiled lazily, 'Yeah, I'm definitely alright,' I said suggestively.

'Alright, then,' he smiled. 'Thanks for the wine, I better let you get some sleep,' he said emptying his glass. He kissed the top of my head. 'I hope we'll meet again, this was fun,' he said, leaving his card on the dining table as he let himself out.

As soon as the door closed, it all came crashing down around me. The enormity of it, what I'd done, that it wasn't with Jack, that I desperately wanted it to be with Jack but it wasn't. It was some other man who had pleasured me according to a set of rules and procedures he'd been given. It was another man, a man whose name I didn't even know, who had given me the desired conclusion. Even though I hadn't wanted it to happen, my body had orgasmed against my will. I could never take it back and next week I'd have to do it all over again with another stranger. Over and over until the end of time and I raced for the toilet and vomited every grain of rice from my paella.

When my stomach was empty, I stepped into a boiling hot shower and tried scrubbing him off me. Tried sweating out the memory of his mouth on my body. It didn't work. I still felt dirty, used and I hated myself. I hated the President. I hated my country, the war, the stupid regeneration of our nation. I hated it all.

Mostly I hated myself, my body for betraying my mind, my heart and Jack.

I dried myself, found my contraband nightdress still buried in the back of my pyjama drawer and slipped it on, feeling the familiar comfort of the cotton, relishing in it, needing it as though the familiarity was all that would get me through the night.

Back in the kitchen, I picked the bottle of wine off the bench and drank it on the balcony looking up at the stars. At least Jack and I saw the same stars, the same moon, breathed the same thick, moisture-filled air.

That was something, wasn't it? It had to be something. But I began to wonder which fate really was the worst as I swallowed the last drops of wine before stumbling into my bedroom.

I ripped the sheets from the bed, the pillowcases, the quilt cover, all of it. I couldn't sleep with the smell of a stranger. I'd never again sleep with the smell of Jack on the pillow beside me, this stranger had replaced Jack's smell with his own and I'd never get it back. I threw the spare pillow across the room and fell asleep, tears wetting my pillow and the naked quilt pulled over me.

CHAPTER 15

Dark fat clouds filled the sky the next morning. How appropriate, I thought as I walked around the apartment in a dazed fog. Every detail of the night before ridiculously clear, making me sick to my stomach. The walls were closing in, mocking me. Jack would be waking wherever he was, knowing what I'd done, that I'd slept with someone else. I wondered if he was as repulsed by me as I was.

I wondered if he knew the man who'd pleasured me, if he'd overhear conversations about the girl in the red dress. I glanced over at the lone bottle of wine left in the rack. No, I hadn't even eaten breakfast, I told myself. I had to get out, even if the weather was bad. I'd go for a walk, go to the market, have a coffee. Maybe later, I'd go for a run. That would help. All of it would help.

Ignoring my sore head, I showered, dressed, paid attention to wear a suitable outfit and went to buy groceries. And wine. More wine, hidden in the bottom of the bag under the eggs and chocolate, beef for roasting, potatoes and carrots.

I stopped at my favourite café. Placed an order for a cappuccino and a cake, and went to sit outside and wait for it.

'It's a bit cool out here, isn't it?' asked the waitress.

'Oh no, it's lovely,' I insisted. What else could I say? Being inside makes me want to rip the hair out of my head and my eyes from their sockets in an effort to forget?

'Saw you out last night,' said the waitress.

I nodded. 'Lots of people were out. Sorry, I didn't see you,' I told the girl.

The girl smiled shyly. 'Oh, don't be silly,' she said waving me away, 'Of course not. I was just saying. Actually, I'm not sure what I was saying. He was a good looking one. I hope you had a nice time.'

'I did, thank you, a very nice time,' I lied. 'How about you? Were you there on a date?' I asked.

'Oh, no, not me' said the waitress. 'That sort of thing's not really available in my pay grade,' she smiled sheepishly. 'Sometimes, for my birthday or something, everyone chips in though,' she said brightly.

I nodded, understanding the divide between the classes. Someone called out to her from behind the counter, their tone disapproving, as though the waitress had done something wrong, overstepped the invisible line of societal divide.

'Oh, sorry,' the waitress whispered to me as though finally understanding what she'd done, blushing, having just been reminded of her place by whoever was behind the counter and she scurried back to where she belonged.

It didn't sit well with me. Yet another thing. I appreciated the distraction of something new to hate.

I quickly finished my coffee and cake, needing to leave.

Nowhere was safe from the impact of this world, but at least in my apartment there was no one to speak to me and remind me of what I'd done.

I closed the doors to the balcony, closed all the drapes, curled up on my bed, opened my wine and began soaking my insides until I forgot my name and slept.

I woke sometime in the afternoon. I was tempted to see if the clouds had cleared for Zoë's important date with Jack's mate, for the rendezvous they'd planned with Jack, but I couldn't bring myself to open the drapes. Instead I opened a packet of potato chips and ate them in front of the vision screen, watching a silly comedy about a group of girls on vacation learning to surf.

I opened another bottle of wine and drank some more. It was all that went any way to piecing together my broken heart.

I wondered where Zoë was going. She hadn't told me. Just that she and Jack were going to accidentally meet up while she was on a date with his mate and he was on a date with whoever. Maybe she knew I'd try to be there.

All she'd said was it wasn't her apartment. But it'd have to be eventually, right? Didn't she have pretences to keep up, too? Would Jack go back there too? No, Margie on security would see them, Margie would know. Margie was always watching. I couldn't bear to think about what Jack would be doing once they parted, wondering who he was doing it with, how his mouth would move over their body, between their legs, how he'd move inside them, the things he'd do to help them climax, clear their head, regain their focus.

As the contents of the bottle transferred to my stomach and my thinking became blurred, I realised there wasn't enough wine in the world to make me forget Jack's midnight black hair or the dark blue eyes that looked like the deepest parts of the ocean. The way they darkened to almost black with lust when he drank me in. The way his body squirmed beneath my touch. The way he laughed. How his face lit a whole room. How every cell in my body came alive at the sight of him. How he made me whole and real and how I'd never again know what that felt like. I remembered all of it, until I passed out.

I woke with a start, my heart pounding out of my chest as something stung my face. What? Why? Huh? Was all my brain was managing as it tried to comprehend what was happening, assessing the danger through the fog and the wine sloshing through my brain, confusing it, slurring it, making me wonder if I'd dreamt it, imagined it, totally lost my mind.

I tried opening my eyes but they hurt. My head hurt, it pounded. My mouth was as dry as sand. What time was it, anyway? I tried to think. The vision screen was no longer talking to me. The room was quiet. I could hear bottles crashing into bins on the street below. People laughing too loud. The train whistling in the distance. Maybe the last train of the night? It had to be late, perhaps midnight or around about.

I heard the slapping of skin on skin a second before my face stung from the impact. I tried looking, focussing my eyes and my brain on what was happening. I needed to wake up. I knew I needed to wake up. But it didn't make sense. Why would anyone be hitting me in my living room in the middle of the night?

'Shit,' mumbled a woman softly. 'Come on, Courtney, wake up.'

I knew that voice. Zoë. It was Zoë. No need to panic. I forced my eyes open even though the lids scraped across my eyeballs.

Zoë looked down at me, her face scowling, furious.

'Whaaat?' I stumbled.

'Courtney, come on,' Zoë said, pulling me up.

'What's going on? How did you get in here?' I asked, finally becoming coherent.

'You weren't answering your door. I was worried. I got access from Margie. I'll tell her later that you'd just fallen asleep and were dead to the world after last night. But come on, what's going on, you're drunk again?'

'I am not,' I defended, trying unsuccessfully to sit up.

'I can see the bottles.'

'I'm fine, I'm fine,' I insisted, concentrating and finally managing to sit up even though the room spun and my stomach and head swirled in opposing directions.

'You're asleep in your clothes, on the couch, in the middle of the night. You can hardly speak and you stink,' Zoë said smugly.

'So,' I defended. 'Since when are you the pyjama police? What are you doing here, anyway?' I asked and then it all flooded back. Who I was. What I'd done. Where she'd been. I'd have given anything to see him, just for a minute.

'There you go,' said Zoë as she watched my face fall. 'Come on, let me get you a coffee and we'll talk about it.'

I couldn't walk very well. I felt sick. My body ached. It begged for sleep. Zoë helped me to the bathroom and left me to pee. I splashed my face with water, brushed my teeth, drank water from the tap. I felt a little better. I could stand and walk without help at least. I put on some less crumpled, better smelling clothes and went back to the kitchen as Zoë was pouring coffee.

'Sorry,' I said, sheepishly. 'Was a bad day.'

'Was your date that bad?' Zoë asked.

I shrugged. 'I felt dirty. He wasn't, well, you know,' I said, leaving the unspoken words hanging in the air. 'Speaking of which, dare I ask?' I asked, my face and eyes squinting, only one eye open as though Zoë was going to give me a visual.

Zoë handed me a coffee and led me to the dining table. 'You have nothing to worry about. I didn't touch him,' she smiled. 'His mate on the other hand,' she giggled.

I exhaled as though I'd been holding my breath for days. 'How is he? Jack. Is he okay?' I asked.

Zoë shrugged. 'Much the same as you really, just without the luxury to indulge,' she answered. 'But he's fine. He's fine,' she insisted as my face must have shown how worried I was.

'Did they know anything about Rachel?'

'No,' Zoë said, shaking her head. 'But his mate's heard rumblings. Apparently, they'd planned to run, not that night, but they'd planned to. There's a rumour, an urban legend really, that there's a place, a community, hidden somewhere where they don't live by the President's rules. He thinks that's where they were going. He thinks something happened that night at the club. Someone must have seen them outside the club. They've stopped questioning everyone now, so he thinks they found them. They got lazy and careless and they got caught,' she said.

'Well at least they're safe, right?'

Zoë shrugged, 'It's still all just a theory, but it looks promising. If we can find where they're being kept maybe we can get them out.'

'We?' I asked hopeful.

'No. Not you, newbie. Still not you. Me and Jack.'

'Jack? No, not Jack,' I insisted, terrified that something might happen to him. I couldn't bare it. I couldn't.

'He's my only access to information. It flows better in his world. But it's still just a rumour. We have to find out for sure. They may have been shipped to the islands already, for all we know.'

I nodded. 'How did he look?' I asked, desperate for more information on Jack.

'He's really handsome, isn't he?' Zoë said. 'He asked a million questions about you, too. I could hardly get him to shut up once his date finally went to the bathroom.'

I smiled, he was thinking of me and it somehow soothed my aching soul.

'Shit, Courtney,' Zoë said, shaking her head.

'I know,' I said, hanging my head, still drunk, in too much pain for the pretence of faking. 'Maybe we should just not speak of it, the less you know the better.'

'I'm not going to say anything,' Zoë insisted. 'I do know when to shut up,' she laughed. 'But you really need to get yourself sorted out. You can't go on like this. You're a bloody flashing beacon of rule breaking. Not to mention, if Jack sees you like this, it'll break him.'

'What am I going to do?' I asked, tears falling from my eyes, down my face. 'I just don't know how to fix it. I just don't know what to do without him.'

Zoë gathered me into her arms. 'I don't know, but we'll figure it out. You just have to do it sober, okay?'

I nodded and laughed. 'Three weeks and I'm a bloody drunken mess. Some perfect society Sheila has going on, hey?'

'Perfect, huh,' she scoffed.

'I thought you liked the way things were,' I asked, surprised.

'Accept, yes. Make the best of, yes. Like, no.'

'Really?' I asked. 'What was all that you said about breeders?'

'Oh, that bit I agree with. The rest, not so much. You're not the only one with secrets, you know. Some of us are just better at hiding them,' she winked. 'Why do you think my family, Rachel, you, are so important to me?'

I nodded.

'We're pack animals designed to mate for life. No one's immune. Some are just better at acclimatising or are fortunate enough to not meet their mate, the one among many who changes everything. Who knows why but I guess they're the lucky ones,' she shrugged.

'What happened to him?' I asked, finally catching her meaning.

Zoë shrugged. 'Trish had him moved down south.'

'Trish knew?'

'We never spoke of it, she just 'accidentally' left her tablet open showing me his transfer document so I'd know. Simple as that. Done. Gone. Now I just get through and play the game as I'm supposed to.'

'So how come you were just separated and not imprisoned like Rachel and Leo?'

'We never got caught. We never flaunted it in public. I just had too many dates with him and the anomaly was buried in one of the analysts' reports that crossed Trish's desk. Like Penny, I was lucky Trish and I have the relationship we have and she spotted it before anyone else,' Zoë said. 'Anyway, are you going to be okay? I've gotta go get some sleep.'

'Yeah, I'll be fine. Thanks,' I said, hugging her.

'You're welcome. Get some sleep yourself and no more wine,' she admonished before walking out the door with the last bottle from my supply.

I sat in the quiet, realising how bad a job I was doing. What it could cost me. I could lose Jack so easily, in the blink of an eye, the tap of a few keys, a single memo from someone like Trish and he'd be gone. One of us could be sent anywhere without even the chance of a goodbye. Just gone. Reallocated in the middle of the night. No fuss, no muss.

I might never see him again. I couldn't let that happen. I had to do better. I had to be stronger. Once all this fuss over Rachel and Leo died down, we'd be free to meet under the bridge again once in a while, maybe have occasional dates. It wasn't enough. It would never be enough, but it was better than nothing, better than having him sent somewhere. I'd never be able to find him and have to live the rest of my life like Zoë. I couldn't do it. I couldn't live without hope, without Jack, without knowing he was some-where.

CHAPTER 16

Anna barged into the reception area as I was finishing up a call. Clearly Anna was not used to waiting, but she waited none-the-less, one muscle twitch short of tapping her foot.

'Hi Anna,' I greeted her brightly when I'd hung up my call. 'How are you?' It was forced merriment but I was not going to let Anna get the better of me or give her any reason to continue sus-pecting whatever she suspected about me and my friends and our character.

Anna 'hmphed' her reply before shoving forward a trolley with a big box on it. 'It's for Saturday's party. You need to do this in between your work. Someone will come by and clear it through-out the day.' She didn't bother with any other pleasantries, she shoved the box off her trolley with the pointy end of a shiny patent stiletto and then barged out as she'd barged in with as much dramatic air as possible.

I waited a minute after Anna left to make sure she wasn't com-ing back and then opened the box. Inside was a hand pump and bags of deflated balloons. It didn't take a genius to work out my task so I pulled out a handful of balloons and one by one stuck them on the end of the machine and manually pumped air into the balloons until they were a decent size then pulled them off, tied a knot and set them free.

When Zoë came into reception, she had to wade through a sea of purple and silver balloons to reach my desk. 'What's all this, then?' she asked.

'Anna gave me a job to do for the party,' I smirked.

'Of course she did,' Zoë laughed. 'You know Christina hates balloons, right? They belong at children's birthday parties not adult gatherings,' she said.

'What do you mean? When did she say that? It's her party,' I said.

Zoë shrugged. 'I read an interview once about her parties. Come on, it's lunch time. Surely you're allowed to eat?'

I happily left all the equipment on my desk and carefully stepped through the balloons and closed the door on it all to eat my roasted pumpkin and fetta salad.

When I returned from lunch, some mysterious person had taken away the balloons I'd spent the morning blowing up. They'd left a box of pink napkins on my desk. Beside the box was one napkin in the shape of a swan. In between calls, I spent the afternoon trying to figure out how to replicate the swan napkin with the help of a tutorial on my tablet.

That night with a head full of swan napkin origami, I headed off to learn how to cook scampi with garlic butter and pineapple salsa and coconut pana cotta with Pauline. Afterwards, we had a beer at the pub across the road then I lied to my friend and said I had some errands to run before heading home and I'd catch her next week.

Pauline and cooking were my only reprieve and respite in my messed up world. I hated lying to her. She was kind and lovely to me, so it was a horrible thing to do, but I enjoyed the anonymity, the easiness of who I was with her and I didn't want to lose that just yet.

I spent the next few days folding swans. When the girls came to watch Tuesday's farmer harvest, they could barely find space amongst trolleys full of all I'd already done since starting the early shift.

'You know it's not a dinner party, right,' laughed Rosie.

'I give up,' I laughed, throwing my hands in the air and settling in for the farmer.

'Don't forget your appointment this arvo with Dr Grace,' Tess said as they were all leaving.

'Sure, sure,' I said.

Zoë hung back. 'What appointment?' she asked.

'My blood pressure was a bit high when she scanned me last week after the saline treatment.'

'Why did she scan you?'

'I don't know but now I have to have it rechecked.'

'Well make sure you have no stress all day and stop thinking and stuff. If it's high a second time, it'll ring bells.'

'Already on it,' I insisted. Although really, I had no idea how to bring my blood pressure down.

I did everything I knew how to do. I guzzled so much water, I spent most of the morning peeing. I ate no sugar and laid off the coffee, the only vices I had left, but it was necessary. I cut off every and all thought of Jack and instead thought of running through lovely gardens with the sun shining, warming my skin, those per-fect days that made you smile. It would have to do.

I instamessaged Zoë just before two to let her know she had the phones and began the long walk down the hallway to Dr Grace's office. I wondered if they did it on purpose, if all Drs' offices were at the end of long corridors so you got yourself worked up on the way?

'How's your week going?' Dr Grace asked casually.

'Oh, fine, fine,' I said.

'I hear you're helping out with the Director's party,' she said.

'Yes, helping Anna.'

'Is that causing much stress?' she asked, getting her scanner out of the drawer.

'Nope, not really, I don't think. I don't mind helping out,' I said, wondering if anything said was in fact confidential. I was getting the impression nothing was.

'Well, let's have a look then, hey?' Dr Grace said, scanning my arm. Although it occurred to me the scanner was more a prop than anything because now I was loaded into her system, she could just tap a few keys and see everything going on in my body anyway, she could probably track every time I ran, every orgasm, every laugh, every change to my insides whenever Jack had kissed me under the bridge. I couldn't think about it or I'd get worked up. I needed to remain calm, peaceful, content.

I watched the screen over on her desk, watched each of the green ticks appear. I couldn't read which line said what from where I sat so I didn't know which one was blood pressure. I didn't breathe a sigh of relief until the last green tick appeared in the last box.

'Ah, very good then,' she said. Must have just been all those new things you were getting used to after all, like you said,' Dr Grace said with a smile.

I smiled back even though I suspected Dr Grace's was fake and that she was in fact either surprised or disappointed. I couldn't quite tell which. Either way, I had passed and that was all that mattered.

I thanked Dr Grace for her time and went back to my desk where I all but flopped in my chair, grateful for the quiet and solitude. I had an instamessage from Zoë with just a question mark. Who knew at this point who was reading or listening to anything? I replied with 'ok' and went back to work, taking calls and folding napkins for a dinner party that wasn't happening but the task was cathartic and calming. I'd dodged a bullet, but only just. I had to do better.

It took enormous effort during Wednesday night's game to not think of Jack, to not look for him in the stands, on the concourse and in the queues. I had to put him out of my mind before I got us both into trouble. I wondered if anyone had connected us. Were they watching him, too? Coordinating what times we were out and where we ran?

I focussed on the game, on the team, Zoë and our champagne. Distractions. Perfect distractions. I was getting good at it. I'd distracted myself all day, keeping my hands busy and every time I thought his name, saw his eyes in my mind, I chastised myself and thought of something else and concentrated on my tasks at hand. It wasn't easy but wallowing was going to show up on a scan and I couldn't go through that again. I couldn't risk it. I mightn't make it through next time. I mightn't be so lucky. So, I cheered. I cheered loud. I refused to look around the stadium even though it tore at something inside me and I knew I'd regret it when I laid down in my empty bed to sleep.

I was only mildly bleary eyed from my bedtime wallowing on Thursday morning as we all gathered for the morning harvest. We'd all just sat, the farmer had just begun when Anna walked in and scoffed. 'Seriously,' she huffed.

'Oh, like you don't all do it,' smirked Zoë.

Anna pretended not to hear her, addressing only me. 'You need to help set up Saturday at one. We have two hours to set up so you'd better work fast.'

'Sure, no problem,' I smiled amenably which seemed to only infuriate Anna more.

As Anna was about to walk away, she turned, annoyed, her face looking as though she'd smelt something bad. 'Oh, Christina said seeing as you've done all this work you should be invited, so consider yourself invited,' she moaned and left.

'Oh my,' Tessa drawled after the door closed behind Anna. 'I can't believe you've been invited to one of Christina's parties. How on earth did you manage that? How did you get in on any of it for that matter?' she asked.

'I've no idea,' I said. 'One minute I was being grilled about Rachel, next thing I know the Director's asking for my help and snippy Anna is giving me grief about it.'

'That's because you stole Bridget's job,' Rosie said. 'I've heard she's furious. She usually chips in so she gets an invite. We never get an invite down here. It's only ever execs and Anna and Bridget. You've seriously stomped on some toes,' Rosie said.

'What was I supposed to do? It's not like I could say no, is it?' I defended.

'There was definitely no way out,' Zoë said. 'But why you were included in the first place is the mystery. Not that you're not capable mind, but there's something going on. Christina would never have pissed off her own girls for no reason. Even if you were on the fast track everyone says you're on, she would have waited until you got there, or added you to a project team or something. This, this screams ulterior motives, I just don't know what. It's not like you were even that friendly with Rachel.'

'I know, right?'

After the others had wheeled their chairs back to the pod, I grabbed Zoë before she left and asked, 'You don't think this whole thing with Christina and Anna is because of, you know,' I asked.

'I don't think so. You haven't seen him enough to raise any flags. You lucky dipped that first date you had with him, right? And the second one I actually booked in as a group and no one can see who had who so they shouldn't have enough to go on, two dates is nothing.'

When I didn't confirm, Zoë's eyebrows raised. 'That was it, right?' she demanded even though her voice was hushed.

'Officially,' I said sheepishly.

'Officially? Fuck Courtney, what did you do?'

As I was about to answer, to tell Zoë about the meetings under the bridge, Zoë stopped me. 'No, not now, we'll talk about it later,' she whispered and wheeled her chair out.

My mouth went dry and my heart beat too fast, panic surging through my body. What if they knew? What if I'd been followed? Stupid Margie on security was recording and reporting stuff to someone. I felt it. But who? Who was she spying for?

I'd packed up for the night and was about to leave when Zoë appeared, hooking her arm through mine, 'Come on, I'm getting the water taxi with you today and we're going to talk over a pizza and water,'

'Water?' I asked suspiciously.

'You're way too fond of the booze right now,' Zoë said. 'So yes, water.'

'Fine,' I groaned, wishing Zoë wasn't so observant after all.

The pizza place was busy, a small, dimly lit long rectangle with red-sponged walls, a dark wooden counter and black vinyl seats. Lots of chatter in a small space bounced off the walls, drowning everyone out but it wasn't too loud that we couldn't hear each other. We ordered two large pizzas, one with the lot and one with ham and pineapple and two bottles of water.

The water arrived only seconds later and the same waiter put plates in front of us, a basket of garlic bread, laid out the cutlery, smiled politely and left.

'So, how many?' Zoë asked as though she was asking after something as simple as how many chocolate bars have you eaten.

I shrugged. 'A few. Four, five, plus the dates,' I answered, without looking up from my food.

'Where?'

'Bridge.'

'How?'

'By accident. A note under the door. I went for a run,' I told her.

'Anyone notice?'

'Margie on security, the last time she asked, a late-night run? I hadn't run in a while. I was trying. But he'd left a note. I'd been on call that night, so told her I couldn't sleep and I needed to clear my head. She seemed fine but she made a note. Might have been unrelated. I don't know.'

Zoë nodded. 'It may just be a suspicion then. After the other business.'

'Fine,' I said.

'You'll have to be on guard at the party,' Zoë told her.

I nodded. I'd already suspected so.

'They'll be watching you. For whatever reason. It might just be that they think you'll be easier to break than me. If so, that's fine, you don't know anything, anyway.'

I nodded again.

'You'll have to flirt your arse off with whatever party favours they have there. None of this being shy and holding out for you know who or making yourself sick after being with someone else. You have to do it, you have to like it and you have to smile afterwards, no moping.'

'Party favours?' I asked suspiciously, my stomach sinking.

'Christina is famous for her party favours. In the old days, before the war, the famous and powerful had drugs and expensive booze to share, now they have men, nothing but top shelf men to play with and do as you please with as many as you please, open buffet. You flirt your arse off, be happy, play, disappear with one or two.'

'Two?' I asked, horrified. I doubted I could manage one after my last attempt.

'Fine, one will do,' laughed Zoë. 'Just make it look good. Play with a few, have fun.'

'Zoë, I don't even think I can do one. I can't do it again. Not after last time. I hated myself. I wanted to tear my own skin from my bones.' I was sick from the thought of it. 'I can't do it again. I don't think I can have another man touch me. The thought of it repulses me. I can't. I just can't,' I said, trying not to cry.

She put her hand on mine in comfort. 'I know. I know. But you have to. We'll get through it together. Afterwards we'll figure it out, I'll help you. I'll be here for you. But Saturday, you have to do it for your own safety, his too,' she insisted as our pizzas arrived.

We waited for the waiter to remove the empty basket of garlic bread, rearrange the condiments and our drinks to fit the pizzas onto the table. I served myself a piece of each, as did Zoë. It was hot and the cheese was stretchy and gooey, the crust thin and crunchy.

'Surely after 20 years of the breeding program there's enough men to go around now? I think Sheila just likes having total control over this world she's created. She's as egotistical as all the men that came before her. It makes me sick. How is it different to any other communist country from the pre-war time? How did that happen to our country?' I asked as I filled my mouth with ham and pineapple pizza.

'I guess it sounded good at the time. People were afraid and vulnerable. It makes them susceptible to people like Sheila. But I'm not even sure Sheila knew she'd go down this path or for this long when she began. Power is addictive and it's addiction, addiction's not gender specific. Now no one's stupid enough to stand up to Sheila. Or brave enough,' she added between mouthfuls.

'Zoë, what if he's there?' I asked, terrified.

'I don't think he's high enough up on their radar scale yet. You saw him at Ora's your first week advertising, right?'

'Yeah, so?'

'So, if he was in with Christina's selection of top shelf men, if he was up to their level, he'd be too busy to advertise and I wouldn't have been able to book him at all. They're very protective of their entertainers. They don't like having them soiled by any old riff raff,' she said.

'You're kidding, right?'

'No. I'm not. Let that be a warning, too. When you're at the party, know your place. Watch to see who's a part of their inner circle and don't overstep your mark, don't touch anything not meant for you.'

'Fine. Know my place. Got it,' I mumbled, reaching for more pizza.

'It won't be all bad,' Zoë suggested. 'Her parties are supposed to be incredible and who knows, you may just score a little bit of intel and we could use some of that,' she said. 'But don't go trying to get it. You're the least manipulative person on the planet. You'll get busted in a heartbeat,' she laughed.

'Fine, fine,' I said, finally smiling. 'Now, what the hell am I supposed to wear to this bloody shindig?'

'Now you're talking,' smiled Zoë. 'I'm at your service. You finish setting up at three, right? I shall see you at four then and I'll work my magic,' she insisted.

'Thanks,' I said and then we turned our conversation to gossiping about the hideously super slutty suit Anna had been wearing that day and how unnecessary it was in an era where there were no men to impress, no need to be flashing your boobs about that way.

'She's decades behind the time. Where'd she even find it?' Zoë asked as she piled more pizza onto her plate.

As the pizza slices on the table dwindled and we mellowed from full tummies, we laughed about all things Anna. She certainly made it easy enough. We both filled our mouths. While we chewed there was a rare moment of quiet between us and I noticed that the noise level was rising around us. People were becoming agitated, their movements animated, their voices high pitched with the excitement of something out of the ordinary happening.

They began jumping from their tables, leaving half eaten pizza as they rushed for the door. A buzz filled the room, people sharing worried looks and speaking in panicked tones as whatever was going on flowed through the room in a silent whisper.

'What's happening?' I asked Zoë.

'I don't know,' she said, concerned.

'What's going on?' I asked someone rushing past but they ignored me, in too much of a hurry to leave. People started running out of the pizza place, as swarms of people outside began running towards the river.

'What's going on?' Zoë demanded, grabbing the arm of another passer-by.

'They've found a body,' she said. 'They're pulling it out of the river now,' she added, hurrying away to see what she could see.

Zoë and I stared at each other, frozen, no words, no nothing. Then Zoë mumbled, 'What if it's Rach?' and we were both out of our seats and Zoë was doing her thing, shoving people out of the way, telling them to, 'watch it,' as she stormed a path towards the river.

I followed quickly in the path she created. The river was crowded with people trying to see around each other, standing on tippy toes to see over heads blocking their view. You'd have thought the President herself was passing by. My stomach roiled with fear for what we would find and revulsion at the degradation of human behaviour from the eager eyes around me.

Zoë pushed her way to the front and I offered an apologetic half smile to the girl who served me my weekend coffee as Zoë shoved her aside. Standing side by side, we held each other's hand, held our breaths, even our hearts stopped mid beat as a woman in a green and white ambulance coat dragged the bloated body out of the water, letting it fall on the grass. Fish had nibbled at the face. There was all sorts of damage to her naked body. Some damage where the fish had feasted, but the purple and blue bruises were clearly inflicted by a person. Both had left enough of the woman intact for immediate identification. We both exhaled simultaneously as we realised it wasn't Rachel. This woman, petite despite the bloating, her face long, her wet hair too dark.

'That's that newspaper lady,' breathed the girl from the café still beside me, to no one in particular. 'The one that wrote those articles about the war being over.'

Zoë began pushing her way back through the crowd. If it wasn't Rachel, it was none of our business. I know I needed air. I needed to be away from this gawking, shoving crowd breathing on me, shoving into my back for a look, too excited by anything out of the ordinary to maintain a scrap of humanity.

Once we reached the front of our building where we were clear of people, we could finally breathe.

'It wasn't her. Oh, thank God, it wasn't her,' breathed Zoë, her hand gripping her chest. 'It wasn't her, Courtney,' she said, tears falling from her eyes.

I hugged her to me. 'No, it wasn't her.'

She took a moment to compose herself and take some breaths, held her head high and we walked into the building with a courtesy nod to Margie as we walked to the bay of lifts and waited for one.

I wished I'd gone to yoga. Yoga would have been better than seeing that body I thought as I let myself into my home. Anything would have been better than seeing that body. I suspected it was going to haunt me along with everything else that was haunting me, and I didn't even have any wine to numb my brain from thinking, from seeing.

CHAPTER 17

The blue mottled body they'd pulled from the river had haunted my dreams. How could such a thing have happened in today's society? Who would have killed a journalist? Why? It made no sense.

To get to the water taxi dock, I had to pass by where she'd lain, dripping, gawked upon by entertainment starved passers-by. Nothing remained from the night before. If I hadn't seen it, I'd have had no idea it had happened at all.

I tried reading the newspaper over the shoulder of a woman in front of me on the water taxi. Suicidal journalist, a DNA glitch, the heading said. The rest of the text was too small. I looked outside at the water as we approached the other side of the river. What other information could they even pass on to alleviate our fears and explain the inexplicable. People didn't suicide in a perfect society where everything down to our DNA was monitored and controlled. Nothing they could say would change what was though. A woman had died. She'd had purple bruises on her neck and body. Someone had dumped her in the river. I knew so because you didn't just dump yourself in a river after a beating, did you? No words, no explanation could change it or make the images go away.

The haunting showed on my face, the sleeplessness showed in the black rings under my eyes. You couldn't unsee what you'd already seen. Now the image of the journalist was stuck in my brain, there was nothing I could do to remove it. Like all the other things I'd seen and done and learnt since I'd arrived, I'd have to learn to live with it, to coexist but somehow I still had to smile, still had to offer good cheer and the professionalism I'd been taught to show at all times, no matter what else was happening.

We lived in a society that had removed every opportunity for stress and misery, to experience either was an indication you were up to no good. But this wasn't the world I thought it was. It was crumbling and no one was paying attention. No one wanted to know. They'd pulled the body of a beaten woman out of the river. People were pretending they didn't see, they didn't know.

'Still seeing that body?' Zoë asked when she saw me.

I nodded.

'It's her eyes that get me,' Zoë said quietly. 'Open, milky, bloodshot, unseeing but you know they saw. They saw what happened to her. They knew it all before she was choked to death.'

'She was choked?' I asked.

'She must have been. Didn't you see the bruising on her neck? Who would do such a thing?' she asked.

'I don't know,' I whispered, comprehending the fear she'd have felt in her final moments. I was sad for her. So incredibly sad.

'Anyway, I should go to my desk,' Zoë said as I took my coffee to my desk, both of us walking away as though in a daze.

I answered calls, made bookings on auto pilot for the morning. Nothing made sense, my voice sounded like it came from someone else and my eyes begged to close, but when I allowed them to for just a second, I saw her, the journalist whose name I didn't know. So, I stared ahead, as unseeing as her blood-soaked eyes had been and pretended to care about the needs of the women who called.

I lazily, sleepily hung up the call I was on and looked up from my tablet to see Stacey in all her lovely perkiness standing at my desk.

'Oh, hey,' I said, mustering as much cheer for my relocation specialist as I could while she smiled back at me like sunshine.

'You ready?' she asked cheerily, as though there was nothing at all wrong with the world.

'Ready?' I asked, unable to recall any meetings scheduled.

'Lunch, you silly duffer,' she giggled. 'We have to talk about the party, prepare, talk dresses and what to and not to do.'

'Oh, right,' I said, suddenly remembering the message I'd seen from her this morning but had forgotten as quickly as I'd seen it. Thoughts of lunch had disappeared somewhere around images of blood-soaked eyes and purple skin and beautiful men I couldn't have. I didn't care for lunch but I gathered my things and transferred the phones to Zoë anyway and smiled as brightly as my face would allow.

Stacey chattered oblivious to my inner turmoil as we walked to a local restaurant. It was a brightly lit café, the sort of thing that was only open during work days. Three cheery waiters greeted us before we'd even reached the hostess. The hostess summoned yet another waiter to show us to a table even though the café was mostly empty. They must have been expecting a crowd.

'I'm June, here are some menus. I'll be back for your order in a few minutes,' she said.

'What do you fancy, my treat?' said Stacey.

I hadn't even picked up the menu yet. I did so, just as the waitress returned.

'What can I get you ladies?' she asked.

Stacey ordered a salad. I was stuck on all the weird food on the menu so ordered the first thing I saw, a vegan risotto.

'No,' interrupted Stacey. 'She'll have the pumpkin soup and a green smoothie,' she ordered for me.

After the waitress had left I asked Stacey, 'Why couldn't I have the risotto?'

'Because you have the biggest party of your life tomorrow, you do not need to be eating that many carbs,' she admonished.

Right, so instead I had liquid food. I was even more depressed now than before. I didn't dare tell her about the stash of chocolate in my bag.

'So, do we need to go over anything for tomorrow?' she asked.

'Nope, I think Zoë's covered most of it,' I said.

'Right. And what exactly has Zoë told you?' she asked sceptically.

'To mind my manners, don't step on anyone's toes, play with the entertainers, the party favours, have a good time, look fabulous.'

'Hmph,' she said, unimpressed Zoë had beaten her to it. 'That sounds about right,' she said. 'There'll be a car to collect you at 7pm, don't be late. Another will return you when the party is over. The door lady at the party will flag it for you. Don't eat anything that might fall apart or has sauce. Avoid the blue cocktails, they'll make your mouth as blue as a four-year-old with an ice block. That's not attractive or suitable for an IT girl. Don't drink too much. You need to be in control at all times. There'll be a lot of people there, a lot of people watching, you need to represent yourself and the company to the highest of standards. Oh, and look amazing. What are you going to wear?'

'Zoë is coming over tomorrow afternoon to help me. She says she saw just the dress in my wardrobe, some little black strappy thing.'

'Right, I know the one,' she said nodding.

'She'll help me with my hair and makeup, too,' I said.

'Excellent. She does know her stuff, that's for sure.'

I took long gulps of my green smoothie when it arrived. I didn't dare ask what was in it. I suspected I didn't want to know. But Stacey assured me it would help my skin glow.

'What about the whole beauty regime, how's that going?' she asked.

'I have an appointment tonight,' I told her.

'Excellent,' she said. 'I think that about covers tomorrow then,' she said with a smile.

I wanted to tell her she hadn't even scratched the surface about tomorrow. She had no idea of the underhanded manipulation involved, that I was Anna's new target, her enemy, that she was determined to bring down, for whatever warped reason she told herself.

What about Rachel missing?

A woman being pulled from the river?

Where was the mentoring on how to deal with that? It was so far from everything that was going on in my life but I didn't dare ruin her illusion of perfection. She was far too chipper to bring down to the depths of misery I now occupied, the dark reality of the world we lived in.

Our lunch arrived and I sipped the hot pumpkin soup that would have been delicious with a bit of cream, a bit of something, maybe some crunchy bread but instead it was plain liquid pumpkin.

Stacey continued to chatter away about pleasant things but my mind couldn't focus on them. Too much had happened, was happening to listen to frivolous chatter. She meant well, it's just who she was. She was light and sunshine and happiness, not dead people and missing friends and rule breaking.

'Good, huh?' she said as she finished her salad.

'Ahuh,' I lied, sipping the last spoonfuls of my soup.

I was glad to be back at my desk, in the quiet of reception. There were people coming in to see Dr Grace and calls for entertainers to tend to, but I didn't have to engage, I didn't have to smile, I just had to be well mannered, professional and polite. That I could manage for the few necessary seconds each interaction required.

After the last visitor had seen Dr Grace the office was quiet, the phones were finally quiet, everyone had presumably sorted their weekends. I nearly jumped out of my seat when Zoë called my name. I was staring out the window, my mind finally blank. She giggled. She looked surprised at herself and I doubted she'd laughed all day. Not by choice anyway.

I smiled back. 'What's up?' I asked.

'Drinks,' she said, her brow furrowing.

'Oh, of course,' I said, suddenly excited that I could finally have a wine, already imaging the pure goodness of being numb.

I loaded bottles of wine, the white from the fridge, the red from the rack in the cupboard, into the crook of my arm, my hands shaking, the sleeplessness, the knowing, the fear of tomorrow, the longing for the wine I was carrying, all taking its toll. No one questioned me though. I held my goods tight to stop the shaking as I approached the break out sofas and unloaded it all onto the coffee table.

Zoë apprehensively offered me a half-filled glass of wine.

'Zoë, you skimped on the poor girl's wine, top it up,' laughed Rosie, from across the other side of the coffee table.

I smiled. Zoë scowled but she topped up my wine and I took a long sip that felt so good.

'Don't drink too much or you'll be dehydrated after your scrub,' Zoë admonished before walking away.

'Oh, she's right,' Jules agreed. 'Those things suck all the toxins out but they'll dehydrate you in a flash too so you best just have the one wine and then a couple of bottles of water,' she suggested.

'Great tip, thanks,' I smiled, then scowled at Zoë who walked away smirking. *Little sneak she is*, I thought, smiling to myself.

I left them after finishing my wine. Trish walked me to the door. 'Zoë told me about last night, how are you doing with that?' she asked.

'Oh fine,' I smiled. 'That poor woman,' I sympathised.

'Indeed,' Trish said. 'And what about tomorrow night, you alright?'

'Yes, I think so' I said. 'I've got Zoë helping me and I had a great chat with Stacey at lunch,' I told her, hoping to alleviate any worries she had.

'Excellent. Well I should be around there somewhere tomorrow night, say hi if you see me. But don't worry if you don't. Those things get pretty crazy. It's hard to find anyone. Just have a good time, alright?' she said.

'Sure, thanks,' I said, leaving her at the front door where she turned to go back inside to finish Friday night drinks and I headed for the river and the water taxi.

I spent the next few hours having my body scrubbed from top to bottom, buffed and moisturised until my skin glowed. The softly spoken and kind lady in pink waxed away any stray hairs I'd accumulated in unwanted places since my last visit and I hoped someone in the new generation of graduates would invent a way to make it a more pleasant experience. Then she shaped my eyebrows, tinting them while a gloopy treatment sat in my hair. Then she gave my fingernails a French polish, painted my toenails a sweet, pale pink, rinsed and dried off my hair and sent me on my way with a smile and wishes of luck for my party.

At home I found a note from Stacey. I wasn't happy she'd been in my apartment but there was nothing I could say, she was my relocation specialist and I wasn't supposed to have anything to hide.

She'd left a note on the bench, saying she'd put dinner in the fridge for me. I opened the fridge apprehensively and found a row of coloured smoothies, green, purple, bright red. Apparently the smoothies made it easier for my body to absorb all the necessary nutrients without wasting time and energy on digestion, which prevented my stomach from bloating, keeping me thin and fabulous for my big event. I wasn't a fan, it wasn't like I was larger than I should be, fat genes had been removed from our DNA.

Even though I'd have preferred another form of liquid refreshment at this point in time, I opened a green smoothie and camped on the sofa to watch the end of a game show on the vision screen.

I was too exhausted to sit up once the show finished. The lack of sleep had well and truly caught up with me. My hands still shook from fear, nerves, for what was to come, from overexposure to this crazy world.

My body twitched and jumped at every shout, hoot of laughter and bottle crashing into a bin on the promenade below. I was fast approaching my breaking point and there was still so much more to come, that I had to handle, that I had to champion, endorse and smile through. I finished my smoothie, dug out my contraband nightdress and did my best to sleep off the horrors of this world in an effort to look fresh and amazing for the director's big soirée.

CHAPTER 18

———

I ordered a flat white coffee from my regular Saturday café. The usual girl, the one Zoë had shoved aside by the river, served me and we shared a look, a look you can only share with someone with whom you've seen a dead body with. There were no words to say, only looks of sadness, understanding. I tried smiling, I had to try but really, we just shared a nod of empathy as I took my coffee with me and I tried enjoying the sunshine as I walked across the bridge to the director's house.

The sun was nice. There wasn't too much moisture, not like that first day, I thought as I crossed the bridge, remembering that first time with Stacey. I stopped and looked out over the water. This was exactly where I stood the first time I saw Jack. I smiled. It was all for Jack. Everything I was about to do was to keep him safe. As long as I remembered that, I'd be okay. Nothing else mattered. Not Anna, not dead journalists, not even Rachel. Not when it came to Jack, everything else, everyone else paled in comparison.

———

I followed the directions Anna had instamessaged me. They took me to the old building Stacey had pointed out that first day on the bridge. She'd gushed then about the parties the Director had. Now I was on the guest list for one of the Director's fancy parties. We'd never have guessed that day that so much could happen in such a short time. Regardless of the reasoning behind my invitation, I had an invitation to one of the Director's infamous parties. It didn't make any sense at all.

The Director's building was old. Even before the war, it'd have been old. Victorian. Edwardian. One of those styles. You only learnt the difference if you were in the architecture program. But it had big stone columns and arching balconies, grand windows edged with thick drapes you could see from the street. It was a big and square, almost regal building, large enough for wings and floors and servant quarters. There was no indication as to what the big cream building had been in its other life. But I was sure it had been grand.

Perhaps it was once a parliamentary building before President Sheila moved parliament to the middle of the country? They lived and worked there now, deep under the red dirt. It might have been hotter to run a country from the middle of one of the hottest, driest continents on earth but finding and bombing what you can't see is near impossible. If you could even get a plane past the coastline without being shot down.

They gave these big, beautiful old buildings to important people now. They lived in them with their similarly important friends and their house staff. There was enough room for everyone to have their own wings, plenty of basement space for the staff to live, to ensure the residents didn't have to lift a finger to do anything.

I channelled Stacey and Zoë as I strutted up the footpath to the front door and knocked on the big metal door. A maid in uniform answered the door and it took every ounce of wisdom not to roll my eyes at the opulence, the societal divide we weren't supposed to have in our perfect society.

'Ah, Miss Courtney, Miss Anna is waiting for you in the ballroom,' the maid said, leading me down the hallway.

A ballroom? Who even knew they still existed? Surely they got converted into something more useful, something more practical?

'Here you are,' the maid said after leading me to the ballroom, just short of bowing before walking away.

Anna stood in the middle of the room, a swarm of staff fussing while she stood there commanding them all like a queen

'Oh, it's you,' Anna huffed, when she saw me.

'Hi Anna,' I called cheerily, making myself ill from being so damned nice.

I walked over to stand beside Anna, awaiting my instructions but she mostly ignored me while commanding others, pointing at things, snapping at all and sundry.

As I watched the many staff scurrying about, hanging fancy glass lanterns, scattering silk cushions, setting up a punch bowl and glasses and arranging overstuffed suede couches in darkened nooks. I wondered what I was even doing here. What job could Anna have for me that the staff, who were clearly more than accustomed to setting up for these parties, couldn't do?

I continued to stand there, quietly waiting but she said nothing. I might as well have been invisible. I saw a woman in uniform straining to move a table and went to help her.

'Stop that,' Anna said, smacking my hand as though I were a two-year-old.

'Ow,' I shrieked. 'What is your problem?'

'We do not do the work of house staff. Who the hell do you think you are?'

'I'm sorry, but I felt useless just standing there. Give me an appropriate job to do then,' I begged.

'There isn't any, so you'll just have to stand next to me and watch and learn.'

'That's why I'm here?' I asked.

'No,' snapped Anna. 'You're here because the Director said you had to be.'

'Right,' I said. 'No problem then. I'm happy to watch and learn,' I smiled.

I stood there and watched Anna boss people around for an hour until one of the maids brought in refreshments.

'I have to go to the bathroom. Don't touch anything. Don't talk to anyone,' Anna snapped, putting her tablet on the table.

She'd forgotten to switch her screen off and it glowed right in front of me. I couldn't help looking. I expected it to show a list of tasks that needed completing for the party. But the first thing I saw was the word Rachel followed by a genetic code, bolded amongst the text. Rachel? My eyes quickly scanned the screen for more information. But the words were too small and I couldn't move closer in case she came back and saw me. The word transfer was in bold type, centred at the top of the page. There was a gold embossed kangaroo in the right-hand corner but that was it, it wasn't enough. Then Anna's long thin, bony hand reached in front of my face snatching the tablet away.

'What did you see?' she demanded. 'Tell me!'

'Nothing, just a kangaroo,' I lied.

'Do you know what it means?' she asked.

I shrugged, 'Just something from the Director, I guess. I don't know,' I said.

'Good. Forget you saw it and if I hear you've said anything to anyone, I'll personally make sure your life is not worth living. Do you understand me?' she demanded.

'Absolutely,' I smiled innocently.

'Good,' Anna snapped, taking her tablet to the other side of the room with her to drink her tea and boss someone else around.

I continued watching Anna, learning how to pull together a party of this size, after the maid had removed our refreshments. My feet hurt, my legs ached from standing so still but I refused to show it. Eventually though, she waved her hand at me and said, 'Just go, I'm done with you.'

I stood shocked for a minute but she began gathering her own things so I said goodbye and left.

I walked back across the bridge, hoping that it would help burn off my frustrations and give me a chance to work out what that document was and what to do with the information. By the time I returned to my apartment, I wasn't any closer to understanding any of it, but I had burnt off some of the frustrations of my time spent with Anna. As I rode up in the lift I decided I'd just offload it all to Zoë and she'd know what to do with it. She'd know what the letter was, what it meant and why Rachel's name was on it and if it was referring to our Rachel at all.

Zoë was sitting on the floor in front of my apartment when I stepped out of the lift. 'Hey,' she sang when she saw me. 'About time!'

'Sorry, I walked back,' I told her. 'You haven't been waiting too long have you?' I asked, swiping my wrist over the scanner to unlock my door.

'No, not too long,' she said, following me inside. 'Well?' Zoë demanded as soon as she closed the door. 'Tell me everything.'

I thought about Anna's warning for half a second then spilled every word she said and everything that had happened, and finished with Anna's warning and details of the document I'd seen on Anna's tablet.

'Are you kidding?' Zoë asked.

'What does it mean?' I asked. 'I wasn't kidding when I said I didn't know what it was.'

'The gold embossed kangaroo is the symbol of the Kangaroo Island Detention Facility. It's a detention island. There's a bunch of huts, a weekly food drop but other than that, they're on their own. It's a women's facility so it means that's where they're shipping Rachel. It means she's still here. I don't suppose you saw any dates in the body of the document?' she asked.

'There was an S word that looked like a day of the week, but I couldn't tell if it was Saturday or Sunday, it was just too far away, but I didn't see any numbers to indicate a date,' I told her as I tried desperately to recall any other fragments I'd seen.

'It wouldn't be a Saturday, that's today and there's too much else going on for anyone to bother moving them today. It'd be a Sunday, while the buildings are empty and everyone in town is enjoying some R&R and hangovers. It can only mean this Sunday. Otherwise it'll be too long. They don't hold anyone that long, she's been gone too long already.'

'What are you thinking? What are you going to do?' I asked.

'I'm going to try and break her out, that's what I'm going to do.'

'Are you kidding? How?'

'I don't know. Perhaps while everyone who's anyone is at the party tonight, they won't notice if I sneak in.'

'Excellent, how do we do it?'

'We? No way Courtney, you have to go to that party tonight. They're watching you too closely. If you don't show, they'll be looking for you in a second.'

'And they'll know I'm with you,' I thought out loud.

'Probably,' Zoë nodded. 'So, you just have to go to that party and put on your best winning smile and play nice. Leave the rest up to me.'

'You'll call me if you need anything though, won't you?'

'Of course, I'm not a fool,' winked Zoë. 'Now, let's get you frocked up.'

I looked like a movie star when Zoë had finished with me. She'd curled my long hair and it hung elegantly around my shoulders, softly cascading down my back like an old black and white movie star in the picture books. I wore a black slip of a dress, straps so thin they were only just holding the dress up, a low scooped neck line and a hem that only just covered the necessary bits. I wore black strappy stilettos with straps that wound up my ankle and looked dangerous. Zoë had given me dark smoky eyes and soft pink, glossy lips. I barely recognised myself in the bathroom mirror.

'Anna is going to have kittens when she sees you,' Zoë laughed.

'Are you sure about the dress? It looks way too short and slutty,' I protested.

'No!' Zoë exclaimed. 'I've seen the photos from these things and trust me, it's perfect,' she insisted.

Margie from security buzzed my intercom to let me know my car had arrived. There was no train or water taxi for an event like this. Cars were organised and paparazzi hid in the shadows in front of the Director's home so I was told, and I didn't even want to know what else happened. I'd have been much happier putting on my jeans and helping Zoë break Rachel out of captivity but I figured in my own way I was helping. I had to make them believe I was playing along, that Zoë was behaving. It had to work. I had to do whatever I could so that Zoë could rescue Rachel.

I hugged Zoë in front of the building. 'Good luck,' I whispered. 'Don't do anything crazy, you have to be okay, too,' I told her.

'I'll be careful, don't worry. Don't you be worrying about me tonight, you just enjoy the party and I'll see you in the morning,' she insisted.

'Promise?'

'I promise.'

Then she was gone. She headed back into the building to plot her rescue and the handsome, albeit ageing driver, held out his white-gloved hand to me.

CHAPTER 19

I slid into the smooth leather of the back seat and readied myself for what was ahead. I had no idea how Zoë's rescue was going to go but there was nothing at all I could do about it. I felt so useless going to a silly party when Zoë was risking her life to save Rachel. I couldn't even be sure she'd still be around when I got home and I hated that thought. I hated that that could happen while I was dancing and drinking and playing with the director's party favours.

The car drove over the big bridge and I watched the river to my left, quiet and dark. Ahead the bright lights of the city proper sparkled. We turned right before we headed into the city and pulled up almost to the front door of the Director's home. An attendant opened my door and I stepped out. Lights blinded me as they flashed from across the street, and I hurried towards the front door following all the others heading in the same direction.

One of the house staff from earlier in the day recognised me, smiled and waved me through, ticking my name off her sheet. I followed the flow of people down the hallway to the grand ball-room I'd helped set up earlier. As I walked into the room though, I had to wonder what had happened since I'd been there in the afternoon. It looked nothing like the room Anna and I had been watching over.

Soft pink curtains draped over the ceiling. Black and pink glass lanterns hung like teardrops giving out the softest glow of light. The sofas were where we'd left them but now soft, gauzy, black curtains surrounded each one, creating little bubbles of privacy. Finely dressed ladies gathered around tall tables spread through-out the room. Handsome men wandered between the tables offer-ing finger food and pretty coloured cocktails from the shiny silver trays they carried.

Entertainers, party favours, dressed in beautifully cut black suits with megawatt smiles worked the room. They were there to make the women feel beautiful and desirable, let them play however they chose. It was working too, going by the giggles and unnecessarily coquettish eye-batting looks the women were giv-ing them in return. The pointless ridiculousness of the game they were playing made me smirk.

From the other side of the dance floor, a sexy jazz tune filled the air, played by a massive orchestra full of incredibly handsome men who were no doubt as near impossible to book as the sports-men. The sound filled your soul with happiness and goodness. A couple of ladies had already selected some party favours, and were dancing seductively on the dance floor at the other end of the room, their flimsily covered bodies swaying in time with the music, playing close to the men whose hands were roaming freely over the women's bodies.

Concertina glass doors to the right of the dance floor led onto a rich green-grassed area dripping in fairy lights. More beautiful, skimpily dressed ladies, sipped Bellini's and laughed haughtily around more tall tables. White leather sofas edged the garden area ready for canoodling couples to play under the bright moonlight.

Zoë had been right about the dress code. Everyone wore tiny chic dresses leaving nothing to the imagination, accentuating all their assets and going by the guys groping the girls on the dance floor, the dresses provided easy access to usually well protected areas. The women were coiffed to perfection in their skimpy dresses and enormous stilettos that made their legs look longer than they were. They were comfortable in their bodies. They were comfortable with most of their bodies on show and when they saw something they liked, a party favour they'd like to play with, they brazenly walked up, grabbed them by the tie or through some other slightly sleazy pre-war time manoeuvre, and led them away from the crowds to a quiet corner or sofa to make the most of the free offerings.

I stood only steps inside the room, taking it all in, my senses overwhelmed. Anna spotted me almost immediately, a scowl covering what would be a pretty face if she stopped contorting it through jealousy. She walked over, looking me up and down as she did, as though I were something dirty someone had brought in on their shoe. She was about to say something and from the scowl twisting her beautiful face, I doubted it was anything nice but a guest tugged on her arm, whispering something in her ear. It must have been an important guest. Anna scowled at me a moment more and walked away with the other woman in tow.

I breathed a sigh of relief. I wasn't ready to confront her yet. I needed some more minutes to take it all in, find my footing. I didn't need Anna's crap. I was on edge enough as it was. I reached for a Bellini on a passing tray, sharing a smile with the very young man carrying the tray, perhaps an entertainer in training? Whoever he was, I was grateful for the drink and hoped the smile I gave him meant he might pass a little more regularly. I didn't care what Zoë and Stacey had said about limiting my intake. I didn't see how I was going to get through the night without the drinks to give me strength.

I slowly moved through the room, sipping my drink. People were filling the room, greeting friends, colleagues, acquaintances, crowding around the tall tables sipping their Bellini's, some with the forbidden blue cocktails. After their initial greetings, they appeared to pay no attention to each other, their eyes greedily scanning the room instead, looking for something more interesting and entertaining to play with than the friends and colleagues beside them.

The Director held court against a wall in the far corner, submerged in her own arrangement of sofas, surrounded by shirtless, beautiful men and her similarly important friends. She revelled in the attention the men were giving her as she sipped her Bellini. She saw me, held her glass aloft in a toast and smiled one of her fake smiles. I toasted her back as one of the men bent to kiss her and another reached between her legs. Holy shit, I thought, quickly averting my eyes to look anywhere but there. Seriously, does she have no sense of pride or privacy?

What kind of party was this?

Well, I knew. Stacey and Zoë had been very clear, but being confronted with the reality, having my face smacked with the reality of it, having to see it, was a whole other story. I refused to let them break me, if I was going to crumble, it wouldn't be here, it wouldn't be in front of them and it wouldn't be because the Director was getting felt up by a party favour.

Men and women were dancing intimately on the dance floor to the sexy jazz sounds. Their hands greedily groping, their mouths taking from each other, knees pushing suggestively between legs, hands reaching for parts that should be private, particularly in public. Watching them was no better than watching the Director being groped. Did nothing we'd been taught apply anymore?

I felt myself blending into the shadows against the wall, feeling like a fish out of water. This was not the place for me. This, I didn't even know what this was. But it didn't feel right. Everywhere I looked men and women were groping each other. Groups were now filling the sofas behind the gauzy curtains. Even the outside area draped in its pretty fairy lights was becoming a scene of unabashed debauchery.

Then I saw him. Moving across the floor towards me, his eyes locked on mine, his expression tight, giving away nothing. My heart leapt to my throat, my body pulsated with heat as he approached.

'Shit,' smirked Jack, shaking his head as he looked me up and down.

I blushed, turning away.

His finger tilted my face back to his, 'Na uh, I've waited too long to see that beautiful face, you're not turning it away from me now,' he demanded, his face only millimetres from mine, our mouths close to touching.

'What are you even doing here?' I asked him, breathless from the warmth of his breath on my mouth.

'I could ask you the same question!' he said, raising an eyebrow.

'The Director is watching me for some reason, so she's had me helping Anna, her assistant organise this shindig.'

'The Director is watching you? That's not good, Coté,' he said, concerned.

I shrugged. 'I've no idea why. But ever since Rachel and Leo got caught, it's been weird and it's me they seem to be watching like a hawk.'

'You're the weakest link,' he said.

'The weakest link to what?' I asked.

'Remember I said there's a theory about people living outside of the President's rule? They think the numbers are growing. People, important people, are getting worried, they're getting desperate. But still, no one knows where they are or how to find them. They've tried, they keep trying but these people are always one step ahead. So the rumour has it. Anyway, they think Rachel knew and that's where she was going with Leo, that maybe you'll lead them there. They probably figure if she mentioned anything to you, even something small, you'd be too stupid or too unaware to keep it to yourself for long. Or maybe a few those Bellini's would be enough to loosen your naïve tongue.'

'Well that's just insulting.'

He smiled. 'I know you're neither naïve or stupid. They'll learn.'

'Do you think any of it's real?' I asked him.

Before he could tell me there was a tap on his shoulder. We both looked to see Anna smirking back. 'I think I'll take this one,' she said, victoriously.

When neither of us moved, she added, 'I outrank her and I believe this is your first time on the Director's list. I get first choice and she gets what's left,' Anna spat, grabbing Jack's hand and leading him over to an oversized couch right in front of me, not even bothering to pull the curtains. I couldn't help but see as Anna slid her hand into his waistband and pulled him to her, taking his mouth as though she had the right.

My breath was stuck in my chest. I couldn't move. I was frozen, my eyes stuck on Jack and Anna as he followed protocol and did his job, his hands moving over her breasts, moving up the outside of her legs, between her legs. I felt my stomach turn, thought I was going to vomit as fury and rage took over my body.

I reached for another cocktail as a handsome underage waiter passed by and almost sculled it, closing my eyes, trying to get the vision of Anna and Jack out of my head, but nothing was ever going to erase those images from my brain. I had to move so I couldn't see them but my legs wouldn't work, the traitorous things were stuck to the spot, my masochistic eyes, frozen on the view in front of me.

'Are you alright?' asked a kind, dimpled man who was probably one of the most beautiful men I'd ever seen. He had neat black hair with a slight wave, tanned skin, chocolate brown eyes, kind eyes and the most adorable dimples when he smiled.

I nodded even though it wasn't even nearly true. Would never be true again. But what could I say? There was nothing I could say or do. Nothing. I was helpless again to what was going on around me, nothing but a pawn, a casualty of a perfect world.

'I saw the lovely Anna stole your toy, but why are you so sad when there's so many to choose from?' he asked softly.

I smiled, knowing it was game time, that if this man and his lovely dimples, had noticed my reaction to Anna stealing Jack, then so had everyone else.

Somehow, I had to pretend I didn't care. Somehow, I had to play this stupid game. 'Oh, it's not that at all. It's all just so overwhelming, it's my first party,' I said, giving him one of the smiles that made Jack roll his eyes in frustration. 'But, I think you and your lovely dimples might make everything better,' I said, batting my eyelids.

'Well,' he smiled, 'me and my dimples would be happy to oblige,' he winked. 'Shall we dance?' he suggested.

I nodded. Wanting to do anything but dance but seeing it was part of the game, I danced. I could see the Director over Mr Dimple's shoulder, watching me. I didn't resist when Mr Dimples pulled me close. If the Director wanted to watch, I'd just give her a show. I slid my body against his, following the lead of the other women on the dance floor.

'It seems we have an audience,' Mr Dimples whispered as we moved around the dance floor.

'I'm getting used to it,' I mumbled absently.

'Why exactly do you have an audience?' he asked, curiously.

I shrugged nonchalantly.

'Well, if they want to watch, we should give them something to see, hey?' he smiled, those dimples of his dancing, making me smile. At least I'd landed a fun guy, some of them looked pretty sleazy, pretty intent on just doing their job and moving onto the next woman. The thought turned my stomach.

Mr Dimples twirled me and I laughed. I couldn't help it. He swung me back to him, dipped and kissed me chastely before twirling me again. As he brought me back against him, he put his leg between mine, forcing me to move slow and sexy against him. That'd give The Director something to see.

I didn't dare look over to where Anna and Jack were. I focussed on the man in front of me, trying to replace the images of Jack and

Anna burnt into my brain, and the knowing of what was happening if I looked over this man's shoulder.

As the song we were dancing to ended and the music picked up pace with a pop song, my companion asked, 'Sit?'

I nodded and let him lead me to an empty sofa away from the throng of people. I could still see Jack kissing Anna's neck but at least they weren't in my direct eye line any more.

Mr Dimples started kissing my neck and sliding his hand up the outside of my leg. He whispered, 'Going by your reaction earlier, the fact I'm practically forcing you to enjoy my wicked ways and of course the fact that Jack is not attending to that woman with any gusto at all, I assume you're Courtney,' he whispered, continuing to do his job.

'I beg your pardon?' I asked.

'It's okay,' he said as he continued to do his thing. 'I'm friends with Jack. I'll look after you and make it look good but I won't do anything you don't want me to do.'

'What? I don't understand,' I said.

'Anyone who's watching will think you're having the time of your life, I promise.'

'How do you know who I am?' I whispered, suddenly filled with fear. Who had sent him, The Director? Anna?

'When you walked in and Jack nearly spat out his beer, I guessed,' he said, his hand massaging my breast.

'But how do you know I exist?' I asked, not wanting to say too much, not knowing who this guy was or who his alliances were truly with.

'I'm Jack's roommate. I know everything, but for goodness sake, please groan a little and pretend you're enjoying this,' he said, taking my mouth in his.

'I still don't understand why you're doing what you're doing,' I said, trailing my fingers along his mouth as though his lips were delectable and beautiful and I couldn't decide what I wanted them to do first.

'Jack's going to kill me for touching you but he knows I'll just make it look good. But if he saw another bloke even close to fucking you, I don't think he'd be able to help himself. He'd go mental and that'd be the end for both of you. I promise. I'm doing you both a favour, he's my mate, he's my family,' he said and with one word I understood, I trusted. He was Jack's Zoë and I breathed a sigh of relief and relaxed.

'Now, I'm going to have to reach up under your dress,' he said and I felt his hands move up the inside of my thighs resting on the sensitive softness right before reaching their destination. 'Now, if you wouldn't mind letting your head fall back and opening your mouth a little as though I'm working my magic, I'd really appreciate it,' he smiled.

I did exactly as he asked. Every time he moved his mouth or head or hand, I did as he asked. When we reached the point in proceedings where things would get hotter and heavier and finales were imminent, he stood, taking my hand, smirking, and led me to one of the elaborate boudoirs hidden behind the paintings on the wall. Small rooms with ornate beds covered with rich, luxurious bedding and with soft pink silk canopies draped across the top.

Mr Dimples led me to the bed, removing his suit jacket and draping it over the chair beside the bed. He removed his pants and crept over me.

Burying his head in my hair, he whispered, 'There are cameras in here to prevent people from doing and talking about things they shouldn't, so just make it look good, alright.'

'Ahuh,' I mumbled, groaning my best sexy groan.

He pushed my dress up as would have been the case if he'd been going to finish the job for real and as he slid his semi hard penis between my thighs, apologising, 'sorry, it's an automatic reaction, you're incredibly beautiful,' he winked as he rested his penis there but moved his body as though going about the regular motions.

I moaned and groaned and did all the things I'd done with the mystery blonde the week before, and then when the time was right, the necessary exclamations made, he sorted himself out and pulled my dress back down.

'That should keep the wolves away for the rest of the night,' he suggested, whispering in my ear.

'What do you mean?' I asked, pulling his face in front of mine so the cameras couldn't read my lips.

'It's our job to keep you happy and make sure every woman has an adequate conclusion to the evening. Yours has probably come a little earlier than most, who'll spend the night sampling the offerings before deciding who will do the concluding but you're new, to both the party scene and this whole fabulous world of ours, so you'll be excused for keeping things simple and getting it over with early.'

'Is this your first party?' I asked.

'No, third. I thought that's why Jack was invited but now I'm wondering if this whole thing wasn't a ploy. If they're watching him as carefully as you, keeping an eye on Rachel and Leo's friends, maybe even seeing how you two interact together, see if there's a rebellion brewing. Maybe I'm being watched too. We were both friends with Leo,' he said as though he were whispering sweet nothings. 'We all need to be careful and play the game,' he said.

'What am I expected to do now?' I asked

'Have a rest. Have a cocktail. Talk to some people. Have another dance. Make sure you thank the Director and when she's otherwise occupied, when Anna is otherwise occupied, slip out, but make sure you're not seen. They'll just think you've disappeared with another guy. But make sure you don't go home until a respectable time, otherwise, if you're being watched, security will be reporting back and if they find out you left such an event early, they'll want to know why.'

I nodded.

He stood, reaching for my hand, playfully pulling me off the bed and led me back into the ballroom. 'We are here for your pleasure and entertainment, milady,' he said, bowing and kissing my hand. Then he whispered, 'Just play along, you get into trouble, come find me,' he said, before kissing my hand again. 'I have to go,' he said, kissing me long and hard. 'Sorry, we're being watched,' he whispered close to my ear. Stay here for a few minutes as though catching your breath, have a cocktail and then dance with someone,' he said, trailing his finger across my collar bone and then between my breasts. 'Will you be okay?' he asked.

I noticed then the Director watching me with Anna by her side. They were the least discreet people I had ever seen, so I kissed Jack's friend as though he was Jack, moved my hands over his body as though it was Jack's and then walked away, picking another cocktail off a passing tray, leaving Mr Dimples to go and find someone else to play with.

I stood against the wall sipping a cocktail, doing my best to keep a smirk on my face, watching the world before me. I took a bite-sized piece of bruschetta from the tray of a passing waiter and then a meatball on the end of a toothpick from another.

I sipped my cocktail as slowly as I could, wondering how Zoë was getting on, praying she was alright, that Rachel was alright, that Zoë had some idea of what she was doing.

The hairs on the back of my neck prickled. They were still watching. I didn't have to look up to know it was the Director. I placed my empty glass on a passing tray then reached into the fray of roaming men and selected the first one my hand found, leading him to the dance floor. If the Director wanted me to play her stupid game, I'd play. For Jack. For Zoë and Rachel, I'd play.

This one didn't know Jack, not that I asked but by the vigour with which he pawed at me and kissed my neck, I knew he was doing his job right. As if things weren't bad enough, I looked up and found a smirking Anna gyrating nearby against a furious Jack. His face looked like it might explode as my dance partner slid his hand up my thigh and I faked the appropriate facial expressions.

When the song was over, I offered the man my hand. He kissed it as was their way and I excused myself.

I picked a pink cocktail off a passing tray, ignoring the blue ones that Stacey had warned would make me look like a child after an ice block, they were the Director's way of testing who was worthy, she said. It was much stronger than the Bellini's and much needed if I was going to keep up this charade. The liquor coursing through my veins, gave me courage. While I was full of courage, I thought it was time to go over and thank the Director.

She looked up from her loyal horde of men and friends as I approached. 'Courtney, dear,' she cooed as though we were the closest of companions.

'Christina,' I cooed back. 'Thank you so much for the invitation, I'm truly honoured,' I said, squatting to air kiss the Director on each cheek while she barely stretched up from her reclining position.

'You're very welcome, dear. Are you having a lovely time?' she asked, an eyebrow raised.

'Oh yes,' I gushed. 'I never knew such beautiful parties could even exist. It really is a wonderful party,' I said.

'I saw you've already made good on the party favours,' the Director smiled.

I hung my head as though sheepish. 'I did. My head is still spinning from all that's on offer,' I smiled.

'Well, I'm glad you're enjoying yourself,' the Director said.

'Well, well,' cooed Anna joining us with her arm linked through Jack's as though she owned him and was never letting him go. Why didn't she have to play by the rules and sample everything on offer? But I knew it was a ploy to try and rile me or Jack, or both, and Anna looked like she was really going to bust a vein from the effort. 'How was your little visit to the boudoir?' Anna asked.

'Sensational,' I gushed with a smile, ignoring the pained look on Jack's face.

'And how's your friend, Zoë? What's she up to tonight while you're here enjoying yourself?' Anna asked.

'I don't know. Why?' I asked, wondering why on earth Anna would care what Zoë was doing.

Anna leaned forward as though to share a secret. 'You didn't tell her about what you saw on my tablet now, did you?' she smirked.

'I didn't see anything to tell of,' I smiled, my stomach dropping like lead as realisation dawned on me. I suddenly realised what had happened. It was a setup, the whole thing. They'd used me to bait Zoë, knowing exactly what would happen. They knew I'd tell her what I saw and they knew exactly what Zoë would do with the information, that she'd try to rescue Rachel while she thought everyone else was preoccupied with the Director's party.

I looked from the Director to Anna and smiled, 'Well, I see you both have party favours of your own, so I'll let you get back to it. I see one over in the corner I wouldn't mind playing with,' I smirked. Then I looked at Anna, 'Oh you'll have a fun ride with this one, enjoy,' I winked as though I wasn't about to hurl all over her bloody stilettos from the idea but playing the part I knew I needed to play.

It seemed neither the Director nor Anna had much to say to that. The Director managed a 'have a lovely night, dear,' as I sauntered off, just as I imagined Stacey would saunter, as though she owned the world and I headed to a blonde in the corner.

I could hardly breathe as I let the blonde kiss my neck and run his hands over my body but not because he was touching me, I barely noticed he was there at all, I could only think of Zoë. How was I going to get a message to her to abort the whole plan? Let her know that Anna had set us up. I had to do something. I had to stop her.

Jack's friend, Mr Dimples was passing so I reached for his hand, pulling him towards me. He raised his eyebrows at me as though asking if I was sure. I already had a man draped over me, after all, but it wasn't an uncommon circumstance I noticed as some women allowed themselves to be tantalised by more than one party favour at a time. I'd even seen one of the Director's friends disappear into a boudoir with two men.

Jack's friend nuzzled my ear, whispering, 'Are you okay?'

'No,' I whispered back. 'They set a trap, for Zoë,' I told him. 'I have to get word to her.'

I looked over his shoulder and saw Anna going into a boudoir with Jack, with a smirk on her face as she looked in my direction. I knew better than to give a reaction so kissed the man that had been nuzzling my neck instead.

'Don't think about it, I've got it,' Jack's friend told me.

I looked at him questioningly.

'I promised Ryan before he was shipped down south I'd keep an eye on her. I've got it,' he insisted. 'I'll go to the men's and make a call. I know a guy headed to her building tonight, I'll see if he can stop by.'

'Thanks,' I said, kissing him.

Jack's friend left, I thanked the man who had been slobbering all over me and went to get a cocktail. I stood by the door opening onto the beautiful patio but I didn't dare go out there while the Director was watching me.

I was slipping away, nervously awaiting the return of Mr Dimples. Finally, he passed by and whispered, 'sorry, she wasn't there,' then he kept walking, straight up to a beautiful blonde who'd been eyeing him.

I let another man flirt with me until I finally saw the Director go into a boudoir with her harem of men in tow. I thought this might be my only chance with both the Director and Anna indisposed, so I excused myself and slipped out onto the patio. Everyone was busy doing their own thing under the stars and it wasn't hard for me to slowly disappear into the shadows, then the bushes and out the other side.

I took off my shoes and ran down the bank to the edge of the river, quickly slipping into the shadows under the big bridge.

Walking around the river would take twice as long to get home than if I walked across the bridge but it was the safest way. No one could know I'd left the party early, and I had to get to the other side and find Zoë. I didn't even know where Zoë had gone and if she wasn't home then what was I going to do, anyway? But I had to do something.

When I finally reached the other side of the big bridge, my legs hurting, my feet scratched and sore, I stopped in its shadows to rest, think. I couldn't go to my own home for another few hours, so I had to think of how to find Zoë without going into our building. I went to go sit on the ledge I'd last occupied with Jack but then stopped as something moved in the shadows.

'Hello?' I called uncertainly, fear rippling through my crackling voice.

'Courtney?' whispered the voice in return.

'Zoë? Is that you?'

'Quickly, get up here,' she demanded.

'What's going on?' I asked when I reached Zoë shrinking into the shadows like a ghost.

'I was being followed, that's what. It was a set up. They used you to set me up,' she said.

'I know.'

'What? You knew?' she spat.

'Just now, about an hour ago, I figured it out. I came looking for you.'

'You left the party before it was over? Did anyone see you leave?'

'I don't think so. The Director and Anna had gone into the boudoirs.'

'The boudoirs? They're real?'

285

'Very,' I said.

'You went in one, didn't you?'

'Only for show. Jack was there and Anna was all over him. They are playing us Zoë and I don't know why,' I told her.

'Because Rachel knew things,' Zoë said

'So Jack said.'

'He did?'

'Yes, but not a lot of details about what and I sure as hell don't know what she knew,' I grumbled

'Of course not. But they think I do,' she confessed.

'Do you?'

'No. Well, not really. Sort of. But it was all rumour anyway, no one even knows if any of it's real.'

'The communities that don't live by the President's rule?' I asked.

'Yes.'

'What are we going to do?'

'I don't know. We still have to rescue Rachel. I just don't know how.'

'We?'

'Hmph,' sulked Zoë.

We passed the time talking about the party. 'You wouldn't believe these people if I told you,' I told her. 'Seriously, I just can't wait to get home and wash all the bloody slobber off me. How do they find that a turn on? How is any of it sexy?'

'I don't know,' laughed Zoë. 'I think really they all do it for show too, to prove their loyalty to the President. There's a rumour that Christina and more than one or two other highly placed elite have contraband men in their basements and they just hire in the hordes of men to deflect suspicion.'

'Are you serious? How do they manage that?'

'They say the men have committed a crime, have them shipped somewhere far away but intercept the transport vans and steal them back for themselves and keep them in the basement.'

'That sounds rather barbaric and inhumane,' I said.

'It might well be, but it's better than sharing or being split up and having the man you love sent to the other side of the country and never seeing them again.'

'So, you're saying these aren't just men they fancy but men they've fallen in love with?'

'Of course. Why else would they risk hiding contraband men? Who knows what else they have hidden down there. The Director went through a phase of wearing really baggy dresses and disappearing for weeks at a time. Rosie joked she had a seed planted in her but we'd all laughed. It wasn't possible with the implants in our arms. But you know, I don't know anymore. All I know is I know nothing and anything is possible.'

'But,' I said, thinking, taking it all in, my brain ticking over. 'That also means there's a way to intercept the transport buses. How do you think they manage it?'

'Well, for them it's easy. They have power and money. They can do as they please because they can ruin a person's life with the click of a finger or a single accusation.'

'Right,' I said. 'So how can we intercept the transport bus? Aren't we some sort of powerful women in this region, controllers of entertainers and all that?' I asked.

Zoë was about to answer when we heard voices. 'Shhh...' whispered Zoë as though I hadn't heard them too.

They were male voices and it took a minute before they came under the bridge. Before they became submerged in the shadows, the light reflected off the water catching their faces just for a second. I was off our perch before Zoë could grab me and I nearly slipped, racing down the rocks as I ran, smacking into Jack's arms.

Jack's arms wrapped around me even before he could have fully comprehended what was happening, then he was pulling me to him, burying his face in my hair.

'Hey, hey,' he soothed as I sobbed from the sheer relief of seeing him. 'Are you okay?' he asked, concerned, holding me at arm's length to check.

'I'm okay,' I smiled. 'I'm okay now,' I clarified.

Zoë climbed down the rocky descent a little more carefully and said, 'Hey,' to Jack and his friend.

'You must be Zoë,' Jack's friend said. 'You're far more beautiful in person than Ryan said, he was definitely playing it down,' he smiled, shaking her hand.

'Ryan?' she asked.

'I'm Seth. Ryan was my roommate. I promised I'd keep an eye on you. I have, kept tabs through the guys. Just wish I could let Ryan know you were okay.'

Zoë nodded, smiled tightly, sadly. 'What are you guys doing here?' Zoë asked.

'Hoping to find you two,' said Jack. 'Or at least Coté. Seth told her not to go home until an appropriate time and I hoped this is where she'd go,' he said, pulling me to him and kissing the top of my head.

'We're very glad to see you, though,' Seth said to Zoë. 'When Courtney told me you'd been set up, I thought you were gone for sure. How did you end up here?' he asked.

'I can spot a tail when I see one, so I didn't get any further than the train, waited for everyone to get on board then rummaged through my bag, sighed as though I'd left something at home, and jumped off right before it departed so they couldn't follow me off. So just to be safe, I've been hanging out here killing time, until Courtney showed up. What are you guys doing here? The party can't be over yet? Besides, don't you all get shipped back to La Ferme like cattle after one of those shindigs?' she asked.

'Our shift was up, we were being replaced by fresh faces and we needed a run,' Jack said, his hand indicating their running gear. 'A lot of us run or hit the gym after such an event, it helps clear our heads and keep us away from the bottle.'

'I can imagine,' Zoë said, shaking her head. 'Ryan hated those things, made him sick to his stomach,' she said.

'That they do,' Jack and Seth agreed as Jack pulled me a bit closer.

'So, what now?' asked Seth.

'Not sure,' Zoë said. 'Any ideas? Courtney thinks we can intercept the bus transfer. You've all heard the rumours that the Director of La Ferme and some of the President's cohorts intercept the buses and steal their beloveds and hide them in their basements, right? Well, Courtney here thinks we can do something similar.'

'She mightn't be altogether wrong,' Seth said. 'If they're in fact shipping them out of town, then they'll have to use the trains, right? They're not going to bus them for two days to the other side of the country. That's just ridiculous. And I've seen them transporting prisoners, a bunch at a time by train. They've gotten cocky, so usually only have one or two guards. If we can somehow be on the train at the right time, then maybe, just maybe there's a way.'

'We need to know where they're being sent,' Jack said.

'The document Courtney saw said Rach was being sent to Kangaroo Island tomorrow.'

'But seeing it was a setup, who's to say the destination and day aren't also fake?' I suggested

'Courtney's right,' Seth agreed. 'There's not even a train going south on Sundays. It goes Monday, Wednesday and Friday,' he said.

'How do you know that?' Zoë asked.

'I had a few dates with a scheduler from the railways. The maps and schedules are on the walls all over her apartment,' he smiled.

'Well, how handy for us,' Zoë smiled.

'Also handy,' Seth started. 'Is it's the same train that goes past the bay. Any chance you have some leave days owing?'

'Trish has been insisting I take a break for ages. Ever since Ryan left but it was easier if I just kept working. So I think I could manage a few days,' she confirmed.

'Excellent. If we plan a nice little getaway then we'll have the perfect excuse to be on the train and we jump, taking Rachel and Leo with us in the hinterland before the train gets to the Bay. There's another train in the afternoon, that'll take us to the Bay where we can spend the rest of the week lying on the beach while Rachel and Leo run free.'

'And what happens in the meantime when they realise both Rachel and Leo are gone and so are we?'

'She has a point, as soon as they realise they're gone, they'll stop the train and do a count,' Jack said.

'So, we separate Rachel and Leo from their guards, push them off the train in the hinterlands and we stay on and continue to the beach as though nothing has happened?'

'That's better,' winked Seth. 'Unless you want to be travelling down south yourself?' he suggested.

She shrugged, sadness clouding her face. 'Who's to say he's even still there, and if I was on the run there's no way I could even contact him.'

Seth nodded. 'Well, we'll have to keep each other company, then,' he smiled kindly.

'So how am I supposed to book in a holiday by Monday without arousing suspicion?'.

'Are we sure it will be this Monday they're transported?' Seth asked. 'Has Dr Grace been out to the correctional farm yet to do the health checks? She always does that before prisoners are transported.'

'How do you know that?' Zoë asked. 'Actually, no, I don't want to know,' she smiled.

'Smart thinking,' Seth smirked.

'But no, I don't think so, but how would I know?' she asked.

'She always takes an assistant when she goes offsite, the same as when she goes to the breeder village,' he said.

'Then no, none of us have left the office,' Zoë confirmed.

'Then we have some time. Keep your ears to the ground and book me when you need,' Seth said.

'What about us?' I asked.

'No way babe, we're both being watched. I don't know what it is they think they know about us, or whether it was just the way I looked at you tonight that had that witch up in arms but we've caught their attention. We have to be on our best behaviour,' Jack insisted, taking my face in his hands. 'Promise me,' he begged.

'I promise,' I agreed, breathlessly as his mouth met mine.

Then Zoë dragged me away and I wondered if I'd ever see either of them again. My heart filled with heaviness but I didn't know what else I could do.

'He's pretty darn hot when he gets all protective, isn't he?' smirked Zoë when we started walking for home.

'He's pretty darn hot just breathing,' I smiled.

'He's right, though. You have to be on your best behaviour. Leave the rest to me and Seth. Now I know they're watching me, I can work with that but you just have to do your thing.'

'I know,' I said, sadly. I certainly didn't want it to be that way but I knew it had to be whether I liked it or not.

As we approached the dock, a water taxi arrived, piles of people, mostly drunk, were disembarking after their nights' out and we blended in with the masses as we made our way towards home.

'Will you come by for Sunday dinner tomorrow?' I asked Zoë as we approached our building and indulged in our last minutes of privacy

'I'd love to, but I better not, just in case. It'll be easier for you if things go wrong, if we're not seen together outside of work any-more,' Zoë suggested. 'And this way, I'll be sure not to accidentally give you any details.'

'Are you kidding?' I asked.

'It's just for the next week, or until everything's sorted, cer-tainly not forever. You're my family, it won't be forever,' she said, hugging me. 'Alright, you hang around here for a few minutes while I go in first,' she said walking away.

I didn't like the sinking feeling in my stomach. Zoë was making it up as she went. No one had any idea what was going to happen when they were on that train and the fear of what could happen rippled through my veins. I watched my friend walking away, holding onto the hope she'd given me, praying everything was going to be okay. It had to be okay. I couldn't do this without her.

'Courtney,' nodded Margie as she opened the door for me. 'How was the party?' she asked, her voice laced with unasked questions and ulterior motives.

I turned on the charm, the drama, the exuberance, 'Oh, it was just like a fairy tale. I've never seen anything so beautiful,' I smiled.

'Why didn't you return by car?' she asked suspiciously, looking over my shoulder as though a car would magically appear and I realised I'd totally forgotten I'd been chauffeured to the event.

I recovered quickly though telling Margie, 'I was riding so high and I knew I'd never sleep so I took a long walk home across the bridge. 'Really, it was the most wonderful night. My head is still spinning,' I smiled. 'Well, good night,' I said, walking towards the bay of lifts with my head held high like Stacey would do. I was fast understanding that people didn't question you so much if you behaved as though you were right, that you had the right, if you held your head high and your posture strong.

I lent in the corner of the lift, smiling as though I had a naughty secret, remembering the cameras. But once I was in the safety of my apartment, I finally exhaled, emptied a bottle of wine into a glass, drank, showered, washing off the slobber and grime and disgustingness of the night until my skin was pink and stung then got ready for bed.

CHAPTER 20

I didn't feel like seeing outside on Sunday. I just wanted to close the blinds and lie on the couch in front of the vision screen. I was tired, exhausted, emotionally ripped to shreds. I'd survived the Director's party but only just. It had taken so much out of me to play that game, to see Jack with Anna, to know what they did in the boudoir to have those men slobber on me.

It took away something I couldn't put back and I'd only just started recovering from the blonde I'd had to allow into my bed. It was too much and I just couldn't face the world. I couldn't face myself. I don't know how Jack was still able to kiss me but he had last night, and I didn't know if or when he'd ever kiss me again.

I searched the cupboards. All of them. I hunted in the backs of the pantry, even rummaged through the storage cupboards in the dining room that housed my ironing board and cleaning supplies. Not a single bottle of wine remained. Zoë had taken them all.

I considered going to the shop to buy more. It wasn't far. It'd be easy, no one could stop me. But it meant I'd have to shower, dress, leave the apartment and look at people, have them look at me and I couldn't stand the thought of it. I couldn't have them see me, have them know who I'd become. Staying inside was the only way I could regain my strength, any semblance of who I was.

I'd never really be the same. I'd been irrevocably altered by so many things, Jack, Rachel, the blonde guy, the party, all the slobber and game playing, all of it. I needed some time away from the world, to remember me, find the new version of me, whoever she is.

I took a giant, party-sized packet of potato chips out of the pantry, tucking them under my arm and reaching for the box of chocolate cereal puffs, a bowl, and getting a carton of milk out of the fridge, I took it all to the couch and alternated between the two as the afternoon progressed. I watched game show after game show, nice, easy, unthinking, unemotional entertainment. I wondered if Jack was watching them too, and I imagined him shouting answers at the screen. It was comforting.

I must have fallen asleep. I woke when heavy footsteps and shrill laughter passed by my front door, heading into a neighbour's apartment. Sunshine no longer shone through the sides of the drapes. It was night time. I was out of chips. I was thirsty. I unearthed a selection of chocolate in the pantry, some with nuts and some with nougat and some with biscuits and some just plain chocolate. I tucked a bottle of peach flavoured iced tea under my arm and returned to the couch.

Despite the sugar rush, or perhaps because of it, I fell asleep again, waking with a start when the sun stretched in, warming my face. My first, my only thought was what is the time? I stretched up, my brain still catching up with the rest of me and checked the time that glowed on the oven. Shoot! I was late.

I bounded off the couch and into the shower. 'Shit, shit, shit,' I mumbled to myself as the water beat down on me. It was the quickest shower I'd had in my life and I was dressed, my hair pulled back into a ponytail and walking out the door while scoffing a muesli bar in next to no time.

When I got to work I went to the pod for a coffee. They kept the best stuff there and I needed the good stuff today. I needed something to give me some cheer and filling my veins with caffeine was a pretty good start.

The girls were in the kitchenette making their own coffees. You could feel the excited buzz emanating from them across the room. Weekend gossip was often the order of the day for a Monday morning. I wondered what they'd all been up to. Not enough to ask. I wanted to avoid this morning's encounter and hide at my desk, but they were there and I was here and I needed the coffee. There was no turning back now, so I just had to listen with as much cheer as I could muster.

'Oh, there you are,' Trish said when she saw me. 'You looked amazing, love, well done,' she gushed with a smile.

I nodded politely. 'Thanks,' I said, reaching for a mug, wondering what the hell Trish was talking about. I hadn't seen her Saturday night even though I knew all the execs had been there, somewhere, amongst the hundreds of other well connected, important society women.

'You haven't seen it, have you?' asked Rosie with a smile.

'Seen what?' I asked wearily.

'Yesterday's paper,' Jules said.

'No,' I said. 'I kind of camped out on the couch yesterday,' I told them, wondering. 'What's in the paper?' I asked.

'You, silly,' laughed Tess.

'Me?' I stammered. What on earth was I doing in the Sunday paper? Surely there were other more interesting people at the party to photograph for their newspapers?

'I'll find you a copy, you have to see it,' insisted Rosie.

'Thanks,' I said. 'Well, I better get out to the front,' I said, taking my fresh, steaming coffee with me.

People came in and out all morning gushing about how fabulous I looked. Customers came in for health checks with Dr Grace and watched me with peculiar expressions from the visitors' chairs against the walls.

I returned to the pod at lunch, grateful to escape the fuss and the probing looks from the masses. How did the drama and music people stand it? How did they not want to shrivel under the gazes, the admiring ones, the scowls of jealousy, all of them? I just wanted to scream at them to stop looking at me, just stop.

I looked forward to seeing Zoë at lunch. I already missed her. I could certainly use her wisdom. She'd make sense of it all. She'd tell the gawkers to bugger off. She'd make it right, make me feel right. But when I arrived in the pod, she wasn't on the sofa eating or at her desk working. *She had errands to run,* Jules said.

'Here, I found one. There was a stray copy of yesterday's paper in the nest common room,' Rosie said, handing me a crumpled newspaper already opened to a page of coloured photographs.

There were a lot of photos. An array of photos of all different sizes filled the first couple of pages with captions below them saying who the women were with witty one liners about them or what they were wearing. Two pages of full-length colour photos followed with names and critiques of their dresses. And there I was, amongst the big names, important women everyone knew, a full length shot showing just how miniscule my dress was and how long my legs were. I don't even know how they'd gotten the shot. The caption and critique underneath read, 'Up and coming IT girl from La Ferme wows the crowds in an amazing Crystal LBD that shows why this girl is one to watch.'

'Wow,' I said, unable to muster up any other words.

'It looks fantastic. You look amazing,' Rosie insisted.

'Thanks,' I said, quietly accepting the compliment.

'Alright, well, I gotta go. Somehow, I've been drafted to be Dr Grace's bloody bag carrier to an offsite health check on Wednesday, apparently the new girl's now too important for such menial work,' she joked, nudging me. 'Anyway, I have a lot of work to do before I go so best get on with it,' Rosie said, removing the cling film from her sandwich to take it and eat at her desk.

'Well thanks for tracking down a copy for me,' I said, handing back the paper, still struggling to comprehend I was in there beside the Director, even Anna had only featured in one of the small pictures with a witty one liner. Anna was really going to hate me now, I groaned inside.

'Oh, keep it, it's yours,' Rosie smiled.

'Thanks.' I had to find Zoë. I had to tell her about Rosie's offsite. She had to be going to the correctional farm. It had to be. The timing was too perfect.

I didn't see Zoë all day. I kept trying to run into her by making all my coffees in the pod. But she was always away from her desk. I didn't know if anyone was listening into my phone calls or reading my emails, so I couldn't give her the information that way. Who knew how closely they were paying attention now. I just had to wait for my chance to come and hope it came soon.

As I was packing up to leave at the end of the day, I finally crossed paths with Zoë as we were leaving the building. I checked no one else was around and as though I was saying nothing more than how are you going, I mumbled, 'Dr Grace is taking Rosie to an offsite on Wednesday.'

'Thanks,' Zoë replied. 'I'll match the timing against the train schedule that magically appeared under my door last night,' she said, laughing as though we shared a joke, then she turned left towards the train station and I headed for the cooking school.

'Well, well,' grumbled Pauline as I stood next to her at our usual bench. 'Can't believe you actually showed up.'

'Sorry,' I whispered, ignoring the stares and mumbles coming from our classmates. I had hoped she didn't read the paper, but clearly, she did, as did the rest of our classmates.

'Why? Why would you lie?' she asked, looking at me with a face full of hurt.

'Because of this,' I said, indicating the others whispering around us. *I told you it was her,* I heard someone say. 'Because people treat me differently when they find out I work at La Ferme. Even the poor girl who serves me coffee on Saturdays was afraid to speak to me after she found out where I worked. I just wanted to be me.'

Pauline shrugged, 'I suppose that makes some sense,' she said as the instructor began handing out our recipe sheets for the night.

The instructor clearly didn't read the paper or perhaps she just didn't associate that version with the version of ordinary that stood before her in a pink stripy apron ready to learn how to cook whatever delicacy she had in mind for tonight. Something with potatoes and carrots going by the supplies laid out on the bench.

'I really am sorry,' I said to Pauline.

'Fine,' she eventually smiled. 'Was everything else the real you?'

'Yep, that was all me,'

'Then alright,' she smiled properly. 'I guess we can still be friends, then.'

'Good,' I smiled, picking up the recipe.

We left a couple of hours later with our leftover containers filled with lamb curry and cupcakes. When we got to the pub I handed Pauline a cupcake I'd made for her with a yellow sun on the top. 'For you,' I smiled.

She smiled gratefully, 'Thanks.'

We ordered a couple of ciders and found an empty table.

'Shouldn't you be drinking something fancier?' she asked.

I shrugged. She laughed. And that was it. We were just two friends having a laugh at the end of the day.

As we were parting ways she said, 'I'm having a party on Friday, for my birthday, will you come?' she asked.

I hesitated for a minute.

'It's okay if you can't. I know there are rules.'

'No, no, it's not that at all,' I insisted.

'Oh, you have a date?' she asked.

'Not yet,' I said. 'I was just thinking I might have something else on but no, I'm sure I don't. I would love to come,' I said.

'You know I was inviting you anyway, before I saw you in the paper. It's not because of where you work,' she clarified.

I laughed. 'I know,' I said, hugging her. 'I'll see you Friday,' I said, and left to get the water taxi home.

Life was quiet without Zoë. Without late night runs to the bridge to look forward to. I bought groceries on the way home from work on Tuesday and despite Zoë's warnings about my drinking too much, I bought a few bottles of wine.

Back in the quiet of my apartment, I ate leftover curry and a cupcake and sat on the stool with a glass of wine staring at my very yellow canvas trying to think of what I could do with it. I have no idea how long I stared at it, long enough to drink half a bottle of wine. I decided to add some pink splotches, left it at that and went to bed.

Wednesday, the phones started getting busy as the weekend loomed and everyone started booking in their dates. There was no basketball to look forward to. Zoë was still steering clear of me, so she'd talked Jules into going with her. So instead of watching the handsome men run around the court and eat nachos and drink lovely fizzy champagne while having my hand kissed by the beautiful man with coffee-coloured skin and dreadlocks, I ate pizza and watched the game on the vision screen, until I'd consumed the rest of the open bottle of wine from the night before and was sleepy enough to turn out the lights without unwanted pictures filling my head.

I vowed to make the most of yoga on Thursday night after a busy day booking everyone's entertainment. But once I was there and trying to stand on one foot like a flamingo with my hands in prayer position, I couldn't concentrate. My head was too full, too distracted. The instructor was getting cross as I kept falling out of position with accompanying little squeals of surprise and disrupting everyone. People began to whisper their frustrations on top of the gossiping they'd done when I walked in. I left and vowed never to return. I quickly changed back into my work clothes and went to meet Stacey at Ora's for dinner.

We took a walk along the riverbank after dinner, just chatting about things, the basketball, how La Ferme was treating me and more so, Stacey was getting as much goss as she possibly could about the party. 'Was it as amazing as everyone says?' she gushed, starry eyed.

'It was,' I told her, smiling at her enthusiasm and gave her as many of the polite details as I could to satisfy her curiosity.

We passed a boutique on the way back to my apartment and with some fake cheer and merriment I bought a new dress and a work suit. By the time the shop assistant handed the bag over the counter, I'd already forgotten what I'd bought. It didn't really matter anyway. It was just stuff. Part of this silly game.

When we reached my building, Stacey pulled me in for a hug. 'You keep laying low and stay out of everyone's line of sight, alright?' she whispered.

I wanted to talk more, ask her questions. What did she mean? What had she heard? But then Margie was standing at the door, watching us, opening the door, absently greeting another tenant but paying us too much attention. I smiled brightly, nodded and thanked Stacey for dinner and help shopping and we went our separate ways.

Something was off in my apartment. I felt it as soon as I closed the door. The energy had changed somehow. The hairs on my neck prickled. I casually wandered through each of the rooms, opening cupboards and drawers, but nothing appeared out of place. My washing basket was empty, the clothes I'd worn over the weekend now hanging in my wardrobe. The cleaning lady, I realised, feeling silly. She'd been in and done my washing and what not. That was all. Geez, I thought, how paranoid was I becoming?

I ate a leftover cupcake and had a glass of wine on the balcony. I couldn't help thinking about what Stacey had said. I desperately wished I could have spoken to her some more about whatever she'd heard. Why hadn't she said anything over dinner? I wondered, absently pouring myself another glass of wine. There'd been plenty of time to discuss any concerns she had but she'd said nothing, not even a hint that she knew something. No, she'd waited until no one could see her face, until no one could hear her words or read her lips.

'Shit,' I said out loud. How closely were they watching? Were they really everywhere, eavesdropping on my conversations with everyone? How far would they actually go to keep tabs on me and my friends? To find out what they thought I knew? I went back into the kitchen, putting the wine away. I needed my wits. I needed all my brain cells in perfect working order.

I switched on the kettle and went about making some peppermint tea. While I waited for the kettle to boil, I gazed around, thinking, wondering, how far would they really go? *What was it Rachel knew that was so important to everyone that they'd have me, the newbie, fresh off the train, under such scrutiny, that they'd listen in to everything I said and watch everything I did?*

As I glanced around, something shiny glinted in the air-conditioning vent, catching my eye. I looked away, pouring hot water onto my tea leaves. What was that? My brain rumbled like a runaway train. What would be in the vent? A listening device? A camera? Really? Would they do that? Could they do that? Surely, they wouldn't have put cameras in my apartment? Surely they wouldn't have gone that far? Would they? Did they really think I knew enough to go to that much effort? I glanced back, hoping it had just been my eyes playing tricks on me, maybe it had always been there but no, I'd have seen the light bounce off that before. Was it my cleaning lady? Or was her visit today just a convenience? Then my heart pounded as I wondered, how long it had actually been there?

'It's your imagination,' I tried telling myself. It had to be, surely. But I knew it wasn't. Deep inside I knew the truth. The cleaning lady had been here before and she hadn't changed the feel of my apartment, she hadn't sent the hairs on the back of my neck prickling before.

I wondered how many there were? I wanted to check but I didn't want whoever was watching me to know I'd seen it, that I knew what they'd done. I did the only thing that was safe to do. I put on appropriate pyjamas and went to bed. They couldn't see inside my thoughts. As I closed my eyes, I didn't dare imagine how long those cameras had been there or how much they'd seen.

CHAPTER 21

F eeling overexposed with nowhere to hide, I left the apartment early in the morning. I kept telling myself the camera was just my imagination but the idea of it still creeped me out and I couldn't stay in there a second longer than I had to. The sun was already high and people were beginning their days as I walked to the local café. The girl who served me my Saturday coffee smiled when she saw me.

'We don't normally get to see you on a weekday,' she said. 'I saw you in the paper. You looked amazing,' she gushed.

'Thank you, but aren't we all, isn't that how we're designed?' I commented then smiled brightly because I liked her and I didn't want to cause her any concern with my snide remark. She was nice. I hated that there was this societal divide between our lives. I'm sure I would have enjoyed having a coffee and a casual banter with her, listening to her view on our crazy, messed up world.

Instead of a chat, I could only thank her for her compliment and order coffee and eggs before finding a table outside. It felt safer at the small table on the patio, watching the passers-by than it did in my own apartment but now as I watched the passers-by, people chatting at the other tables, many glancing in my direction as they recognised me from the paper, I wondered who was watching. Who was listening? Not that there was anything to listen to while I waited alone for my breakfast but if Stacey had been afraid to talk too over dinner she must have known they were listening. Somewhere. Somehow.

My friendly waitress brought me my breakfast. As she put everything on the table she dropped some sugar packets.

'Shoot, I'm so sorry,' she apologised profusely, bending down to collect them. 'There was a girl,' she whispered while slowly gathering the sugar packets. 'Asking about you. She wanted me to watch you, listen and report on stuff,' she told me.

'What girl?' I asked, absently stirring my coffee.

'Blonde, sort of tall, beautiful,' she said.

Well, that described half the women in the country. 'What did you tell her?'

'I told her we get very busy and my manager doesn't like me talking to customers, especially important ones. She told me to try anyway and gave me a phone number. But I wanted you to know about her and that I'd never use it.'

'Thanks,' I said as her boss called her back to the counter.

Great, so that's how they were getting information on me, listening in, they were following me, seeing where I went, paying people I came into contact with. Who else were they paying? My yoga instructor? The people at the cooking school? Pauline? Bree at the paint supplies shop? They could have recruited anyone, my beautician, the driver of the water taxi. I adjusted my sunglasses, determined not to crumble under their scrutiny, under their oppression. I knew nothing anyway, so they were wasting their time. They'd be very disappointed with the meagre scraps I had for them.

When I arrived at the office, Trish was behind my desk. 'Oh, there you are,' she smiled as though I'd been missing or was late instead of ten minutes early.

'Hi Trish, what's up,' I said, surprised to find her there.

'Nothing much. Zoë's taking a long weekend, she's gone away to the beach or something, says she needs some sun and R&R with everything that's been going on and about time, too. I've been bugging her for a year or more to take some time off and get some sun. So I just wanted to let you know you were on your own today. Give Rosie or one of the girls a call if you get too stuck, but you should be fine.'

'Oh, okay, no problem,' I said, wanting to ask more questions but knew it was best if I didn't. Zoë had gone away for the weekend. No problem, I tried telling myself.

'So, how's it all going?' Trish probed.

'Great,' I replied.

'Excellent,' Trish answered. 'You getting out and about, finding things to do in your spare time?'

'Absolutely. I've been learning to cook, doing some yoga and painting, it's been great,' I told her.

'Very good. I'll leave you to it, then. I'm around if you need me,' she said with nothing much else to be said and left me to get on with my day.

I maintained the required facial expression but inside my head was doing somersaults. So, this was it. Zoë and Seth were going to rescue Rachel and Leo. I mentally wished them every luck imaginable, because I knew the odds were against them, and we all needed them to succeed so Zoë could come home safe. She and Seth both and Rachel and Leo needed to be free.

There were no actual clocks in the room but I still heard the ticking. Tick, tick, tick, every second echoing through my body as I wondered what Zoë was doing, as I waited. For what I didn't know. Would I know when it was over? If they'd succeeded? How long would it take to hear any news? Would I hear or would I just see it on the weekend news, 'prisoners escape train,' as though just a side note to the frivolity of regular activities? Or would I have to wait until Zoë was back, going about her business as usual with a fresh suntanned glow?

The day went on as usual around me. I tried going with it as best I could, as though it was an ordinary day, trying not to think of Zoë and Rachel, Seth and Leo, all in harm's way. I took calls and made bookings and typed some things and sent some emails for Trish. All normal, everyday things and I did them with a smile, a 'so what my best friends saving the world and might get caught but it's all good,' kind of smile.

I went to the pod for lunch like normal and ate with Rosie, Tess and Jules. We talked about our weekend plans, which reminded me I was supposed to go to Pauline's birthday party after work. Shit, was this one of those things you took a date to? Or was that not something that happened in her group? Someone really needed to write the rules down. I asked the girls without giving too much away about the party. I certainly wasn't supposed to be accepting invitations from people like Pauline.

'Definitely,' they all agreed. 'You can't go to a party without a date,' they insisted.

I still wasn't sure they were right, sure dates weren't in the pay grades of people like Pauline, but I needed to book a date this weekend anyway, so figured it'd cover two birds and all and if I was the only one with a date, I'd just offer him up as a birthday gift. That was acceptable, right? I had access and discount and all that, what else would someone from La Ferme bring someone like Pauline?

Rosie thankfully changed the subject soon enough, suggesting a nice weekend market I might enjoy and gave me the details of the train to catch. She was right, it sounded great. But I didn't imagine I'd have the capacity for a market this weekend. I doubted I'd be able to do anything without my brain exploding until I knew Zoë was okay, but then I thought of that camera in my vent and wondered how many more were in my apartment, was there anywhere to hide? A day out at the market suddenly sounded like a great idea and it would show whoever was watching me, I wasn't worried about Zoë, that I was just going about my life as though nothing was out of the ordinary.

I told everyone about the cooking class I was taking to make it look like I had a full and healthy life without Zoë. Tess started telling us of some pasta sauce secrets she'd learnt from a class she'd taken a while ago. She was mid-sentence when the door to the pod flew open and the Director and Anna stormed in like an angry hive of bees set free.

'You,' the Director shouted, pointing at me. 'Trish's office. Now,' she spat, storming into Trish's office without bothering to knock, Anna scowling behind her.

'Shit! What did you do?' Jules asked in a whisper.

'Nothing,' I whispered, standing, my insides shaking, guessing it had something to do with Zoë and Rachel.

I slowly walked to Trish's office as though walking to my death, my stomach sinking in anticipation of what turmoil awaited.

'Hello,' I greeted everyone quietly as I took the only seat available and sat looking into the fuming faces of the Director, Trish and a smirking Anna. 'What's going on?' I asked.

'Oh, I think you know,' scoffed Anna.

'Enough,' Christina said. 'You, young lady, had better start talking. Where are they?'

'I'm sorry, where's who?' I asked innocently.

'Don't play dumb with me. Zoë. Rachel. The men. Where are they?' she demanded.

'Zoë's at the beach having a long weekend and Rachel, I don't know. I haven't seen her since that night we went dancing,' I told them.

The Director scoffed and snorted. 'You know more. I know you do. Come on, out with it. What was the plan? They have a cabin somewhere? What?'

'What are you talking about?' I asked, trying not to sound smart.

'Christina, I really don't think she knows,' Trish said.

'Knows what?' I asked. 'What is going on?'

Trish sighed. 'Rachel and her male companion have been in custody for breaking the unauthorised fraternisation rules. Guards were transferring them to detention centres today. They were on a train headed south. The man was to be transferred west once they arrived in Sydney and Rachel was to continue south but somewhere in the hinterlands they disappeared, as did Zoë and her date.'

'Zoë's gone?' I whispered.

'You really didn't know?' the Director asked.

'Oh, she knew,' Anna spat.

'What is your problem?' I demanded, too upset to mind my manners. 'What'd I ever do to you?'

Anna hmphed and turned her face away.

'Enough,' Christina insisted. 'Did Zoë mention anything, anything at all about what she was planning?'

'No. I haven't really seen her lately,' I said, grateful for the truth now my insides were reeling and my heart was breaking. She wasn't supposed to disappear, too. She and Seth were supposed to stay on the train. It wasn't supposed to turn out this way.

'Why is that?' asked Trish.

I shrugged. 'Just busy, I guess. I don't know,' I said, trying to make it sound like it was no big deal.

'What I want to know, is how she knew when Rachel was being transferred,' the Director asked, almost to no one.

'I'm still figuring out how to exist in this world. I'm sorry, I wouldn't even know where to begin to figure any of that out. I'm really sorry, I can't help you,' I told them.

'Are you? Really?' mumbled Anna.

'You really are a bitch, aren't you?' I said, unable to stop myself. Anna, on top of everything else, was just too much. 'I am nothing to you, no one. Why are you so mean to me?'

'Yes, why exactly?' asked the Director.

Anna refused to give a worthwhile answer, just shrugged and grumbled, 'I just don't like her, alright? And you can't say it's just a coincidence that all this trouble started right after she showed up?'

'What's that supposed to mean?' I asked.

'What exactly are you insinuating, Anna? Are you suggesting impropriety on Courtney's behalf?' Trish asked.

Anna shrugged. 'I think she likes one of the entertainers a little too much,' Anna smirked.

'Who?' I demanded as though the idea was ridiculous.

'Yeah, who?' asked Trish. 'She hasn't been here long enough to fancy anyone. She's only had a few dates for goodness sake.'

'And how many with one particular entertainer? It's not his fault. He doesn't get a say in where he goes or who books him, does he? No, it's her digging her grubby little mits into him, stalking him, mysteriously showing up wherever he is. And where exactly does she go on her midnight runs?'

'Who is she referring to?' asked Trish.

I shrugged. 'I saw one guy twice. He was my first. I lucky dipped him the first time and then the next night after dinner and too much sangria with Zoë and Rachel, Zoë booked him for me as a joke because I didn't tell her enough juicy details. I didn't even know he'd been booked until he arrived and I still don't know whose name he was booked to. Three guys rocked up. Zoë and Rachel took what they wanted and left me with one, eight, five, nine. I didn't mind, I was still new to the whole sex thing and he was nice to me.

'But I haven't seen him again. Well, I saw him at the Director's party and he said hello, asked how I was going because he knew I was fresh off the train but then Anna selected him and I found some others to play with. They were very nice too, thank you again for inviting me,' I said to the Director.

'You're welcome,' the Director said. 'I really don't think she's done anything improper,' she told Anna.

Anna hmphed again but said nothing else.

'Why do you even care, Anna? You don't fancy him yourself, do you?' asked Trish in my defence.

'Don't be ridiculous,' Anna scoffed with less venom than usual, her face turning just a little bit pink. 'What about the running?' she asked desperately.

'I like to run,' I said. 'It's how I clear my head. I've always done it. I ran late at night at the college too, it's quiet at night, peaceful. I don't see the problem.'

'You run at midnight, sometimes at two in the morning. Margie times you, you know,' she smirked.

'So?' I shrugged nonchalantly. 'I run to the bridge, rest for a few minutes. I like the quiet. Then I run home, same as I've always done,' I said.

'I don't think there's anything going on here, Anna,' the Director confirmed.

'I really think you need to lay off Courtney,' Trish said angrily.

'I'll deal with Anna,' Christina said. 'Alright, well it doesn't sound like you know anything useful so we're done here. If you hear anything though, you'd better be upfront and let Trish or myself know immediately. Protecting them won't do anyone any good,' she insisted. 'Meanwhile, I suppose you get to do your job and Zoë's, until a new booker can be recruited. Congratulations on your promotion,' the Director spat, stood and left with Anna scurrying behind her.

I looked at Trish dumbfounded, still taking it all in. Zoë was gone. I didn't want her job. I wanted Zoë back. I wanted everything to stay the same. Nothing was making sense anymore and I didn't even have Jack to help make sense of it all. I was alone. I had no one.

'Are you alright?' Trish asked.

'Yeah, sure. I just can't believe Zoë's gone, that she would do that,' I said.

'I know. It was a bloody stupid thing for her to do. But like I said, sometimes it all gets too much for some people, sometimes they get more emotionally invested than they're supposed to and I guess for Zoë, losing Rachel was just too much,' She said sadly, disappointed.

I shrugged, 'I guess. So, what do you want me to do?' I asked.

'Just stay out the front for now. If I need some help, I'll let you know. But you'll have to take on Zoë's out of hours shifts on the roster. I think she was working tomorrow. I know it's late notice but you'll need to step into that shift.'

'Sure, no worries,' I smiled politely. 'I'll be at my desk if you need me.'

I resisted the urge to slump at my desk. No matter how worried I was, I had to keep a smile on my face and behave as though everything was fine, as though nothing had happened, as though my best friend hadn't ditched me in this giant pile of crap. But someone somewhere was watching me, watching everything I did. I now knew Anna was one of those people, but was she the only one? Did it stop with her? Whoever was watching I had to show them they weren't going to win. I opened the booking screen and booked a lucky dip date to take to Pauline's party. If it wasn't the done thing in her circle of friends then I'd be the best gift giver on the planet. To anyone spying on me, it looked like I was just going about my business as usual, unaffected by Zoë leaving me.

CHAPTER 22

Pauline lived in one of the older, pre-war apartment buildings. A five-story red brick square building. Only the red bricks remained on the ground floor, for character no doubt. Four stories of duck egg blue render sat on top of the red bricks looking pretty as a picture. Planter boxes filled with produce hung at the base of the windows, and big solar panels glittered on top of the building amongst the lush greenery of whatever produce they were growing up there. It was a quarter of the height of my building and looked much cosier, much friendlier. I bet Pauline knew her neighbours. I'd still never actually seen mine.

There was no security in Pauline's building. I doubted she realised how lucky she was to not have a Margie watching her every move. I wondered what she'd think if she knew how jealous I was of her life. I pushed open the door and my handsome date and I walked through the vinyl laid lobby to the lift bay that only had one lift. It was probably a blessing there was one at all, considering she lived on the fifth floor. I didn't fancy walking up that many stairs in heels.

'Do you come to these buildings often?' I asked my date, one, four, nine, two, it took all my energy not to call him the bearded stud as we'd named him after he'd rattled Zoë's bones.

'Not often but I went to one down the road in my first quarter,' he said, guiding me by the small of my back as we stepped out of the lift and onto a hallway laid with cheap, serviceable carpet.

Pauline's door was ordinary and plain, non-descript, white. No wrist scanner to gain entry, just an old-style pin pad. I smiled apologetically to my date. I still wasn't sure if this was a date party but I'd needed to hire a date, none the less, just to have one in my calendar.

I doubted I'd have been able to focus on him one bit with all that was going on, so even though I'd rather wallowed and worried in my apartment, I was here, showing the Director and Anna and whoever else was watching, that it was business as usual, that I was completely unaffected by whatever had happened to Zoë and Rachel, Leo and Seth.

'Oh, you brought a date,' Pauline, smiled, trying not to look surprised when she opened the door wearing a tiara with a flashing happy birthday in place of diamantes.

I could see inside enough to see there were no men in there. 'For you,' I smiled. 'Happy birthday.'

'Really?' she gushed, her eyes wide with excitement. 'Oh my goodness, thank you,' she said hugging me.

'Of course,' I chuckled. 'What else would your friend from La Ferme bring?' I grinned before shrugging my apologies to my date when Pauline turned back to lead us into the room. He shrugged in return and smoothly switched his attentions to Pauline. She'd be pretty happy I was sure, if what Zoë said was anything to go by.

Pauline introduced me to an array of people who mostly watched me suspiciously. The apartment wasn't too unlike mine, open plan living space, galley kitchen to the right beside the dining room, the living room in front, bedrooms and bath beyond. It was all just a little smaller, no stone counter tops, no leather, no balcony but there big windows that showed the city buildings.

'Oh, and this is my flatmate, Kylie,' Pauline said introducing us and reminding how far apart our lives were.

'Hey, aren't you that new up and coming IT girl from La Ferme we saw in the paper?' Kylie asked, suspiciously.

Everyone turned to look as though suddenly realising who I was, clearly, they hadn't even looked at me properly when I arrived. I guess that's what happened when you infiltrated existing friend groups. I'd been lucky to have found Zoë and Rachel, to have them welcome me so easily. I suddenly saw how hard it would have been without them. How hard it would now be without them.

I nodded because the girl, the flatmate, Kylie, along with all the others watching on, appeared to be waiting for confirmation. I smiled, held my head high and said, 'Yes, but don't believe all the hype you read in the paper.'

'Oh sure,' said Kylie doubtfully. She raised her eyebrows at Pauline as though I couldn't see and walked away and went to join the others. Everyone was in the living room amongst a jumble of chairs and cushions in a rough circle so they could talk.

'Sorry about that,' Pauline said, apologising for her flatmate. 'Margarita?'

'Sure. And don't worry about it. It's all crap though, you know that, right? The way they allocate us into groups and who's who and societal cliques.'

'I know,' she smiled, pouring me and one, four, nine, two icy margaritas in plastic cocktail glasses. One, four, nine, two, smiled at me over his glass.

'I'll be right back,' said Pauline. 'Don't you go anywhere,' she smiled brightly to one, four, nine two and disappeared through the door leading to the bedrooms and bathroom.

'That was very nice of you,' he told me.

'What?'

'Giving me away like that. You know I'm not in her price bracket, right?'

'I shrugged. She's good people,' I told him, not wanting to give away anything more.

'Well, it was still nice. You know, I have a mate, you might remember him from Zoë's the other week, dark hair, blue eyes,' he winked. 'He's on a job nearby, I could call him later, see if he's free to walk you home.'

I raised my eyebrows. 'You people are unbelievable,' I laughed. 'But we both know that is not allowed and in this perfect crimeless society of ours, there is no danger at all in me walking home alone,' I said frankly, even though my insides were churning knowing Jack was nearby.

'It would be quite accidental of course, two people crossing paths as they walked.'

I shook my head. I was confirming nothing to him, agreeing to nothing, and walked away to join the party, even though everything inside me had screamed, 'yes, yes, call him now.'

I sat on the outskirts of the group on a cheap timber dining chair with a purple upholstered seat that was a little lacking on the cushioning. As the group's frostiness wafted off them towards me, on the outside was where I suspected I was going to spend a great deal of time in the coming years. Without Zoë, without my little tribe of people, my family, I'd always be on the outside because no one welcomed a La Ferme girl into their group.

'Don't worry, they'll be nicer once they get those margaritas into them, once they let their guards down and get to know you,' Pauline smiled beside me.

One, four, nine, two, did his job perfectly, sitting on the other side of Pauline and putting his hand on her knee, laughing at her poor attempt at making jokes and politely joining conversations only when required. I was suddenly sad. This was no life for this man. He was a fun guy. He had thoughts and ideas and contributions to make, not only to this group of women, but to society, the world. I bet he had more to offer than sex. I bet they all could do more than entertain, breed or farm.

But this was all he could be. A well-mannered party favour that played by the rules and knew his place. It wasn't enough. It wasn't good enough. We couldn't keep treating our men this way. Surely there was enough by now to start giving them jobs and lives beyond what they were? They mightn't talk about it, but I knew, I'd learnt from my time at La Ferme, from Jules, that in the early days of the program, they controlled what was in those petri dishes, controlled how many boys and how many girls were born. One girl for every four boys, Jules had said. I'd done the calculations in my head. There had to be enough by now. Even with natural selection, there'd have been enough to go back to the way it used to be. Dr Grace's voice echoed in my head 'We only breed what we need.' What if this was all they needed, all they wanted? What if this was the President's plan all along?

'What about you Courtney?' asked a girl with choppy, short black hair from a bean bag in the corner opposite me.

'Sorry, what?' I asked, realising I hadn't been paying attention to any of the conversations but I was looking at them as though I was.

'What do you think of this perfect society of ours?' she asked from her bean-filled perch.

'I've only just arrived. I don't really have any thoughts,' I lied.

'Did you know those two girls from La Ferme who've mysteriously vanished,' she asked with explosive hand movements to insinuate their magical vanishing.

I shrugged.

'Shame, thought maybe you were one of us,' she said.

'One of what?' I asked, not liking her tone and feeling an odd discomfort in the pit of my stomach from the curious way she was looking at me.

'Never mind,' she said, observing me curiously before going back to her friends.

I went to the kitchen counter, poured another margarita and ate a piece of pizza. What was she playing at? Which side was she on? Were there even sides? All I knew was she made me feel uncomfortable the way she looked at me, the way she digested and analysed the words I spoke and mostly the way she dismissed me. I didn't want preferential treatment because of who I was or where I worked, but I still deserved to be treated like a person.

The hairs on the back of my neck prickled. I looked over to the woman and she was watching me from her bean bag perch in the corner. Watching me too carefully, not even trying to hide it. She raised her eyebrows at me and went back to her conversation. Why was I so interesting to these people? It was more than

La Ferme. I could feel it. There was something else going on, an underlying objective that I felt I was supposed to get but I didn't.

As I stood there, trying to make sense of it all, I couldn't help but overhear Kylie talking to a petite, pretty brunette by the big windows, 'It doesn't matter what they do, it won't silence us. Her work will go on. I promise. Margaret didn't die for nothing,' I over-heard the girl saying to Kylie.

I wondered who Margaret was. Then I saw a newspaper on the end of the bench with a picture of a beautiful, sunny looking woman above a lengthy article. I picked it up, reading it. The pic-ture was of Margaret. She was the journalist I'd seen pulled from the river. My heart broke for her. For what had become of her.

'It's terribly sad isn't it?' asked Pauline as Kylie and her friend stopped their conversation to watch me.

'It is. She was really beautiful,' I said. 'What happened to her? She looked nothing like this in the water. How does that even happen?' I asked.

'You saw her?' Pauline asked.

I nodded. 'I was eating with Zoë at the pizza place by the river when there was all this commotion. We thought maybe it was Rachel and we pushed through to the riverbank. I've never seen anything like it. I never want to again,' I said, taking a drink, clos-ing my eyes, trying to block the memory.

Opening my eyes, I read the beginning of the article. It said Margaret had committed suicide, had jumped to her death. 'This isn't right though,' I said.

'What do you mean?' Pauline asked.

I could feel too many eyes on me as I answered her. 'The bruis-ing. There was bruising. It was dark, on her arms, on her neck.

Her eyes, I'll never forget how much blood was in them, how they stared. She couldn't have done that to herself,' I said.

'I knew it,' I heard Kylie say. I wasn't looking at her though, I was stuck, staring at the picture of Margaret, trying to match it to the woman I'd seen pulled from the river.

'I'm sorry,' I said to Pauline when I realised how many people were watching me, their faces showing how uncomfortable they were. I felt too conspicuous. 'I didn't mean to ruin your party with talk of such things. I think I might just go,' I said, looking at the angry, hate filled eyes turned my way. It wasn't proper party talk, sure, but their response was a little unnecessary.

'No, don't go yet,' she begged.

I looked around at the group glaring at me. 'No, no, I think it's better if I leave,' I told her. 'You have a happy birthday though. Thank you so much for inviting me,' I said, hugging her. 'And you,' I said, pointing at one, four, nine, two, 'you make sure her bones are rattled,' I said, smiling.

He laughed at our shared joke. 'That I can do. Sure you don't need me to make that call,' he said conspiratorially.

I smiled kindly. 'Thank you, but no, I'll be fine,' I said, regretfully.

He nodded, understanding. I put my hand on his shoulder in thanks. Thanks for understanding. Thanks for agreeing to be someone's birthday gift as though you were a piece of meat to be shared and traded. Thank you for thinking of my safety and my heart and Jack's heart, and thank you for understanding I couldn't put him in danger, not right now. Thank you for being a truly decent human being.

When I got home, I ordered up a pizza. I only had the one slice at Pauline's in the end. I was too distracted, too busy putting up the appropriate front in amongst all that iciness, and all I'd managed was a slice of pizza and a few margaritas. Just one of those was too many on an empty stomach and it would be such a waste to puke up those lovely drinks that helped numb my insides.

I ate in front of the vision screen with my bottle of Shiraz beside me for company, but with the camera above my head, I was smart enough to drink it out of a glass, no more guzzling from the bottle. If I kept busy, if I kept my brain distracted with other things, I wouldn't keep worrying and I'd be okay.

If I could slosh my brain into numbness, I'd forget that my best friend had just left me. Zoë had left me even though she'd have to know the fallout I would face. She had to know how much grief I'd get from the Director. Even though she'd promised she'd come back. Who the hell was going to help me through this life now? Pauline? The girl from the coffee shop? Unlikely. They were too sweet and kind. I couldn't drag them into this sordid mess I'd created. The mess Zoë and Rachel had dumped me in. I couldn't do it to them. I had to go it alone. Somehow.

But no matter how angry I was, no matter how sad I was, I had to put it all out of my head. I had to pretend I knew nothing, felt nothing. Which wasn't too hard when I actually knew very little of the actual details. They'd left me out of their decision-making process on purpose, left me out of more than I'd even imagined it turned out. Yet still, there were cameras above my head watching my every move, probably listening to my every conversation in the hope I could lead them to the escapees. So just in case I let something I didn't even know I knew slip, in case I gave any indication I should be watched any closer. I had to clear it all out of my head and pretend everything was just fine. I couldn't arouse suspicion. I couldn't fall apart. I just had to be numb.

I drank the rest of the wine, pouring big glugs into the oversized glass, swallowing big gulps with every mouthful and stumbled to bed to sleep like the dead until my alarm screamed for my Saturday shift. Again, another perk thanks to Zoë.

CHAPTER 23

———

I put Zoë out of my mind. I had to. I went to the local café and ordered a coffee and a cake.

'You're up early,' the girl behind the counter greeted me. 'No date last night?' she asked with a cheeky smile.

'I had a party,' I told her warmly. 'Now I'm off to work,' I told her, happy enough to chat. She was a nice girl. She was protecting me from Anna and whoever else was watching me, trying to find out my every move and conversation. I didn't like that she'd been admonished by her boss for talking to me, and I didn't like that there was such a divide between my life and hers. It wasn't fair. There was not much in our world that was fair it seemed.

I walked to the train station with my coffee. Trish had upgraded my travel fund in line with my promotion into Zoë's position, so I no longer had to worry about water spray and climbing into the wobbly boat in my heels. But I was too sad about Zoë to care. I didn't want a promotion if this was the price. I didn't want to lose my best friends, my only two friends. Nothing was worth that.

———

The office was eerily quiet without all the other bodies to fill the space. Even though I couldn't see anyone else from my desk out the front, the nest workers even had their own rear entrance, their presence and now the absence of them altered the feeling of the space, leaving it quiet. Too quiet. Even Jen was off enjoying her weekend, her office locked.

Dr Grace had a steady stream of visitors. Weekday workers coming in for their health checks before they were allowed to book entertainers, updating data, getting the all clear and having their implants reset after a cold or something or having their annual implant scans and hormone top ups. But their appointments lasted long enough to leave quiet time between where there was too much time to think.

I filled it as best I could by booking entertainers, reading books and playing games on my tablet, but it seemed my brain was able to do multiple things at once and it continued churning through my worry and sadness and disappointment.

'Here,' Dr Grace said at midday after the last patient left, handing me a sandwich. 'It's your first Saturday shift, I guessed no one would have told you the cafeteria would be closed,' she said, kindly.

'Thank you,' I said, grateful because no, no one had told me. Zoë would have told me, I thought sadly.

Dr Grace brought over one of the visitor's chairs and we ate our sandwiches at my desk.

'It's been a busy morning for you,' I said, making conversation.

'Saturday's often are,' Dr Grace said. 'Most people can't get time off to come in during the week, so I have to book them in on Saturdays.'

'Do you work every Saturday then?'

'Most,' she said. 'I get another day off during the week though, often Monday's, just depends on what's going on. Like when you started, I took Tuesday instead, so I could transfer your health records and update your implant and stuff when you arrived.'

'Do you have many more for this afternoon?' I asked.

'Nope, that's it for today. I'll need you to give me a hand after lunch though if you don't mind, to take some things downstairs. It's a good time to test the entertainers,' she said. 'Have to make sure they're all shipshape,' she winked.

'That must be a really tough part of your job,' I joked, even though I knew Dr Grace would be nothing but professional, but she wasn't a robot and those men were beautiful.

'Very tough indeed,' smiled Dr Grace. 'Come on,' she said as we finished eating. 'It won't take long, I just need you to help carry some boxes of supplies and then you can come back up and camp out here until four.'

'Won't you need help bringing it all back up again?' I asked.

'Most of it will all be used while I'm there, so I'll just get one of the boys to help me dump the cartons in the incinerator.'

'What exactly will you be doing to them?' I asked curious.

Dr Grace smiled. 'It's just blood tests and breath tests and urine tests to make sure everyone's clean and healthy, check their implants, that sort of thing. Nothing serious, I promise. No probing today,' she laughed.

I didn't even want to know what the probing was for or why any of it was necessary if they had implants. Maybe Dr Grace just liked getting up close and personal. She was only human, after all.

I followed Dr Grace out of reception and down the long hallway to Dr Grace's office. There were three small to medium boxes of supplies ready to go. Dr Grace loaded two of the boxes into my arms, hooked her stethoscope around her neck, which I figured was mostly for show as everything was done electronically, removing the risk of human error. Then she folded her tablet, dropping it into the pocket of her white coat and picked up the last box.

'This way,' she said, leading me through another door that required Dr Grace's wrist swipe to access.

We walked down another dimly lit hallway. There was no art adorning the walls, the carpet was coarser, the ambience more utilitarian than the hallways I was used to. We went around a bend and stopped at a foyer with one set of elevator doors.

Dr Grace pressed the call button for the lift. 'I hope you're paying attention,' she told me as we waited. 'You're going to need to remember the way back, okay?'

'Yeah, sure, no problem,' I assured her, running through the route so far in my head.

'Now stay close,' Dr Grace said when we stepped out of the elevator into another dimly lit hallway. The walls were darker, the carpet darker, the smells manly, the sounds coming from the rooms along the hallway distinctly male.

'The rec rooms,' smiled Dr Grace as a cheer went up from behind the walls.

As we walked down the dimly lit hallway, the sounds of laughter and chatter, video games and vision screens squealed from the rooms either side until we reached Dr Grace's office at the end.

'You can just pop them on the desk there, thanks and unpack that one onto the shelf for me,' Dr Grace asked.

It only took a few minutes and she'd kept herself busy organising other things onto the desk. 'All done,' I told her.

'Excellent, thank you.' She took her tablet out of her pocket, tapping a few things on the screen then said, 'Alright, then, I've given you one-way access back up to the ground floor, you won't need it to get back into the hallway though, the door will open for you from the inside. Will you be alright?' she asked.

'Absolutely, no problem at all,' I smiled, visualising the route in my mind.

'Excellent. Thanks for your help, I'll see you Tuesday.'

'No worries. Have a great weekend,' I said, closing the door and heading back down the hallway.

I walked quickly, not daring to dawdle or think about who was behind the doors or the curtain-covered windows, I was passing. Were any of those people Jack? Could he feel me passing by?

I didn't dare consider it further, there were cameras all the way along the hallway, I could see their little red lights blinking. I knew Jen had the day off but someone had to be monitoring those cameras from somewhere and I wasn't sure if I'd be able to manage any restraint at all if I saw Jack hanging out in his natural environment. If I saw him at all.

There was a dark stairwell leading down to the next level just outside the lobby that housed the lift that would return me to my own floor. As I passed, I tried not to think about where it led, who it might lead to. If the rec rooms were here, were their bedrooms down those stairs? Is that where he slept? As I hesitated, a hand reached out from the dark, wrapping around my mouth, muffling my screams for help and dragged me down into the stairwell and out of sight.

'Shhhh... shhhhh...' my assailant begged before setting my mouth free.

I turned to hurl abuse at him but instead, grabbed Jack's face, pulling his mouth to mine. 'You scared the crap out of me,' I laughed when we parted for air.

'I'm sorry. I just had to see you. Just for a second, to be sure you were okay. Are you okay?' he asked, holding his breath as he waited for the answer.

'I'm fine, I'm fine,' I promised.

He pulled my mouth to his again as though I was air he desperately needed for survival and he exhaled when he released me. 'That's better,' he smiled.

'I knew it,' shouted Anna from the steps above, stomping down to confront us. 'I bloody knew it,' she scoffed.

Shit, I hadn't heard a single sound other than the pounding of my heart, the sound of Jack's voice.

'Anna,' Jack mumbled. 'What are you doing here?'

'Keeping an eye on her,' she spat at me. 'I knew she was after you,' she said to Jack.

'She's not after anyone, we were just having a conversation,' he told her.

'Oh, I saw,' she smirked. 'Don't let her drag you into her web,' she begged, trying to muscle in between us.

'What are you doing?' I asked.

'None of your business, is it? Especially not once I tell the Director what I saw. And don't think she'll dismiss me so easily this time because the cameras would have caught you coming down here,' she smirked.

I was dumbstruck. I didn't know what to say.

'You can't say anything,' Jack begged. 'What good will that do? They'll just send us both away,' he told her.

'No, they won't,' she insisted. 'They'll send her away and you won't have her bothering you anymore,' she said.

'She wasn't bothering me,' Jack told her.

'Jack, shut up,' I said, suddenly realising the gravity of the situation. He had to shut up before he bought himself a ticket to the islands or Anna's bloody basement. I couldn't stand the idea of it. I couldn't stand it if anything happened to him. Me? I could handle that. I no longer cared what happened to me, but not him.

'Don't be ridiculous,' Anna said with less venom than she'd begun with. 'You don't fancy her. You fancy me,' she said, her face dropping with the understanding she might be wrong.

'Do you really believe that?' Jack asked. 'Is that really why you get so up in arms around Courtney? Why us talking at the party bothered you so much? Why you monitored our goings on to see if anything matched?'

Anna looked as though he'd slapped her across the face. Once she regained her venomous composure she said, 'I'm phoning the Director now.' She clipped the earpiece to her ear, 'and you,' she said, pinning me to the wall with her forearm, 'are staying put.'

I struggled against her arm, trying to get air into my lungs. I couldn't breathe and my chest hurt where her arm pinned me. I had to get past her. I had to get to the elevators and back to my desk. If I could get back to my desk, maybe I could pretend none of this had happened. It was a stupid, naïve, fanciful thought but it's what my brain latched onto. I just had to get free. I just had to breathe.

Anna fought hard to keep me pinned, crushing my chest then her forearm relaxed a little, as she tried to press the Director's phone number on her tablet, she released her hold just enough so I could suck in some air. Once I could breathe, I knew I'd be okay, I was stronger and as Anna was distracted with what she was doing, I pushed her off me, freeing myself from her stronghold, gasping for air.

Anna lost her balance, falling towards Jack but he stepped out of the way and she tumbled, all arms and legs, bouncing down the stairs and out of sight.

'Shit,' I said, frozen to the spot. 'Bloody hell. Is she okay? Do you think she's okay?' I babbled.

'I don't know,' Jack said, just as stunned.

He went down the stairs to check on her while I stood frozen to the spot.

'Well?' I asked when he came back.

'It's not good. She's out cold but she seems to be breathing, just. She's beat up though. Her arm looks broken. I think. Either way, we're screwed.'

'What do you mean?' I asked.

'She's Anna, Assistant to the Director with bruises and broken limbs to prove her case against you. She's right, the cameras would have seen you pulled down, they would have seen me come in here a few minutes ago, but it wouldn't take much for her to pin this on you, and if she's not okay, there'll be an all-out man hunt for you. For both of us, if she's dead and can't defend me.'

'What do I do?' I asked, my eyes welling with tears, panic surging through my body and stealing my breath.

'You have to leave. Go upstairs, get your handbag and leave. There's a freight train that comes down from the north, it passes just on nightfall. You have to stay hidden until you get on that train. You'll have to run and jump. The train won't stop but it'll slow down enough for you to grab a rain and hoist yourself as it nears the station. It slows to protect itself from jumpers, it will be your only chance. You have to be brave, you'll have to be strong enough do it. I don't know any other way to get you out of town, to keep you safe. I'll meet you there, I swear it,' he said breathlessly, pulling my mouth to his.

'No, you can't risk it,' I said, gasping, resting my forehead against his, 'You have to stay here and be safe, she'll protect you if you let her, if you let me go,' I insisted.

'I will be there,' he vowed. 'Now go before your lift access times out.'

I nodded, took a good long look at him in case it was the last time I'd ever see his beautiful face and I ran up the stairs and into the lift lobby where the lift waited where Anna had left it.

Back on my floor, I walked casually, my heart beating a million beats a second, to my desk, picked up my bag and strolled out, my head high as Stacey had taught me.

The warm thick air smacked me in the face. What had I done? What was I doing? I wanted to double over on the footpath. I wanted to curl up into a ball and cry. I wanted Jack's arms around me in my bed, safe from the world. I didn't have the luxury of any of those things. I had to survive. Is this what had happened to Zoë? Some unforeseen interruption to her carefully laid plan? Was she, too, having to survive on a whim?

I had to keep going, that's all I knew. I had to keep my face impassive, just popping down the street on an errand, impassive. I couldn't permit myself to fall apart. Not yet. But I would. At some point, I would. Especially if Jack did as I asked and stayed behind, let me take the fall and kept himself safe. I would fall apart and I wasn't sure I'd ever be able to repair myself. But now was not that time. Now I had to do as he asked because at least if he thought I was safe, at least if I didn't wash up in the river, at least if my dead face didn't show up on the front page of a newspaper, he'd survive and I needed to believe he was okay. No matter what happened from here, no matter what happened to me, I needed him to be okay.

The mall was full of people on weekend errands, shopping with friends, drinking coffee, lunching, laughing. It was easy to blend in with the masses enjoying their Saturday. There would be too many faces for someone watching a security monitor to quickly pick out just me.

I ducked into a little shop selling leisurewear and bought a black hoodie, tracksuit pants and runners. I bought a few supplies, chocolate bars, a coffee, water, from a street vendor. Then all I needed was somewhere to change, to re-emerge as someone else. I just had to blend into the shadows with everyone else and find a bathroom in which to change my clothes. I was thinking, trying to remember where I'd seen signs for public bathrooms, then, remembering where I'd seen one, I turned, on a mission, smacking into someone so hard I bounced off. Instinctively I looked up to apologise and saw Pauline looking down at me with a big stupid grin that could only come from celebrating her birthday with some bone rattling.

'What's the matter?' she asked when she saw my face.

'Nothing, nothing. Sorry, Pauline, but I really have to go.' All I could think about was finding a bathroom and changing and getting the hell out of the mall, getting the hell away from Pauline before someone saw us together.

'No,' she said, grabbing my arm so hard I could feel her fingers bruising my skin.

'Ow,' I cried out. 'What are you doing?'

'You're in trouble, aren't you?' she asked.

'No, it's nothing. I just have to go,' I insisted.

'Is it to do with your friends?'

'What? No,' I said, surprising myself that this had nothing at all to do with Zoë and Rachel, yet would look as though it did when I disappeared.

'Let me help you,' she whispered close to my ear.

'What? No, no way.'

'Please, I can help you,' she insisted.

'Pauline, I'm sorry, but right now, no one can help me,' I told her, saying more than I wanted to, trying to keep the tears at bay.

'Tell me what happened?' she asked, dragging me out of the throng of people to a secluded alley. 'This is a camera black spot. Tell me,' she insisted.

'How do you know that?' I asked, surprised.

She shrugged. 'What happened?' she repeated.

'I was downstairs. Helping Dr Grace. It was an accident,' I said, tears finally overflowing from my eyes. 'I didn't mean to push Anna but she cut off the air to my lungs, she was going to phone the Director and split Jack and I up, and I didn't mean to hurt her. I just wanted to breathe. To reason with her, protect Jack and she fell down the stairs and now I have to go. You have to let me go,' I pleaded, struggling to pull free the arm she was still gripping.

'I can help you. I told you I can and I will,' she insisted. 'What's in the bag?' she asked, indicating my bag of purchases.

'A change of clothes, tracksuit pants, a hoodie, runners,' I told her, wondering why she cared.

'Good, put them on,' she instructed.

'What? Here?'

'Yes, here. I told you, it's a blind spot.'

'Fine,' I grumbled as I quickly pulled the track pants on under my skirt, pulled off my skirt. I unbuttoned and took of my shirt, pulled the hoodie on over my bra, kicked off my heels and laced up the runners.

'Good. Now, is there anything sentimental in your handbag?'

'I don't know. The bracelet my sisters made me for my fifth birthday,' I said, remembering the shell bracelet they'd given me. Goodness, it seemed a lifetime ago now.

'Good, take it out and throw the bag and your clothes in the bin,' she said, pointing to a nearby rubbish bin.

'What? Are you kidding?' I asked.

'You don't know what has trackers in it. If this Anna knew you were downstairs and where exactly you were, she was watching you, maybe even tracking you. You can't know to what extent.'

'I think there were cameras in my apartment,' I said.

'There you go, take out the bracelet and ditch the rest,' she instructed. 'Wait, do you have anything in there worth trading?' she asked.

'What do you mean?'

'Anything of value?'

I shrugged. Then I remembered the jewellery I'd worn to the spa that I'd taken off and forgotten about. I brought out the diamond studs, the tennis bracelet I'd worn that day. 'What about these?' I asked.

'Perfect,' she said, taking them from me.

'Wait,' I said, suddenly concerned about what she was going to do with my jewellery. 'What exactly are we trading them for?'

'You'll see,' she said with a mischievous smile as she put her earpiece in and dialled a number on her tablet. 'Throw the rest,' she said, indicating the bin with her head while she waited for whoever she was calling to pick up on the other end.

I did as she asked, sad to be throwing the beautiful tote in the bin with my lovely clothes and shoes like they were rubbish. But she was right, who knew to what extent Anna had gone to keep tabs on me. I'd heard you could put trackers in the buttons of shirts and the heels of shoes, Helen had told me on the bus the day we left the college. She probably had no idea she was giving away secrets that would someday be useful to me as I ran, after I'd injured or even killed the Assistant to the Director of La Ferme.

Pauline was just packing up her tablet when I returned. 'Okay, let's go,' she said. 'Hood up. We have to hurry,' she added, sliding a pair of oversized sunglasses onto my face.

I scurried along beside her as we hurried, weaving and dodging through the busy mall being as inconspicuous as possible, hopefully hidden amongst the masses of people going about their Saturday afternoon business.

At the end of the mall, we left the shopping district and all the laughing, jovial people behind and entered the business centre. We blended into the cool shadows of tall buildings as I hurried beside Pauline and we headed towards the botanic gardens.

'Wait here,' she instructed when we reached the fence of the gardens, pushing me under the cover of a wide tree as she hurried off to a person hiding under the boughs of another tree. I couldn't see who it was. They had a cap on covering their hair, sunglasses, a baggy top and baggy pants disguising their body shape. I wondered if that's how I looked, indistinguishable. I hoped.

I watched Pauline pull my jewels out of her pocket and offer them to the woman. I assumed it was a woman considering our men rarely roamed without anyone knowing where they were. Then the woman looked over at me and even though she'd done a good job disguising her face, her contempt was as recognisable as some people's faces. I could see enough, feel enough, to know it was the woman from the party with short choppy black hair, the one who'd watched me that way that made my stomach turn as it did again now. I didn't like her and I didn't want her help but I had no idea what Pauline was trading with her and could only wait for her to return.

I was in no position to be choosy about who helped me. The woman argued with Pauline a moment, then handed her something that looked like a black chunk of plastic, took my jewels and she scurried away in the opposite direction.

'Come on,' Pauline said, when she returned, without explaining herself or the trade and ushered me into the gardens.

The sun had gone and it was only as I realised the trees weren't bathed in it that I noticed it wasn't there, and the sky, was in fact, filled with fat, dark grey clouds instead. It didn't stop people from going about their day though. There was still a group of women doing yoga in the gardens. There were women picnicking together and a group of women torturing themselves with boot camp but none of them paid us any attention as we hurried through the shadows.

When we were far away from all the people, Pauline pushed me into some bushes, 'give me your wrist,' she said.

'What?'

'Your wrist, come on, hurry, we don't have all day,' she said frustrated.

I held up my wrist, implant side up, not really sure what she was about to do.

Pauline pulled the black plastic thing she'd traded my jewels for out of her pocket. It was the size of an old, pre-war phone. She wiped it over my wrist and my arm the way Dr Grace wiped her implant scanner. It made a buzzing noise. I felt a sharp zap as though I'd been stung by a bee, once, then again when she waved it over my health implant, then it was quiet.

'Ow, what was that?' I asked.

'A scrambler,' she said, handing it to me. 'It's just fried the electronics in your implants. Are you meeting him?' she asked.

I nodded, even though I secretly hoped he saw sense and stayed where he was.

'Here then, keep it, he'll need it,' she said.

'Thanks,' I said, grateful.

'Your friends' trackers have been deactivated too, in case you were wondering. The first one, she was caught because of her implant. They've all deactivated their implants now. Somehow. All four of them are off the grid.'

'How do you know this? Do you know someone in security inside La Ferme?'

'No. We were hoping that would be you,' she winked. 'We hacked our way in. Everything they can see, we can see and for those four, they can't see a thing.'

'Hacked?'

She smiled. 'While they continue to underestimate us, we'll continue to outsmart them,' she smiled. 'Unfortunately, they can track me,' she said. She pushed open a door hidden in the bushes with her hip. 'This is where we part ways, I'm afraid. There's an exit on the other side when you're ready, it'll lead you to the trains. I assume that's your plan? Good luck.'

'Pauline, thank you. I don't know how I can ever thank you,' I said.

She laughed. 'Trust me, your birthday gift was thanks enough.'

I laughed.

'You do have a plan, right?' she asked.

I shrugged. 'Sort of.'

'Alright then, this place will give you some time to think or whatever. Good luck, Courtney,' she said, hugging me.

'Do I even dare ask how you made all this happen?'

She smiled. 'We're the Resistance.' And then she was gone. Just like that, gone, melted into the shadows like a ghost.

The Resistance? Then the conversations of the night before at Pauline's party came back to me. They're the bloody Resistance. I laughed. Of course there was a resistance. If I'd known, if they'd just come out and said something, I'd have put my hand up in a second. But maybe they couldn't, maybe bringing one, four, nine, two had changed things? It didn't matter now anyway. Nothing mattered now.

I sat alone in the hidden oasis, surrounded by bamboo walls and tall trees. There was a pond in the corner with big fat goldfish. But otherwise, I was alone. I sat on the green grass listening to the birds, watching the sky change colour as I waited for the day to end and night to come.

There were hours to think. To think of what I'd done. To wonder how the hell I'd gotten here. To think of the people I'd always thought of as my sisters, and wonder if they'd know, if someone would tell them what had become of me. That after such promise, the brightest new recruit in a decade, I'd become what I'd become. Unpatriotic. A killer. That I'd so easily, so quickly and so stupidly, fallen in love. I wished I could tell them the truth. That Jack was worth it. That what I felt for Jack shouldn't be wrong, shouldn't be unlawful.

I wished I could tell them about the men made in petri dishes, about the Resistance, about the stupidity of our world, unnecessary divides, the extremes taken by those in power, the degradation of our men, of our society, of humanity. But I couldn't forewarn them about any of it. I couldn't help them, protect them or save them. They still had some years to go at the college. Perhaps the Resistance would change our world before my sisters were set free?

I hoped so. I mostly hoped they wouldn't hate me. Would anyone tell them? I doubted it now I knew things. Perhaps Miss Milly would hear though, maybe read it in a newspaper. I hoped when all this was over, I didn't look in the mirror and hate myself. If I bothered to look in the mirror at all. There was no point reflecting. What was done was done. I had to live with it. I would live with it.

I'd chosen life over death, over incarceration, that's all there was to it. I hadn't meant to hurt Anna, she'd put herself in that position. I had to remind myself of it before guilt ate my insides.

I watched the clouds and snippets of sky change colour and knew I should be making a plan, getting ready for what came next. But I didn't even know where the train went. I had no idea how to plan to survive. But I would. I'd find a way. Perhaps if I found my way to the hinterland, I'd find Zoë and Rachel? But I suspected it would be equal to finding a needle in a haystack. Impossible. And too risky. The further away I went the better. I'd just have to stay on the train until it stopped. Wherever it stopped. But it would be far away from here and I could drift into the shadows and find a way. I suppose that was my plan, the only one I could come up with without Jack.

Finally, pink claimed what there was of the blue sky, then purple claimed the pink. Then the purple darkened as it changed to black. It was time. I pushed open the door on the other side of the hidden oasis, I hadn't had the mind to even appreciate. It opened onto a thick grove of trees lining the upper end of the train track I needed.

As I made my way through the trees, I could see the glow of the nearby station a little way down. It wasn't my station and I prayed that when Jack didn't find me near my own station that he'd give up, think I'd changed my mind, gone somewhere else and he'd stay at La Ferme where he'd be safe and could get on with his life. I wondered if he knew of the Resistance. If any of them knew?

The whistle blew from somewhere up the tracks. This was it, I thought as I readied myself for the challenge of jumping onto a moving train. No turning back now. It was my only chance at freedom. I had to get as far away from here, from Anna, from what I'd done, as possible. And fast.

The freight train slowed as it neared the station, not to stop but just in case someone tried to run across the tracks, for some, it was the only way out Jack had said. This was my chance. My only chance. I spotted the hand rail beside an open compartment filled with boxes of produce and kept my eye on it as I came out of the tree cover and ran, reaching up for the handle, grabbing hold with everything I had, holding on as the train tried to rip my arms from my body and finally, summoning the strength to swing myself on board, almost popping my shoulder from the socket as I did.

The blood in my veins pumped as my body tried desperately to get air and my heart regained a regular pace. As I saw the people hovering in front of the station waiting for the passenger train that would be along soon, I ducked into the compartment and sat amongst the boxes, falling against the wall.

I'd done it. What I was going to do now was anyone's guess. I didn't even know where the train went or what I'd do when I got off or how on earth I was going to survive on the run, on my own.

All I knew was that I was free and I was alone and nothing would ever be the same again.

'This isn't the place for a lady like you,' said a deep, gravelly voice from the dark corner opposite.

'Who's there?' I asked.

He laughed, a hard, menacing laugh.

Fear rippled through my veins. I couldn't breathe. How soon could I jump? I wondered. Not soon enough, I suspected. I, had to wait until we were at least weaving our way through the hinterlands and well out of the way of people but that was a long time to be alone with a man who laughed that way.

I looked out the doorway and wondered if jumping back out there and facing up to whatever fate awaited me would be a better option than facing whatever was in store with this man. Maybe Anna wasn't as badly hurt as I thought and she'd just get over it? Realise she'd lost and not bother to harass me any further? Even as I thought it, I knew it was ridiculous. Anna had been desperate to see me gone the second we'd met and if she was alive, she was never going to let go of an opportunity like this. She wouldn't rest until I was rotting on an island. Until she could have Jack all to herself. The idea of it made me ill. To think of Anna and Jack together at all. To think of Anna in love with Jack. To know she probably had designs of her own to rescue him and lock him in her own basement. It filled me with rage.

As I passed my own station there was still no Jack beside me. I'd expected it, hoped for it but it didn't make it easier, didn't make my heart weigh any less. I couldn't go back. I couldn't face whatever Anna had in store for me. But I knew she'd look after Jack, love him, care for him, even if he didn't want her to. That was something, right? He'd be safe and warm and fed, that was enough, enough to keep me sane through whatever was to come.

Just as I was wishing someone had told me where this freight train went, where it stopped, how to find food and mostly, wishing someone had told me where these secret communities were instead of protecting me, as the train was about to enter an endless stretch of darkness and I was doing my best to somehow come to terms with what awaited me, a body flung itself into the compartment and turned to me with a grin illuminated from the full moon shining through a gap in the parting clouds.

'There you are, babe,' Jack smiled, swinging himself onto the floor beside me. 'Where we going?' he asked with a smile in his voice and I pulled his mouth to mine and kissed him like it was all that would keep me breathing.

'Don't think I care where we're going if you're going to kiss me like that,' he laughed.

'You two aren't going to do the nasty on the floor in front of me, are you?' asked our companion from the shadows.

I'd forgotten he was there but I no longer cared. I had Jack. Everything would be okay as long as we were together. I scrambled his implants and settled in for the ride.

Alexandra Deen

Read on for a sample of Alexandra Deen

A Harrington Family Story

Beside me, the River Seine bubbled like a witch's brew. Fat raindrops soaked my clothes, chilling me right through to the bone. Tears streaked what remained of my make up and I was glad I couldn't see my own face. I'd become a version of myself I no longer recognised. Not just in the last couple of hours, but the last few years if I were honest. If I were brave enough to face the reality of who I'd become, who I'd allowed myself to become because it would be easier. It was expected.

The streets of the most romantic city in the world were suspiciously quiet, as though it were ashamed it hadn't lived up to the hype. My feet hurt, from the cold, from the wet, from poorly chosen pretty ballet flats. I shivered, unable to stop the quivering of my lip.

A car horn blared, my heart near leapt from my chest.

I stepped back onto the kerb. 'Pay attention, Lexi,' I scolded myself. Billy bloody McCrae certainly wasn't worth getting run down on a dark Parisian street. So my life was officially in the gutter, it wasn't reason enough to die. Or worse, end up in a Parisian hospital all alone and having to call my mother to come and get me.

Catching my breath, I wiped my tear-stained face, checked the street for traffic and trundled across the road towards the music, the laughter, the dry roof of the hostel matching the map on the now bedraggled pamphlet in my hand.

I was angry and sad and so disappointed the weight of it crushed my lungs, stealing my breath as I stood before the big blue doors, the rain falling in sheets around me, my clothes soaked and heavy. I watched a piece of peeling paint flapping in the breeze, resisting the urge to pull at it and wondered if I should I knock on the door or should I just walk in? I'd never stayed in such a place before, somewhere without a doorman to direct me. Was there an etiquette I should have been aware of? The paint chipped doors suggested etiquette didn't rule this little corner of Paris.

Looking for guidance, for something, I spotted a girl with wild black curls sitting on the balustrade of a small verandah heaving with jovial young people, drinking beer from bottles, unaware the world was full of misery and cheating bastard boyfriends. She laughed, her whole body shaking from the happiness. I wondered if it would feel as good as it looked, to laugh that way, to be that happy. I wondered if I'd ever been that happy. If I'd ever laughed that freely. I couldn't remember.

The girl looked over her sun-kissed shoulder, smiled and nodded towards the door. I turned away, embarrassed. What was wrong with me? I don't stand on streets in the middle of the night, lurking, staring at strangers. I was losing my bloody mind.

I sucked in a deep, fortifying breath. It wasn't a palatial hotel with marble floors, but it would do until I could get the hell out of Paris, I reminded myself and pulled open the door.

The foyer was sparse but clean and dry. A worn timber chair sat beneath a phone attached to the wall. A staircase opposite wound its way up into the hidden heart of the hostel. The well-worn reception desk was directly in front. Behind the desk, sat a girl with red hair so bright it almost glowed, framing a face as perfect as porcelain. The girl chuckled at something Homer Simpson said in French on the television beside her, completely oblivious or perhaps purposely ignoring the fact that I'd just stumbled in and was dripping all over the streaked timber floor.

I walked towards the desk, my shoes squelching loudly in the quiet, my insides cringing from embarrassment. She finally looked up from the television as I reached the counter, raising her eyebrows, trying not to smile at the makeup streaked all over my face and hair stuck to my head like paint and dripping all over her counter.

'Dorm or single, hon?' she asked with a poetic French accent.

'Whatever's cheapest?' I stammered, tears choking my vocal chords as I pulled scrunched, damp euros from my handbag.

'Dorm it is, then. Room two, bunk three.' She put a key attached to a block of wood atop a pile of linen and a towel and handed the pile over the counter as though I were an army recruit reporting for duty. She sent me up the stairs with no further question, as though I'd stood before her in a sundress in the middle of the afternoon instead of a drowned, miserable version of a person in the middle of the night. But maybe that's what happened in places like this? Vagrants, society's misfits and those spat out by the world, appeared at all hours so often, it was accepted as the norm?

Four bunk beds had been crammed into the room she sent me to, each flanked at the foot with a metal locker. Flimsy curtains covered the long, short, rectangular windows that were too high up to see out of. The dull light from the bulb hidden under the white plastic shade on the ceiling wasn't dull enough to hide the worn timber floor covered with the debris of the room's missing inhabitants; a discarded towel, a pair of thongs, backpacks, socks and a navy blue hoodie.

They had squeezed the tiniest bathroom I'd ever seen into the far corner, just big enough for a toilet, basin and shower. It was a far cry from the fancy hotel I'd woken in with its giant bathtub and shiny white tiles and luxury complimentary bath products, but it didn't matter. Not much mattered right now other than getting through the night and thinking about tomorrow when tomorrow showed up.

As I organised my things, my mind flashed to the morning when I'd strolled the streets of Paris, the bridges that arched over the Seine, hand in hand, happy, in love. I'd seen the Eiffel Tower rising above the trees in the distance, wondered if it would be there that Billy would sink to one knee on the grass and ask me to be his wife. I'd have said yes, too. I'd been a fool. Of course I'd been a fool. I'd been a fool for years. Now I had to find the strength to go home and face my family, my friends. What friends? They'd all known, I'd seen it on their faces in the fancy Parisian restaurant where we were dining, when my life had unravelled at my feet. They'd eaten dinner in my home, eaten my food and drunk my wine laughing in my face, laughing behind my back.

No, they were Billy's friends and he could keep them. I didn't want them. Friends don't allow you to be blindsided in foreign countries. Friends save you, they protect you, they look out for you. They don't just sit back and watch your life crumble. No, I had no friends. I didn't have much of anything now. Perhaps just the scrap of dignity I'd held onto when I'd told Billy to go to hell and walked out of the fancy restaurant where he'd sat with that woman draped across his lap and the revelations had unfolded, piece by piece in seconds but what had felt like hours. I'd walked out with nothing, no friends, no savings, nowhere to go, nothing.

I dug around in my suitcase for something to wear to bed but almost everything was damp. I knew I should have bought the one with the hard shell case, I thought to myself as I began pulling things out. After hanging my wet clothes over the edges of my bed, over my suitcase, from the open locker door, I squeezed between the bunks to the bathroom. The cubicle was small but the water was hot and I thawed, movement returning to my fingertips and toes. I leant on the wall, letting the hot water beat on my body, glad to be feeling something other than devastation or misery or self hatred.

Careful not to overuse the hot water, I reluctantly stepped out of the shower, my bones finally warmed, my skin red, raw, and shiny new. I threw on an almost dry t-shirt and undies, already imagining the sweet perfection of the warm bed and the desperate bout of indulgent wallowing that waited.

With my towel and wet clothes gathered in my arms, I squeezed between the bunks and found the girl with the wild black curls sitting on my bed, absently picking at a hang nail and swinging her leg as though to a tune only she could hear.

She looked up as I dropped my loot onto my suitcase.

'Hey,' she said in an Australian accent, holding out a bottle of beer.

'Hello,' I replied as though in question, but taking the beer she offered anyway.

'You alright?' she asked.

I shrugged.

'Wanna talk about it?' she asked.

'Not really.'

'That means you really should. It'd be better than wallowing or letting it eat you up all night. It might help you sleep at least,' she offered.

I shrugged. She had some good points and really, what did I have to lose? Pride? I couldn't lose much more and maybe once I hit bottom I could start building myself back up. Somehow.

'I got duped, that's all. Utterly blindsided. The man I loved wasn't who I thought he was. My friends let me down, let me fall. I just, I don't know, my head's still spinning.'

'Are there actual details in there? Come on, sit, spit them out, otherwise you'll keep seeing them every time you close your eyes.'

'I sure as hell don't need that,' I laughed, surprising myself. 'We came for a wedding. We were at dinner with some of our friends. I went to the toilet, stopped to take a phone call from mum. I'd called her earlier but forgot the time difference. Anyway, we only talked for a few minutes. When I came back into the restaurant, there was this girl, I'd seen her a couple of times at the footy, never paid her any attention, knew she knew some of our friends but had no idea her and Billy knew each other as anything more than passing acquaintances. I'll never forget her, tall, lanky, all arms and legs, Kardashian hair and a laugh like a strangled hyena. She was draped all over my boyfriend. His hands were all over her and his face was buried in her hair. I don't know what he was doing, kissing her neck, whispering something. I don't know. I just froze and when he saw me he just laughed. He was drunk I guess, just enough to not care what I saw or what he said. Suggested a ménage a trois. Said it'd be very French of us.'

'What did your friends do?'

'They just sat there. Fuckers,' I laughed, taking a long sip of cold beer.

'Fuckers,' agreed my new friend, tapping her bottle to mine.

'She wasn't the only one. She laughed when I thought she was. Then it all began falling into place, the late nights, the 2am showers, the unanswered calls and I asked the questions. Turns out he's been all over the place with anyone who'd take him for years. None of it was real. We weren't real and I just don't know who I am now without him. Everything has been him. Everything I'd planned for the rest of my life had been with him. Now it's just me and I don't know what to do. He chose everything, decided everything and I let him because he was usually right and it was easier than hearing I told you so. So I let him and now I feel so stupid and lost.'

'Did you notice you never said you loved him or that your heart was broken? You've just been humiliated and horribly inconvenienced,' she smiled.

'Really? Huh,' I mumbled, realising she was exactly right. I was pissed off. I was annoyed. I was afraid and utterly humiliated. But I wasn't sad. I wasn't brokenhearted. How was that possible? I'd loved him, didn't I? We shared a home, a bed, a future. I'd planned babies and old age with him. I had to have loved him. But this bringer of beer and kind shoulders was right, my heart didn't feel broken. I wanted to wallow but I didn't feel the need to cry for him. I'd cried from the surprise, the devastation, for who I'd become, but the thought of never seeing Billy again, never having to listen to his obnoxious lectures or be bossed around, left me with nothing but relief.

As I finished my beer, my new friend said, 'Come on, plenty more of those downstairs. Your new life starts now. A new life where you're in charge,' she smiled.

I liked the sound of that.

'We'll be gentle, I promise,' she offered, holding her hand out to me.

I took her hand and let her pull me up.

'I'm Lydia,' she said, finally introducing herself.

'Alexandra.'

'Come on Alex, let's go see if you're in there somewhere.'

I laughed, forgiving her for the choice of nickname. I hated

Alex, it was a boy's name. My friends and family call me Lexi, but for one night, what did it matter? For one night I could be anyone and at that moment I was pretty done with Lexi the lovely door-mat.

I followed Lydia onto the verandah and into the throng of people still enjoying the night and thanked my beer buzz when she called everyone to attention, commanding the spotlight.

'Alex, this is everyone. Everyone, this is Alex. She needs beer and kindness and it's our duty as fellow travelers, to provide her with both,' she insisted as I tried smiling.

Mumbles of agreement followed sympathetic nods. Beers were passed forward through the crowd of people with words of sympathy and welcome. Lydia draped a kind, friendly, comforting arm around me and led me to the balustrade she'd occupied earlier.

'What a bastard. Forget him,' Lydia said. 'Everything will be better now you've left him, you'll see. You'll pick yourself back up and find a new way now you've found the strength to stand up for yourself.'

'He has to be a real asshole to bring you all this way and then do that,' claimed a bright, bubbly girl with blonde dreadlocks when Lydia told her my boyfriend had turned out to be an ass. She was another Aussie. In fact, they mostly seemed to be Aussies, like the hostel was a magnet for lost Aussie souls, although I seemed to be the only one truly lost.

'Thanks,' I said, taking deep breaths, waiting for the tears welling in my eyes to evaporate. It would take some getting used to, figuring out who I was without him, thinking of how I would move forward alone, it had all happened so suddenly it was a lot to comprehend. Six years with the same man was a long time. He's all I knew, we'd been together my entire adult life.

A few beers in and I couldn't believe the world I'd landed in. These people spoke of adventures and places that sounded too good to be true, surfing in places I'd never heard of, finding treasure in small European towns where no one spoke English, cycling along the coastline in remote villages, the sun kissing their skin, falling in love, eating incredible food. They laughed loud, they wore simple cotton summer dresses and crazy board shorts, the men with permanent five o'clock shadows, living in a world so far removed from my grey cubicle and suburban life back home that I could hardly comprehend any of it and now here they were, welcoming me into their fold, commiserating with me over beers as though we were old friends.

I leant on the balustrade, looking out over the dark road, slick and wet under the moon's bright rays now the clouds had moved on. Had I really stood out there on the footpath in the rain? Now I was dry and warm and comforted, sipping cold beer amongst the laughter and camaraderie, I couldn't believe that had been me. Who was that person? In fact, who was that person I'd become over the last six years? Not someone I recognised. Not someone I particularly liked and I hadn't even realised it was happening. Somewhere it'd just been easier to give me up and go with the flow, abide by everyone else's expectations, my boss, my mother, Billy. I didn't even know which bits were me and which were Billy. All I knew was Lydia was right. It was time to find out who I was.

'What's with all the thinking?' asked Lydia, twisting the top off another beer.

'Oh, nothing,' I half smiled. 'Just thinking how different the day's ended to how I'd expected.'

'Yeah, life does that,' she smiled.

'I've been here one bloody day and my life's been turned upside down. How does that even happen? This trip was not supposed to go this way.'

'Maybe it was and you just didn't realise it. The universe has a way of kicking us up the behind when we don't pay attention.'

I laughed a huffy laugh because she was probably right. 'It was easy to ignore it all.'

'Isn't it always,' she grinned. 'Until the kicking comes and you have no choice.'

'So, what are your plans from here?' a man asked, joining us at the balustrade.

I turned away from the rain soaked street, looked up and our eyes locked. It was him. My knight, my saviour who'd given me the pamphlet that had led me here. The waiter with the sun bleached shaggy hair, broad shoulders, wide smile and laughing grey green eyes that knew things, that loved things, that loved life. He wore a loose fitting, faded yellow tank top with bright, multi-coloured board shorts and blue thongs on his sun drenched feet.

The sun had soaked his body, from his biceps to his beautiful broad shoulders. I tried not to look but my eyes wanted to linger, to drink him in. Where did men that beautiful even come from? What was I even doing noticing? I was supposed to be crying into my beer not admiring handsome strangers that help damsels in distress find refuge. But for just one second, everything stood still and my breath caught in my chest.

'You?' I asked softly.

He smiled.

'You know each other?' Lydia asked.

I wanted to laugh, as if I know men that look like him. Billy was alright, handsome enough, a good catch even, so everyone kept telling me, but Billy had nothing on this bloke. This bloke was tall, slightly rugged, his strong jaw covered lightly in stubble, everything about him was strong, then there was his lovely mouth and puppy dog eyes that smiled without trying. I mentally shook my head clear to stop from staring.

'It was my restaurant she was at earlier,' he told Lydia. 'Well not mine,' he said to me, 'the one where I was working. Just filling in actually, not really my thing waiting tables, prefer pouring beers, but a mate needed a favour, they were short and needed a hand.'

'Well, thanks,' I said. 'I've no idea where I'd have gone without the pamphlet you gave me.'

'Oh a regular knight, huh,' joked Lydia.

'I'm Tom by the way,' he smiled, his whole face lighting up as though lit from the inside by his own personal sun. Then, his right bicep flexed beautifully as he stretched his arm around Lydia's shoulders, draping it there casually, as though he'd done it a thousand times. I felt my heart sink all the way down to my toes.

Don't be ridiculous, I told myself. Of course he has a girlfriend. What was wrong with me? What was wrong with my brain? I'd just left Billy, the supposed love of my life, the man I'd shared intimate moments with, cared for when he was sick, gone to birthday parties with, hosted barbeques with, told all my deepest secrets and wishes to, the man I'd expected a bloody proposal from under the Eiffel Tower. My head was still spinning with everything that had happened, where I'd ended up, what lay ahead. I couldn't fancy someone else already. My traumatised brain was just confused, that was all.

'Um, I'll see if I can get a flight home in the morning, I suppose,' I said, answering Tom's question

'Home? No!' cried Lydia. 'You're in Paris, Alex. You've only been here a day. You can't go yet. This is one of the most beautiful cities you'll ever see.'

I shrugged. She was right. But I was short on funds now I had a life to rebuild and really, no inclination to wander the streets alone.

'You know what you should do,' Tom said, looking at Lydia as though he'd solved the most intricate puzzles of the universe.

'Absolutely!' she cried, reading his mind.

I watched them, waiting for an explanation.

'Come down the coast with us, Alex. Oh you have to. It's just what you need, a bit of sun and sand, the ocean will heal all those wounds and you'll be good as new in no time. France is incredible, you can't miss out now that you're here. Please. Please say *oui*,' Lydia begged, gripping my arm in anticipation.

'What? No, no. We just met. You don't want me imposing on your trip,' I insisted, despite how nice the prospect of forgetting my life and laying on a beach in a foreign country sounded.

'Don't be ridiculous, the more the merrier. We'd love you to come with us. I promise, we're relatively normal, non murdering types, you have to come and balance out all the testosterone,' she insisted with a smile that left me both nervous and more excited than I could remember ever being.

'We have a car,' Tom added proudly.

'That's so nice, really it is but I don't think my failing funds will allow me to stay much longer than tonight anyway, I'm afraid. This was Billy's trip. He paid for the flights, the accommodation. I've just got a little spending money for bits and bobs, souvenirs, snacks, maybe a dinner or two, that sort of thing,' I admitted sadly.

'That doesn't matter,' Lydia said, waving my worries away. 'None of us have any money, but we get by, that's half the fun.'

'Really?' I couldn't believe it. They were all so happy. They didn't look hungry and the travel stories they'd shared in the last hour were so mind blowing they didn't even seem real; how could they all have no money? Living the life they lived cost money, surely? Billy and I had spent nights planning and budgeting for this trip. But what if all this time I'd had it backwards? 'But how?' I had to ask.

'Ah, you have to come for us to share all our secrets,' Lydia winked, laughing.

'C'mon, Alex, it'll be fun. You need some fun. We leave first thing tomorrow and it's just for a few days. It will cost next to nothing, I promise. We have a spare bed in the villa, and I am pretty sure it has your name on it,' Tom insisted.

'You can't go home yet, you have to come,' begged Lydia.

All the usual thoughts ran through my head again as though on repeat. Blah, blah, blah. What I really wanted to do was blow off my life and go to the bloody beach with this group of the coolest, most amazing people I'd ever met. To have the much needed fun Tom spoke of. To lay in the sun and pretend none of it had happened, that I hadn't been so humiliated I was afraid to look people in the eye. Forget it all and laugh. It'd been so long since I'd just let go and laughed, I'd forgotten what it felt like. These people were reminding me and I wasn't ready to let it go, to go back.

So, after taking a long sip of beer for courage, I ignored that annoying voice in my head, the one that had led me down this path in the first place. 'Fine, fine, okay, *oui*,' I agreed, panicking as soon as the words were out despite my newfound courage and resolution.

I couldn't drive to some French coast with these people. I'd just met them. It was crazy. Lydia was crazy. Tom was crazy. They were all crazy. But it did seem silly to waste the airfare Billy had paid for and they were right, I was in Paris, anything was possible in Paris, right?

Also By Tamara Martin

Alexandra Deen – A Harrington Family Story
Mrs May's Tea and Toast – A Harrington Family Story
The Rise of Jaz – Harrington Family Christmas (eBook only)
The Fall of Jaz – A Harrington Family Story

Thank you

Thank you to everyone who believed in this story. Amanda and Kelly for loving the words and the journey right from the start. Carly for keeping me on the right path and being my Barossa Buddy. My family for their love and support. Mum for pimping my work. Fiona for the long lunches. My RWA family for their incredible support, sharing their wisdom and crazy late nights at conferences, particularly, Kaye and Brooke, you ladies are my people. Cathleen Ross for making everything in this book better. Kristyn McQuiggan for her genius covers. And to all the readers who have been sharing their love of The Harringtons, I hope you enjoyed this little shift in worlds. I'm incredibly lucky that I get to do what I do, so thank you for taking the ride with me ♥♥♥

About Tamara

Writer, hiker, food lover, tv addict and book nerd. Tamara lives in beautiful South Australia and knows where all the best wineries are hidden. She is fuelled by Doritos, Chocolate Sultanas and Shiraz but on a cold wintry night may morph into an old man and pour a nip of port and drink it in her jammies by the fire with a book in hand.

You can join Tamara's member newsletter list on her website www.tamaramartinauthor.com to receive exclusive content, behind the scenes stories and be the first to know of upcoming releases and all the other good member only stuff. You'll also find a link to her blog, Postcards From Here, there as well.